DISCARDED
D0284417

None Shall Look Back

Southern Classics Series

M. E. Bradford, Editor

Southern Classics Series

M. E. Bradford, Series Editor

Donald Davidson	The Tennessee, Volume I
Donald Davidson	The Tennessee, Volume II
Caroline Gordon	Green Centuries
Caroline Gordon	None Shall Look Back
Caroline Gordon	Penhally
Augustus Baldwin Longstreet	Georgia Scenes
Andrew Nelson Lytle	Bedford Forrest and His Critter Company
Andrew Nelson Lytle	A Wake for the Living
Thomas Nelson Page	In Ole Virginia
William Pratt, Editor	The Fugitive Poets
Elizabeth Madox Roberts	The Great Meadow
Allen Tate	Stonewall Jackson
Robert Penn Warren	Night Rider
Owen Wister	Lady Baltimore
Stark Young	So Red the Rose

None Shall Look Back

CAROLINE GORDON

with a preface by Eileen Gregory

"Stand, stand, shall they cry; but none shall look back."
—NAHUM, Chap. II, Verse 8.

J. S. Sanders & Company
NASHVILLE

Originally Published 1937

Published by arrangement with
Farrar, Straus & Giroux, Inc.

Library of Congress Catalog Card Number:
92-089827

ISBN: 1-879941-11-2

Published in the United States by
J. S. Sanders & Company
P. O. Box 50331
Nashville, Tennessee 37205

Distributed to the trade by
National Book Network
4720-A Boston Way
Lanham, Maryland 20706

1992 printing
Manufactured in the United States of America

To Allen Tate

Preface

When Caroline Gordon in late 1934 embarked upon a novel about the Civil War—originally to be called "The Cup of Fury," and finally entitled *None Shall Look Back*—the subject matter might have appeared a natural one, given her family heritage and her intellectual affiliations. However, to a writer of her seriousness it posed considerable problems, and she did not lightly take it on. When she did, she chose the most demanding of stories—the story of a soldier—depending upon no easy devices of narrative, and crafting her work with models in mind that far transcended the genre of Civil War romance.

That she should turn eventually to the materials of the Civil War might seem, in retrospect, almost inevitable. By 1934 she had already clearly revealed in her two published novels—*Penhally* (1931) and *Aleck Maury, Sportsman* (1934)—an intent to mine the resources of her own family's history. And in the context of that immediate fund of memory, the Civil War had something of a mythic stature—a "general catastrophe" in the past, as she put it in a late memoir, that, at least in part, explained why "life was a desperate affair." Her acceptance of the matter of familial memory opened her to the need to imagine and enact again that original catastrophe.

Moreover, the need to come to terms with this store of memory was shared by a generation of Southern writers. Her husband, Allen Tate, as well as Andrew Lytle, Robert Penn Warren, and others, was publicly involved in the Agrarian movement before and after the publication in 1930 of *I'll Take My Stand*, a polemical, intellectual defense of the Old South. In addition, Tate had written biographies of Stonewall Jackson (1928) and Jefferson Davis (1929); and Lytle had published a biography of Nathan Bedford Forrest (1931). Not coincidentally, this period also witnessed a new surge of fiction about the Civil War. While Gordon was writing *None Shall Look Back* (from December 1934 until October 1936), Lytle completed his novel set during the war, *The Long Night* (1936), and Tate began *The Fathers* (1938). These titles joined others of some seriousness emerging around the same time, novels by Evelyn Scott, DuBose Heyward, Stark Young, and William Faulkner.

Though the Civil War forms part of the story in *Penhally*, Gordon's choice to address the material of the war directly was long and carefully contemplated, because she fully understood the demands it would impose upon her. To grasp her achievement in *None Shall Look Back*, we need to see clearly the technical problems she confronted, as well as the scope of her conception. While on a Guggenheim in Paris in 1933 Gordon wrote to a friend that she had long cherished a desire to take a soldier through the four years of the war, but that she didn't think it could be done, at least not by a woman. Her remark suggests that she had a particular kind of narrative in mind: one that, among the hundreds of published Civil War novels, had not yet been done and might still be impossible to do; and one that she saw as particularly "masculine" in its demands on the writer.

What story did Gordon imagine, and what were the impediments she may have foreseen? First of all, the genre of Civil War novels, which continued to thrive into the first decades of the twentieth century, itself constituted a serious problem: the task of bringing romance into the confines of naturalism and historical accuracy. For Civil War novels, almost by definition, are romances, characterized by tendencies which are deadliest to the serious novelist—idealization, sentimentality, and polemicism. Ironically, the publication of *None Shall Look Back* was delayed because of the success of the greatest war romance of them all, Margaret Mitchell's *Gone with the Wind* (1936).

Clearly, then, Gordon's first instinct as a writer in imagining the story of a soldier would be an insistence upon careful naturalism. But another, even larger, aspiration complicates this instinct. From the beginning she seems to have envisioned a narrative difficult to achieve, one that would be epic in spirit—a tale memorializing the deeds of a hero, set in the context of the concrete, valuable, though flawed world for which he is willing to die. "Her story," said Katherine Anne Porter in reviewing *None Shall Look Back*, "is a legend in praise of heroes, of those who lost their battle, and their lives." As Porter keenly discerns, it attempts to give homage to the ancient assertion of "*dulce et decorum est pro patria mori*," uttered in the novel by an old classics teacher as his students leave the academy for war. This unqualified affirmation of the heroic was to some extent scandalous even in its own day, when anti-heroes were the norm and when the writer, according to Porter, was under considerable pressure to adopt a "form of opportunism . . . called 'interpreting history correctly.' " Even more so does it seem scandalous today, with our still more exacting criteria of negation.

The desire to chronicle the hero is hard indeed for any novelist to fulfill. The naturalism at the roots of the novel is essentially skeptical, resistant to the easy appeal of public beliefs and of heroic gestures: irony is its dominant tone. Thus, as much as Gordon admired Crane's *The Red Badge of Courage*, its narrator, who continually deflates the pretensions of the main character and who views "courage"—both as a human gesture and as a public "badge"—with steady skepticism, cannot serve as a guide in her effort to render the hero. Crane's irony must be eschewed, as well as the sentimentality of the romance.

Gordon was conscious too of the anomaly of a woman's choosing this kind of artistic task: women do not generally write epic narratives. And, in technical terms, though the world of the home and of lovers is relatively accessible to the imagination, to write a narrative of the experience of a soldier in war requires more: an assured mastery of a "masculine" domain, the highly technical language of warcraft—strategy and maneuver, both overt and covert; disposition of forces; the technical nature, force, and impact of weapons; the pragmatic care of the army, the movement of vehicles, the feeding of men and of horses; the physical symptoms of hunger, thirst, disease, and exposure; the nature and variety of wounds, the postures of the dead, the cries of the dying, the effects of putrefaction, the disposition of bodies; and, perhaps most essentially, a language attentive to the individual characters of horses and of men as they show themselves in gesture—that is to say, a language ordered to the discrimination of spirit and courage. We should note, indeed, that the mastery of this kind of detail is not typical of male writers either: it simply requires too much work.

Thus in writing this novel, Gordon did not turn for paradigms to the romance writers that preceded her. For her narrative discipline and for the factual record she depended upon the study of historical writers—Civil War documents such as the Forrest biographies of John Wyeth and Andrew Lytle and the collection of eyewitness accounts in *Battles and Leaders of the Civil War*; and, as models of perspective, classical battle narratives, such as those of Plutarch and Thucydides. But beyond these disciplinary guides, she chose imaginative company with no less than Tolstoy and Homer. Indeed, the considerable technical achievement of *None Shall Look Back* is to make the devices of fictional naturalism serve the purposes of a classical heroic narrative. As in Homer, the bareness and simplicity of the style, the quiet, reiterative use of epithets, and the play between nearness and distance, give great dignity and poignancy to the tragic events described. The narrative stance in the novel, Ford Madox Ford said, suggested that of Athene among the armies in the *Iliad*, the narrator standing beside the reader with calm impartiality and clear-sighted premonition.

We must emphasize the technical matters of *None Shall Look Back* in part because the style is so conspicuous a part of its force, but also because craft, for Gordon, was in some mysterious way identical with, or at least inseparable from, imaginative vision. In her late memoir "Cock-Crow," she sees the pattern of her life's work in terms that make *None Shall Look Back* appear a fable of her career: "War which, now under one disguise, now another, pits a man against his arch enemy, Death, has always provided a favorable climate for the growth of the hero, as well as for the study of his ways and deeds. The novelist, like the soldier, is committed by his profession to a life-long study of wars and warriors." The novelist and soldier are alike in commitment: and thus the author's attention to the details of military craft as well as to the passion of the soldier's life reflexively signifies the inexorable demands, the austerity and sacrifice, of her own art.

If *None Shall Look Back* renders the catastrophe of the South, we are brought to the question, as with Troy in the *Iliad*, of why this "city" falls. Concerning the war itself, the loss of Confederate to Union forces in the western campaigns, Gordon is quite clear. Its leaders relied excessively on an abstract knowledge of military procedure and insufficiently on specific and original strategies and inspired leaders: "The problem," Forrest thinks when he sees that the generals at Fort Donelson plan to surrender, "was how to convey to these men a certain knowledge which he had and which they did not seem to possess," a knowledge based on concrete and intuitive engagement with all the actualities of the moment. Gordon does not give commentary on the generals and battles, but only renders the historical account, which itself clearly conveys the imprudence and blindness that lost the Confederate army its opportunities at Fort Donelson and Chickamauga and which caused unnecessary slaughter at the battle of Franklin. Nor does she obscure these failures by vilifying the enemy or ridiculing its leaders. On the contrary, Sherman in particular, unlike Jefferson Davis or Generals Bragg and Hood, is depicted as recognizing a military genius when he sees one, and from the beginning considered Forrest one of his most formidable adversaries.

Apart from this large arena of pride and error, in the private sphere of family and desire, do we also find premonitory signs of the eventual fall of this world? We are led to this question in part because of the title of the book. An apocalyptic sense is suggested both in the original title—"The Cup of Fury," from Jeremiah 25:15—as well as in the final title, taken, as the epigraph tells us, from Nahum 2:8: "But Ninevah is of old like a pool of water: yet they shall flee away. Stand, stand, shall they cry; but none shall look back." In the verses alluded to, both Jeremiah and Nahum speak prophetically of the wrath of God descending upon unrighteous peoples. The verse from Nahum, in particular, describes the warriors in the last line of the city's defense breaking in terror. The novel closes with just such a scene of panic in battle, when Forrest yells to his retreating men: " 'Rally, men, rally! For God's sake, rally!' But they would not listen." Though the title of the novel may be read ambivalently—as referring to the kingdom of the invaders (the oppressor Ninevah) rather than to the South (Israel)—the parallel between the biblical text and the last scene clearly suggests that the defeat of the South is a kind of retribution, that it collapses out of some ultimate weakness of spirit. However, the ending just as clearly points to the heroic figure, for Rives does "stand," and our last image of the war is of Forrest charging the line alone.

To understand the importance of the hero in the world of the novel, we must first contemplate the problem of courage—that is, the problem of facing death—which his presence brings into focus. As we attempt to discern the possible weakness within this world—or more specifically within the Allard family—the flaw is not obvious, but so deeply embedded in a stable and elegant way of life as to be almost invisible. Critics have located this flaw as part of a defense or attack of the presumed agrarian beliefs of the author, and their diagnoses seem inadequate: the polemical is as alien to this novel as is the sentimental. As the author renders it, the chief flaw does not appear to be the encroachment from within of "Yankee" entrepreneurs like Joe Bradley, or industrialists-to-be like Jim Allard. Nor is the flaw of the Allards and of the South to be found in the institution of slavery as such, which appears to be a symptom of a deeper spiritual problem, rather than the problem itself. The novel reflects a deliberate choice by the author to avoid the question of slavery as an abstract issue—for such reductive abstraction on both sides was, after all, a main cause of the war—and to confront it as a concrete and therefore complex aspect of the South, reflecting its hierarchy and economics, but also its values and its unresolved moral perplexities.

The flaw of the Allard world might best be seen in the figure of its patriarch. Fontaine Allard's love of land and his sense of responsibility to his ancestors and descendants are presented as a kind of sacred piety; and as one who breeds horses, he is associated with the heroic pattern of the whole novel (two of the Confederate generals who escaped from Fort Donelson were on his horses). But this sense of piety and proprietorship should not be taken as an unqualified moral measure. Though he is basically a good and generous man, the narrator makes us aware that Fontaine Allard is unable to be happy where he cannot command; that he is slightly pompous, complacent in his sense of his family's superiority, and intolerant of difference. He thinks to himself at the beginning of the novel that "Youth must always regard itself as imperishable"; but there is little sign that he does not participate in the same naivete, the same inability to appreciate the mutable and transient. Even his awareness of familial continuity in time is associated with the transient, the fragrance of flowers from the garden, which "spoke to him of pleasures past and of pleasures to come." His identification with land, lineage, and ownership is so complete and unconscious that, like the crazy dwarfish Old Ben who haunts the stables where he used to ride as a jockey, Fontaine becomes a helpless idiot at the moment his house falls, roused from torpor only at the mention of horses.

The flaw in the fabric of the ample and contented Allards of Kentucky might be put in simple and proverbial terms: they live a life whose happiness (well-being, good fortune) is apparently never seriously examined in relation to death and mutability, and never rooted in any order beyond the natural. The South, Allen Tate suggests in *I'll Take My Stand*, failed in being a feudal society without a correspondingly articulate structure of religion; its way of life to some extent was an end in itself. Something of the same insistence is made in *None Shall Look Back*, as it presents a world of gracious and decorous pleasures and passions, having no apparent ends beyond the moment, except its own perpetuation in the family. The implied questions throughout the novel, thus, are simple, stark, and ancient ones: in what does human happiness consist, and what are the ends by which it is measured? War and catastrophe bring us to a remembrance of these ultimate questions; and the hero points to an answer, if we are able to read it.

The novel establishes a persistent questioning all along, in pointing to ambiguous figures like Forrest who possess an incommunicable and invaluable knowledge. In this light, we must reconsider two of the Allard connection that are taken by the Fontaine Allards to be "eccentric," but that prove, paradoxically, to be central: Edmund Rowan, who ignores the life of the farmer in order to pursue the life of sport; and Susan Allard, the wife of Thomas Allard, whose father Garrett Allard, concerned with his soul, in his old age gave up the raising of tobacco and tried to dispose of his slaves. These two figures are alike in important ways: each lives austerely, minimally sustained by an agrarian life, with no concern for possessions; each manifests an intensity or a "passion" that transcends the pursuit of ordinary pleasure—for Susan Allard, the care of the sick and needy, and for Edmund Rowan, the hunt (if, as Gordon suggests elsewhere, we take the hunt as an heroic quest, a ritual confrontation with death); and each is happy and self-sufficient, as are no other characters in the novel.

Susan Allard's character, in particular, deserves closer attention, since her household provides the chief counterpoint to that of Fontaine Allard, and since Rives Allard inherits her intense and austere disposition. Her significance in the novel is almost uniformly misread, because critics take the condescension and prejudices of the Kentucky Allards as somehow normative—and surely this is not entirely justified. Seen without prejudice, Susan Allard is clearly a good and selfless woman: she takes in orphans; cares for the sick, the poor, the homeless, and the wounded; refuses to participate in the retribution for her husband's murder, referring vengeance to God, not to men; compels her sons to work in the fields part of each day with the slaves; gives away her possessions continuously, the family heirlooms as well as the fresh pudding at dinner. None of these things is scandalous in itself; but certainly they appear so to a society bound in its identity to various codes—hierarchy, legality, ownership—which she ignores and transgresses.

Susan Allard is, like the Allards of her husband's family, concerned with the soul and with the good. She is apparently possessed by a sense of mission that wholly preoccupies her attention, to the exclusion of domestic affairs. But there is nothing abstract or puritanical about her ministrations: she is active, pragmatic, and effective. After seeing his mother tend to the wounded on the battlefield of Chickamauga, Rives thinks: "You could not set her down as belonging to one of those [ladies'] associations. She was a host in herself. A 'captain' the negroes called it."

What they mean in this phrase is that she has the mysterious quality of "authority." Within this chronicle of a confused and death-filled world, where the heroic is often difficult to discern, the author surprisingly points to an essential kinship between Susan Allard and General Forrest: as those engaged in concrete, directed action, both move instinctively, in ways that call into question the codes within which they move. They are distant and strange to those who surround them. Nothing makes clearer the hidden affiliation of these characters than Rives Allard, who has his mother's disquieting eyes, "at once cold and passionate," who like his mother is seen often reflectively gazing into the flames of the fire; but who also feels an affinity for Forrest like that of a son for his father, and who becomes inextricably linked with Forrest in the last heroic gesture of the novel. George Rowan, thinking of the "dangerous lot" of the Forrest brothers, wild and reckless, places Rives among them, echoing the chauvinism of all the Kentucky Allards: "Well, Rives Allard had always been a queer cuss. It was only natural that he should land in a queer branch of the service. For it [spying] was a queer way of fighting." Rives, along with Susan, belongs to the "peculiar" branch of the family; and that strangeness is identified with the "queerness" of Forrest's scouts.

Finally, both Susan Allard and Forrest are associated in the novel through the image of the horse. Susan Allard is called "Mammy Horse" by one of her children, so constantly is she mounted and moving. "She goes up and down the yearth," Rivanna says of Susan Allard: "She just gets on her horse and waits till the spirit move her." Likewise the last image of Forrest on his gigantic horse King Philip is a culmination of the constant presence of horses throughout the novel, beginning with Fontaine Allard's race horses, and moving through the incessant changing of mounts in the cavalry, as the horses are driven to their limits and collapse or die of wounds. The horse and the hero are inextricable, joined especially in battle as a sign of intensity, power, and mysterious spiritedness.

There emerges, then, in the novel an implicit argument suggesting the limitation and the transparency of the "happiness" of Fontaine Allard and his family. What they disdain about Good Range, the land of the Georgia Allards—that they would "hate to live in a country where [their] grave was already dug"—points precisely to their blindness. For the simplest piety tells us that in some sense our grave *is* already dug. The author points to characters marginal to the accepted agrarian structures who possess compelling passions rooted in the spirit, and rooted in a constant and candid engagement with death. Nowhere is the innocence of the Allards shown more vividly than in the marriage of Rives and Lucy Churchill, which joins the two branches of the family. Their momentary passionate happiness possesses no ground sufficient to sustain it in the face of despair and death.

The story of marriages made quickly in the midst of war is an ancient one: the woman, in her passion for the warrior, becomes in a sense the bride of Hades, and the marriage bed and deathbed become one. The warrior, lost in the vastness of the underworld, mesmerized by the constant gaze on death, loses the orientation toward life that his bride might give him. That mythical dimension is fully amplified in *None Shall Look Back*. Here, as so many characters say in the *Iliad*, it seems wrong to assign blame where fate has had inexorable control. Rendering the first days of their marriage, the narrator captures their doomed story in an image: "One of the logs that Rives had just laid on [the fire] was green. From one end of it little drops of moisture formed and fell hissing into the ashes."

However, the special poignancy of this union is that it possesses a spiritual possibility never realized. When Rives first recognizes his attraction to Lucy, he recalls George Rowan's phrase for her, and she is associated in his heart with that exaltation of spirit causing him to go to war: "*Clarissima . . . Most clear*! The name suited her, a sort of brightness about her, a quick, proud way she had of turning her head. When he looked at her he got back the feeling he had had about the war before all this talk came to confuse him." On Lucy's part, the necessities of her own spirit cause her to reject the conventional George Rowan and to be attracted to the silent intensity of Rives, to his fieriness and pride. However, as so often happens in Gordon's work, their choice to marry is not quite a choice, but an event brought about by circumstance. Moreover, their union seems consistently defined in terms of passion: "I *want* you, more than anything," Rives says to Lucy, as they decide to marry; and when he leaves a final time for battle, Lucy thinks (unable to utter it), "I may never see you again, but I will *desire* you all my life" (emphasis added). The consuming, mortal passion that defines their love is most clearly seen in their physical union in a "dark cedared ravine" on the death-filled battlefield of Chickamauga.

In their passion, circumscribed by loss and hardship as well as by the weary desperation of battle, the question of "happiness" arises repeatedly and hauntingly. Each time it does, it brings with it more vividly a sense of the fragility and inadequacy of the happiness sought so fiercely. As heir to the innocence of the Kentucky Allards, Lucy Churchill naively expects happiness from the future, an animated and rich fullness of the moment, such as the dance brings her. The narrator shows us the repeated frustrations of Lucy's expectations, and her persistent unwillingness to accept the darkness and confusion that those disappointments bring. Reflecting on her own inexplicable behavior toward George Rowan and on the "ruined life" of her aunt Cally, Lucy sees "in a flash . . . what a precarious business life—and particularly love—is and how impalpable the forces which make for success or disaster. And it now seemed to her as improbable that she could be happy in this life as it had once seemed certain." Though her insight here is genuine, her disillusion is to some extent self-fulfilling. Her instinct is to shut her eyes and raise a barrier of pride at the first sign of the betrayal of her happiness—and life itself, as Lytle points out, is her betrayer.

Lucy's story consists of a series of "descents" which she fails to negotiate. When she goes down the dark, sunken lane to Cabin Row where her own slaves live, she refuses to take in the human, moral darkness signified in Della's brutal beating by the overseer, and instead she feels revulsion for the beaten woman herself. Later when she travels down to Georgia to Rives' home after their marriage, she is oppressed by the darkness of the woods, and by the bare, austere house. When alone with Rives, she turns passionately to him, "her eyes tightly closed as if to shut out the room." When he asks her then, "Are you happy?" she whispers "yes" passionately. The device of using passion in order to escape from circumstances she does not want to see is in fact at the origin of her hasty marriage to Rives, which takes place immediately following the destruction of Brackets, the Allards' home in Kentucky. Later, her descent with Rives into the "dark, cedared ravine" on the battlefield, in the midst of death and disease, represents a more desperate escape into passion. All the while, Lucy impatiently endures her condition—her separation from Rives, the hardship of work and hunger, the increasing presence of death in her life—in proud and increasing bitterness that she has been betrayed. Needless to say, Lucy finds her mother-in-law Susan Allard "disquieting," and is fearful that Rives shares in her nature; for Susan Allard is clearly drawn to a happiness entirely other than the one Lucy desires.

Rives' sense of happiness centers from the beginning upon the spiritedness associated with the thought of going to war: he reflects on the day he leaves that no one "could possibly know how happy he was." His orientation, which draws from the quiet spiritual intensity of his mother, stands in contrast to that of Lucy and her family. His reasons for fighting are not intellectual or abstract but simple: to defend an invaded country. But more profoundly his exaltation in anticipation of battle involves the mystery of courage, the nature of which is impossible to know except in concrete action. But like Lucy's initial happiness in the animated moment, Rives' expectations too must come to a fall. When he begins to experience battle, the reflective character inherited from his mother draws him increasingly into a fascination with death. Especially, the prospect of the South's defeat accentuates the appeal of death. Rives thinks, after General Bragg's refusal of an appeal by Forrest seals the doom of the Confederate forces: "If the Confederate cause failed . . . there could be no happiness for him except the grave."

The dilemma of the hero's desire for "happiness" is a subtle one. For him, we might say, happiness consists in that moment of selfless, spirited release which goes under the name of courage. But in the anger and weariness of continual defeat and loss, death would seem to offer another release and another mystery. So courage is confused by Death that relentlessly shadows it; and the act of the hero may seem an act of despairing rage, or even an act of suicide, and thus of cowardice. This situation—the ambiguous appeals to the hero that draw him between courage and the darkness of despair—may be what Gordon means when she says (in "Cock-Crow") that each hero stands "at the edge of the abyss. An abyss so deep and dark that no human eye has ever penetrated it."

This mystery within the nature of courage, with its shadow life of rage and despair, is what Rives Allard faces more and more intently throughout his story. It comes to a climax when, after his brother Jeffrey is killed in battle, General Forrest charges in a blind rage toward the enemy lines. An officer, his eyes "bright with fear," whispers, "Be killed. That's what he wants. Be killed." Riding away, Rives curses the officer violently: "God damn. . . . lying . . . dirty . . . *coward*!" Then, waving his arms crazily, he shouts, "Every man. Got the right. To get killed," and collapses with the thought that Forrest himself may already be dead. Is Forrest's charge an act of courage, despair, or cowardice? Does the officer accusing Forrest of wanting to die do so because the hero's courage, his unhesitating surrender to possible death, is terrifying? Forrest in this scene stands at the abyss, and Rives recognizes it as the place where he too stands.

Though *None Shall Look Back* ends, like the *Iliad,* with an austere and uncompromising sense of loss and grief, it also, like the *Iliad*, wholeheartedly praises the hero, whose central task is to act as fully and selflessly as possible, with awareness of the ultimate stakes of his action. Speaking of this novel, Porter says, "The hero is forever the same, then and forever unanswerable, the man who throws his life away as if he hated living, in defense of one thing, whatever it may be, that he cares to live for." Porter keenly recognizes the ambiguity of paradox of the hero's gesture: "as if he hated living . . . in defense of the one thing . . . he cares to live for." Rives Allard in the last scene of the novel successfully, it seems to me, negotiates the precarious territory of his own spirit. When the line of battle breaks and all the soldiers flee, Rives does stand; after shooting the fleeing color-bearer, he seizes the flag and furiously charges the enemy line to his death. At this point Forrest—recognizing Rives with pity and grief, and seeing in him his own fallen brother Jeffrey—in his turn takes up the fallen flag and charges the line alone.

Rives' action to stand against the impossible onslaught of the enemy is simple, instinctive,and unhesitating. If at the end we ask what he dies for, and thus what he cares to live for, whether his act is not simply one of rage and despair, the answer is given not in any commentary or in any words spoken by Rives, but in the image of the "colors." The cowardice of the color-bearer—entrusted to bear the honor of his people in the vanguard—is the unbearable outrage. Rives unhesitatingly kills him (as in one historical account of this battle Forrest himself did) and mounts the flag on his saddle; so absolutely is his attention fixed on the flag and the battle line that he never knows he has been shot and is dying.

That Rives' gesture in this scene is completed by Forrest suggests its participation in the full dimension of the heroic. The last image of war in the book is of Forrest: "He put spurs to King Philip. The great war-horse bounded forward. Forrest stood in his stirrups. The rose-colored flag danced above him then dipped. It veiled his face for a moment from the men's sight but they heard his voice sounding back over the windy plain and saw him gallop toward the fort." Though the novel suggests why the cause of the South failed, the ending clearly points to the endurance of its heroes and its heroic gestures in the face of death. The hero Forrest on his powerful horse, always obscure and unaccountable, partially veiled from our vision, enters into memory here, joining other, ancient heroes on the "windy plain." In the last scene of the novel, Lucy after hearing of Rives' death, sees clearly enough, despite her grief and bitterness, to recognize the ancient battle in which Rives has been engaged: "She had been staring at the dark woods. . . . They took strange shapes, a boy in a peaked cap fleeing a giant along a forest road, a man on horseback contending with a dragon."

When Homer in the *Iliad* has Achilles bear the shield depicting the whole of the human cosmos, it is to remind his audience that the happiness of any world has no ground without the hero's struggle with death. *None Shall Look Back*, rendering the catastrophe of the Allards, and of the South, consistently points to the same truth.

Irving, Texas EILEEN GREGORY

Part One

PRINCIPAL CHARACTERS

FONTAINE ALLARD, *Kentucky tobacco planter, sixty-five years old.*

CHARLOTTE ALLARD, *his wife.*

JOHN MCLEAN, *Charlotte's brother, planter, opposed to Secession.*

LUCY CHURCHILL, LOVE MINOR } *Allard's orphan grand-daughters.*

JIM ALLARD, *elder son of Fontaine Allard.*

NED ALLARD, *Confederate officer, younger son of Fontaine Allard.*

BELLE BRADLEY ALLARD, *Jim's wife.*

JOE BRADLEY, *a wealthy merchant of Clarksville.*

ARTHUR BRADLEY, *Joe's son.*

CAROLINE ("CALLY") HOBART, *Fontaine Allard's divorced daughter.*

JENNY MORRIS HOBART, *Cally's ten-year-old daughter.*

GEORGE ROWAN, *cousin to the Allards, aide to General Deshler.*

EDMUND ROWAN, *George's father, planter and sportsman.*

SPENCER ROWE, *cousin to the Kentucky Allards, prisoner at Johnson's Island.*

RIVES ALLARD, *of Georgia, cousin to the Kentucky Allards, scout under General Forrest.*

SUSAN ALLARD, *of Georgia, mother of Rives.*

MARION ("MITTY") ALLARD, *Rives' sister.*

BEN BIGSTAFF, *scout under General Forrest.*

WINSTON MCLEAN, *butler to Fontaine Allard.*

NATHAN BEDFORD FORREST, *Lieutenant-General, C. S. A.*

Confederate Generals BRAGG, BUCKNER, FLOYD, PILLOW, LONGSTREET, HILL, DESHLER, BRECKINRIDGE, POLK, *and other Confederate officers.*

Federal Generals THOMAS, GRANT, GRANGER, *and other Federal officers.*

1

FONTAINE ALLARD watched the three vehicles move down the drive. Colonel Whitcomb's grays and Mr. Harris' match were abreast now—they'd be racing time they hit the big road. And behind them rolled old Mrs. Spencer's victoria. She had been half an hour making her adieux but she was gone at last. Perhaps some of the other ladies would follow her example now and leave. He drew his handkerchief out and mopped his face then took a quick look around. In the hall his wife stood talking to Cousin Cissy Masters and Mrs. Latham, and Cally over there held the Pleasant Grove ladies in tow. The young people, gathered around the millstone table under the cedar tree, could take care of themselves and somebody, Cally, probably, had carried old Cousin Lydia off for her afternoon nap. There was nobody just now who seemed to need his attention. He thrust his handkerchief back into his pocket, took another cautious look around, then went quietly down the steps and made off across the lawn.

His goal was a little summerhouse that stood on the far southern slope, beyond the last tree. It was octagonal in shape, built of cedar posts, its sides bare except for the northern exposure which was matted thickly with cinnamon vine. Allard, walking fast, gained the shelter of the green wall, stepped inside. His great split-bottomed chair was there. He pulled it over into the middle of the earthen floor and was about to sit down when his foot came in contact with some soft, yielding object. He looked down. A little negro boy, curled in a ball, lay sleeping on the ground. He opened his eyes drowsily, looked up at his master and was going back to sleep when Allard bent over and touched him with the tip of his cane. "Dolphus, run in the house and get me a julep."

The little boy rose, stretched himself, yawned, then moved off at a slow dogtrot. Allard slanted his hat brim over his eyes and sank back in his chair. From where he sat the main part of the house was invisible but he could see the long west wing. The leaves of the Virginia creeper that covered it were scarlet; there had been enough frost to redden them but the trees on the lawn were still green and the air today was as balmy as summer. He shifted his gaze to the south lawn. A group of ladies had come down from the porch and were walking about. He could distinguish his wife's dark dress among the lighter ones, thought he occasionally heard the sound of her laughter. He knew where she was taking them. To the rose garden. There was a yellow-hearted rose blooming that at this season of the year was Charlotte's delight and marvel. She went out to look at it a dozen times a day.

The little boy was back with the julep. Allard took the glass from him and, still looking out over the lawn, tilted it to his lips. The ladies had moved out of his field of vision but he could hear the click of the garden gate as they passed through, the sudden burst of animated chatter as they came upon the yellow rosebush and then the voices dying away as they scattered upon the garden paths.

He sighed, stretching his heavy limbs in his deep chair. It had been a long day and tiring. But everything had gone off well. He shook his glass absently to and fro, reviewing the events of the annual celebration. Edmund Rowan who never drank after breakfast had come according to his custom at dawn. They two had had several drinks together before the family assembled for breakfast. After breakfast Rowan had ridden off on one of his fishing excursions. He, Fount, had barely had time to give his overseer some necessary orders before the carriages had begun rolling up the drive. The Spencers had come first and after them the Bathursts and then the Pleasant Grove people. He mentally ticked them off on his fingers. Yes, there must have been twenty ladies to sit down at the long table in the dining room. The children and nurses, as was the custom, had been served on picnic tables spread under the trees. And off there in the grove thirty or forty men of the community, his friends and neighbors, had eaten a barbecue dinner. Not to mention the four carcasses served up to the negroes in the quarters.

The little boy, standing at his side, silently stretched out his hand. Allard looked down, saw that the glass was empty save for the yellowish, sweetened fragments of ice. He handed the glass to the child who at once lifted it to his lips. Allard watched the pulse in the small throat leap as the boy greedily drained the few drops of syrup. He smiled, made a flicking motion with his cane. "Run 'long. Run 'long now and play. I'm going to take a nap."

He settled himself deeper in his chair, was about to close his eyes when he heard footsteps on the path. His wife was approaching with their little granddaughter, Jenny Morris. The child saw him and, breaking away from her grandmother, ran up beside his chair. "Guess who's here?" she cried.

Allard reached out and encircled the dancing figure with his arm. "Mister Robert Alexander Minor," he said, naming an eleven-year-old boy of the neighborhood who was sometimes accused of being Jenny Morris' beau.

She shook her head, still dancing. "Not any old Robert Aleck Minor. It's a grown gentleman."

Something in her tone made Allard look enquiringly at his wife who just then had come up beside his chair. She smiled, though her expression a moment before had been grave. "He thinks he's a mighty fine gentleman," she said.

He got heavily to his feet. "Ned," he said, "he's come home."

She laid her hand on his arm. "George Rowan is with him. And they've brought another boy. One of those Georgia Allards."

They stood there together a moment. Her hand was still on his arm. Her eyes were fixed on his face. His gaze was bent on the ground. Each knew what the other was thinking. They had believed their younger son, Ned, safe, for a few months at least, at the seminary, but his sudden arrival—with George Rowan of all people—could mean only one thing. The boys had come home to go to war.

Mrs. Allard even as she realized this knew that her husband wanted to disguise his own anxiety from her, so she said only: "We'd better go see them," resisting the impulse to add, "and get some sense into their heads."

They left the summerhouse, the child running on ahead, and walked toward the house. As they approached, a slender, dark-haired boy of seventeen broke away from a group of people on the steps and came running toward them. He kissed his father impetuously, then realizing perhaps that it was considered unmanly for men to kiss each other, blushed scarlet, but retaining his father's arm squeezed it hard. "I got home for your birthday," he said.

Allard looked down at him. Ned was dark where all the other children were fair. His father, greeting him after any separation, was always surprised to notice how much he resembled his mother. "I suppose you know where you ought to be this minute, sir," he said sternly.

Another dark-haired young man, taller by a head than Ned, had come up. George Rowan. Edmund's wild young son. He was grinning but his voice was properly respectful. "You mean at school, sir?" he asked before Ned could answer.

Allard nodded. "No business coming off home without consulting anybody." He looked at Rowan. "Does your father know you're here?"

"No, sir. But he will. I'm on my way there now. Had to stop and drink your health." And the young scoundrel grinned again.

Mrs. Allard came up, slipped her arm through George's. "Not tonight," she said authoritatively. "Your father can wait till morning to see you. Fount, these boys have ridden fifty miles today."

"Killed their horses?" Allard asked.

"Oh, Pa, there aren't a dozen boys left in the seminary!" Ned said excitedly. He squeezed his father's arm again. "Pa, that's Rives over there under the tree."

Allard looked over to where under the great oak tree three or four men stood talking. His brother-in-law, John McLean, was still there, talking with Frank Leffingwell. The square-shouldered, well set up young man in travel-stained clothes must be Rives. "Aye," he said, "I'll go speak to him," and he moved off with the two boys across the lawn.

Captain Leffingwell, a handsome, military-looking man of fifty, remained silent until the introductions had been accomplished then resumed his discourse. He was talking about the Louisiana country from which he had just returned.

"I'm glad I went," he said. "Why, I hadn't any idea what was going on until I went down there." He made a sweeping gesture with his right hand then brought it up, fingers clenched. "War," he said, "nobody down there is thinking of anything but war."

George Rowan, whose eyes had been fixed on the captain all the time he was speaking, nodded emphatically. "The country's at war and the people in Kentucky don't even know it's going on. Well, we'll ride out of the state and enlist."

Fontaine Allard was not listening to the talk. He was looking at the visitor. He had been trying to place this boy in his family connection and it had suddenly come to him who he was: Tom Allard's son. Yes, he was Tom's boy, all right, with those eyes. He was about to move over beside him, to tell him that he had gone to school with his father when an old gentleman, who up to now had taken no part in the conversation, stepped forward. Mr. McLean's dress, a suit of homespun with blue linsey woollen vest, presented quite a contrast to that of the other guests, but his appearance and carriage were those of a person who is accustomed to being listened to with respect. He eyed the speaker critically now and shook his head so vigorously that his pendulous jowls quivered.

"I declare, Frank Leffingwell," he said, "you're a bigger fool than I gave you credit for. What do you want to get all the young men in the country killed off for?"

Captain Leffingwell did not answer and the old man struck his fat hand on the side of the tree trunk. "Gilfillan Brothers," he said, "biggest tobacco firm in London. Been furnishing me and my father before me with all the credit we needed. You reckon they going to keep on sending me my bill of exchange the first of every April now this blockade's on? How's a man going to sell his tobacco if he can't ship it? You stay here and let Fount Allard support you. It don't make any difference to you but other people have got to make a living. A pack of fools out to ruin commerce, that's all you are. I ain't got any more use for you than I got for the Yankees."

Captain Leffingwell was shaking his head irritably. "The blockade's on, whether we like it or not. When the country's at war a man's got to take sides."

Fontaine Allard had been looking off over the lawn as if absorbed by the quiet evening scene before him, but now he turned to face Leffingwell. "A man's got to take sides," he said slowly. "At least he's got to take a stand. But those people 'way down south are different from us. I was down there in '55, visiting Cousin Joe. I often think of it." He paused, his clear blue eyes, untouched as yet by age, going from the face of one to the other as if he were not certain he could make his meaning clear. "Why, there was one fellow, Old Man Trotter Simpson's son, raised right here in Todd County, Kentucky, on hog and hominy, like all the Simpsons. Why, that fellow—I made Joe drive me in to see his place one day just out of curiosity. He was living in a mansion with six thousand acres of good cotton land, waited on hand and foot by negroes. And all bought with two years' cotton crops Joe told me."

Captain Leffingwell nodded. "It's a rich country. I saw 'em plowing in the fields and water splashing high as a mule's knee. Can't cake the land they tell me. Too fat."

"That's it," old Mr. McLean said testily. "It's too rich. Now this country, we been a long time building it up. Those fellows down there got rich too quick and it's gone to their heads. If somebody don't hold them down they'll ruin the country."

He clapped his hat on his head as he spoke, put out his hand to his cousin. "Well, I must be going. . . . Fount, many happy returns."

They walked over to where his low-slung buggy stood waiting on the drive. The negro boy who drove him had gathered up his reins and was clucking to his horse when Mr. McLean turned around, bawling as if he were already a mile away: "Good dinner, Fount, but tell your nigger Jim he put a mite too much vinegar in that sauce."

George Rowan's laugh rang out over the rattle of the departing wheels. "If that ain't Cousin John for you. Don't reckon anything in this world ever was made to suit him." He turned to Rives whom he evidently considered his particular guest. "Come on, let's go down to the office."

Allard watched them move away across the lawn. The "office" which stood in the far corner was the young men's special domain. There would be half a dozen of them in there tonight and Cicero whose duty it was to clean up the three rooms and wait on the visitors would grumble mightily.

Frank Leffingwell had started toward the house. Allard walked on and caught up with him. As he went he glanced about him, savoring as he liked to do the sights and sounds of evening. The air had freshened as it turned toward twilight. Above the oak tree one star was out. Allard looked toward the house. The wing was dark but in the parlor candles were lit and figures could be seen moving about. The strains of a violin were heard and a moment later a girl's voice rose in song. The young girl stood so close to one of the windows that they could discern the folds of her white dress, see the light shine on her neck and upturned face as she sang:

> "Believe me, if all those endearing young charms
> Which I gaze on so fondly today . . ."

The young voice, very high and pure, floated out on the evening air. The young men, halfway across the lawn, stopped as if arrested by the sound. Frank Leffingwell had stopped too and stood quite still until she had finished the second verse. "Lovely voice," he said and then meditatively, "Lucy's getting to be quite a young lady."

Fount Allard looked up at his granddaughter just then turning away from the window. Her dead mother, Honoria, had been his favorite among his children. He wondered if that was the reason he had a peculiarly tender feeling for Lucy. The words of the song were still in his ears: *"Let thy loveliness fade as it will . . ."* Lucy was eighteen this year. Honoria had not been much older when she had died at Lucy's birth. It was strange to know that she had been dead all these years and here was this young thing, her daughter, standing up there with the candlelight shining on her, singing of loveliness that must fade.

The young men still stood as if hoping the singer would continue. He wondered if any meaning from the song reached them or whether it were merely the sound of the fresh, pure voice floating out on the air and decided that it was. Youth must always regard itself as imperishable.

Frank was talking again, about the political situation. ". . . One thing they've done, they've put a soldier at the head of the state." And then his thoughts evidently going back to his conversation with old John McLean: "It don't matter how rich they are or what they raise. They're all fighting for one thing. Freedom. . . ."

Allard stepped up on the porch beside him. As they had come across the lawn some fragrance from the garden, roses, probably, but mingled with some other flower, had been wafted to them on the breeze. It spoke to him of pleasures past and pleasures to come. He realized that he was sixty-five years old and that all his life he had been peculiarly blessed. In the same instant he remembered an experience he had had many years before. He had been walking through a woodland—"the far woods" they called it. He had been in a part of the woods which he had never to his knowledge traversed before. And then suddenly walking along through those trees over ground covered by their dead leaves he had had the strange feeling, as if a voice had said to him: "These are your father's and your father's before him." The emotion had been as immediate, as passionate as desire or hate. He had actually for a moment been overcome by his attachment for that earth, those trees. Something of that same feeling was on him tonight as he stood on the porch looking out over the lawn where the trees were now only cloudy shapes under the soft sky.

He turned to Leffingwell. "Aye," he said, "that's what we all want. Freedom."

2

MR. ALLARD, rising a little in his chair, carved the last slice from the breast of the peacock and laid it on the plate that would go to his wife. She herself had finished serving butter beans and creamed potatoes from the two steaming tureens before her and Uncle Winston was already handing around the second plate of hot biscuits. She relaxed a little her erect posture, looked down the long table. Her granddaughters, Love and Lucy with Ned and George Rowan were on her right. On her left was the young cousin who had just arrived and her youngest granddaughter, Jenny Morris. She lifted a slice of the peacock breast now and laid it on Jenny Morris' plate. "Eat that, honey, it'll put meat on your bones."

Jenny Morris, who was already as plump as a little partridge, obediently lifted the dark, gamey morsel to her lips. She should have been in bed an hour ago but she had been allowed to stay up for the grown folks' supper, partly because it was her grandfather's birthday and partly because her young uncle, Ned, had just come home.

Mrs. Allard saw that her eyes, gray and shining, were fixed now on one, now on the other of the two girls. She reached a hand under the table and gave the child's knee an affectionate pinch. Jenny Morris leaned forward confidingly: "Mammy say Cousin Lucy'd be real pretty if she warn't so buck-eyed," she whispered.

"Mammy *said,*" Mrs. Allard corrected mechanically, repressing a laugh as she thought what Lucy would have to say to such a remark. She glanced at the two girls who tonight happened to be dressed alike in pale yellow tarleton with coronals of red roses in their hair. Love, she supposed, was the better-looking. She had a really beautiful nose, delicately aquiline, hair that was exactly the color of honey, the sloping shoulders that seemed made to display a shawl, but she was one of those people—Mrs. Allard numbered some of her nearest and dearest among them—whom privately she labelled as "tiresome." Lucy was different. Her mouth was too large, her nose too short, her only real beauty the unusually large, shining, gray eyes which Mammy decried, but she was more popular in the family circle because of her liveliness. It was a quality of imagination that lent excitement to whatever was going on. Mrs. Allard smiled now, remembering that it was Lucy who discovered that Cousin Thomas Mason did everything by the clock. Louisa Bathurst, a little on the tiresome side Mrs. Allard thought her too, had been shocked by Lucy's portrayal of Cousin Thomas chewing tobacco—spitting it out and throwing it into the bushes with a "Here, I ought to a thrown this thing away five minutes ago!"—but the rest of the family had shouted with laughter and all the rest of that summer it had amused them to keep imaginary track of Cousin Thomas' day. "Nine o'clock. Cousin Thomas has just taken off his left sock. Or ten. Cousin Tom is turning over on his right side now."

She turned her attention to the other young people. There had been a little flurry when they sat down. She realized now what it was. The visiting cousin had innocently been going to take his place beside Lucy but George Rowan had dexterously guided him to a place farther down the table and he himself sat now beside the girl. George had refused half a dozen dishes as they were passed and sat turned half sidewise in his seat as if supper were over. His long fingers fiddled with a salt cellar that was in front of him. He kept his eyes fixed intently upon it except when he would look up, smiling or sometimes very intent and grave at Lucy. "The rascal," Mrs. Allard told herself, "making love to the child right here at the table." He had been waiting on Louisa Bathurst last year and now here he was paying court to Lucy. She found herself studying his face, wondering what sort of husband he would make. George wore his hair rather long, and thrown back romantically from the high Rowan forehead. He had a long face, dark eyes full of light and sensitive, mobile lips. Just the sort she told herself that women made fools of themselves over, and recalled an incident of last summer to which she had paid little attention at the time. Fanny Latimer had been staying at Brackets. It was no secret that pretty, languishing Fanny would have preferred to stay on at Brackets and never return to her grim Scotch merchant of a husband. George had openly professed his admiration and had got up a tournament in her honor, he himself going as the "Black Knight." But Mrs. Allard rather thought that there had been more to it than that. A rambling house like Brackets affords plenty of opportunity for philandering. Wandering through the hall one night when it was too hot to sleep she had met George who by rights should have been down in the office, and there had been another time when she had been positive that an empty and seldom used bed chamber in the guest wing had had recent occupants.

Her eyes went to her younger son. Uncle Winston, handing around the hot biscuits, had just got as far as Ned. The boy was twisting around in his chair to smile up into the old man's face. Uncle Winston put a hand on his shoulder and pushed him down as if he were a child. Winston was always very stern with the children about their table manners. *Children!* Ever since she had come to the table she had been trying to put one thought out of her mind. Ned, barely seventeen, was going to war. The two boys, Ned and George had come into her room just before supper. Ned had a copy of the Memphis *Daily Appeal* worn from much folding which he had shown to her:

A CHANCE FOR ACTIVE SERVICE

MOUNTED RANGERS

Having been authorized by Governor Harris to raise a battalion of mounted rangers for the war, I desire to enlist five hundred able-bodied men, mounted and equipped with such arms as they can procure (shot-guns and pistols preferable) suitable to the service. Those who cannot entirely equip themselves will be furnished arms by the State. When mustered in, a valuation of the property in horses and arms will be made, and the amount credited to the volunteers. Those wishing to enlist are requested to report themselves at the Gayoso House, where quarters will be assigned until such time as the battalion is raised.

N. B. Forrest

The paper had been circulated at the school. She ought to be thankful that the boys had not got on the cars then and gone straight to Memphis. They confessed that they had been tempted but George, when he went off to school that fall, had promised his father that he would not enlist without first coming home. They had not needed to go to Memphis, however. This same Colonel Forrest—she had heard of him as a negro trader of unusual probity—had come to Louisville. He had come secretly, making his presence known only to Southern sympathizers to whom he had confidential letters. While he was there he had collected pistols, guns, saddle blankets and all the cavalry equipment that could be purchased without attracting attention. Her two boys—she thought of George Rowan as her own son—had been among the volunteers—none of them over eighteen years of age!—who had met him by appointment at a livery stable late in the night. The colonel had not taken them off with him then. He had to use secrecy in his movements. He had judged it best to divide his recruits into small bands which would rendezvous later on the border of the state, so the boys had come on home and would probably not go off to war for another week yet.

Jenny Morris had overcome her shyness enough to address a remark to the young man on her left.

"Cousin Rives, where do you sleep when you go to war?"

He smiled at her. "Don't know. I haven't gone yet."

"On the cold ground," George Rowan said, "on the cold, cold ground. Ask Cousin Frank. He was sleeping with his head on his saddle one night and a bunch of Indians came along and stole the saddle out from under him and he had to shoot them to get it back."

The little girl eyed her military cousin at the other end of the table. "I don't believe that," she said candidly. "I don't believe Cousin Frank could wake up that easy. They have to ring three bells down at the office to get him up every morning."

There was a shout of laughter. Under cover of it Mrs. Allard regarded her cousin thoughtfully. Captain Frank Leffingwell had come out from Virginia years ago, had bought a tract of land and was erecting a house on it when the Mexican War broke out. He was a man who liked fighting and he had left the logs for his house half rolled while he hurried to the war. Coming home from the war he had stopped a night at Brackets to see his cousin and had been there ever since, preferring the comforts of such an establishment to the austerities of a bachelor's hall.

Mrs. Allard knew his history. She was one of the few persons in the room who knew that Frank Leffingwell had been in the center of the square that broke the charge at Buena Vista. He thought a lot of having been an officer of the United States Army and he was an old-line Whig. His politics had kept him out of the Confederate Army so far but of late there was a new energy, a vitality about him that surprised her. "He's just like an old hound," she thought, "he's caught the scent. All he's thinking about now is striking the trail."

She turned away and her glance fell on the visiting cousin. Rives Allard was a young man of about twenty, well set up, with a brown moustache and brown, curling hair. There was nothing remarkable about his face except the eyes. Set under large, firmly modelled lids, they were of that sparkling blue-gray that can look at once cold and passionate. Mrs. Allard, who knew the ramifications of the Allard connection quite as well as her husband did, reflected that those eyes were peculiar to the Georgia Allards. That branch of the family had always been—or at least had always been regarded by the Brackets Allards—as peculiar. Old Garrett Allard, this boy's great-grandfather, had travelled out from Virginia with Fontaine Allard's grandfather. Younger sons, they had purchased tracts of tobacco land within ten miles of each other. Each had prospered. Fount's grandfather had imported a fine stallion from England and had raised fine horses. Garrett Allard had been a good farmer but all his life he had been mightily concerned about his soul. In his old age he had quit raising tobacco, thinking it wrong to pander to what he considered a vice and had planted his land in mulberry trees and bought a lot of silk worms. He could not find any factory that would convert the raw silk into the finished product and so he had just sent it around to his friends. He had been mightily concerned too about his negroes—and well he might be with them all living there idle on his hands—and had sent a lot of them back to Africa. Finally he had sold out his land here and gone down to north Georgia, where he settled. Fount always said that settling on that poor, washed-out land was the crowning folly of his life.

Fount had gone down there when he was a child, visiting with his mother who was much attached to Garrett Allard's wife, and he always quoted what she said when she looked out of the carriage and saw the red gullies stretching away on every side. "Humph, I'd hate to live in a country where my grave was already dug for me."

Mrs. Allard, smiling to herself over the ancient jest, became aware that Jenny Morris was looking at her with a peculiar, intent expression. It came to her what the child wanted. She glanced around the table to make sure that everybody was through, then slipped from her seat and broke into a dance step that carried her out of the dining room into the hall. Immediately there was a burst of laughter from the dining room and people pushed back their chairs and poured into the hall. She revolved before them slowly, her finger tips resting on her crinoline. The pose seemed to her histrionic, she was conscious that the smile on her face was too wide, too fixed. "But shucks," she told herself, "no use in children missing their fun just because the old people are worried."

3

IN the long ballroom on the second floor the young people were dancing to old Mr. McCulloch's fiddling. At ten o'clock Mrs. Allard noticed that the visiting cousin was alone, and crossed over to him. He was half-leaning, half-sitting against a window sill. She took her place on a sofa near the window without speaking, then reached up and lightly touched him on the arm with her fan.

"Tell me about your mother," she said.

He started. When he turned to her he seemed to be scowling; then his face cleared. He said: "She is very well. When she heard I was coming here she told me I must go to Hayslope and get her a sprig from the box tree by the gate. Do you know whether the tree is still standing?"

She considered. "I don't know. It may be. It's been years since I was at Hayslope." While she smiled into the handsome, and it seemed to her, gloomy young face, she was thinking that she would never have suspected Susan Allard of that much sentiment. She remembered Susan very well, a small woman with enormous gray eyes in a pale face, indefatigable, eternally dressed in a riding habit—she stayed on horseback so much that her youngest child when he was a baby had provoked laughter by stretching his hands to her and calling, "Mammy Horse, take Miles!" Charlotte Allard, who had herself often been accused of being too fond of horses, reflected complacently that she had never been that bad. But then all those Georgia Allards were peculiar.

She turned back to the boy. "I used to go to Hayslope a great deal when I was a child. It was very exciting. Old Maum Allie, she was the one that looked after the children, always took us out to the tobacco barns. Your grandfather didn't believe in raising tobacco, you know, and he had the whole place planted in mulberry trees. The negro men used to bring great branches of mulberry into the barn for the silk worms to feed on. When you went in there you could hear the worms cutting on the leaves. It sounded like a high wind blowing. Some people thought it was like the sea."

She was pleased with the fancy and looked up at him, smiling out of dark eyes that were almost as bright as when she had been a girl. He smiled back politely but he made no comment. He had been leaning a little over her. When he resumed his erect posture Mrs. Allard, who was already tired and more than a little worried, gave him up as a bad job and turned her attention to old Cousin Lydia on her other side.

Rives Allard stood, meanwhile, his arms folded, looking out over the dancers. He had been startled when Mrs. Allard addressed a question to him about his mother, for as he stood there he was thinking of her for the first time in many months. He had left the family plantation, "Good Range," over a year ago to go off to school. His vacations he had spent in the houses of his Kentucky kin. The only connection he had with his home had been through letters. Lately he had been telling himself that he never wanted to go back.

Rives Allard's father had died when he was nine years old. There had been a mystery about his death. Rives was approaching adolescence when he heard from an older cousin all the circumstances. Thomas Allard had gone in the late fall to a near-by city to sell some cotton. He had sold it, for a good price, and with the money, seven or eight hundred dollars in his pocket, had started home. A stranger who had spent the night in the same tavern had accompanied him. The man was afoot so Allard had taken turns with him, walking and riding. They progressed as far as a swamp which ever since had been called "Dead Man's Swamp." The stranger killed Allard there and made off with his money. The horse, escaping, had been instrumental in bringing the murderer to justice. Tom Allard's family had not been able to find his body and had finally relinquished the search, but one day his widow, riding the horse, noticed that nothing would induce him to pass by a trail that led into the swamp. Her curiosity was aroused. She got two negro men to lead the rearing, plunging horse along the trail. Penetrating into the swamp a few hundred yards the party came upon Allard's still recognizable body, flung down at the foot of a tree.

Susan Allard had the body brought home and buried. She made no attempt to find the murderer. The community was aroused, however, and *posses* scoured the country. The man was brought back from the next state, hastily tried and hanged. Susan Allard refused to attend the trial and on the day of the murderer's execution remained in her house with the blinds drawn. She had no doubt of the man's guilt, she said, but vengeance belonged to the Lord, and she quoted something about giving the stranger thy cloak also. She always maintained that her husband was quite right in sharing his horse with the stranger even though he turned out to be his murderer.

Rives, growing up, had heard confused accounts of this affair. He knew that his family was alien to the community in which they lived. As a very small child he had thought that this was because his father had been murdered—the proceeding to his childish mind somehow seemed to reflect disgrace on the family. As he grew older he realized that it was his mother's character and way of life that set the Allards apart.

Susan Allard, after her husband's death, went on farming her land with the help of old Uncle Mack as overseer. Uncle Mack—he was one of the few negroes who had refused to go to Liberia when Garrett Allard gave the others their freedom—was more like a member of the family than a servant. He and his wife, Rivanna, had as Uncle Mack was fond of saying "an arrow *full* of quivers." Their descendants had multiplied until there was an adequate field force at Good Range. Susan Allard believed, however, that work was salutary. Her sons—and her foster sons

—were required to work in the field along with the negroes for half of every day.

There were other aspects of life at Good Range at which the young and pleasure-loving rebelled. Susan was in the saddle from early morning on, overseeing the work in her fields or attending to the wants of her neighbors—she was indefatigable in her charities. The housekeeping was left to Aunt Rivanna and Mitty, a sweet-faced, ineffectual girl of twenty.

The house, a rambling log structure, was commodious but bare. It had long ago been stripped of most of the handsome furniture which old Garrett Allard and his wife had brought down from Kentucky. Susan herself could not have told where these things had gone. A carved rosewood sofa carried out to a negro cabin because rheumatic old Aunt Dolly liked to sit up close to the fire; the cherry "missy" bed put in a wagon and hauled over to the Crabtrees who were all down with fever; silver spoons carried off to invalid neighbors in the same basket that held the broths and jellies.

Visits away from home had showed the young Allards that everybody didn't live as they did. Rosalie, the pretty, dark-haired second sister, had been the first to defy her mother, after a prolonged visit to some cousins in lower Georgia. Susan came back from one of her rides one day announcing that the Proctors had had their house burned down last night. They were on the way, the whole seven of them, to Good Range, where they would remain until their house could be rebuilt. Rosalie stared at the news and murmured: "But Mama, where can we *put* them? In my room?"

Susan Allard had a swift way with such questions. She had stared back coldly at pretty Rosalie. "Pray, Madam, would you like for Mrs. Proctor and her young baby to sleep on the ground?"

Rosalie had sulked but she slept on a pallet on the gallery for that and many subsequent nights.

The result of all this was that the girls—the pretty ones—had married young. The older boys, marrying young too, had set up their own establishments on the land which Susan had divided out among them as soon as the oldest son came of age. There were left at home now only Rives, his sister, Mitty, and the youngest brother, Miles.

Rives, growing up, had been aware not so much of the inconveniences and privations of life at Good Range as of its moral compulsions. A burden seemed to have been laid upon all the members of his family to do good, as Rosalie sometimes irreverently said, "whether they wanted to or not." When Rives went off to school that burden had been a little lifted. Suddenly a few days ago it had been lifted entirely, when he realized that he was going to war. There had been a great deal of talk, of course. The boys argued about what would have happened if Beauregard, after Manassas, had followed the Union Army into Washington, about the merits of Albert Sidney Johnston as a commander, about whether Kentucky would not finally secede. One boy who was a cousin of John Cabell Breckinridge held interminable debates in his room in the long spring evenings. Rives had listened to all the talk and the Southern cause was already taking shape in his mind as a thing to be fought for. But it had not occurred to him that he, himself, could go and fight for the South until two evenings ago when he and three other boys were sitting in his room construing their Latin for the next day's classes. They had studied an hour or so and were about to put up their books when George Rowan burst into the room. Charley Button was in town, he said. He wanted them all to come over to Grogan's livery stable.

Albert Rush, a fair-haired, slow-witted boy, looked up, his mouth a little open. "What for?" he demanded.

"To go to war," George said simply.

It was ten o'clock by that time and lights were out in most of the academy buildings. They swung down out of the window by the tough old wistaria vine, padded silently off over the campus and made their way across town by obscure streets and alleys. Grogan's livery stable, lit only by a single lantern, was crowded with men and boys. The four boys slipping into the crowd had looked about in vain for an officer in uniform. There was no one in command unless it was a dark-haired, stern-looking man of middle age who stood in a corner of the stable beside a great pile of saddles, bridles, pistols, and other gear. The various objects of equipment had all been counted and the numbers noted down in a little book before he turned to the crowd that faced him in the smoky light. He had made them a very brief speech.

"Men"—there was hardly any one in the room over twenty but he called them "men" without a smile for their youth—"Men, your country has been invaded. She needs you to defend her. How many are prepared to enlist as rangers tonight?"

Thirty boys—half of them from the academy—had come forward. Six of these recruits had been detailed immediately to pack the articles of equipment in coffee sacks and carry them out into the alley where they were loaded into wagons and started out on the Elizabethtown pike.

George and the two Allard boys, Rives and Ned, had not been lucky enough to be selected for this duty. They had had to return to the academy that night. Colonel Forrest had talked with them a moment, however, before dismissing them. He was in correspondence with Captain Leffingwell, he said. The company which Captain Leffingwell was organizing would probably be under his command. The three Clarksville boys—he had taken it for granted that Rives came from there too—could go to their homes now and join him a few weeks later. He intended to divide his company into small detachments which would start out on different dates and travel through the country by different routes until they could rendezvous at some place on the border.

The boys had returned to the academy that night—but not to sleep. They had packed their belongings. George had had the idea of entrusting them to old Zack, his body servant, to bring on the cars. Then he and Rives and Ned got old Professor Masters out of bed to bid him good-by. George, who for all his wildness had an instinct for convention, had insisted that they must not sneak off, as he dramatically put it, "like thieves in the night."

The old professor, his gray hair ruffled, a shawl over his night shirt, came out and stood on the steps. He turned his ironic classroom smile on them, raised a thin hand:

"Gentlemen, I appreciate your thoughtfulness in coming to bid me farewell. . . . Yes, I quite understand. . . . *Dulce et decorum est. . . .*"

But after they had turned away he still stood on the doorstep staring after them until his daughter came and led him back into the house.

There had been half a dozen Clarksville boys in the cavalcade. It was a moonlight night. Their spirits were too high to allow them to sleep so they had ridden for half of it, until the moon was down. They stopped in the middle of the night at a little country inn. The host was at first angry at being awakened, then frightened when he saw a body of horsemen before his door and finally placated at the thought of the fees he would get. Yes, the gentlemen could have every convenience the hotel afforded. Breakfast? Fried chicken or, if they preferred, fish caught fresh from the river.

They had slept until ten o'clock and after a hearty breakfast—platters of fried bream and corn muffins—were on the road by eleven o'clock. There was some hard riding after that, on country roads thick with dust, but they had ridden into the front gate at Brackets just before sundown.

Rives' exalted mood had lasted through the moonlight night and the hot dusty afternoon, but in the last few hours it had gone from him. Standing there, his arms folded, looking out over the dancers, he found himself listening to conversations among the older people. They had talked about the war before supper there on the lawn and now they were talking again; Captain Leffingwell and Mr. Allard just behind him.

Cousin Fount seemed to be concerned about slavery though he was discussing it for the moment humorously:

"The Abolitionists remind me of old Henry Sampson. They

were talking down at the store the other day about sending the negroes back to Africa. Henry was perfectly agreeable but he didn't see any sense in hiring boats to take them. 'Hell,' he said, 'let the damn negroes walk.' "

They had turned so as to include the young man in their conversation. Aware of Mr. Allard's fine, humorous eye upon him he smiled briefly at the pleasantry.

Frank Leffingwell said, "Hmm, just like old Henry." He spoke to Spencer Rowe at his side, "You may be right when you say this war is going to be fought with picks and axes instead of bayonets. I agree that methods of warfare have changed much, even since the Mexican War, but all the old methods aren't obsolete. You'll always have cavalry charges and the cavalry will always be important for reconnaissance. The cavalry is the eyes of the army. Napier says . . ."

Rives half turned so that though he was still included in the circle he could look out over the room. He had danced dutifully with half a dozen girls—he thought his cousin, Love Minor, was the prettiest one there—but he was beginning to feel the effects of his long ride. It seemed pleasanter to stand and look on for awhile.

All this talk about slavery, the tariff, the Hartford Convention of 1815 when the East had wanted to secede from the Union, even the discussion of methods of warfare confused him, took away from the exaltation he had felt at the thought of going to war. With an effort he found his way back to that feeling. No, it was not a question of slavery—his own family, for instance, did not think it right to own slaves—and he did not understand all this business about the tariff. He thought with a kind of obstinateness that he had that it was really just as that Colonel Forrest said. Our country had been invaded—it did not much matter on what grounds the invaders had come. Men, he thought shrewdly, could always find sufficient pretext for taking something they wanted, like Henry the Eighth who upset church and state whenever he wanted a new wife. The country had been invaded. Men were wanted for her defense. He was glad to go.

A little wind coming in at the window made the candles flicker. Old Mr. McCulloch was playing softly a dreamy waltz. The girls in their pale-colored dresses drifted by in the wavering light like great moths. He found himself dwelling with pleasure on this or that face. He was not in love but he would like to be. George Rowan was in love, with Lucy Churchill. *Clarissima* he called her in the sonnets he was perpetually writing. Bob Petrie said that George always gave his charmers classical names so he could discuss their charms with at least some measure of decorum. Rives recalled some verses George had labored over about Lucy:

"*. . . your eyes, lustrous as morn*" or had it finally turned out "*Dawn?*" The verses, anyhow, had given him the idea that the girl was dark-eyed. But she had gray eyes, very large and shining, looking almost black in the candlelight. *Clarissima . . . Most clear!* The name suited her, a sort of brightness about her, a quick, proud way she had of turning her head. When he looked at her he got back the feeling that he had had about the war before all this talk came to confuse him. He was still standing there, following the girl about the room with his eyes when there was a flurry among the dancers, and one or two voices were suddenly raised. Mr. McCulloch stopped playing. Cousin Fount had lifted his hand as if to command silence. Everybody listened. From far down the road the unmistakable beat of horses' hooves. Not one, or two or even a dozen. A body of mounted men was steadily approaching.

Mr. Allard let his hand sink to his side. He looked about the room, met the questioning eyes.

"It is the rangers," he said, "Colonel Forrest's mounted rangers. I have invited them to stop here for the night."

4

LUCY stood on the front porch looking out over the lawn where two negro men were at work with rakes and baskets. They were raking up the litter left by the soldiers and piling it in the great hickory split baskets. Lucy, watching them, had a frown on her face. It was strange to see the traces of the soldiers' visit obliterated so quickly. They had camped there in front of the office, three or four officers and forty mounted men.

A shiver of excitement ran up her back as she remembered how they had ridden into the yard last night. Mr. McCulloch had been playing a waltz and everybody was dancing and then suddenly they had heard the hoof beats down the road and a few minutes later the place was full of mounted men. Her grandmother, for once, had been disconcerted. She kept saying, "But Fount, where can I *put* them?" Grandpa had been very calm. The officers, Colonel Forrest—the girls hadn't liked him much; he was too stern—Captain May and the two lieutenants—she preferred the one with the moustache though the other girls raved about the blue-eyed one—the officers would make themselves as comfortable as possible in the three bedrooms of the office. The men would have to make out as best they could, sleeping on the ground.

Grandma had thought that seemed very inhospitable but Cousin Frank laughed. "Soft turf on a warm night! I assure you, Charlotte, that is luxury for a campaigner."

Grandma had been tart with him. "They aren't campaigners yet, just boys away from home. I wish I could give every last one of them my own bed."

They had all laughed at that. "Well, since you can't, my dear, just concentrate on feeding them," Grandpa said.

Feeding them that morning had been a problem. Grandma had been up long before daybreak and she had got every other woman on the place up. "Come on, girls, this is your chance to do something for the soldiers." Love and Lucy and little Jenny Morris as well as the visiting girls had run errands till their feet ached. They had cooked on every fireplace on the plantation. A fire had even been kindled out of doors and corn meal mush had been cooked over it in the great scalding kettle. Boys had been running back and forth from the summer kitchen with platters of fried ham and chicken. All the late corn had been stripped from the garden and Uncle Winston moaned that there wasn't a tomato left on the place. Still the soldiers had been fed and fed well. They had gone off smiling, privates and officers alike. The black-browed colonel—somebody said that he had been a nigger-trader before the war!—was riding the Diomed colt. Grandpa had given him to the colonel.

Now that they were all gone it seemed like a dream. There were those places where the turf was torn up by wheeling hooves, of course, and the litter of newspapers—the soldiers had all been liberally supplied with newspapers. But except for the litter and those marks on the lawn it was as if they had never been there. She wondered if she would ever see the brown-moustached lieutenant again. He had a very agreeable baritone voice.

There were steps behind her. Her Uncle Jim had come out on the porch. He smiled at her. "Well, Lucy, you girls will have to go back to your old beaux now. No more handsome lieutenants."

Lucy smiled back into the blue eyes which as usual when they were bent on her had a twinkle in them. Jim was her favorite among all the younger members of the family connection. When she was a little child he had taken her riding all over the place in the front of his saddle and now that she was grown and he married the affection between them still persisted. She thought that but for his limp—he had been crippled by a fall from a horse as a boy—he would be the handsomest man she had ever seen. Certainly he was handsome enough, even with the limp. He had fine blue eyes, regular features and his moustache and hair were the color of cornsilk. Lucy had been a little dismayed by his marriage a few weeks ago to Belle Bradley, the daughter of a Clarksville merchant, but she was gradually becoming reconciled. The Bradleys were perfectly respectable people though they had never until lately come out to Brackets and Belle was as pretty as a picture. And besides, where could Uncle Jim find *anybody* good enough to marry him?

She went over and slipped her arm through his and then wished she had not for Jim's bride, Belle, was just then coming through the door. Although it was so early in the morning Belle was elegantly dressed in light brown silk and a bonnet of the same color sat on her golden hair. Jim and Belle had spent the night at Brackets and they proposed to drive in to Clarksville before returning to their own farm three miles distant. "There's an extra seat in the trap," Jim said now, "which one of you girls is going with us?"

"Yes," Belle said, "but we may stay to dinner at Papa's, so be prepared. He says it's too far out here to turn right around and come back," and she smiled at Lucy with the happy superiority of a spoiled daughter and a happy bride.

Mr. Allard, who at the other end of the gallery had seemed absorbed in his thoughts, glanced at her, then looked quickly away. He never looked at Belle without being reminded of the old merchant, her father. He was not yet reconciled to his son's marriage. He himself had followed his own fancy in choosing a wife (though the Allard and the McLean properties, lying as they did on either side of the road to Trenton had joined very prettily). He had supposed when the time came that his Jim too would follow his fancy, only, he told himself bitterly, he had never thought that that fancy would lead him behind a counter.

Fount Allard regarded himself as a very democratic man because when he rode into town on county court day he was hail fellow well met with everybody, including some very rough customers. In reality, he was governed entirely by the instincts and prejudices of his class, that of the landed proprietor. He and his ancestors as far back as he had any knowledge of them had drawn their living from the land. He regarded dependence upon and culture of the soil as the proper state and he had a good-natured contempt for a man engaged in business as one who had to resort to what he privately labelled "tricks" and "shifts." Old Joe Bradley was conspicuous in Clarksville as being a "sharp" man to deal with. Allard actually winced at the thought of the word being applied to any connection of his and he glanced quickly away from Belle for fear the aversion with which she inspired him might appear in his face.

Jim, happily unconscious as yet of his father's feelings, looked at Lucy. "Why don't you come, Lucy?"

Lucy hesitated. She liked the idea of a drive behind her uncle's fast-trotting grays. Then, too, she was a little jealous of the bride. She was pleased now at this evidence of Jim's preference. While she hesitated Mr. Allard got up.

"Lucy," he said, enunciating his words coldly and formally, "can't go gallivanting off. She has to go to Cabin Row."

Lucy made a mouth at this. She had regarded the day as one set apart for pleasure and she had no desire to spend even an hour of it at Cabin Row. She knew, however, that when her grandfather got a certain expression on his face he would not stand for any argument, so without a word she went upstairs to change into her riding habit.

When she came down he was waiting at the horse block where the horses were already standing, saddled. A young man had ridden up and was just dismounting: "the new cousin," Rives, who had spent the night with George Rowan and was only now getting back to Brackets. Lucy was about to mount her horse from the block when he offered her his cupped palm. She placed her foot in it and with a quick, dexterous movement, he sent her up into the saddle. Mr. Allard, mounted himself, smiled genially as he gathered up his reins. "Rives," he said, "you better come along with us. You never have seen the Cabin Row place, have you?"

This was the farm which Fontaine Allard had given Lucy's mother on the occasion of her marriage. It had been managed for many years by an overseer but Mr. Allard always insisted that Lucy should pay regular visits of inspection there. She had known all along that this morning's tour would end up at Cabin Row. Nevertheless she expostulated: "Oh, Grandpa, do we have to go there? I wanted to look at the horses."

"We'll go to the stables," the old man said, "but we'll go to Cabin Row too." His tone which had been severe softened as he turned to Rives. "Boy, what do you think of a farmer who won't even go out to look at her crops?"

"I didn't know Cabin Row was Lucy's," Rives said.

"It's hers," the old man said, "but she don't seem to take much interest in it. I tell you, I believe she thinks Brackets belongs to her and that's enough for one woman to fool with."

"Well, there's nothing at Cabin Row but a lot of old niggers," Lucy said. She was looking at Rives with a touch of coquetry. She had thought last night that he had looked at her once or twice admiringly. She wondered now whether he really had or whether she had just imagined it. "Are you coming with us?" she asked.

He was looking at Mr. Allard but he turned now and looked at Lucy. She had not realized last night how extraordinarily blue his eyes were.

"I'll come," he said abruptly and got back on his horse.

They rode off along the wagon road that bisected the farm. Lucy, who thought now that the young man had come on the expedition solely on her account, was piqued to find that he and her grandfather seemed to have a great deal to talk about, mostly about Rives' family. Fontaine Allard knew this branch of the connection well, and secretly held them in contempt because with all Kentucky to choose from, they had settled on poor land. Still this boy seemed to be a likely fellow. He found himself talking to him as he had talked to all the young men of his acquaintance for thirty years now about the importance of building up the soil, of keeping up the breeds of stock, of watching one's fields constantly for erosion.

"There's a man in Virginia," he said, "Edmund Ruffin, who has the root of the matter in him." He broke off suddenly, his thoughts having come to one of those dead ends to which they so often came these days. "But you young fellows, you ain't thinking of anything these days but going to war."

The boy smiled. "Cousin Frank says he thinks it can't be more than two or three weeks now before we go. You think it'll be that soon?"

Fontaine Allard shook his head. There was a note of irritation in his voice. "I don't know and Frank Leffingwell he don't know any more than anybody else." He looked off at the fields shimmering in the heat of the July sun. When he spoke it was musingly as if trying to capture some memory that eluded him. "The War of 1812 now," he said. "I was sixteen years old when my Uncle Joe went off. I remember the night before and 'em all making egg-nogg because it was Uncle Joe's last night and I remember that morning when he rode off. On a gray horse. With a Captain Somebody. And then I remember him coming back with just one leg. I remember the way the floor shook when he went stumping around." He looked into the boy's eyes as if there he might find the memory he sought. "The War of 1812," he said, "that's all I can remember."

The boy returned the gaze gravely. "There was an old Mr. Robinson at home," he said, "had a bullet still in his arm. He said he had a horse shot under him, but that was all ever happened to him. Just that bullet hit him above the elbow."

Mr. Allard shook his head. "War's a terrible thing," he said gravely.

They had passed the quarters and came now to a cluster of low, whitewashed buildings set in the shade of a grove of poplar trees. There were the plantation shops, each run by a foreman who had under him half a dozen helpers. Fontaine Allard paused to have a word with the saddler, the blacksmith and one or two other foremen. Lucy, wrinkling her nose at the smell that came from the saddlery, had ridden on ahead and was entering the gate which led into the stable lot.

Fount Allard for many years had been engaged in the breeding and racing of horses. He had chosen the site for his stables partly because it was adjacent to a fine pond and partly because the situation pleased his eye. The stables, long low buildings divided into roomy stalls, crowned the crest of a low hill. On one side was the enclosure in which the horses were confined during the winter's severe weather. Immediately below was the pond and a quarter of a mile beyond that, on a smooth circular plateau, lay the race track. The entire enclosure, which included a park in which deer grazed behind a high cedar fence, comprised sixty or seventy acres of rolling green and stretched away to a hedge which marked both the Allard line and the boundary between the states of Tennessee and Kentucky.

Lucy could remember riding here, a tiny child, on the front of her grandfather's saddle and being told to observe the view, which lay, the old gentleman always said, in circles: the pond, the race track, and beyond them toward the Tennessee line an oval-shaped grove of walnut trees. She checked her horse a minute while her eyes took in the familiar scene, then she rode on into the stable lot and dismounted before her escorts had reached the gate.

A bent, dwarfish old negro who had been sitting in the shade of a sycamore tree got to his feet when he saw her coming and half crouching, half running, made off into the bushes. Lucy ran after him. "Uncle Ben, Uncle Ben, where you going?"

The old man paused and still in his crouching attitude looked up at her. "Ise old Ben," he whined. "He ain't hurtin' nothin'."

Fontaine Allard coming up looked down at the old negro. "Unc' Ben," he said sharply, "does Aunt Mimy know you're over here? I told her the other day and I told you, you warn't to come around the stables any more. You hear?" he repeated. "You—ain't—to—hang—around—the stables—any more."

The old dwarf passed his arm over his face in confusion, then still holding it before his face he looked up at his master slyly. "They ain't doin' right," he said. "I keep a-tellin' 'em, Marster, but they ain't doin' right over here." His cracked voice rose high and then trailed off in an indistinguishable murmur about "them young niggers." He took a step toward Rives who stood silently regarding the scene: "Marster," he whispered, while his whole face was animated with an expression of cunning, "does you ever eat any chicken?"

Rives nodded. The dwarf came nearer and laid a hand on the young man's arm. "They'll pizen you," he whispered. "They's always a trying. They don't never git tired. Ole Ben. They want to fix him so he cain't ride them horses."

Lucy gave a "Tchk" of sympathy. "He's crazy," she said to Rives in a low voice. "He used to be Grandpa's best jockey, and now he's got so he can't ride he runs off all the time and comes over here."

They walked around a clump of walnut trees and came out on the other side of the stables. In this enclosure half a dozen stable hands moved about or lolled in the shade of the trees. Several of them when they saw their master coming leaped up and at once began to go through the motions of work. There was only one man who seemed completely undisturbed by the approach of the three white people. This was a tall negro man of about thirty-five years of age, with an intelligent, open face who stood a little apart from the others superintending the fitting of a mare with a bitting rig. He was so absorbed in what he was doing that he did not at first see the three white people coming and when he did look up it was with the abstracted gaze of a man who knows that no interruption can possibly mean as much to him as what he is doing.

"Howdy, Marster," he said, "Howdy, Miss Lucy," and his gaze went back immediately to the mare. Mr. Allard went over and stood beside the man. They remained silent for some time watching the mare step about the lot. After a little Mr. Allard turned to Rives. "That mare," he said, "now her great-granddam was by Gray Medley. And he was by imported Medley."

The boy's face lit up. "We had a Medley stallion once. My father brought him from Kentucky."

Mr. Allard nodded. "Before your time," he said. "But I can remember when he made his first season, up here at Nashville."

"My father saw Gray Medley," the boy said eagerly. "In the pasture when he bought the colt. He went up and ran his hand over him and looked at his teeth and everything."

"If I'd a been there I'd have ridden him," Lucy said. "I'd a got right up on him. Then I could have told my grandchildren, 'Your old mammy here used to ride Barry's Gray Medley.' "

Mr. Allard laughed. "Lucy thinks it's all name." He fell silent, his eyes fixed on the mare's slim, moving legs, then he spoke suddenly: "Dave, I thought we decided not to change those plates."

"I got to studying about it after you went up to the house, Marster," the negro said in his pleasant voice. "Them Fraxy colts got to have weight."

Mr. Allard compressed his lips while his eyes followed the mare's light hooves. "She picks 'em up heavy, seems to me," he said.

The negro looked at his master, then back at the mare. When he spoke it was with finality. "Them Fraxy colts got to have weight." He turned to Lucy, an indulgent smile lighting his face. " 'Ey's a new colt," he said, "come last night."

Lucy gave a squeal. *"Dave!* Horse or mare?"

"Mar. Come about daybreak. They was something told me and I got up and lit my lantern and thar was old Lightfoot out thar under that walnut tree with a nice little filly."

They had been walking toward the farther end of the enclosure. He pushed open a gate and they stepped into the pasture. A sorrel mare with a beautiful head and large, intelligent eyes stood under a tree suckling a new-born colt. She turned her head as they approached and whinneyed. Lucy, catching up her long skirt, went flying over the ground and began patting the mare on her soft nose, pulling her ears, running her hand voluptuously over the long shining barrel. Finally as if these caresses did not satisfy her need to show affection she went up to the colt and embracing him while he was still in the act of suckling his mother, lifted him off the ground. The colt, held up awkwardly off the ground, his long weak legs dangling, plunged from side to side and the mare turned her head in alarm.

"Look out, Lucy," Mr. Allard cried sharply, "that mar's skittish!"

Rives started forward and in two strides came up to the girl and the colt. He spoke more calmly than her grandfather but peremptorily, "Better put him down." Lucy, obstinate in her excitement, continued to embrace the soft, furry side. Her eyes avoided her grandfather's and fixed on Rives as if he were the only person present who could share her rapture.

"Isn't he beautiful?" she cried. "Did you ever see anything as beautiful?" and she buried her face in the colt's furry side before she let him go.

"Fine colt," Mr. Allard said. "Mare all right, Dave?"

"Yes, suh," Dave said, "that mare she don't never have no trouble."

They walked back to the stable. Dave was giving his master a report of some alterations that were being made in some fences. Mr. Allard listened, nodding occasionally. His eyes were fixed on the old dwarf, Ben, who was crouching in his old place against the stable wall. "All right, all right," he said when the foreman had finished. "Dave, if I's you I'd just let old Ben stay around. He ain't doing any harm."

Dave frowned. "Marster, he so pestiferous. Gits these other niggers ever' which way, all time shouting at 'em. I can't do nothin' with that old man around here and that's a fac'."

An expression of annoyance crossed the master's face. He spoke irritably. "Dave, you ought to get a little more work out of these boys. I saw 'em when I come in. Sleepin' under the trees at nine o'clock in the mornin'. Now you know that ain't right."

Dave's expression which had been truculent changed. "Naw, suh, it ain't," he agreed. "But them two boys of Sis Molly's you sent over here last week, they ain't nobody in this country could git any work out of *them*. . . ."

"If they'd tend to their work they wouldn't have time to be worryin' about Old Ben," Mr. Allard interrupted.

"That's right, that's right," Dave said soothingly. "I'll tell them niggers. I'll tell 'em Marster say leave that old man 'lone. He ain't doin' nobody no harm."

"That's right," Mr. Allard said hastily. "Man gets distracted like Ben you can't do anything with him. Best just let him have his own way as long as he ain't doin' harm."

He mounted his horse and joined the young people who had ridden on ahead. Out on the wagon road he took out his watch. "Just time to go to Cabin Row before dinner-time," he said.

Lucy and Rives assented and they took the woodland road through the farm. Mr. Allard, having asserted his authority in the matter of Old Ben, was again his calm, benignant self. As they rode along he spoke to Rives in high praise of Dave Montgomery, congratulating himself on owning such a knowledgeable man. "That's a remarkable nigger. Now some folks might think he was a fool. Can't chop out a row of corn and that's a fact. I've seen him in the field and he'll chop down as much corn as he does weeds. But when it comes to a horse he's got as much judgment as anybody in this country. It's a gift. Been that way ever since he was a little boy." And chuckling at his own cleverness he told Rives how he had acquired Dave. Colonel Miles, next door neighbor to Brackets, was one of those people to whom one nigger was just like another. He, Fontaine Allard, had seen this little boy around the blacksmith shop and had observed that he was skillful in shoeing horses. He had made up his mind to buy him. But he hadn't made the mistake of offering the colonel a fancy price for him. He had remembered that the boy was a grandson of old Aunt Docy—Amos, Aunt Docy's son had had a 'broad wife on the Miles place—and he had told Colonel Miles that the old woman needed somebody to sleep in the cabin with her and keep the boogers off. He had acquired Dave at a very reasonable price and had at once set him to work about the stables. "So now," he chuckled, "when Colonel Miles wants to get Dave to drench a horse or something I let him do it and I let Dave charge him a fancy price. 'This ain't no common nigger,' I tell him. 'This is one of the smartest niggers in the whole country!' "

Rives, riding along the woods road whose dust was patterned with the light and shade of interlacing boughs listened respectfully to the older man. His mind took in what was being said. He thought that Mr. Allard was indeed clever, "smart" he would have said. But even as these thoughts went through his head his eyes went every now and then to Lucy's face. She was riding along, not joining in the conversation, evidently wrapped in her own thoughts. Rives looking at her saw her not as she was but as she had been a few minutes before, when she had looked up at him over the furry side of the little colt. He was nineteen years old and no girl had ever looked at him in just that way before.

5

THE road to Cabin Row lay past the Sampson place. This was a rambling log house, whitewashed and set about with hollyhocks and other summer flowers. Fontaine Allard, who always enjoyed the clean, thrifty look of the premises, stopped to pass the time of day with Mrs. Sampson who was working in the little corner of the yard that had been fenced in for flowers. The old, white-bearded grandfather, Henry Sampson, hobbled down the path to join in their talk. The party from Brackets was about to leave when Mrs. Sampson, twisting her hands in her blue checked apron, gave Mr. Allard a shrewd, daring glance. "You going to Cabin Row? I was saying to Henry last night it was about time some of you all was over."

Allard looked at her in surprise. "Why, Mrs. Sampson?" he asked bluntly, "ain't everything going on all right over there?"

Mrs. Sampson shook her head, compressing her lips. "He uz a beatin' a *woman* last night. You could set right here on this porch and hear her hollerin'. I told Henry it was a wonder y'all didn't hear her clean over to Brackets."

Allard's fine, full-fleshed face colored but he retained his composure. "I have given the overseer orders that none of those negroes is to be touched without my permission," he said in a cold, formal tone of voice, then glancing at the old man as if in him were to be found wisdom superior to that of the woman he asked: "Henry, what do you make of that fellow?"

Old Henry balanced on his cane, spat once or twice and looked at the sky. "Mr. Allard," he said at length, "they ain't a thing to him. I been watchin' him ever since he went over there and they ain't a thing to him."

Allard nodded and gathered up his reins and the three rode on toward Cabin Row. Rives was silent out of sympathy. He was experienced enough in farm management to understand what trouble an irresponsible overseer could cause. Lucy was awed by the unusually stern set of her grandfather's mouth. He was a man who prided himself on conducting all his affairs in order and she knew that he would resent having people like the Sampsons discussing the way any of his negroes were managed. She felt the slight sense of guilt that always came over her when she thought of the Cabin Row place. If she had been a man and could have assumed its management, it would not have been the thorn in her grandfather's side that it had been now for years.

Fontaine Allard had given the four hundred acres of land to his daughter, Honoria, on the occasion of her marriage to Robert Churchill. The young people, anxious to set up their own establishment had gone there to live in the first year of their marriage, had built the four log cabins that gave the place its name. Churchill had not proved a bad farmer, though he always went out to see about everything on the place with his finger keeping its place in his book. But he had died of typhoid fever three months after he went to live at Cabin Row and Honoria had died when her baby was born, and the orphan child had had to be brought up by her grandparents. Allard now as he rode along was thinking of this daughter. Even now he could not bear to think of her as dead.

They left the big road and turned down a narrow lane. This lane, originally part of the old post road, was sunk so low that in many places the roots of the trees that grew along its banks were above the travellers' heads. Lucy, reaching up her hand to break off a stalk of Queen Anne's lace that waved in front of her, thought how different Cabin Row was from Brackets. There the house sat in the midst of its green lawns with the fields stretching away on either side. What flowers and shrubs there were about stood in open, bright light, but the approach to Cabin Row was hidden. It might—if she had not known that it was only a log cabin—have been the house that one finds at the end of a road in a fairy tale.

They came out at the head of the lane and rode toward the house. It sat in a grove of silver poplars, the four cabins in two parallel rows. The lower yard was covered with young poplar shoots but the ground about the house and the open space between the cabins was worn bare and white by passing feet. Two little negroes sat now on the steps of the first cabin which was used by the overseer as his quarters. Mr. Allard, seeing them, motioned peremptorily with his riding whip. He did not believe in negroes making free around the dwelling place of any white people.

A thick-set young man in boots and corduroys came around the corner of the last cabin, George Robbins, the overseer. When he had greeted his employer and the two young people, he sat down on the wood pile and taking his knife out, began to whittle. Mr. Allard had brought his right leg over and was sitting woman fashion on his saddle for greater ease. He too had got out his knife. Robbins, without being asked, handed him up a splinter of freshly cut oak and the two men whittled as they talked. Their talk was chiefly about a very fine ram that Mr. Allard had recently sent over from the other place, which persisted in breaking out of any pasture he was put in. As Mr. Allard talked, he raised his eyes from his whittling occasionally to study the face below him. It struck him now for the first time that there was an unnatural roundness, a smoothness in contour in George Robbins' face, and he found himself questioning his previous judgment of this young man. He had seen him first at a cattle sale in a near-by town and had been impressed by his quiet, knowledgeable manner. Needing an overseer badly for Cabin Row just then he had gone at once to make enquiries about Robbins' character from his previous employer. Squire Downer had spoken enthusiastically about Robbins' ability as a farmer. He was particularly skilful in firing tobacco, a delicate operation which requires natural aptitude as much as experience. Questioned about Robbins' ability to handle labor, Squire

Downer—Allard saw only now—had been evasive. He managed his own negroes he said and therefore was not qualified to pass on a man's qualifications as an overseer.

Allard, looking down, now felt that he had been negligent. He should have examined this man's character further before putting him in charge of negroes. The conversation came to a pause. Mr. Allard swung his leg over, straightened up in the saddle. He spoke authoritatively. "George, I'd be obliged if you'd have those sheep driven up. I'd like to look them over before I go."

The man got up slowly from his place on the wood pile. He looked out at the flock of sheep grazing just then not a hundred yards away. He looked at them and his countenance which had been assured and genial, underwent a change. He looked back at Mr. Allard, a long, deliberately level look, then turned and silently walked toward the pasture.

Mr. Allard, accompanied by Lucy and Rives, rode on down toward the whitewashed cabins of the quarter. The men were all in the field at this time of day but a number of old women and children were on the porches. One or two of them seeing Lucy called out: "Lord now, look at her," or "Ain't she grown?" These were Lucy's own negroes in whom she was supposed to take a special interest, though as a matter of fact she was better acquainted with and more attached to the house servants at Brackets.

One old creature, long past work, hobbled out into the middle of the street, blocking Lucy's passage. "Miss Lucy," she demanded, "when you comin' over here to live?"

Lucy looked down at the wizened figure. "Soon as I get grown, Aunt Em'ly," she said.

The old woman tilting her face up eyed the girl's full yet slender figure. "Grown," she cried. "You done grown now. You mean when you git married. Better watch out now. You goin' to pass through the woods and pick up a crooked stick" and with a sly glance at Rives she withdrew and let the girl pass.

Mr. Allard had ridden on to a cabin at the end of the street. He sat on the porch of this cabin now, talking with an intelligent, elderly looking negro: "Unc' John," he said, "what's the trouble over here?"

"Hit uz that yallow gal, Della, Marster," the old man said slowly.

"Della, hmmm," the master repeated. "Well, what's she been doing?"

The old man put his hand out and plucked a petal from a hollyhock which leaned over the porch railing. "She sassed him, all right," he said. "Hit uz about bringin' water from the spring. He say he tole her three times to fill up that pitcher what set on his washstand and she ain't never done it. He git in there ever' night and they ain't no water to wash with and then he go after Della." His eyes as he spoke were fastened on his master and when he had finished speaking the eyes of master and man held each other in a long look.

"Hmmmm," Mr. Allard said again and took a turn up and down the porch, his hands clasped behind his back. "Well," he said, pausing in front of Uncle John, "did he hurt her?"

"I don't know about that," Uncle John replied. "I hearn some of 'em say he drew blood but I don't know much about that."

Lucy, sitting her horse in the shade of a poplar tree, had heard most of this conversation. At the words "drew blood" she turned to Rives indignantly. "The horrible, brutal creature! Grandpa doesn't allow *anybody* to lay a hand on his negroes."

The next minute she was astonished to see her grandfather step down from the porch and come toward her. "Lucy," he said, "I want you to go into the cabin there and see about that woman. I want you to examine her and see how badly she is hurt."

Lucy got down off her horse in silence and walked toward the cabin her grandfather had indicated. The word "examine" uttered by her grandfather in such a grave tone had frightened her. At the same time she was confused by memories of Della as a bright-skinned lively child who only a few years ago had been her playfellow at Brackets.

The door to the cabin was half ajar, held in place by a brick.

Lucy stepped up on the porch and called, "Della." There was no answer for a moment and then a faint moan came from inside. Lucy pushed open the door and went in. A young mulatto girl who was lying on a bed in the far corner turned over, apparently with an effort and regarded Lucy out of enormous dark eyes. As Lucy approached she half sat up, then sank back.

"Miss Lucy!" she said hoarsely and yet with a joyous note in her voice.

Lucy went swiftly across the room and sitting down on the side of the bed, took the girl's hand in hers. It was hot and feverish. She dropped the wrist, laid her hand on the girl's forehead. "Della!" she cried indignantly. "Why, Della. What's the matter?"

The mulatto smiled faintly. "He's a mean man, Miss Lucy. That's a mean white man. Ain't nobody over here got any use for him."

"I should think not!" Lucy cried indignantly. "Grandpa'll beat *him*. He won't let him stay on this place. Not a minute longer."

The woman moaned and turning over in bed lay looking up at the ceiling. Lucy rose. A touch of embarrassment came into her manner. "Della," she said, "Grandpa told me—get up and let me see how bad he hurt you."

The girl rose silently and with a swift movement stripped down the waist of her linsey woollen gown. There was a purple bruise on her arm and in the middle of her back a great lacerated place clotted with black blood. She put her hand around now to her back, letting it hover over the wound. "'At's where he got me," she said. "He say he goin' to beat me to death."

Lucy was silent, staring fascinated at the wound. She had heard of people whipping negroes. There was a man living not a mile from Brackets who punished unruly negroes by fastening them to the back of a buggy drawn by a fast trotting horse. She had heard people speak of this Colonel Miles all her life in disapproval, had had some vague picture of such goings on but she had never before seen human flesh torn by a lash and the sight sickened her.

Della had finished fastening up her waist and stood in the middle of the floor looking at her mistress. Lucy meeting her gaze suddenly had a revulsion of feeling. She had a sudden memory of Della, her playmate of a few summers ago. Della, then, had been bold and revengeful. When Aunt Mimy, the cook, refused to let the children lick the dasher from the ice-cream freezer one day it was Della who had thought of fastening the wire across the path which Aunt Mimy had to traverse between her cabin and the out-kitchen. People said that you could never be certain that negroes were telling the truth, could never trust them except within certain limits. Perhaps Della had provoked the overseer beyond endurance.

Confused and embarrassed by these thoughts she lowered her eyes, murmured another phrase of sympathy and hastened out into the fresh air where her grandfather and Rives were waiting. Old Mr. Allard glanced at the girl keenly but said nothing. She mounted her horse and they rode off in silence. At the overseer's house Mr. Allard stopped and told a little boy to run find Mr. Robbins, he wanted to speak to him. The urchin, twisting his bare toe in the dust, was silent, but another, larger boy spoke up. "He's done gone, Marster. Done gone. Soon as you went to Unc' John's he come back to the house and got his horse and rode off lickety-split."

Mr. Allard sat a moment, staring, his lips pursed. Then he gave a low whistle. "Jupiter!" he said. "Now what do you think of that?" He called the boy's father to him then and told him that he was in charge of everything on the place until he himself should return on the morrow. The three riders made their way down the sunken lane. Rives and Lucy on ahead talked desultorily. But the old man rode in complete silence, his head sunk in thought. He had not needed to question his granddaughter. One glance at the girl's face had told him that the woman had indeed been cruelly beaten. Tomorrow when Lucy was less upset he would question her more. In the meantime, since the overseer had taken matters into his own hands by leaving, there was nothing to do. The flight, he thought, was certainly a confession of the man's guilt. And yet he wondered. Della was a bold, brassy piece if ever he had seen one. His imagination swiftly constructed scenes that might have been enacted night after night at the cabin. It was significant that she had rebelled at bringing water to the man's house. And yet, Della being what she undoubtedly was, there might be extenuating circumstances. He concluded with a sigh that if anybody was to blame it was himself. He should never have assigned a young and untried man—an unmarried man—to such a responsible post.

They emerged from the sunken lane and took the road that led back to Brackets. As they did so a rider who was sitting his horse in the shade of a tree, evidently waiting for their appearance, plunged toward them in a cloud of dust. It was George Rowan. He had ridden over from Music Hall that morning to talk with his "Aunt" Charlotte about an idea he had had, a splendid idea, he said with a bold glance at Lucy. He was going to have a dance at Music Hall Tuesday night. He had talked it over with Aunt Charlotte and she approved. He had three niggers over there now who could fiddle like the devil and he was going to ride over to Spencer Rowe this afternoon to see if he could borrow his Tom. They would have a fine time. Didn't they think it was a splendid idea, and he glanced quickly from Lucy to Rives, his brown face alight.

Rives said he thought it was a splendid idea and then was silent. Lucy answered joyously, criticising the arrangements, making suggestions. They rode on, Lucy glancing from one to the other of the young men and smiling brightly. A little while before she had been ready to weep over the misery of the world but now riding up the avenue to Brackets between her two cavaliers she was so happy she felt that her heart would burst.

6

DURING the next three or four days preparations went on for the dance at Music Hall. On the evening before the dance the three Robinson girls drove over to Brackets. Their father, who was notoriously niggardly, said that it was too much to expect his horses to make the trip from his house to Music Hall in one day. At the same time he was unwilling to leave his carriage and horses in his daughters' care, so the carriage returned to the Robinsons and the three girls stayed at Brackets. Annie, the eldest, a big-boned, indomitably good-humored girl, said with a laugh that now they'd got this far she supposed Pa expected them to take their foot in their hands and walk the rest of the way. Fount Allard told her not to worry. They would all get to the dance, even if somebody had to ride Old Beck (a mule noted on the place for her incorrigibility and bad temper). When the time came, however, Charlotte Allard was put to it to find conveyances for everybody. The two older ladies of the family with three girls would fill the carriage. Jim and his wife could drive by and squeeze two more into their barouche. There was the trap which would accommodate four. But these arrangements left one or two still unaccounted for. They were beginning to consider the advisability of having one at least of the vehicles make two trips when Lucy suggested that she and Annie Robinson ride over on horseback. They could start a little ahead of the others, taking their party dresses with them and arrive in time to dress for the dance. Annie, with her charming, hoarse laugh, said that she reckoned they could take their party dresses in saddlebags. And that is what they did.

At five o'clock the girls came down dressed in their riding habits. Mr. Allard, in his everyday clothes, was sitting on the gallery reading. Lucy, knowing his passionate fondness for dancing, was surprised to find that he was not going. The old gentleman, when pressed, shook his head, smiling, and said that he would stay at home and look after the place. The young girl could not understand this. She did not know that part of his pleasure in any gathering lay in the fact that it went on under his own roof; he was so used to command that he would not have known how to behave in another man's house.

Music Hall lay on a main road in what the Brackets people, who considered Brackets the center of the universe, called a "back country." The heavy carriages and the trap would have to go "the long way" but there was a short-cut through several adjacent farms which the riders could take. Ned, who knew every lane and by-road of surrounding country for miles, had volunteered to be their guide. They set off, taking the road which ran past Brackets' house into the remote end of the farm. They rode for a mile or so in the hot sun, then entered a woodland and from there on the greater part of the way lay through woods. It was pleasant to ride along, the horses' hooves rustling in the dead leaves, through deep shade. Ned and Lucy found themselves wanting Rives' knowledge of the country to be as perfect as their own, and kept pointing out landmarks as they rode: "There, in that grove of trees. That's Cousin Fenwick's house," or "This woods we're in now is part of the Babylon place." Once, crossing a stream celebrated for its purity and coldness they got off their horses and going down the steep hill to its source bathed their faces and wrists in the green water.

At six o'clock they rode out of deep woods into a wide valley. A little river, the Whip-poor-will, wound through this valley and the bottom lands on either side had been in corn this year. Rives, who had a farmer's eye, commented on the size of the stalks still left standing and Ned told him that these particular bottoms brought the best corn anywhere around there. At the farther end of the valley rose a low, wooded hill on which the Husic Hall house was situated. The young people rode toward it, through the corn fields and over a rattling wooden bridge. Rives looked down, saw a great hole in one of the planks. "That's dangerous," he said. "Why don't they fix it?"

Ned laughed. "'Cousin Edmund doesn't have time to fix anything."

The visitor looked at Lucy. "Why is he so busy?" he asked seriously.

"He isn't busy," she said. "He's just so crazy about fox hunting, he wouldn't care if the house fell down. He never does anything but go fox hunting."

"He does too," Ned said. "Sometimes he goes fishing. And old George," he looked slyly at Lucy, "is going to be just like him."

Lucy tossed her head and did not answer, and they began the ascent of the hill. Lucy had heard of Music Hall all her life but she had never visited it before and she looked about her with interest. The trees, mostly gum and hickory, grew thick. It was only when one emerged on the brow of the hill that one caught sight of the house. It was a rambling, clapboarded structure, rougher looking than most gentlemen's houses of the place and period. The clapboards, originally white, had not been painted for many years. In some places they had dropped off and the naked logs were exposed. One end of the gallery was built up higher off the ground than the other. This recess under the flooring was the sleeping place of dozens of hounds. They had scented the visitors' approach and were rushing out now, baying and jumping about the horses. A dark, sparely built middle-aged man came swiftly down the steps, laying about him with a whip. He stood now, still thrusting at the hounds, and talking with the animation of a man who finds himself in an unfamiliar situation. "That's right. That's right. Get 'em off the horses. Where's George? . . . George . . . George'll be here in a minute . . . ."

George himself came out on the gallery at that moment. He was wearing a blue broadcloth coat and a flowered waistcoat and the ends of his brown moustache were freshly waxed. Laughing and talking excitedly, putting his arms around the girls under the pretense of helping them up the steps, he ushered them through the wide hall and into a bedroom on the right. An old negress, white-turbaned and aproned, came forward to assist the young ladies who at once set about changing into their party dresses. Lucy as she dressed looked about her curiously. The room—large enough to accommodate a tall four poster bed in each corner—had an odd, old-fashioned air, she thought. The wide oak boards of the floor were bare, the canopies that overhung the huge beds ragged in some places, there was no screen before the washhand stand—none of the knickknacks that graced the rooms at Brackets. Still, everything though plain was neat and clean. She decided that Cousin Edmund did not live in as heathenish a fashion as people said.

The other ladies of the party were coming in. Lucy had had first chance at the mirror and had no further concern for her appearance, so she climbed up on the foot of one of the beds and sat watching the others. Love, slow and deliberate in all her movements, had finished arranging her hair and was standing on tiptoe before the mirror shaking out her flounces. Lucy thought she had never seen her look so pretty. It was not so much the dress she wore—a *mousseline de soie* of a blue that exactly matched her eyes—as her expression which tonight was particularly animated as though everything she saw gave her pleasure. Lucy seeing her look over her shoulder now with this unfamiliar, lively expression, thought what a good plan it was to have this, the last dance at Music Hall, instead of any of the places to which they were accustomed to go. And then the realization that this was the last dance, that soon the boys would be going away and there would be nobody left to dance with swept over her, and she jumped down from the bed and ran swiftly out into the hall.

Two or three negro boys were there applying a last sprinkling of wax on the floor and the fiddlers were being installed in their station on the first landing of the stairs. Lucy crossed the hall and entered the parlor. A number of the older ladies were seated in this room, talking in low tones or glancing discreetly about, at the faded carpet, the antiquated furniture, the pictures on the wall. There had been a good deal of discussion about this dance that George was to give. Aunt Molly, the aged negress who kept house, did well enough for a bachelors' hall, but preparations for such an affair as this were another thing. Getting the bridles and saddles and fishing tackle out of the front hall was a feat in itself, the ladies whispered. Lucy, who had heard all this talk, glanced about her now and thought that the room looked well enough if a trifle old-fashioned. Seeing her grandmother standing beside a center table, she crossed over to her. Charlotte Allard could have told the visiting ladies a great deal about the preparations for the dance. She had given old Aunt Molly and her assistants much advice and she had only that morning sent over a hamper of delicacies from Brackets, but she was a woman who often found pleasure in keeping the counsel of others as well as her own. Having rendered all the assistance she could she had decided to conduct herself like any other visitor for the remainder of the evening and she stood now idly turning over the pages of an album.

Edmund Rowan, meanwhile, walked about among the ladies. Before each he paused and made some remark about the weather, her children, her family at large. The ladies, feeling that it was an effort for him to make conversation, were able to give only forced, short replies to his questions, but he would stand listening to each, an attentive smile on his face until it was apparent that she could be induced to say no more, when he would go off squaring his shoulders to present himself before the next one.

Edmund Rowan, a distant cousin of Fontaine Allard, had married twenty-five years ago, a beautiful girl from Albemarle County in Virginia. She died when the boy, George, was five years old. Rowan had adored his wife. While she was living he had led the life of an ordinary planter of the community. After she died he ceased visiting in the neighborhood at all. This did not mean as narrow a life for him as might have been supposed. He had always been passionately fond of sport. His three or four thousand acres provided sufficient cover for birds and foxes; the Whip-poor-will River which ran a quarter of a mile below his house abounded in bass. He had no need to go abroad for sport, and so nowadays rarely left his own land. He did not think of himself as a solitary, however, but merely as a man too busy for visiting. On this occasion he had emerged from his preoccupation and was determined to be agreeable to everybody in his house.

He left Mrs. Spencer now and came toward Mrs. Allard. One of the hounds had slipped into the house and was fawning against him. Feeling the dog's head against his knee he bent down and was about to put her out of the room when Mrs. Allard stayed him with a gesture.

"Which one is that?" she asked with an indulgent smile.

His dark face lit with an answering smile as though it were a relief to him in the midst of so many strange people to speak of his own passionate preoccupations. "Muse," he said, "great granddaughter of the one you used to know."

Mrs. Allard, in turning the pages of the album, had come a moment ago upon a group of names, inscribed in a copperplate hand and encircled with a delicately traced wreath. "Eva, Margaret, Violet, Steve, John, Edmund, May 1836." She remembered the first time he had brought his bride to Brackets. It would have been that day in May. And he would have brought his favorite hound too. "Old Muse," she repeated, smiling. "Is that the one the place was named for?"

He shook his head. "The first Muse came over the mountains with my great-great-grandfather. Ran beside his horse all the way and whelped the morning after they reached this valley, so he named the place after her."

Lucy who had been listening to this conversation suddenly burst out laughing. She was fond of animals but the idea of a whole plantation's being named for a dog seemed to her absurd. Rowan, startled by her sudden laughter, turned and looked at her. His gaze was keen and direct. Lucy had heard Edmund Rowan spoken of as a wastrel and libertine all her life. She was surprised to find herself feeling that her laughter of a moment ago had been frivolous. At the same time it occurred to her that he might be considering how he would like her for a daughter-in-law. She blushed hotly, and was relieved to see George hurrying up.

He came, smiling, his arms extended, as if he were in the midst of a dance. Lucy placed her hand on his arm and they waltzed through the door and into the hall. There half a dozen couples were already revolving. Lucy, who already felt some responsibility for the success of the party, looked about her and was pleased to see that every girl had a partner. George did not seem to feel keenly his duties as a host. His attention was all centered on Lucy. He wanted to know whether she thought the floor was properly waxed, if it would not perhaps be better to move the musicians up to the second landing. Was not the music too loud coming from so near at hand? Lucy, circling the floor, smiling, knowing that she appeared to advantage in the arms of this handsome young man—George was considered the best dancer in the entire connection—was perfectly happy.

At the conclusion of the third or fourth waltz Edmund Rowan who had been leaning against the wall talking to Caroline Allard suddenly stepped with her out among the dancers. There was a candid smile on his usually reserved face. He clapped his hands sharply to ensure attention. "We're going to dance an old-fashioned dance now," he said, and going up to the musicians directed them to play "Louisiana Girls, Won't You Come Out Tonight?"

The music rang through the room, one of the negroes singing the air:

> Oh, Louisiana girls, won't you come out tonight?
> Won't you come out tonight?
> Won't you come out tonight?
> I'll give you half a dollar if you'll come out tonight
> And dance by the light of the moon . . ."

The young girls, still breathless from the waltz, stood swaying and smiling, uncertain whether they were expected to join the set which already included some of the older people. Edmund

Rowan marshalled them all into line, then leading Cally by the hand he took up his position at the head and began calling the figures in a clear, ringing voice: "Hands All . . . Circle to the Left . . . Ladies Cheat and Swing. . . ." Some of the younger guests went through the movements awkwardly at first. Mr. Rowan who seemed to know exactly what he was doing was patient with them, repeating the figures until everybody in the set had gone through them once without making a mistake.

Suddenly he threw up his hand—evidently a prearranged signal to the fiddlers—and the music changed to a faster, rollicking tune. Mr. Rowan no longer showed any patience with mistakes. A couple who blundered were signalled off the dance floor until finally there were left only half a dozen couples led by himself and his partner. These couples all kept their eyes on their leader's face and seemed to move by his volition. He seemed, on the other hand, to make less effort to direct their movements than he had done heretofore. His voice which had been ringing and persuasive sank lower. He called the figures curtly as if wishing to minimize his own part in the performance. At the same time the style of his dancing changed. At first he had danced as the others did with bobbing and swaying motions of the whole body but now he held his torso upright and advanced or retreated with a rigid, almost hieratic motion.

The dancers imitated him as best they could and though the style of their dancing differed from his, they seemed to catch his meaning and progressed from one difficult figure to another. Finally with a wave of his hand he motioned them back to their places. There was a pause in the music then he called: "Cage the Bird!"

The young people took up the cry and the room rang with "Cage the Bird!"

Lucy was not familiar with the figure and hesitated, about to beckon some other lady to take her place when she saw Mr. Rowan approaching with his rigid yet gliding step. He took her by the hand and swung her, but instead of returning her to her place as she expected, he swung her into the middle of the floor. The other dancers immediately closed in, holding their hands high above their heads and calling "Cage the Bird!"

This manœuvre was repeated until every girl in the set had been "caged," when suddenly the spirit that had animated the dance seemed to vanish and the scene resolved itself into a laughing confusion. Edmund Rowan, emerging from the laughing, jostling group of young people, stood a moment, his head on one side, smiling brilliantly, as if to say, "There. That's the way we danced when I was young." Then he walked off the floor.

After supper there was an attempt to repeat the square dance, the young people crying for "Cousin Edmund. Cousin Edmund!" Mr. Rowan, however, shook his head, hardly troubling to smile, and the young people had to go back to their waltzes and polkas. It was during a breathing space between dances that Lucy, sitting in a window seat with George beside her, looked over and saw Love standing between Tom and Rufus Crenshaw. The blue, cloud-like folds of Love's dress had been crumpled in the dance. Her hair, too, was disarranged, the short hairs usually brushed down so smoothly were standing up so that in the candlelight they gave the effect of a halo about her head. Her eyes, ordinarily placid, shone, the pupils seeming almost black. Lucy, looking at her, was struck as she had been struck once before tonight by her unusual animation. Lucy was truly fond of her cousin and accustomed to feeling herself the superior character, was always generous to the young girl, often calling people's attention to something Love had said and lending it perhaps some wit in the telling. On this occasion she felt she was seeing a Love she had never seen before and she turned impulsively to George:

"Did you ever see anything prettier than Love is tonight?"

George turned obediently and glanced at Love as he had done a hundred times before at Lucy's bidding. Love was taking back a fan which Tom had been holding for her. As she did so she glanced at the young man and in lieu of thanks smiled. There was a sweetness about her mouth, an assuredness in the gesture which George had never before observed in her, and he remained gazing at her in unconscious surprise.

Lucy stood up abruptly. She knew from the expression on George's face that he had seen Love in exactly the same light that she herself had seen her and it angered her to know that the man who was devoted to her should respond even for a moment to some other woman's charms. She was about to say something sarcastic about Love's having made a conquest but she was able to reject the impulse and remained silent.

It was now quite late. A good many people had already called for their carriages and gone off. Only ten or twelve dancers were left on the floor. Some of them looked pale and tired but all looked happy. It was evident that they would go on dancing until dawn unless interrupted. Mrs. Allard, who for some minutes had been silently making preparations for departure, came in bonneted and shawled and stood looking on. Once or twice she had made a motion as if to initiate departure, then checked herself, turning to Edmund Rowan with a smile. This smile was apologetic and tender. It told him that she was aware that his guests by staying so late were trespassing on his hospitality and at the same time it asked him to regard the dancers, who, her smile seemed to say, might never be dancing together again in this same hall. Finally musicians and dancers stopped on one note as if exhausted by happiness. Mrs. Allard hurriedly made her adieux and got into her carriage with her daughter, Cally, and two of the Robinson girls. Ned and Annie and Rives rode off behind the carriage but there was some adjustment to be made on the girth of Lucy's saddle and she and George were therefore the last to leave the hall.

Edmund Rowan had come out on the porch to receive the guests' farewells. Lucy as she and George rode off looked back and saw him stretch his arms above his head in the gesture of a man who is calling the finish to a day before he turned and went back into the house. A moment later the last candle went out and the house was in darkness.

They rode down the hill between the black tree trunks. The

horses' hooves slipped every now and then on a loose stone and the young man rode close to the girl to protect and guide her. Below them they could hear the little river winding its way through the corn fields and the last rattle as the carriage and its outriders passed over the loose flooring of the wooden bridge. Lucy's mood had changed abruptly when she looked back and saw the dark house and Edmund Rowan's gesture which said so plainly that everything was over now, the dance finished. She was still giddy with excitement of motion but fatigue was setting in. She swayed a little in the saddle as she rode. It seemed pleasant to be here in the dark with the sounds of the night in place of the lights and confusion of an hour ago.

They had reached the bridge. The horses went slowly over. George, riding close to Lucy, turned and looked back at the dark water that could just be discerned flowing under the bridge. The next moment he spurred his horse and joined her. They rode on in silence for a little, then he said: "We're going—Thursday," and suddenly rode his horse so close that he could lay his hand on the back of her saddle. "Doesn't that mean anything to you?" he asked in a low voice.

She looked away, over the dark fields. She had distinctly felt the little jar when his hand fell on the back of her saddle. In a second, if she said the words he expected her to, his arm would be about her, he would be leaning forward to kiss her. She did not at this moment want that and her feeling was so strong that involuntarily she leaned away from him crying: "No, please, George. . . ."

He at once took his hand from her saddle. They rode forward slowly. George, after a moment's silence, had begun to speak, in a low, constrained voice, and yet passionately as if now that he had begun he must say all that was in his heart. He seemed puzzled by her refusal, for he took it, she saw, as a refusal. He thought that it was perhaps because he had made love to other girls, that he had a reputation for flirting. He was aware, he said, that he had made a fool of himself last summer over Fanny

Latimer. That was the foolish kind of thing that all young men stumble into with an older woman. He could not himself tell how it had happened. Last summer now seemed so long ago. . . .

Lucy, riding along, listened in silence, once or twice putting up her hand in protest. His voice as much as what he said moved her. She wanted to yield to him and yet there was something that held her erect, kept her eyes fixed on the dark fields. "In a minute," she thought, "in a minute now I'll say yes. I won't be able not to. . . ."

They rode on. George had ceased speaking. She hardly knew what she had done, whether or not she had answered him. They came to a gate. He got down and opened it. She passed through. There was the rattle of the chain. He was speaking, in his ordinary tone of voice: "You know, I've trained Prince to go up and lift the chain off a gate with his nose but he won't do it to save me when there's any other horse along."

They left the fields and entered a stretch of woodland. George seemed to find the silence and the dark oppressive. He asked Lucy if she minded his singing. The next minute his voice rang out in an old hunting song. He sang as men sing when they are alone with abandonment, making his voice go as far as it would. In the pauses of his breath Lucy could hear the clop-clop-clop of the horses' hooves on the soft woods road and then the voice would ring out, again covering every other sound. Lucy, listening, had the feeling that there was in this song now all the passion that had been in his words before and that this passion was going away from her, out into the immense night.

7

NED AND GEORGE ROWAN had already gone up the walk with Spencer Rowe. Rives was alone in the office. He finished stowing the last of his belongings in his saddlebags and started toward the open door. On the threshold he paused and looked behind him. This room and the one beyond it were in great confusion. Ned had been packing all morning. At the last minute he had not been able to find a favorite pair of spurs and he had turned the contents of the cupboards out onto the floor and had even dismantled the beds in his search. Rives, alone in the place now, looked about him. The morning sunlight streamed in through the windows and lit up the pile of gear in the middle of the floor. The old setter dog, Joe, curled up in the shaft of light, rose to his feet and came toward Rives, yawning and wagging his tail. Rives stooped to pat him. As he shut the door behind him he reflected that Joe would be here tomorrow while he himself would be gone. In the midst of his elation there was a little sadness. He had been happier here in these rooms than he had been anywhere else in his life.

He went up the walk between the crape myrtle bushes and emerged on the lawn in front of the house. It was full of people. Carriages had been rolling up the drive all morning, people of the neighborhood gathering to see the young men leave for Camp Boone. There were seventy recruits in all. Enough for a company. The Leffingwell Rangers they were going to call it. George Rowan and Spencer were the first and second lieutenants. There had been some talk of electing him, Rives, ensign, but the honor had gone to a young man of the neighborhood, rightly, he thought; he himself was a newcomer.

Captain Leffingwell was already mounted on his big roan, Jupiter. He was wearing a new suit of homespun. The silver-mounted pistols he had carried in the Mexican War were in his saddle holsters and his sword was at his side. George and Spencer with half a dozen of the others were standing beside him. Over on the cedar-bordered drive negroes stood patiently holding the reins of horses.

Rives, carrying his saddlebags, went over and joined a group of people standing under the big oak tree. Ned was there with his father and mother and Edmund Rowan and two or three of the girls stood with them. They had smiles on their faces. Rives followed the direction of their eyes. A wagon was rolling along between the cedars. There were three trunks in it; a young negro was perched on top of each trunk. The wagon reached the gate. The negro who was driving pulled his mules to a halt and began waving his hat to the company on the lawn.

There was laughter and loud cries of Good-by, Zack! 'By, Jim! Good-by, Tom!" and little Jenny Morris created more laughter by slipping away from her mother's restraining hand and running toward the gate to cry "Be good, y'all."

Rives heard Mrs. Allard's low laugh as she turned to Edmund Rowan, "Zack bows exactly like you, Cousin Edmund."

Rowan's eyes were on the retreating figures. "I debated quite a while in my mind which of the negroes to send with George," he said, "in fact I had decided on Sam. He is sound in body and has excellent judgment. Zack is older than Sam but he is inclined to be flighty sometimes."

"Yes," she said, "Zack is a little flighty at times but he is truly devoted to George. I think that makes a difference."

He nodded thoughtfully. "I believe you are right, Cousin Charlotte. But I really had no choice in the matter. George and Zack both came to me this morning and when I saw their faces I knew it would not do to separate them."

"George is looking for you now," she said. He bowed and

walked across the lawn to meet George who came forward, smiling brightly, leading his horse.

Mrs. Allard was standing with one arm linked through Ned's. She laid the other hand on Rives' arm, gave it a light pressure. "Did you put those neckbands in?" she asked.

He said, "Yes, ma'am, thank you." She had given him the neckbands only a half-hour ago when she made her last trip down to the office. She hadn't forgot, she just wanted him to know that his going away meant as much to her as that of these other boys whom she had known all her life. He smiled at her, reflecting that neither she nor anybody else could possibly know how happy he was. When he had waked this morning it hardly seemed possible that the long looked for day was actually here.

Ned had stood quietly beside his mother for some time and now he came around to Rives' side. "Look," he said excitedly.

Another wagon was rolling down the drive. It was driven by one of the Sampson boys and had four outriders. It was apparently a wagonload of potatoes. If you went up you could see the tops of the tow sacks protruding over the wagon bed. Inside those sacks, packed in with the potatoes, were pistols, knives, cartridges and a quantity of other gear. Colonel Forrest had brought the arms that he had collected in the livery stable at Louisville here and had left the guarded wagon standing in the Brackets stables until it was ready to make the trip to Camp Boone.

Jim Allard came up. Jim's eyes were on the wagon too. He was smiling. "Well, General," he said to Ned.

Ned laughed. "I don't see why they keep standing around," he said impatiently. "I don't see why we don't get started."

Jim pulled the boy to him and good naturedly ruffled his dark hair. "You'll get there soon enough, General."

He was smiling at Rives as he spoke. He had taken a great fancy to Rives. Day before yesterday he had taken him down to the shop he had fitted up for himself in one of the out buildings and had showed him an invention he was working on, a machine that would shell corn, he said, as fast as any man could shell it.

They had spent a pleasant afternoon. Jim had grown quite excited in showing Rives how his machine worked or would work when he got one or two things about it adjusted and Rives had been fascinated by the possibilities of the invention. That all seemed very long ago now. Rives, as he stood there, kept his gaze averted from Jim's crippled leg. He was wondering how it would feel to have to stand there and watch all the others go off, knowing that you yourself could not go.

There was a stir in the crowd. Captain Leffingwell, after giving his lieutenants final directions, had got off his horse to bid the members of the household a ceremonious good-by. He stood now at his horse's head, smiling and clasping his gray hat to his breast. Lucy Churchill ran forward and handed him a peacock feather which she had just picked up on the lawn. He stuck it through his hat band and claimed a kiss from the giver. She was running back across the lawn, a light figure in her muslin dress that had little sprigs of roses scattered over it.

Ned, his father and mother on either side of him, was walking toward his horse. George Rowan embraced his father and turned quickly away. Lucy was standing a little remote from the others. Rives had thought that George was going toward her but instead he was making his way to where Love was standing. On an impulse Rives went over to Lucy, holding out his hand. "Cousin Lucy, I want to tell you how much I have enjoyed knowing you."

She looked up. Her face, that had been a little clouded, brightened. She put out a slender hand. "Good-by," she said, and then suddenly she tore a ribbon from her dress, thrust it into his hand and before he could speak again was off over the lawn.

Captain Leffingwell was on his horse and the others were mounting. Rives went over and took his horse's reins from the holder and swung into the saddle. He settled his saddlebags into place, furtively felt the holster which contained his fine new pistol. Shouts went up along the line. Wheeling hooves tore at the turf on the lawn. The cavalcade, seventy strong, was in motion. Rives' horse, a black four-year-old, broke into a canter.

He swept his hat from his head and waved it as they clattered down the drive. The group on the lawn had moved over toward the cedars. They were all waving and calling good-bys. Lucy's arm was upraised and her white handkerchief was waving. Hers was the last face he saw as he swept with the others through the gate.

8

THAT afternoon Lucy was walking alone in the grounds. She had been sewing ever since dinner and now at four o'clock she had come out for a breath of fresh air. Jenny Morris was with her. The child was in one of her enquiring moods and had asked numerous questions, about where the sap went in winter and what became of the old holly leaves when the new ones came out in the spring. Lucy was glad when a little negro peeping around the corner of the house had enticed Jenny off to play.

Lucy unlatched the gate of the little rose garden and stepped in. She went up and down the walks, stopping now and then before some rosebush or flowering shrub, but she could not have told what flower it was she was eyeing so intently. She was thinking of the night when she had ridden home from Music Hall with George Rowan. She could remember the distinct feeling of aversion that she had had when George laid his hand on her saddle and she knew that in a second he would be leaning over to kiss her. But she could not understand why she had felt as she did. She knew that if George were here today she would act very differently. And yet, she told herself, feeling as she felt that night she could not have acted differently. And she would start over the same cycle, beginning with the time they had ridden down the hill and going on to the moment when George had let his voice ring out wildly in the night as if to say it was all finished.

She left the garden and walked toward the house. The east portico as always at this season of the year was hung thick with vines. The white columns could barely be discerned under them.

Growing close to it, so close that its branches brushed the portico steps, was an enormous hemlock tree. Lucy·had played with her dolls in the little cave made by the sweeping branches and this tree, this whole section of the grounds, had always had a special charm for her. A few months ago when she had been away at school she had thought that if she could see the hemlock tree and the white columns under their greenery, she would be perfectly happy. Soon after arriving home she had darted away from the others and had come around to this side of the house merely for the pleasure of traversing the shady path. She stopped now and looked up at the portico. It was just as usual, the vines as green, the shade of the hemlock boughs as thick and yet the whole scene was in some mysterious way altered.

At that moment Cally, tired from bending over the cutting table, came to the ballroom window and looked out. She habitually dressed plainly but today she looked even less glamorous than usual, in a dress of gray poplin with her hair pushed back from her strong, plain face. Lucy, seeing her aunt looking down on her, smiled and made a gesture signifying she would be upstairs in a minute, then looked away. There had come to her one of those moments of discernment in which the whole tenor, the inner meaning of another person's life seems revealed. Lucy had been familiar with her aunt's history ever since she could remember. She had heard older people sighing over Cally's "ruined life" but she had never until this moment conceived what it would be like to have one's life "ruined." Up to now whatever spiritual necessity she had known was that of being true to herself. "That's not like me," she would think sometimes when she had been unkind to Jenny Morris or had thwarted one of the older girls in some petty way. But now she saw in a flash that life was not so simple as she had thought it. Aunt Cally, everybody agreed, had done all she could to make her marriage a success. She had stayed with Charles Hobart as long as she could but he was dissolute as well as weak, forever after other women, dangerous when drinking. She had had no choice finally but to leave him. And yet, Lucy thought, it must have been very bitter to her to have to come home to her father's house, a divorced woman with a child, to live on year after year the futile life that a woman with no household of her own must live. Lucy loved her aunt but she had always thought of her as curiously set apart by her misfortunes. She had never even conceived of such things happening to herself, but in a flash she realized what a precarious business life—and particularly love—is and how impalpable the forces which make for success or disaster. And it now seemed to her as improbable that she could be happy in this life as it had once seemed certain.

She stood still on the path, staring at the white portico and green vines until they were completely obscured by the tears that had sprung to her eyes. Finally she turned around and walked up and down the path. Blinded by tears she did not see a negro boy who approached until he was at her side. She looked up and shaking the tears angrily from her face, said in a cold, strained voice: "Well, Antony, what is it?"

The boy replied that he had come from camp and had a letter for one of the young ladies.

"They're upstairs in the ballroom," Lucy said in the same cold tone.

She watched the boy mount the steps and cross the porch. The idea that had just come to her affected her so powerfully that she could feel her vitals turning over within her and for a moment had to stand perfectly still. Finally she closed her mouth, looked around her with the furtive expression a person has when he fears some alien eye has seen him making a spectacle of himself and started up the steps. She was as violently happy now as she had been miserable a moment ago. She was convinced that the note the boy brought was for her, from George, and it seemed to her that she could hardly wait to get it in her hands.

In the sewing room everything was as she had left it a half-hour before. Cally was out of the room for a few minutes and the negro women had taken advantage of her absence to lay down their shears and stretch themselves. Barbara Clayton and Octavia had put their sewing down too and had gone over to stand beside a window. They looked at Lucy curiously a moment when she came in, then continued their conversation.

Their quick, glancing scrutiny made Lucy conscious of the tears on her face but she was too proud to wipe them off publicly. Sitting down in a low chair she drew her sewing toward her and with unsteady hands tried to thread a needle. The negro women, yawning, bent over their work again. At the window the girls continued their conversation. Lucy managed to get the thread through the eye of the needle and bending forward in a stiff, unnatural posture took the careful stitches she had been trained as a child to take. But her hand, indeed her whole body, shook so that in a minute she had to put the work down.

"What did the boy bring?" she asked finally in a harsh, unnatural voice.

Barbara laughed. "A note from Bob."

She came over to the table and began rolling up some scraps for the rag bag. As she bent over the black ribbon that she usually wore thrust down into the bosom of her dress swung outward. Lucy could see the little gold locket suspended at the end of the ribbon. Bob Summerfield's picture was in it, of course. Everybody knew that she and Bob had been engaged since last summer.

Octavia had come over to the table and was helping Barbara roll up the scraps. "I wonder how that boy knew he'd find you here. We forgot to ask. . . ." She broke off, laughing constrainedly as she saw the expression on Lucy's face.

Lucy hardly heard what the girls were saying. She had suddenly realized what was wrong with the room. Love. Love was not there. She was upstairs, reading a letter. . . .

Head bent forward she took two more trembling stitches, then got up and quit the room. Out in the hall she paused a second, then walked resolutely up the stairs and into the company wing where the young girls all slept these days. Love's door was closed. There was no sound from inside. Lucy knocked and then without waiting for an answer went in.

Love was lying face down on the bed. She sat up when Lucy

came in, smiling tremulously. "Oh, Lucy," she cried, and before Lucy could avoid her she had thrown her arms around her cousin's neck.

Lucy sat rigid, staring at a vase of flowers on a table. After a little she unloosed Love's arms from around her neck and made her sit down.

"Was your letter from George?" she asked in a low voice.

Love was too absorbed in her own emotions to notice that anything was wrong with her cousin. Gazing at her hands clasped in her lap or sometimes raising her head to look dreamily out of the window she recounted the circumstances of her engagement to George: "Thursday night . . . you know just before he and Rives went off on that hunt. He said he wouldn't go unless I promised him and so I did. . . . And then he didn't want to go but I made him . . . I didn't want everybody to know then. . . . I don't know why. . . ."

Lucy, listening, calculated swiftly. Wednesday, no, Thursday had been the night after the dance at Music Hall. He had waited two days after she refused him before paying court to another girl And she, fool, had been convinced that he was still in love with her all that time. Her cheeks burned. She clenched her hands hidden in the folds of her dress.

Love was looking down at her letter. "He wrote this just before they left Hopkinsville. He doesn't know where they go from there. He. . . ." She seemed to be trying to extract the less intimate portions of the letter for her companion's benefit.

Lucy got up. "I told Aunt Cally I'd be back in a minute," she said and walked out of the room, closing the door quietly behind her.

In the hall outside she leaned against the wall, her forehead pressed against the cold plaster, her hands unclenching at her sides. In a few minutes she recovered herself and walked on. From the ballroom she could hear the sound of the girls' voices. She had turned her steps toward that room but when she was almost there she stopped and went swiftly down the stairs and out into the back yard. Her grandmother was there, superintending the activities of three or four negro women who were turning over peaches that had been laid out on long plank tables to dry. Lucy took her place among these women and for an hour she worked turning over the peaches and spreading out those that were still being brought up in sacks. At six o'clock Mrs. Allard, who had been back to the house several times during the afternoon, came out and called to her that it was almost time for supper. Lucy, who was sitting in a low chair peeling peaches, looked up. When Mrs. Allard saw the strained, blank face upturned to hers she thought Lucy was ill and started forward, but Lucy had got up and was walking toward the house and now as she saw her grandmother coming toward her she called out something about the peaches. Mrs. Allard thought that the expression she had seen on the girl's face must have been some trick of the light falling through the peach tree boughs. Lucy, meanwhile, went upstairs and made herself ready for supper. After supper she sat on the gallery with the others until Mr. Allard, yawning, said it was time to go to bed. Lucy took up her candle and mounted the stairs with the others. Alone in her own room she set the candle down and began mechanically moving about in the process of getting ready for the night. After a little she stopped and sat down at the foot of the bed. She remained there a long time, staring before her in the dim light. Suddenly her mouth worked piteously, childishly and she pitched forward on the bed and lay there for a long time.

Part Two

1

EARLY in February, 1862, a Confederate force numbering fourteen thousand was garrisoned at Fort Donelson on the west bank of the Cumberland River. The fort was situated in a big bend of the river a quarter of a mile from the little village of Dover. Two water batteries had been sunk in the northern face of the bluff and a hundred yards above them were the outer parapets of the fort. The ground enclosed in the fort was rugged and covered with dense undergrowth but the fort itself was of good profile, admirably adapted to the ridge it crowned. Around it on the landward side ran the rifle pits, a continuous, irregular line of logs, covered with yellow clay. These pits followed the coping of the ascents, seventy or eighty feet in height up which a foe must charge. Where they were weakest they had been strengthened by trees felled outwards so that their interlacing limbs must offer yet another barrier to the enemy. Above, on the inner slopes of the rugged hills, defended thus from sight of the enemy as well as his shot, were the huts of the garrison and the log cabins which housed its supplies.

At dusk on the evening of February twelfth a group of soldiers were cooking their supper in front of one of these huts. One man, a thickset fellow whose burly figure so filled his trousers that his waist band seemed on the point of bursting every time he bent over, seemed to be leader or chief cook. He had just dispatched two of his comrades to the spring for water and now he stood, stooped over the fire, stirring something in an iron pot and occasionally calling over his shoulder to some men who were squatting on the ground a few feet away. These men were gathered about a basin filled with corn meal mush. As it grew cold enough to handle they patted it into cakes which they laid in rows on a plank. When the plank was full of cakes one of their number carried it over to the fat man who inspected the cakes critically. "Them'll do," he said, and he and a younger man who had stood by as if awaiting directions squatted down beside a pile of corn husks and began wrapping the cakes in the husks and rapidly shoving them into the hot ashes.

When the last cake had been wrapped and placed in the fire, the younger man, Rives Allard, leaned over the fire inhaling the odors from the steaming pot. It seemed to him that he could not wait for the stew to be finished. He looked down at the cakes, half buried in ashes, calculating that it would take them at least a quarter of an hour to get well done. And Ben Bigstaff was a stickler for doing things right. He would not take the stew from the fire or the cakes from the embers a minute before the allotted time.

The men who had gone for water were returning with their brimming buckets. They set them down and coming to the fire stood gazing down at the bubbling pot. There was the same expression on every face. None of them spoke. Once one of the men ventured to lift the lid from the pot with a forked stick, then meekly put it back, feeling Ben Bigstaff's stern eye fixed on him.

Bigstaff alone seemed impervious to the pangs of hunger. He strolled about abstractedly, humming a tune. Once he stopped and endeavored to engage one of the men in conversation. The man looked at him in wonder. "God, Ben," he said, "my stomach and back have growed clean together and you go talking to me about them white oaks!"

Bigstaff laughed and stepped to the fire. There was a moment of hesitation and then he dexterously flipped the lid off the pot. Rives Allard, evidently a privileged helper, caught the handle of the pot on a stick and lifted it off on to the ground. Bigstaff swiftly ladled the hot stew onto the tin plates the men held while another man began raking the husk-wrapped cakes from the embers.

The men squatting on their haunches ravenously devoured the

stew of rice and sow-belly, and then sopped their plates with the hot hoe cakes. Bigstaff meanwhile poured cup after cup of hot coffee into tin cups which were quickly passed down the line.

Finally a long sigh went up almost simultaneously. A burly red-haired fellow gave his plate a final wipe, then set it on the ground.

"Ben," he said, "that was a good one. I don't mind telling you."

Bigstaff stretched his stout limbs while he fumbled in his pockets for tobacco. "Well," he said modestly, "might as well do it right while you're at it. Unless," he added, "you're on the march. You cain't do no cooking then, of course."

Several of the men looked up at him quickly. "You heard anything, Ben?" one of them asked.

Bigstaff silently shook his head. The man who had addressed him turned to another man and asked for the loan of some tobacco and the conversation became general.

The men had been immured in this fort for three months and their gossip was of local matters. They debated as to whether it was easier to fell trees on the brow of the hill or on the outer rims of the *abatis* where they had been working all day, and speculated on how many more trenches would have to be dug before "them crazy engineers" were satisfied. One man provoked laughter by saying that in his opinion it would take a monkey to climb over them parapets now. In the midst of the conversation Bigstaff rose and went into the hut. In a few minutes he emerged, buckling on his pistol belt, then strode off through the trees. The man who had been sitting next to him edged over and took his place by the fire, but no comment was made on his going.

Rives Allard, propped against a tree, smoking, followed the striding figure with speculative eyes until it had disappeared, then turned to find a comrade standing beside him. "Less go see what's going on," this man suggested, and Rives, assenting, got up and went with him on a stroll about the camp.

They brought up on a wooded knoll where a number of men were engaged in a favorite sport known as "devilling Old Fulton."

Old Fulton, a lanky, cadaverous mountaineer had ridden into camp a few weeks before mounted on a sorrel mule. He asserted his age to be thirty-five and said that he had come down from the mountains for the purpose of killing a few Yankees. The commanding officer, seeing the man's lined cheeks and grizzled, flowing beard, had known that he must be at least sixty but he had taken him at his word and had assigned him the same duties as the younger men. Whether because he was disappointed at not being able to kill any Yankees or because he was being taxed beyond his strength in lifting heavy logs and felling trees, Old Fulton, ever since arriving at the fort, had been in a passion of anger. This anger seemed to be directed at the universe rather than at any one object; his curses were muttered to himself and he seemed almost unconscious of the presence of the crowd that was nearly always attendant on him.

Half an hour ago a group of soldiers had stopped to watch him build a fire. The original number had been swelled by ten or fifteen others and now they squatted in two rows, immobile, eyeing the old man like an audience which waits serenely on a favorite entertainer, certain that he will furnish them with amusement.

The old man, meanwhile, had assembled a heap of twigs and was clumsily piling branches on top of them. Kneeling, he struck a match to the pile only to have it go out. He repeated this manœuvre several times before one of the soldiers gravely drew a piece of paper from his pocket. The old man twisted it and stuck it at the base of the pile of twigs. The flames rose bravely for a second then struck wet wood and released a cloud of blinding smoke.

Rising to his full height Old Fulton leaped into the midst of the pile and, cursing violently, kicked the wood in every direction. This was what the soldiers had been waiting for. Laughing uproariously they fell over backwards, their arms about each other's necks. "Go it, Old Fulton. Go it! You ain't said it all yet. Less git Maude."

This was a subject that never failed to rouse the old man's

anger. He cherished his gaited mule, Maude, and was in deadly fear of her being stolen. The suggestion of bringing her up to stamp out the fire provoked a fresh volley of curses the while he kicked the wet wood in every direction.

When the wood had all been scattered and Old Fulton had exhausted himself in cursing, the group began to break up. Some of the soldiers strolled on to other camp fires to see if they couldn't "stir up something." Rives and his companion, tired from their long day's work felling trees, turned their steps back to the hut.

The fire which had burned so brightly an hour ago was now only a heap of smouldering ashes ringed with silent figures. Ed Toulmin, kicking off his boots, wrapped himself in his blanket and was soon asleep. Rives decided to smoke a pipe before turning in.

He pitched another log on the fire and sat down with his back against a tree. He felt a pleasant lassitude after the long day's work with the axe and at the same time his mind was unusually active. Faculties dormant for a long time had suddenly been called into play by an incident of the evening. Something in the tone of Ben Bigstaff's voice when he said that you couldn't cook on the march, the quick look that the other man had given him—these two happenings had combined to lift a veil from the monotony and everyday routine of camp life, and now Rives, like a man who trudges mile after mile of a wearisome journey suddenly to find himself in a strange land, raised his head and surveyed the scene about him with new eyes. The camp fire, the motionless figures at his feet, the long slope down from the cemetery, the single great oak on the crest of the hill which was a landmark for the upward climb every morning, the chimney of their hut which after much discussion they had redaubed only three days ago, working late at night by brush fires, all these things which for months had been as familiar, as unquestioned as the surroundings in which he had passed his childhood, all now seemed unfamiliar, even unsubstantial. *"Where have I been? What am I doing? The war is going on now,"* he told himself and with these thoughts came the same excitement he had known months ago on a fox hunt when, riding home through the wet woods, he had seen the sun rising over the Brackets woods and had asked himself whether going to war would be like the chase or would have in it perhaps some excitement sterner, more terrible than any he had ever imagined.

Carried out of himself by these thoughts he rose and stood over the dying fire, rubbing his hands together as men do in moments of stress. As he stood there in the faint circle of light a man came out from a group of trees and crossed slowly to the camp fire. Rives recognized him as Ben Bigstaff and it seemed to him a confirmation of all he had been thinking that Bigstaff should approach him at this moment.

Rives could remember his first meeting with this man, the morning when he, together with several other men from the recently dismounted cavalry brigade, had reported to their new command wearing spurred boots and with feathers stuck through the bands of their broad-brimmed hats. The majority of the infantrymen had affected to be unconscious of the presence of these newcomers but one stout middle-aged man, with the unmistakable look of the "regular" had walked up and gazed with hard eyes before he called out: "Hey, boys, come help me catch these little birds a worm."

The dismounted cavalrymen had taken the first opportunity to get rid of their spurs and their feathers. It had been two or three days later that the stout regular, bending over the fire, had called out to Rives a friendly "Hey, Boy, fetch me that skillet." Rives did not know that the approbation signified in these condescending words had helped bridge over the gulf between "gentleman" and common soldier. He had been glad to wait on Ben Bigstaff who at that moment was concocting a savory stew for the whole mess. He had been fascinated, too, by something in the man's bearing, an intensity, a precision which he, more than any other man in the regiment, brought to every detail of camp life. Some days later he learned that this man occupied a peculiar position in the regiment. He had been in the United

States Army before, it was rumored, he had knocked his colonel down and had had to flee to the Confederate Army to save his life. There seemed no chance, perhaps because of his history, of his rising from the ranks, but he was known to have friends in high places. General W. H. Jackson, who had been an officer in the United States Army before he sided with the Confederacy, was said to have recommended him to Colonel Heiman as a valuable man for scouting and other desperate work, and Bigstaff's comrades knew when he disappeared as he sometimes did for days at a time that he was on some mission for Colonel Heiman.

Bigstaff had now arrived at the fire. Rives threw another log on and kicked the embers so that they threw up a flare of sparks. Bigstaff acknowledged the kindness with what would have been a smile except that his features were so lined, so drawn with fatigue that they seemed incapable of registering any emotion. He stood for several minutes, turning around at intervals to warm himself through. Once he picked at the dried beggar's-lice, that covered his legs from the knees down, with meditative, stiff fingers; then stopped, hand held halfway in the air, head cocked to one side as if he still heard the sounds that had summoned him out of camp. Finally fatigue seemed to triumph over every other feeling. He gave two or three prodigious yawns. His eyes, which had been bright with excitement or weariness when he first came to the fire, glazed like a child's. He took silently the blanket which Rives had fetched from the tent and almost in one motion wrapped himself in it and sank to the ground. Rives knocked his pipe out, got his own blanket and lay down. Bigstaff who seemed to have settled himself for the night suddenly raised up on one elbow. Light played for a moment in his eye. "Boy," he said, "you'll see fighting tomorrow."

Rives raised himself up. "You think there'll be a battle, Ben?"

Bigstaff gave another great yawn as if he could not forget even for a moment his fatigue. "I don't know what else," he said, "there must be twenty thousand of those devils and they're still coming in, on every road."

2

IN a clearing about two miles from the fort there was a log house occupied by a family named Crisp. This house had been made the headquarters of the general commanding the Federal forces. Bigstaff had been right. Federal forces were coming in to Dover on every road until now fifteen thousand men were bivouacked on the bare, hillocky ridges that lay between the camp and the town.

In the room occupied by the commanding general a dim lamp burned through most of the small hours. The General's aide sat at a table writing letters. Occasionally as he wrote he glanced over at the high-piled feather bed where the General lay sleeping. The back log burned in two and fell on the hearth with a soft thud. There was no other sound in the room except the scratching of the aide's pen and the General's deep, regular breathing. This breathing as the General rolled over on his back became stertorous. Occasionally a snore would break forth in such volume that the aide's train of thought would be broken. When this happened he always glanced toward the bed but not with the expression usually provoked by snores. The aide, a high-strung young fellow, who had got up because he was unable to sleep, was actually pleased by this evidence that his commander whom he whole-heartedly loved and admired was storing up strength for the day to come.

Finally the aide signed his name to his letter, folded and addressed it and placed it with a pile of other papers that would be sent off tomorrow by boat. He stood up, yawned, tightened the belt of his jacket and going to the door stood looking out. It was quite dark but in the light from the cabin doorway dim figures could be seen moving to and fro on the slope. These figures resolved themselves now into a group of men gathering in one spot. The aide knew who they were: Birge's sharpshooters, regularly astir before any other regiment in camp.

A cook had brought up a kettle of coffee and was ladling it out into the tin cups the men held. Two helpers stood behind him with baskets of bread. The men stacked their arms and quickly filed past.

One of these soldiers leaned up against a tree which was directly in the path of light from the doorway, drinking his coffee and munching a handful of biscuits. As he munched, his hard, impersonal gaze was fixed on the man in the doorway. The young assistant adjutant general returned the gaze with astonishment and curiosity. He was fascinated by the soldier's stern, almost insolent bearing. He remembered that these marksmen were experts, carrying, every one of them, long-range Henry rifles with sights delicately adjusted as for target practice. He remembered too that they never manœuvred in a corps but hunted such cover as they could find, behind rocks, stumps or in the tops of trees and from there picked off the enemy, crawling back at night to report in camp the number of men they had slain. Always before he had thought of battles as manœuvres of bodies of men but now he pictured this soldier perched in the limb of a tree, making perhaps during the day the good shots that a man will make in the course of a day's hunting and finding in them the same exultation. As he watched the marksmen crossing and re-crossing the square of light it seemed to him that every one had the same length of limb, the same insolent bearing and he followed them in his imagination down the slopes to the places before the enemy's breastworks where like Indians they would seek cover for the day.

He turned from the doorway, his sunken cheeks flushed and his large, dark eyes glittering. General Grant had awakened and, partially dressed, stood in the middle of the floor talking to two brigadiers who had entered through the other door. He spoke in a harsh, monotonous voice as if reiterating commands that had been given over and over. One of the brigadiers, a handsome, military-looking man with a white curling moustache, listened enthusiastically, occasionally ticking off something that had been said on his outstretched finger as if he had been in a classroom. The other General, a stern-faced man with a graying beard, listened with downcast eyes and a bitter, constrained expression about the mouth.

Grant paused, set his coffee cup down and taking out a cigar lit it. The military-looking General—he had been Grant's instructor at West Point twenty years before—shook himself like a handsome retriever coming out of water. "High time they were moving then," he said and settling his belt about his broad waist left the room with a brisk step. The other General followed.

In a moment the beats of their two horses' hooves were heard, going in opposite directions on the hard road. The general and his aide, left alone, looked at each other thoughtfully. Grant walked to the table, poured himself a second cup of coffee and drank it down. Rawlins, the aide, consumed a biscuit with methodical bites. In his mind he was following the two brigadiers on their way back to their lines which lay at either end of the crescent of Federal troops that now encircled the fort. The hoof beats had died away but now there came a new sound, a far-away stirring that came closer and closer, and grew into a steady hum which was punctuated now and then by sharper sounds: the whole army was in motion.

Grant paced the floor, his hands, one of which held a cigar, clasped behind his back. The young adjutant went to the door. In the gray dawn the rough hillocks about the house were alive with moving men. Infantry regiments were swinging into line. Batteries were setting out to find their postions, the officers going first to choose the vantage ground and calling out the commands to their men or running restlessly up and down while the men hewed a way through the brush with axes and then slowly and painfully hauled the guns and caissons to their places. The crack of the sharpshooters' rifles was heard.

The sun came up. One battery after another opened fire and was instantly answered from the Confederate fort. And all the time, behind the hidden sharpshooters and behind the skirmishers who occasionally paused to take a hand in the fray, the regiments marched after their colonels, route step, with colors flying, up hill and down hollow toward the gray, looming fort.

3

SHORTLY before daylight Rives Allard was roused from a sound sleep. Bigstaff was bending over him, a cup of coffee in his hand. "Get up, boy," he said, "going to be moving here in a minute."

Rives sprang up and buckling on his equipment began to gulp the hot coffee and eat a pork sandwich which Bigstaff had thrust into his hands. As he ate he looked about him marvelling that he could have slept through so much confusion. The whole camp seemed to be in movement. As he watched, guns were being trundled past, the gunners running and shouting alongside and already regiments of infantrymen were marching on their way to the earthworks below. A few minutes later Rives heard his own regiment ordered up and, falling in line, he joined the procession of men plunging down the hill to the rifle pits.

It was still dark when they broke ranks and Rives had difficulty in locating the very trench he had helped to dig a few weeks before. He was standing uncertainly gazing about and wondering what had become of his comrades when he heard a familiar voice: "Come in here, boy."

By the light of a flare he could see Ben Bigstaff smiling up at him and patting the earthen wall against which he was leaning as if it were a cushion. Rives at once slid down beside him. For a few minutes there was silence, all the men in the trenches gripping their rifles and gazing toward that gray plain which up till now had been lit only by the flash of the sharpshooters' rifles.

Suddenly the gray was riven by a streak of fire. There was the roar of cannon. At almost the same moment an answering salvo was heard from the Confederate guns and musketry began to crackle all along the line.

Rives in his excitement stood up. An officer who was walking up and down behind the trenches ran up and slapped him on the shoulder. "Get down, man, get down," he cried impatiently.

Rives obediently crouched down and with shaking fingers began to load his rifle.

The sun was now up and the arena of battle was clearly revealed to the men on the hill. Three divisions of Federal troops were drawn up in a semi-circle in front of the fort but because of the intervention of thickets and ravines this disposition of the troops was not visible to the Confederates. Rather it appeared as if the ground below the fort were occupied by a horde of shining ants that ran now backward now forward, now up, now down the wooded hillocks.

Rives loading, taking aim and firing, noted the movements of these ants absent-mindedly as men in moments of excitement will follow with their eyes any moving objects. He came to have an interest in certain groups and in the intervals of raising and lowering his rifle he would look back to ascertain whether his group had been successful in surmounting a certain obstacle.

The cannonading from the battery above grew stronger and in the valley below all the forces were in motion. The ants had changed into men. Sometimes one would run so far ahead of his line that it was possible for the riflemen to discern the features of a face or catch the glint of buttons on a coat.

Suddenly the men in the trenches all began craning their heads in one direction while ejaculations of wonder and almost of delight broke from them. Every eye was fixed on some regiments of Federal troops who were slowly pushing their way through the undergrowth of a slope a little to the left of the fort. The men in the trenches, however, were looking not so much at the Federals as at the ground that lay before them. This was a large field, hitherto unoccupied by any troops. The Confederates who knew that every foot of this field was under the fire of three batteries now watched this ground with the feeling of men who, on frosty dawns, lie ambushed, hardly daring to hope that the game will break from cover. It did not seem possible that the enemy would try to cross this field under the fire of the batteries and yet all the signs said they were coming on.

Suddenly a long shiver went through Heiman's men. A young lieutenant on the parapet above screamed out in delight. "Look at 'em, boys. They're coming!"

Down the hill the three regiments came, crashing, tearing their way through the underbrush. There was a roar from the Confederate battery on the crest. A moment later Graves' battery below opened fire. The Yankees had arrived at the foot of the slope and without hesitation they rushed across the open field, raked by the fire of the batteries. Men fell rapidly but the living rushed on and up, firing as they came.

It was now seen that the battery on the crest of the hill was their objective. Rives involuntarily cast a glance over his shoulder at Maney's gunners boldly outlined against the sky. Three or four gunners had already fallen. The young lieutenant who had screamed out in delight was tumbled from the parapet by a spent ball and rolled down the slope. His body, living or dead, the men did not know which, lay now with one foot half extended across the trench. Ben Bigstaff pushed the officer's leg out of the way as he leaned forward to rest his rifle on the earthen wall.

The officer who had taken the young lieutenant's place danced about on the heights above shouting: "Aim at their feet, men. Aim at their feet!"

Many of the riflemen, excited at seeing the enemy so close, were firing too high and their bullets whizzed harmlessly over the heads of the Yankees who, arrived now at the foot of the hill were pushing boldly upward. Bigstaff was one of the men who seemed instinctively to adapt himself to this new style of fighting, coolly pointing his rifle far downward each time he fired. He had by this time bitten off the caps of so many cartridges that his cheeks were grimed thick with powder. One of these smears of powder he had rubbed with his sleeve into the shape of a curlicue on one side of his mouth. This half of an upward turning moustache gave him a strangely jaunty appearance when he looked over at Rives, as he did every now and then.

The Yankees had pushed their way through the *abatis* and were within forty yards of the rifle pits. The Confederates with savage yells jumped on the parapets, took deliberate aim, jumped down, reloaded and again delivered their deadly fire. The Yankee leader, a hard-faced man on a gray horse, mounted steadily, never looking up but glancing occasionally over his shoulder to see if his men were following him. A hickory tree felled the night before so that its limbs extended down the hill was now the only barrier between this officer and the breastworks. When his horse's nose brushed the limbs of this tree he looked up once at the men above him, then putting spurs to his horse rode around the tree, two or three hundred men crowding on behind him. Rives rising to his feet to fire looked into the stern, powder-blackened faces of boys of eighteen or twenty, saw them opening their mouths for the yell of victory when suddenly the whole long line of breastworks crackled and broke into yellow flame.

The Yankees staggered, then came on through the rolling smoke. But the leader had gone down, knocked out of his saddle by a musket ball. The men who a moment before had pushed so confidently upward now stood wavering. Three or four ran back, picked up the officer and carried him hurriedly off down the hill. One man stood irresolute, holding the wildly curvetting horse and looking back over his shoulder; then he too joined the men who were pouring back down the hill.

At the foot all was in confusion for some minutes, then the Yankees could be seen rallying around their flags to renew the assault. Pushed down again, again they rallied, this time climbing almost as high as they had climbed before. But the musketry had set fire to the dry leaves and the heat and smoke were now so stifling as to be almost unendurable. Slowly, sullenly, pausing frequently to return a shot the living Yankees withdrew while the dead lay quiet and the wounded shrieked among the charred and burning leaves.

4

THE weather up till now had been balmy and spring-like but late on the afternoon of the thirteenth it began to snow. An icy wind blew, meanwhile, changing the snow into sleet and all during the night a storm of rain mixed with sleet beat upon both armies. When the Confederate soldiers woke in the morning an inch-deep crust of snow covered all the earthworks and whitened the carriages of the black guns that pointed down the river.

The change in the weather was more clearly discernible in the river than anywhere else. Yesterday its slow current had been a tawny yellow. Now, whipped by a steady northeast wind the water where it was not broken into white caps was a slaty gray that seemed to reflect the color of the sky.

Riverwise men, of whom there were many in the Confederate forces, said that the February rise was on and speculated as to whether it would not carry away the lower batteries. Others peering down from the parapets expressed the hope that the Yanks would try it today. "They'd shore have to battle that current."

At nine o'clock a shout went up from one of the sentries posted on the parapets. From far down the river a number of transports could be seen approaching. Men and officers came running and leaned over the parapets to watch the boats plowing their way steadily against the choppy current. The Confederates' attention was fixed, however, not on the steamboats which they knew to be transports coming to unload fresh troops, but on the armored gunboats which formed their escort.

They peered down at these black snub-nosed objects fearfully and with intense curiosity. Warfare by water was as yet comparatively untried and most of the men had never seen a gunboat before. The veterans of Fort Henry now enjoyed a delightful distinction. They moved freely about among their fellows, professing to recognize various boats and speaking of them almost with affection. "There's the *Carondelet,* Bill, and the old *Conestoga.* Remember when we put a shot through her boiler?"

Among these veterans was an old man-of-war's man, Orderly Jones, who enjoyed the melancholy distinction of having climbed the pole to haul down the Confederate colors when the flag halyards had been cut away at Fort Henry. Lounging against the earthworks and picking his teeth with a sliver of pine he praised the *Conestoga,* which he said at Fort Henry had delivered as pretty a broadside as ever he saw flash from a frigate. His comrade, Bill, nodded but expressed the opinion that the *Lexington* had done the greatest damage on that day.

A private who was leaning over the earthworks near the veterans, gazing off at the nearest gunboat, suddenly laughed. "Them things! They look like mud turkles to me. How they ever goin' to put a shot 'way up here?"

Orderly Jones leaned over and tapped the young man on the knee. "See that plank?" He kicked a thin pine board that lay at their feet. "And you see this Colt?" He laid his hand on the Navy colt that swung at his belt. "I can take this Colt and put a shot through that pine plank, cain't I? Well, them guns can put a shot through them earthworks you're a-leanin' on as easy as I can plug that pine board, and don't you forgit it, boy."

Bill nodded. "It ain't *their* guns I mind," he said gloomily.

The green youth who had been about to move away, turned, arrested by the man's tones. "Well, what are you skeered of?" he asked after a moment.

"It's our guns gittin' hot," Bill said gloomily. "I was on the parapet when that rifled gun bust. You could hear it over everything. '*Unh hunh!*' I says and I threw my arm up over my face quick's a cat but I could see around it. I saw 'em go up and I saw 'em hit the water."

The private eyed him intently. "You mean some of our men was blowed clean out of the fort?"

Bill nodded. "They was half a dozen of 'em. They went up like a covey of pa'tridges." He threw his arm up in the air then suddenly curved the hand downwards. "I saw Aaron York whizzing by me. I saw his face and I saw him hit the water. Landed like he's diving and then I saw him trying to swim, with one arm. . . ."

"Did he get out?" the boy asked.

Jones laughed shortly. "If you was to heave a setting of eggs up in the air how many of the chickens would get out?"

During the conversation he had kept his eyes on the parapet and now he leaped to his feet calling, "Yes, sir, coming right now!"

The attitude of the crowd on the parapet had changed in the last few minutes. Men fell back on every side as the longest range gun in the battery was shoved to the highest point of the earthworks. It was being manned now under the direction of a black-haired young captain of artillery. This officer as the gunners came running laughed confidently. "We'll just pepper 'em a little, boys," he said.

A gunner pulled the lanyard. A shell hissed over the water. The Confederates leaped in the air, yelling as they saw the shell strike the gunboat and a second later heard the crash of iron.

The fleet now opened fire. From the gunboat which had been struck came a puff of smoke, and a shell plunged into the river bank fifty yards below the lower battery.

When the Confederates saw it bury itself harmlessly in the bank they laughed again and some of them threw their hats in the air. The young officer who was directing the firing was perhaps the most excited of all. He had taken off his broad-brimmed hat, which had stuck through its band a peacock's feather, and every time the guns boomed over the water he flung the hat out as if he would cast it from him, then swiftly crushed it back, against his breast, waiting for the next shot. Suddenly this officer who had been pacing swiftly back and forth behind his guns stopped short. His mouth opened and he remained standing, staring off over the water, lower lip drooping like a child's who sees some coveted object removed from his reach.

The last troops had been landed and the gunboats which up to a minute ago had kept up a brisk firing were now seen to be turning and making their way downstream.

The Confederates gazed at one another incredulously and then back at the boats.

"Shell 'em, boys, shell 'em!" the young captain cried.

The Confederate gunners redoubled their fire but only a desultory shelling came back from the enemy boats, which continued to make their way downstream like great, wounded animals withdrawing from a conflict.

The Confederates gazed at one another, baffled. They would have liked to believe that their fire had driven the enemy off but even men inexperienced in warfare by water knew that the engagement had been too slight to produce any casualties. They therefore gazed disappointedly after the boats and a murmur of contempt ran through the crowd while the young captain threw his hat on the ground, peacock feather and all, and stamped on it.

"They won't fight, boys!" he cried. "The white-livered hounds. They won't fight!"

The case of the gunboats was very different from what the Confederates imagined. Commander Foote, having landed the troops, had merely withdrawn out of range in order to complete preparations for the battle. These last-minute preparations, which consisted mostly in placing all the hard materials on the vessels such as chains, lumber, bags of coal on the upper decks to protect them from plunging shot, were now concluded, and at three o'clock the fleet, led by the flagship, *St. Louis,* steamed slowly up the river.

The ironclads advanced slowly and steadily. Suddenly in the silent air a whizzing sound was heard. A shell from the bow of the *St. Louis* struck the ground near the lower water battery and exploded, throwing dirt and gravel almost to the level of the parapets above. The Confederates answered with round shot. The other ironclads now opened fire, slowly and deliberately at first and then more rapidly as they advanced. Some of the shells were thrown too high and passing over the fort exploded in the Federal camp beyond. This caused some confusion among the gunboat crews until the offending boat, the *Carondelet,* was hailed by the flagship and ordered to reduce the range of her guns. The air, so calm a few minutes before, was now full of the deafening crack of bursting shells and the crash of solid shot.

Meanwhile the flagship *St. Louis* advanced nearer and nearer to the fort. The decks of this boat to the uninitiated spectator presented a strange spectacle. Her officers and crew, many of them old man-of-war's men, seemed with the greatest coolness and agility to engage in a weird rhythmical exercise, bobbing now up, now down, now back, now forward. The chief gunner had given the men instructions to follow during the engagement his every movement. When he saw a shot coming he called out "Down," and stooped behind the breech of his gun as he did so. At the same instant his men had orders to stand away from the bow ports.

Suddenly a 128-pound solid shot struck the port broadside casemate, passed through it and, striking the upper deck, seemed to bound about it like a wild beast after its prey. Men who a moment before had been cool under fire now ran screaming in every direction. A dozen or so had been knocked down and seven of these were severely wounded. An immense quantity of splinters had been blown through the vessel. These splinters, fine as needles, shot through the clothes of the men. Several, excited by the suddenness of the event and the sufferings of their comrades who lay groaning in a dozen quarters of the boat, were not aware that they themselves had been hurt until they felt blood running down into their shoes.

The shots came faster and faster. Another 128-pounder ripped up the iron plating and glanced over; another took away the remaining boat davits, another struck the pilot house, knocked the plating to pieces and sent fragments of iron and splinters into one of the pilots, who fell mortally wounded. This hail of shell and shot continued for several minutes when there was a sudden diminution in the firing from the fort.

The Union gunners looked up, perplexed at this cessation of hostilities, then a wild yell rose as they realized that one of the two Confederate long-range guns was disabled.

The commander of the fleet quickly took advantage of the Confederate battery's mishap. The gunboats bore in upon the fort as if they would drive into the western bank itself, then at a distance of three hundred yards, swung around, two on the east bank and two on the west and, anchored at this distance, turned loose their broadsides upon the disabled batteries.

The cannonading was devastating. The great projectiles went hurtling through the air almost without cessation, tearing great fissures in the parapets and almost burying the Confederate guns under the débris. It seemed impossible that men could remain alive under such fire. Commander Foote, walking the forward deck of the flagship, told a young officer walking beside him that the engagement could now be only a matter of minutes.

Suddenly a long, wavering cry arose. Ten men had left the Confederate parapets and were making their way down the hill, axe in hand. These men were evidently in search of a tree trunk that would serve as a rammer for the disabled gun. Having found one, they could be seen through a hail of lead, felling the tree and carrying it back, ramming the shot home and then coolly washing out the bore with water before they stepped back over the ramparts.

A moment later the long-range gun was heard thundering over the water. The gunboats were in a perilous situation. Foote, confident that the Confederate gun would remain disabled, had brought his boat within range of the shorter guns. They were exposed to a fire even more withering than that which they had turned on the Confederates. The commander, however, proved as stubborn as he was reckless. His boats instead of retreating pushed in even farther. The flagship was within four hundred yards of the fort and shot and shell hailed on her unprotected decks. These decks were so slippery with blood that the men could hardly work the guns, and powder boys were kept busy scattering sand. One of these, a lad of fourteen, was coolly chalking up the number of shots the boat had received when he fell, mortally wounded.

In such a hail of fire it seemed useless to regard the warnings still mechanically uttered by gunners and officers. One or two of the young men refused to duck, saying that it was useless to dodge cannon balls. An officer running forward screaming remonstrances to one of these men fell to the deck as a cannon ball went over. When he raised himself up the man he had been about to reprimand was being carried past with his head torn off.

A moment later a shot plunged through the pilot house carrying away the wheel and killing the pilot. The vessel, its wheel ropes shot away, drifted helplessly with the current.

The commander of the fleet, wounded slightly by the same shot that had killed the pilot, gave the order to bring the broadside guns to bear. But his orders could not be carried out. The other gunboats were rapidly falling out of line. The *Pittsburgh* in her haste to turn struck the stern of the *Carondelet* and broke its starboard rudder, so that the *Carondelet* was obliged to go ahead to clear the *Pittsburgh* and the points of rock below. The *Louisville* was in as bad a plight as the flagship with its wheel ropes shot away and the men prevented from stering by the tiller ropes at the stern because of shells from the rear boats striking over them. The *St. Louis* and the *Louisville,* unmanageable, were compelled to drop out of the battle and the *Pittsburgh* followed in a moment. The *Carondelet* was the last to keep her head to the enemy, firing into the fort with her bow guns. The enemy concentrated all his fire upon her. Harder and harder fell the battery shot, stripping side armor, cutting boat davits, breaking wheels. Finally her rudder was smashed and she, too, twirled helpless in the current.

5

AT daybreak on the morning of the fifteenth soldiers of the Union line rose, shaking the snow from their frozen garments, and repaired to the fires which were built here and there in the shelter of the little hills. The woods were already ringing with *reveillé* but not a regiment had fallen in. Squatting by the fire or stamping about to restore circulation in half-frozen feet the soldiers drank hot coffee and ate bacon and hoe cake, turning occasionally to stare off in the direction of the fort.

A lank New Yorker who was unpopular in the regiment for the reason that he was a New Yorker and not an Illinoisan kept his eyes fixed on the woods as he stirred his coffee with a frozen twig. "I hear horses," he said solemnly.

The man who had slept next to him laughed. "You heard 'em all night," he declared. "I had to get up and lambaste you two, three times to get any sleep."

At that moment a vidette came dashing out of the woods. He came like a hunted hare, swerving now and then so that he passed various groups of men at their fires. As he passed the Illinoisans he beat his knees and yelled: "Battle! Battle! Woods 'live with 'em."

The Illinois soldiers grasped their rifles, buckling on their equipment as they ran. Some men carried their tin cups with them and gulped coffee or chewed on sandwiches of pork and bread. Others started so quickly that they forgot their rifles and had to come back for them.

Arrived in line they stood panting and looking about, some men fixing their eyes on the dark forest, others glancing wildly around as if expecting that the attack might come from the rear. All around regiments were forming in line and the shouts of officers rang out over the galloping hooves of horses and the rattle of artillery being drawn into position.

Suddenly a hundred yards ahead there was a yellow line of flame. A band of horsemen burst out of the woods firing as they came and yelling. Their shouting, which seemed to come from one rather than many brazen throats, was incessant and hideous. It filled the whole woods with its clangor and rolled back upon the men in echo. In the void left by its dying away the captain's voice sounded punily: "Steady, men, steady. Don't let them rattle you. *Steady!*"

The men were indeed standing as steadily as he could have wished, returning the fire of the yelling horsemen. Half a dozen had fallen but the ranks closed up quickly. The captain, who, with the terrible initiation of the Rebel yell, had already arrived at that state of detachment which usually comes only after a long period of fighting, now looked at them coolly, calculating whether he could drive them to advance instead of standing to receive the volley of musketry.

At that moment his attention was distracted by a new development in the battle. A tall column of smoke veiled the combatants from each other, then drifted off to hang in plumes from the trees. A second later came the sound of the explosion, deep and jarring. The captain instinctively turned his head to where on a hillside behind the line a dull cloud of smoke and dust sullenly arose. The shell had passed a hundred feet to his left.

He now returned his attention to the advancing horsemen and found to his amazement that they had disappeared. In their place an infantry battalion came steadily forward, the early morning sunlight glinting on the barrels of its rifles. There was another roar from a cannon and smoke again veiled the combatants from each other. When it cleared away the two armies were revealed blazing away at each other like boys swinging gigantic firecrackers.

The Illinoisans in the intervals of firing glance at one another out of eyes that look unnaturally light in powder-grimed faces. There has been a moment of consternation at the beginning of the encounter—they are not accustomed to being charged by cavalry. But it is give and take now, infantry against infantry. The men know this business and in the course of the next few minutes—minutes which might be spanned by years in the ordinary life of a man—they come to find a relish in it. Here and there a man falls. His companions with terrible care step over his body and advance doggedly, loading, firing, reloading. Reinforcements come up. The men, looking over their shoulders and seeing them, yell with joy and before the word of command can be given, advance to a piece of rising ground. It is the same hillock behind which they were breakfasting half an hour ago. They stamp unseeing over the ashes of their own camp fire. One man treads on the tin cup out of which he drank his coffee and with an oath kicks it aside while, half crouching, he rushes on.

A little to the left of the Illinois regiments a Federal general sits his gray horse on top of a little hill. There he commands a view of almost the whole battle-line. He reflectively munches a sandwich and turns his head now this way, now that, like a man at a circus who finds himself unable to concentrate on one ring for fear of missing what is going on in the others.

Men on horseback ride up to this general, salute and scream something about ammunition. The General nods punctiliously. Occasionally he screams something back. Once or twice he shrugs his shoulders and raises both hands with palms flung wide, then lets them sink to his sides. After a little his aide heads these unwelcome visitors off at the brow of the hill. The General is left to study the scene before him.

His gaze is oftenest drawn to a regiment on his right, the 31st Illinois. The Colonel of this regiment, who is personally known to the General, can be seen galloping back and forth behind his men crying to them in fierce entreaty. The General raises his glasses to his eyes and studies the contorted face framed therein as if closer vision would bring him the sounds of the man's voice.

Then the General shifts his gaze to the next regiment which seems, seen through his glasses, engaged in a game of checkers with the regiment adjacent. Men are falling fast and the action of their comrades in stepping over them is absurdly like "taking" a man at draughts. But no such frivolous thought enters the General's mind. He is absorbed in noting that these two regiments with soldier-like precision close up each gap, always toward the colors. "Pretty work," he murmurs once and strikes his hand on his broad knee.

Suddenly he gives a low grunt as if of pain. The aide rushes to him thinking he has been wounded by a piece of flying shell. The General shakes off the helping hand, holds the glasses to his own eyes a moment, then hands them to the aide. The aide looks and sees approaching galloping horsemen, the same band of cavalry that had led the attack earlier in the day.

The General shakes his head with the air of a man who washes his hands of a business of which he has never approved. "Front and flank!" he mutters and then with sudden savagery, "My God, Davenport, how're you going to keep men under fire, front and flank?"

The aide does not even trouble to reply to his chief. He seems to have appropriated the glasses for his own use, and he now follows the movements of the approaching horsemen. Once he shakes his head, compressing his lips.

"Well, what is it, Davenport?" the General demands irritably. "What is it, man?"

The aide takes the glasses away from his eyes. An expression of tenderness dwells briefly on his face. "They're running," he says, "but they're holding up their empty cartridge boxes as they run."

The General seizes the glasses away from his subordinate. Gazing, his face too is illumined with the same tenderness. "It's a damn good retreat, Davenport," he cried. "You never saw a better retreat."

The regiments which a moment before had stood so valiantly now present a singular and, to the military men beholding, a not unpleasing sight. There is first of all a wave-like motion to the right. Regiment after regiment, retreating, uncovers its comrades' regiment. And this regiment thus uncovered shifts to keep from being turned. These manœuvres, under the hottest fire, are being executed in the most orderly fashion. One regiment, that led by the galloping colonel in the midst of bursting shells and musket fire, shifts front to rear, as coolly as if on parade.

The General and his aide are so absorbed in watching these manœuvres that they are oblivious of danger. Suddenly the aide notices that the Confederate cavalry have approached near enough to engage in actual conflict with the flank of the Federal forces. He calls sharply to the General and the two, attended by a courier who has been a silent witness of the manœuvres, trot rapidly toward the rear.

The cavalrymen came on, yelling and brandishing their sabers. The leader who was a good hundred yards in advance of his men, halted on the very hillock which the Federal general had just vacated. As if realizing that this was a vantage point to be held, he pulled his horse up and sat for a moment breathing hard and looking about. This black-haired man in the prime of life seemed to be in a very ecstasy of fury. His whole face was deeply flushed and the veins in his temples were so swollen with blood that they seemed about to burst. His eyes, grayish-blue, large, ranged restlessly back and forth in his head. Sitting his trembling horse there on the hill he looked like a wild beast suddenly balked of its prey.

There was indeed no prey at that moment for the Confederate colonel of cavalry. The little hill, the field below were vacant of all save the dead and wounded. The Confederate colonel with the passage of minutes seemed to realize this, for suddenly calling out a word of command to his men he turned and galloped back toward the Confederate lines.

A few minutes later he can be seen behind the Confederate lines, talking to a Confederate general. This general, a benevolent-looking man with a brown, spade-shaped beard, listens to what the officer says, compressing his lips but gazing obediently in the direction in which the fierce interlocutor is pointing. It can be seen from the sweeping motion of the cavalryman's hand that he is urging an immediate attack all along the line. The General seems to consider the cavalryman's recommendation, then suddenly and with finality he shakes his head, uttering words indistinguishable in the roar.

The cavalryman nods impatiently as the other speaks, then as if he had heard enough gallops off. The General looks after him, an indulgent smile on his face as if saying that no good will come of such impetuosity; then resumes his study of the scene before him.

While the Confederate soldiers yelled, driving, they thought, everything before them, another Confederate general, Gideon Pillow, studied the same scene through a pair of field glasses. He had hoped to roll the Federal forces back into the swamps of Hickman's Creek, leaving the road to Nashville—the road that meant safety to the beleaguered garrison—clear. He saw now, however, that the Union right had recovered from its momentary panic and was re-forming behind the Illinois troops. This meant a counter-attack within the next half-hour. But there was still a chance, he thought, of withdrawing in safety to Nashville. And this chance depended on the Confederates' possessing themselves of that part of the Wynn's Ferry road that lay directly in front of the lines. General Pillow surveyed the scene, looked down hastily at the map which he held in his hand, and came always to the same conclusion. The Wynn's Ferry road must be taken.

At that moment he caught sight of the discontented colonel of cavalry galloping now toward the center. General Pillow rode out to meet him. As he approached he saw blood dripping from the saddle skirts and at the same time caught sight of the cavalryman's sleeve which was half torn away. "Wounded, Colonel?" he asked in concern.

The Colonel shook his head. "Horse got hit but he's all right. Still going, anyhow." And he fixed his stern gray eyes impatiently on the leader.

The General rode closer so that his voice might carry to the other's ear. He pointed out the one obstacle to the advance that he was now convinced must be made: a section of artillery that the Confederate gunners so far had been unable to dislodge.

The Colonel's eyes followed the pointing finger. He studied the hill on which the Federal battery was planted and then his eye ranged down the ravine which sloped away from it. It was up this avenue, exposed to direct fire, every inch of it, that the charge would have to be made. The prospect seemed to daunt even the reckless Colonel. He studied the scene in silence for several minutes.

The General looked down. The snow near his own charger's hooves was reddened with the blood that kept dropping from the Colonel's wounded horse. As the General watched, another great drop of blackish blood fell. The General found himself wondering how long a horse could hold up under what was probably a major wound, and as if the dripping blood brought home to him the dangerous passage of time, he spoke, decisively: "Colonel Forrest, it will have to be done."

Colonel Forrest nodded as if he too had just come to the same conclusion. "I'll try it," he said.

Immediately turning off he drew a part of his command up in an open space, in columns of squadrons. Looking back he saw a regiment of Kentuckians standing idle. Knowing that cavalry might take the guns but could never hold them without infantry support, he sent a courier to ask for the Kentucky colonel's co-operation.

The Kentuckians came on the run. They were given their instructions. The first and second cavalry companies were to deploy to the right and left as they advanced. The Kentuckians were to follow, holding their fire until the decisive moment. The order to charge was given. The cavalry went forward at a gallop, the infantrymen following.

The gunners on the hill saw the Confederates coming and opened fire. The smoke of battle rolled out and hung over the ravine. The hail of lead rattled in the vines and undergrowth, then fell, melting little holes in the frozen ground. The Confederates meanwhile poured up the ravine. Many of the cavalrymen had already fallen and here and there a horse went down. When this happened its rider kicked his feet free from the stirrups and went forward on foot looking for the next empty saddle.

They reached a narrow clearing. The leader, rising in his stirrups, swung his blade high and charged the hill. The cavalrymen followed yelling and a hand to hand conflict ensued about the guns which still belched fire as some of the gunners stuck to their posts.

The gray infantry line had ascended the hill within fifty yards of the battery without moving their guns from their right shoulders. Fifty men had already dropped from the ranks but they still came on, holding their fire according to orders. Suddenly the hilltop above burst into flame. Simultaneously their leader's voice rang out and they poured a destructive fire into the regiment of infantrymen supporting the stricken battery.

In the meantime the hand to hand struggle still went on about the battery. The Yankee gunners fought hard. They dropped in heaps about their guns. The hooves of the artillery horses splashed in the blood of the wounded and slain until, blackened, it froze along the surface of the snow.

Forrest's horse had been shot out from under him. A shell crashing through the horse's body just behind the rider's leg had torn the already wounded animal to pieces. The rider, disentangling himself, went forward on foot. He was splashed with blood and his overcoat had fifteen bullet holes in it, but he was uninjured. Placing his hand on one of the bloody gun carriages he threw back his head and yelled with triumph. His men yelling too gave him back his own name: "Forrest! Forrest!" Then still hysterical with joy they ran about over the field, gathering up the arms of the enemy's dead and wounded.

It was almost at this moment that the Confederate general, Pillow, decided to abandon the advance on the Wynn's Ferry road and he gave the order, soon to be relayed to these men drunk with victory, that they were to return to the fort.

6

ON a hillside within the fort a group of soldiers had built their camp fire high and now sat around it in various attitudes of relaxation or exhaustion. These men an hour or so ago had come up the hill dragging the arms they had stripped from the bodies of dead or wounded Federal soldiers. Some of them, too exhausted even to eat, crawled at once into their huts or fell log-like to the ground. The veterans, however, at once set about building fires and frying skillets of hoe cake and sow-belly. Coffee was made and passed around in tin cups. Gradually as the hot coffee did its work excitement and the consciousness of victory triumphed over exhaustion. The men's eyes brightened. They began to live over the victory and speculate on what the morrow would bring forth.

The private soldier never knows where he is going next or why. But there are times when the issues involved are so clear that the army feels as one man. And this was the case at Donelson. Every soldier in the ranks, down to the greenest recruit, knew that he was fighting to clear a way out of the fort, knew even the goal of the last charge, the Wynn's Ferry road, and they cheered the cavalrymen on wildly, thinking that now the last barrier to escape was removed. When on the heels of the successful charge the order came to return to the fort, which many of them thought they had seen for the last time, they looked at one another in amazement, and some grumbled, asking what all the fighting had been for, anyway.

In a few minutes the docility of the trained soldier asserted itself. This new move was regarded as part of the mysterious manœuvres that had led them to victory. Many men were glad to return to the fort for a night's rest before starting, as they confidently expected to start, for Nashville on the morrow.

Some of these men now, having warmed and fed themselves, were taking thought of the morrow by conducting on an old army blanket an auction of articles they had accumulated during their stay in the fort. Playing cards, frying pans, minute pieces of wood carving were scattered over a blanket. Presiding over them was a dejected-looking coon which one of the soldiers had caught and tamed. When trade was dull the auctioneer whipped it up by sonorously offering him for sale under the title of the "One and Only Genuwine and G'aranteed Ring Tail Roarer from Lick and Indian Creeks and the Owl Bottoms."

Rives Allard sat with his back propped against a tree, his legs spread wide before him. A rifle that he had taken from a wounded Yankee lay across his knees. He was too weary to move his head to look at it but he allowed his fingers to glide over the stock for the pleasure of the feel. His head would slip sidewise from the tree and he would appear to be sinking to sleep and then he would sit bolt upright, roused by something one of the men had said.

In the expansive spirit of the hour a fair-haired, short-set young private had found the courage to dwell on his impressions of this, his first battle:

"After we got up over them trenches and started toward them Yankees you know all I could think of was how many of 'em they was. I had a notion that if they'd known they was that many Yankees they wouldn't a sent us in there. And then all of a sudden I says to myself, 'Joe Gowan, you better stop standin' here and arguin' with yourself. You better go on there and git to fightin' or some of them officers'll come up and shoot you from behind.' And I looks over and what do I see but Old Bill Shackelford runnin' along beside me. Old Bill Shackelford, and I'd been runnin' right 'long with him all the time and thought I was standin' stone still." He looked around the group in smiling wonder. "Ain't it funny the notions a man'll git in his head?"

A lean veteran of Fort Henry smiled grimly. "I was just coming down the hill when that first shell burst. The Old Man was sitting there on his horse and it hit right in front of him. Knocked the gravel up all over him. If he wasn't mad. I could hear him cussin' clear down the hill. 'Damn my —— if it ain't goin' to be hot in there today,' he says. 'Old Man,' I thought, 'it's going to be a heap hotter for mine than 'tis for your'n', but I kep' on." He paused and laughed. "They was one funny thing. As I come down that hill I saw the whites of one man's eyes. I saw the whites of his eyes and I saw him chewin' and I says to myself, 'Yank, I'll knock that corn bread down your throat there in a minute.' I kep' him in sight and I fetched right up against him. I fixed my bay'net and made a pass at his shoulder. Then I run on and was about to bay'net another when durned if *he* wasn't chewin'. I thought to myself, 'This whole Yankee army is still a-eatin' its breakfast,' and then I saw 'twas the same feller. He'd run around behind another feller and come right up in my path."

The group guffawed. "I reckon he'd had enough of you by that time. Did you git him?"

The speaker shook his head. "I was in such a tight myself by that time I didn't know whether I was gittin' or bein' got."

Rives listened, fingering the stock of his rifle. He wished that he could contribute something to the conversation but he could not think of any incident of the day that seemed worth relating. Somebody had complimented him a minute ago on the capture of his fine rifle, but even that would not make a story. He had seen the barrel glinting and had run over, hoping to secure a good weapon—his own had got water soaked in a hard rain marching down from Bowling Green. The Yankee soldier who carried the rifle was not dead but he was dying. Rives could tell that by the rolling of his eyes and the convulsive movement of his hands. The rifle lay half under the man. Rives had to lift his leg to get it out. The dying soldier had raised one hand in a sudden, irascible gesture, his eyes had rested on Rives for a second before they rolled upward. Rives fancied that the man had died in that instant, but he could not be sure for he had run on immediately, hailed by a comrade who was unbuckling from a huge, dead corporal a holster belt with two pistols. The corporal lying there, shot apparently through the heart, for only a small, round stain disfigured his new blue tunic, had been almost as splendid a specimen as his pistols. A full-fleshed, blond man in the prime of life. Rives, as he leaned down across the dead man to help extricate the pistols, had felt regretful that this splendid body would not, like the pistols, be put to some use, but would go to waste there on the field.

It seemed to him, listening, that the other men were in possession of some knowledge of which he had only a part, and he thought that if they only went on talking long enough he would know all about the battle. He now felt the greatest curiosity to know the whole of it and he listened with attention to what each one said. Then after a little he realized that one of his legs, from being left in one position too long, had gone to sleep and he got up and walked mechanically up and down outside the circle, still listening.

As he walked he became aware of the repetition of a phrase that had evidently been going on for some time at his side.

"Anybody here seen Jim Rollow?"

The speaker was a small, gaunt man with a heavy moustache. He uttered the words in a voice made hoarse by repetition, but his eyes went to the face of every man in the group before he turned away, asking again forlornly:

"Anybody here seen Jim Rollow?"

There was a moment's silence. The tall veteran leaned forward and spat into the fire. "I seen him about sundown. He was heading back to the fort. With some of the boys from the Tenth Alabama."

"And where's the Tenth Alabama?"

The tall man made a gesture to the right. "Over there somewhere behind that hill. Ask Corporal Wiley. He'll know. He knows everything."

There was a burst of laughter as the men's eyes followed the gaunt figure. "What'd you send that pore little feller over there for, Tom?" one man asked.

Tom did not answer until the man had disappeared over the hill. Then he spoke reflectively: "Last time I seen Jim Rollow he was layin' up against a tree with a shot through both legs."

"Well, why didn't you tell him? What you let him walk his laigs off for?"

The tall man shook his head. "I know that feller, I know that Ira Holt. If I's to tell him Jim was layin' out there, for Jim couldn't a lasted long after I saw him, why, that feller'd start right out there after him. He's little but he's a jim dandy, full of fire. He'd go right out there after Jim Rollow and then there'd be two of 'em. Naw, better just let him go on walkin' around." Rives had stood eyeing the speaker. Now as the talk sprang up again about the fire he turned and made off for his hut. There was the forlorn little man in search of his lost comrade, and the victory no longer seemed glorious. The warm, excited, curious feeling about the battle that he had had a few minutes before was gone. He thought dully that there had been a battle and that our arms, we were told, had been victorious. But he wanted only to stretch out, to sink into oblivion. Within a few minutes after entering his hut he was asleep.

7

THAT night between one and two o'clock a group of men sat in a room of the house that was being occupied as the headquarters of the Confederate commander-in-chief. The negro servant of the host had made the fire up brightly, had ranged decanter and glasses on the table, and now withdrawing left the room to the council, for the men gathered there were regimental and field officers met to decide the fate of the fort.

The commanding general and the two senior brigadiers sat at a table upon which lay a litter of papers and maps. Scattered about the room were various regimental officers, among them one or two surgeons, who kept up a low-voiced conversation. On a stool by the fire, communing evidently with his own thoughts, sat the black-browed colonel of cavalry who had so distinguished himself during the day's fighting.

The commanding general, John B. Floyd, a handsome, full-blooded man in the prime of life, sat at the head of the table. He had been delivering now for some minutes a speech to which every man in the room, with the exception of the gray-bearded brigadier, listened respectfully.

The enemy, the commanding general said, had received heavy reinforcements during the night and had now returned to the position from which he had been dislodged during the day. He had suspected this for some hours and had confirmed his suspicions an hour ago. Scouts sent out to reconnoitre reported seeing heavy lines of armed men and camp fires blazing in the very position from which the enemy had that afternoon been driven.

There was silence. The gray-bearded brigadier—he was an

older man than Floyd and had about him the unmistakable air of the trained and veteran soldier—glanced at his colleague, a handsome, dogged-looking man, as if he expected him to speak. When he did not speak, the gray-bearded brigadier leaned forward, rapping nervously on the table. "I cannot believe that all avenues of escape are closed, General. In fact I have evidence to the contrary. Eh, Colonel Forrest?" And he turned and smiled kindly at the cavalry colonel who had just returned from a scouting expedition.

Colonel Forrest now rose and came slowly toward the table, his eyes fixed on the eyes of the commanding general. "Those are not new camp fires," he said. "They are old camp fires which the wounded have kindled up to keep from freezing. Men of my command have been over that field as late as nine o'clock and they saw no sign of the enemy. Besides," he added bluntly, "Grant is no fool. If he was going to reinvest he would have done it earlier. The Yankee right was cut clean to pieces, I tell you."

The gray-bearded man, General Pillow, nodded. "I think," he said eagerly, "that we should make another attack at dawn, or at least make enough fight to hold the fort another day. By that time the boats that took the wounded to Clarksville will be back and they can ferry the command to Nashville."

The dogged-looking general, who up to now had taken no part in the discussion, spoke in a flat, dissenting voice: "I cannot hold my command half an hour after the attack."

Pillow stirred restlessly in his seat. "Why so, General Buckner?"

"Because I can bring into action only four thousand men and they are demoralized by long exposure and fighting. The enemy can bring any number of fresh troops to the attack." Buckner spoke in the dogmatical tone that a slow-thinking man often employs when he is uttering an indisputable truth.

Pillow eyed Buckner as if he were studying not what he had said but the man himself. "I differ with you," he said mechanically, "I think you can hold your lines. I think you can, sir."

Buckner looked sullen. "I know my position and I know that

the lines *cannot* be held with my troops in their present condition."

"Then," said Pillow eagerly, "we must cut our way out."

"If you do," Buckner returned, "you will be seen by the enemy and followed and cut to pieces."

Colonel Forrest, who had remained standing in the exact position in which he had been when he last spoke, now intervened coolly: "You can withdraw your men under cover of my cavalry."

Buckner, as if he had not heard the cavalryman, turned to the table and with an exaggerated air of patience took a pencil and made on a sheet of paper a dot then drew in front of it a half moon. "You can't get out *here,*" he said and then moving his finger along the line of the half moon: "Your only chance is *here* and while you are trying to cut your way through that one small avenue they can bring all their forces to bear on your retreat."

The handsome commander, Floyd, looked down, nodding. "It would be wrong to sacrifice three-fourths of the army to save one-fourth," he said sententiously.

The cavalry colonel stood silently regarding the scene. He was not awed by the presence of his superiors, and though he was an unlettered man he was not overcome by their display of superior knowledge. But as he stood there, one leg advanced toward the table, he was bringing all his faculties to bear on the problem that confronted him. The problem was how to convey to these men a certain knowledge which he had and which they did not seem to possess. He *knew,* from the temper of his own men, from the temper of the troops as a whole and from certain other signs that he had begun half superstitiously and half practically to look for in every battle he engaged in, that the victory belonged to the Confederates, or rather that victory hung just within their grasp if they would only reach out their hands and claim it. He knew these things, but as his knowledge proceeded partly from some deep conviction within himself which he could not put into words, he had no way of conveying it to the generals.

With an impatient sigh and knitting his brows, he strode forward to the table and laid the tip of his finger on the half-moon that Buckner had traced. "I will cut my way out through any part of this line that you will designate," he said, "and I will undertake to see that the enemy does not harass your flank or rear while you are retreating."

Buckner gazed straight before him and did not speak. The veteran Pillow's gray cheeks flushed at the bold words but the flush died when he saw how the other generals regarded them. The senior brigadier, Floyd, continued as impassively as if the cavalry colonel were not in the room.

He said that for reasons peculiar to himself * it was impossible for him to surrender to the Federals. He therefore proposed to turn over the command to his subordinates and leave by boat with the Virginia troops.

Pillow, whose reason was always at the mercy of his sanguine temperament, now seemed to change front entirely. He was willing to fight but he could not face the prospect of a Northern prison camp. "It is true," he said, nodding rapidly. "There are no two men in the Confederacy whom the Yankees would rather have than the General," and here he bowed to Floyd, "and myself. Will it be proper for me to retire with the commanding general?"

Buckner, who had squared his shoulders as if to receive the burden laid upon them, now smiled dryly, either at the generals' estimate of their own value or at the willingness with which they shifted responsibility, and said that he thought the two senior generals might properly depart if they left the fort before negotiations were opened with the enemy.

The cavalry colonel was looking from one to the other as if he could not believe his ears. "You mean you are going to surrender the army?" he asked.

Pillow raised his hand in a deprecatory gesture, but Buckner eyed the enraged colonel with displeasure. "I think there is no more to be said, Colonel Forrest," he intoned icily.

The cavalryman advanced until his face, darkly flushed as it

* He was under indictment by the Federal government.

had been in battle, hung immediately over the General's. "I didn't come out to surrender," he cried boldly. "I came out to fight. I promised the parents of my boys that I'd take care of them, and I'm not going to have them rot in Yankee prison camps."

Buckner, perhaps with the idea of reprimanding his subordinate, got slowly to his feet, but with a powerful thrust of his foot Forrest sent table, glasses and decanter spinning, then strode from the room.

At the door he stopped and looked back. "You can surrender the infantry," he said, "but you can't surrender my cavalry. I'll take 'em out if it's the last thing I do."

8

RIVES had been asleep for hours but it seemed to him only a few minutes before he was awakened. Ned was leaning over him, shaking his shoulder and saying, "Get up, get up, quick. There's something going on."

Rives, with confused ideas of the Yankees having captured the fort in the middle of the night, sat up and drew on his boots, then with fingers trembling from fright and cold he buckled on his pistol belt and, stooping, followed Ned through the door of the hut.

The whole valley, lit up by the red embers of camp fires, seemed to be in wildest confusion. Here and there men wrapped in their blankets still lay sleeping the sleep of exhaustion but for the most part every man in camp seemed to be awake. Some to Rives' startled gaze were packing their equipment. Others sat and stared or caught hold of the first man running past to ask what the bustle was about. As Rives gazed he saw that the confusion had a center. The noise, the talk, the moving to and fro all came from the head of the valley, and it was there that men's glances were directed. He beckoned to Ned. "Come on. Let's go see what it's all about."

They made their way through the crowd, pressing as far up toward the head of the valley as they could. The cause of the confusion was now revealed: a body of mounted and armed men drawn up on a slope of the little hill that faced the valley. Some officers sat their horses a little apart from the mounted troops, seeming to be in consultation. As Rives and Ned came up, one of the officers, a black-haired man on a powerful horse, rode forward and sat looking over the crowd. His appearance was in great contrast to that of the sleepy, jaded men before him. He seemed in the dead of night like a man who had just come from a battle. His face was flushed and his cold gray eyes glittered metallically in the light of the camp fires. He swept his broad-brimmed hat from his head and addressed the men in a great voice that rang out over the valley:

"Soldiers, they are going to surrender the fort."

There was a great outcry. The men surged forward protesting. "Surrender the fort! But we beat. We beat 'em, didn't we?" and they turned toward one another, muttering angrily.

The officer caught the words of some of the men. He rode his horse in among them. "You fought bravely," he cried, "and you won a victory. But they are going to surrender the fort just the same. You know what that means. A Yankee prison camp for you."

There was a dead silence. The men gazed at one another uncertainly. The officer had been looking over the crowd as if to ascertain the effect of his speech and now he waved his hat in the air, so vigorously that his startled horse reared upright and then plunged wildly to and fro. Reigning him in negligently, he repeated the gesture and cried in his bold voice:

"The cavalry is going out. How many infantrymen are going with us?"

A yell went up and the crowd began to press toward him. Here and there men broke from the crowd and ran wildly toward their bivouacks. In a few minutes some of them could be seen returning, knapsacks strapped on their backs, ready for the march. These men immediately took up their stand with the mounted forces ranged to the left of the leader.

Rives felt a hand on his arm. Ned's face was suddenly thrust before him. "I'm going out," Ned said calmly. "No use staying here to be taken prisoner."

"Yes, yes," Rives muttered and hurried after him back to the hut. They collected their few belongings and then going to the shed got out their horses. The horses, not having been ridden for weeks, were frisky in the keen night air. The soldiers subdued them mechanically, threw the saddles on, and galloped back to the hillside where the forces were gathering.

Columns were forming as they rode up. Officers rode back and forth along the lines giving commands. After a few minutes the unwieldy body of troops, half cavalry, half infantry, had assembled, cavalry in front, infantry column in the rear. The officer who had made the speech was directing the formation, now uttering a sharp command, now threatening some hesitant man with the flat of his sword.

The order to fall in was given. The cavalcade started. The men rode forward, over the slope of the hill and then down a ravine. The lights of the fort were visible for a minute, then another hill rose and blotted them from sight. The column moved slowly; the troopers could hardly see beyond the horses' heads. Once the word to halt went down the lines while a subaltern and three men were sent ahead to reconnoitre. They returned. There was a low-voiced consultation and then a rider, the leader, attended by a single other officer, pushed off suddenly into the night. The men waited. There was silence except for the creaking of saddle leather and here and there a low-voiced order from an officer. Finally the leader and his aide rode up and the order to march on was given.

They came up over a rise. Suddenly all along the line horses came to a stumbling halt. The soldiers reared back instinctively, then leaned forward, peering. Here and there a laugh rang out as men discovered that they had mistaken the fires that the wounded had kindled to keep from freezing for a bivouac of the enemy.

They were now on that portion of the field that had seen the most stubborn fighting of the day. Some men looked with professional curiosity at places that they themselves had covered in the dawn advance. Others looked with astonishment at the faces of the dead.

The men who had died here lay as they had fallen. Some with drawn faces, on their backs, lay gazing at the sky as if awaiting the approach of day. Others seemed to have been frozen in action, one man fallen sidewise against a tree, his body resting awkwardly on a crooked elbow. Another, with compressed mouth, a gaping hole in his head, still seemed in the light of the flames to strive against the enemy, his hands fiercely tight about his musket butt plunging the bayonet up to its hilt in the ground. One of the soldiers of the cavalcade cried out as he passed. "It's Old Fulton," he said and then turned to stare back at the terrible and grotesque figure. "Boys, isn't that Old Fulton?"

There was no answer. All along the line men were riding faster. They had come now to a part of the field where there were many wounded. Most of these men seeming to realize that no help could come from the cavalcade, only gazed grimly. Others in the delirium of their wounds dragged themselves forward, painfully, inch by inch, calling hoarsely for water. The men passing only rode faster. Rives rode with his face averted.

The procession dipped down into a little glade and came up another rise. On the far side of this a fire, just replenished, crackled brightly. It was attended by a single man. He sat leaning back against a tree, at ease, except for a certain stiffness in his position. Rives, riding a little out of the way to avoid a hole made by the explosion of a shell, could see that blood stained all one side of the man's jacket and was matted on his right trouser leg. He noticed too that one of his arms hung unnaturally straight at his side. As Rives approached, the man reached over and dragging up a canteen held it awkwardly to his lips. He repeated this manœuvre several times while the cavalcade was approaching. There was a deliberation, a sureness in all his movements, but the fingers that held the canteen trembled and once he had to set it down. "He's crawled all the way to the branch for that water," Rives thought.

The man as if arrested by Rives' scrutiny suddenly looked up over the edge of the canteen. His eyes, enormous in the shadow of his peaked cap, met Rives' for a moment, then his lids fell. Rives could see the pulse in his throat leap as he greedily drank the water.

From up ahead had come the order to "Move faster." Descending a hill, they came to a swollen stream whose banks were lined with ice. The colonel in command had called for a volunteer to test its depth. When none came forth he himself rode quickly in. When it was seen that the water came no higher than his saddle skirts the command splashed in after him, a rear guard remaining until all had crossed.

Rives, as his horse breasted the icy water, thought that it must have been to this stream that the man by the fire had crawled. He did not see how a wounded man could have accomplished the feat, for he would have had to go out on the thick ice a little way before he could get through to water. As he rode on he thought of this man who had expended his last strength getting water and dragging up boughs for his fire. He would bleed to death before morning, his dark glance had said. But there had been a quietness, almost a relish in all his movements, the way he leaned back against his tree or nursed his failing strength in picking up the canteen. And there had been a strange lack of curiosity in his gaze, a meditativeness about it as of a man shut in on a winter night. It seemed to Rives now that the wounded soldier gazing, and then letting his lids fall, had turned away much as he had turned away from the wounded men by the other fires. The dark glance had been enigmatic but there had been in it a flicker of the hostility which men look on at unbearable suffering. It was as if the man dying in the circle of the firelight could not endure the spectacle of the living, who were only riding toward death.

The cavalcade rode on, splashing sometimes through shallow branches, sometimes through backwater deep enough to swim the horses. The gray was lifting. It was possible now to see the road they were travelling. They raised their haggard faces and stared at one another. As they came out of a bridle path on to the main road a bugle sounded off, clear but subdued in tone. It was opening negotiations for capitulation, the surrender of the fort and 10,271 men.

9

ON the second day after the fall of Fort Donelson, citizens of Clarksville—all those who had not fled from the town—were gathered on their balconies, wharves and private docks along the river front. Every eye was fixed on the same object, a broad ribbon of smoke which hanging low over the river slowly advanced toward the town. The gunboats had been expected hourly for two days, and for two days the whole town had been in a panic. Business had long ago ceased, mills and foundries were closed, railroad rolling stock had all been sent south. Even the wharf boat, *The Captain O. M. Davis,* had been towed to a place of safety far up the stream. Meanwhile the riverside was black with throngs of runaway negroes, and there was talk of a servile insurrection. Many people, fearing this as much as the approach of the Yankees, had taken what gold they had and fled over the border into Kentucky.

The first gunboat arrived and dropped anchor far out in the high water. The crowd watched in silence as the transports began feeling their way in to the bank; then a faint cry arose as the portholes of one of the gun boats was suddenly opened and a broadside of cannon thrust out. No sound, however, came from the gunboats. In silence the gangplank was laid down and in the same dead silence a group of officers, headed by a thickset, bearded man in a rusty general's uniform stepped over the gangplank and out onto the square.

Far back on the edge of the crowd a voice rose, "Grant! That's General Grant!"

There was a loud hiss from somewhere in the vicinity from which the voice came, then people could be seen scurrying to change their position. The General lifted his black felt hat, which had on it a slightly draggled plume, but his face remained impassive. The soldiers disembarking behind him formed columns of fours and rapidly wheeling into line, their guns at right shoulder shift, marched through the square and out onto College Street.

A murmur ran ahead of them, rose on the heels of the marching men. As the columns passed the balconies of the Arlington Hotel, a young girl's nervous laugh suddenly rang out. "Here they come. Look at the blue-bellied Yankees!"

The officers at the head of the column marched on, looking neither to right nor left, but a private's grinning face was suddenly upturned as he passed under the balcony. "I thank you, madam, my belly is as white as yours."

Out on the Red River bridge a fat old man in a tight blue coat and a striped linsey woollen vest and pantaloons sat in a trap, holding the reins over two steaming horses. When a negro came in sight, running down the road at full speed he rose to his feet yelling: "They here yet? They coming?"

The negro coming on pattering feet shouted that there were thousands of them. Done took the square and marched all over College Street. Some said they was going to hang the mayor and all the council. . . . Old Mr. McLean did not wait to hear the rest. He turned his trap around so quickly that the negro had barely time to clamber on in the back, and belaboring the already foaming horses, he set off in a gallop up the Trenton pike.

An hour later he drove into the yard at Brackets, shouting "Fount! Fount!"

Mr. Allard came out on the porch, followed by all the rest of his family. Old Mr. McLean, while he extricated himself from the trap, commanded his servant to go straight to the stable and get the fastest pair of horses—this with hardly a side glance at his brother-in-law. While the negro was gone he recited some details of the invasion as he had heard them from the negro. The riverside was swarming with negroes and white rabble.

They had already looted the great warehouse of thousands of pounds of salt pork and flour and were starting now on the storehouses of private homes. The Yankee soldiers were already established in barracks at the college. They would be on the warpath tomorrow. Spread over the country like locusts. But he—and here a smile trembled on his pendulous lips—he was not worried. He had foreseen it. He had arranged. Day before yesterday he had started them driving all his stock up to a little farm he had over the border. His money—he patted his broad waist with another secret smile—he was taking that along too. He might even go to Canada before he was through with it.

Mrs. Allard, as her half-brother was speaking, was pacing up and down the gallery. As she turned and came toward him he got up from the chair in which he had sat down, and groaning, clumsily patted her on her shoulder. "You can come with me in the trap, Charlotte," he said. "And Fount," he looked about distractedly, "Fount can bring the rest in the carriage."

Mrs. Allard smiled faintly, put her hand up and let it rest on his. Her eyes were on her husband. Fontaine Allard had sat down in his big split-bottom chair. He was looking out at the road. "I declare," he said, "people already started running out from town."

Mr. McLean glanced at the road where a motley procession of vehicles could be seen, then looked back at his brother-in-law. "Well, what you going to do?" he demanded. "You going or ain't you?"

"I'm going to sit right here," Allard said coolly. "If the Yankees want me they'll know where to find me."

"Charlotte?" McLean asked.

She shook her head. "I couldn't leave, Brother John."

The trap was at the door. Old McLean climbed in. As the horses started off he leaned forward and shook his fat fist. "Pair of damn fools," he yelled, "and always were. Hope the Yankees git you."

Allard watched the team plunge down the drive. "Hope he don't kill my horses," he said.

Behind him Lucy's laugh rang out, infectious, almost gay. She had been standing there, silent as befitted a young person in the presence of her elders, but her vivid imagination had been busy. She saw the town in the panic and confusion which her grand uncle had just described, visualized the river front swarming with negroes, the warehouse looted, the houses along Second Street deserted or filled with terror-stricken people. She pictured it all but she got from it not a sense of confusion and terror but a feeling of new, up-springing life.

In the twinkling of an eye a change had come over her whole being. She who yesterday had been so sluggish that it was an effort for her to move, to answer a question, now felt capable of concentrating upon anything, everything. This feeling was so strong in her that she felt the necessity to discharge it by physical action. Walking swiftly over to where the others stood looking anxiously into each other's faces, she laid her hand on her grandmother's arm. "I'm glad we're going to stay," she said. "I'm glad we're not going with Uncle John," and she gave each of them a brilliant smile, not because she had at that moment any concern for their welfare or her own, but because she felt the necessity of scattering some of this abundant life about her as people do when they are very happy or are intensely living.

10

THE next morning Mrs. Allard awoke at dawn. She lay for a few minutes waiting drowsily for certain sounds which would tell her that the servants had assembled and were preparing breakfast. The old cook, Aunt Mimy, as soon as she entered the house was in the habit of going into the dining room and flinging the blinds wide, and Mrs. Allard for many years had wakened to the creaking of the blinds on their hinges. Now as the minutes wore on and this sound did not come she became vaguely uncomfortable. She raised herself up in bed, alarmed, and looked over at her husband. He was lying on his back, one arm flung up over his head, his brown beard rising and falling with his even breaths. Mrs. Allard put her hand on his shoulder and shook him gently.

"Fount, I don't hear any sounds from the kitchen."

His eyes opened suddenly: he stared not at her but through the window which gave on the lawn. "Yes," he said. "Yes, I expect so."

"Expect what?" his wife demanded sharply.

He remained silent, lying propped on his elbow, staring out of the window. Mrs. Allard after a moment slipped out of bed, dressed herself and went across the hall.

The dining room, still darkened for the night, was deserted. In the kitchen old Winston knelt before the great range laboriously kindling a fire. He looked over his shoulder as Mrs. Allard came in, murmured a "Mawnin', Ole Miss," and turned back to his work.

Mrs. Allard stood still in the doorway. "Where is Mimy, Winston?" she asked.

He let the stick of wood he was holding drop to the floor. "She's gone," he said. "Dey all gone. To Clarksville."

"To Clarksville?" she repeated.

The old man got to his feet. His wrinkled face was working. He chuckled, on a high, malicious note. "Bre'r John sont you word he still here. And old Sis Dep down in her cabin. She's taking care of them chillun they left." He took a step toward his mistress, eyeing her as if accusingly. "What's goin' to become of things around here?" he demanded. "Who gwine do them niggers' work? Old John, he cain't git down his front steps and Sis Dep, she so crippled up with rheumatism folks have to be waitin' on her."

Mrs. Allard's face had flushed a painful red, as it might have flushed at an insult or personal rebuff. She looked at the old man as he spoke, then turned away with a visible effort at self-control. "I'll send Dep and John down their breakfast directly. Now, Winston, you get me some flour and I'll make some batter cakes for breakfast. Then soon as you get your fire to burning you go down to the spring house and bring up some milk. We can see about the milking after breakfast."

The old man turned quietly to his tasks, his mistress to hers, and by the time the rest of the family was assembled a tolerable breakfast was on the table.

Fontaine Allard came in as they sat down, reporting that he had just made the rounds of the quarters. Uncle Winston was correct. Of all the negroes on the place there were left only a dozen children, Old Maum Dep, who acted as nurse for the mothers who worked in the field, and the octagenarian, Uncle John. Even a young mulatto girl, Lissy, who had been bed ridden for years, was gone with the rest.

Mrs. Allard was aghast at this. "Lissy!" she exclaimed. "Fount, she'll die, out in this weather."

Cally, more practical, enquired of her father if any stock were missing.

"Six mules," he replied, "the best on the place, of course."

Belle gave a short laugh. "Catch these lazy Brackets niggers walking!"

There was a little silence. Everybody knew that the Allards were thought to spoil their negroes but nobody had ever before charged Fontaine Allard with it to his face. Belle, herself, as if feeling that she had gone too far, looked down and toyed with something on her plate while Love gave the involuntary laugh with which nervous people sometimes greet a breach of decorum. Lucy glanced angrily at Belle, then kept her eyes fixed steadfastly on her grandfather's face.

He, too, had glanced down for a moment after Belle spoke as if he could hardly credit what he heard. But now he looked up, fixing Belle with a level glance. "I have never found," he said coldly, "that overworking darkies on week days makes them any more willing to walk on Sundays. As for the mules, I think you will find your cousin, Colonel Miles, has lost as much stock as I have."

Belle kept her eyes on her plate and did not answer. Mrs. Allard began to speak quietly of the tasks that would have to be performed if the stock were not to suffer and after a little everybody rose from the table. Lucy, being more active and used to out doors, had been assigned the care of the poultry. Getting down her bonnet and shawl and drawing on a pair of woollen mittens, she went out into the yard and entered the poultry runs. The chickens, ducks and turkeys all came crowding around her. When she had filled all the pans with water and buttermilk she crossed the yard to the granary. Opening the door with the great brass key she passed into the compartment where wheat was stored. It had been years since Lucy had been inside the granary but she and Love and Ned as children used to come here often to "play in the wheat." Standing now beside the great bin and scooping out wheat into a tow sack she remembered how they would step on top of the pile and then allow themselves to sink in until they were buried, sometimes to the neck. She recalled the excitement when the mass of grain began to yield under foot and the delicious sensation of the grain rushing up over the bare feet and legs. But though she could recall the sensations and the consequent excitement as distinctly as if it had been yesterday, she could not recapture the mood of that far-off time. It seemed to her strange that even children could have been delighted by so trivial a pastime.

She finished filling her sack with grain and dragged it across the yard to the poultry runs. The sack was heavy. Lucy might better have filled it half-full and made several trips, but she found a perverse pleasure in the effort to drag the heavy weight over the ground. It was a relief to have something to do with her hands. Ever since she left the house she had been struggling against a feeling of oppression. As she flung handful after handful of grain to the fowls she went over in her mind the encounter between Belle and her grandfather. When she came out of the house her chief emotion had been distaste for what she considered Belle's impertinence to Mr. Allard. But now analyzing what had occurred she realized that that was not what troubled her. Belle, after all, had been guilty only of a slip of the tongue. Whatever her private opinions she would never have aspersed Mr. Allard's handling of his negroes if she had paused at all to consider. But Mr. Allard's rejoinder to Belle! That was what amazed Lucy. He had stooped—she found herself putting the matter into words—he had stooped not only to defend himself to Belle but to strike out against her. "Your cousin, Colonel Miles." Lucy had known of the relationship—it was one of the objections Mr. Allard had had to his son's marriage to Joe Bradley's daughter—but she could never remember hearing it mentioned before. *"Your cousin, Colonel Miles. . . ."* He must have wanted to hurt Belle or he would never have said that. The idea of her grandfather, whom she could not remember to have seen out of temper, being provoked to retaliation like an ordinary mortal filled Lucy with a feeling of desolation such as she had never before experienced.

She glanced down at the fat white ducks who were waddling at her feet, and scooping up with their spoon-shaped bills the grain she had thrown down for the chickens. These ducks, unlike the other fowls, were allowed to wander at will over the place and often made a procession across the lawn. Lucy was accustomed to look out on them often from her bedroom and to delight in the dazzling white of their plumage, but now the white feathers seemed cold and unattractive, the black eyes greedy.

She flung down the remaining grains of wheat and started toward the stable with the intention of helping her grandfather feed the horses. Halfway there she turned aside on an impulse and went instead toward the quarters. The approach to the quarters, leading as it did through an alley of pawlonia trees, was pleasant and the cabins themselves, neatly whitewashed and set about with the broad green leaves of hollyhocks, presented the appearance of a village street. Today, however, the scene was one of extraordinary confusion. The negroes had departed in great haste. It was apparent that they had tried to take some of their belongings with them and then had abandoned the effort as too great. A feather pillow was tossed into a bed of hollyhocks, a rocking chair sat forlornly under a tree, a child's wagon beside it. Lucy saw something shining at her feet and stooping found a little pocket mirror she had given to one of the maids a few days before, its glass shattered, its pretty, embroidered case fouled by mud. She went on down the street and stopped before the open door of Aunt Mimy's cabin. The hearth was cold and the room in disorder. Fallen in the middle of the floor was the great feather bed with a rope half-tied around it. Lucy stood looking down at the bed with an astonishment almost childlike. Always before she had seen it, high on its bedstead, the covers, the blue and white patchwork quilt on top, drawn up smoothly, the bolster topped by the huge pillows with their embroidered shams. Her eyes roved about the room which she had known from childhood and in which she had received some of her earliest lessons in order. "Larroes to catch meddlars. You want me smack yo hans?" She could hear Aunt Mimy now when she or Love, standing beside the high dresser, had reached for two tiny china shepherdesses that always stood there. The shepherdesses were gone, the drawers of the dresser gaping wide disclosed only folded newspapers. It was hard to believe the dignified, precise old woman had ever lived in this room. Lucy was lost in a wonder not so much how Aunt Mimy could have left her home but how she could have left it in such undignified haste. The sight of the gaping dresser drawers, the tumbled mattress, all increased the sadness which was already upon her. As she stepped down from the porch and started toward the stable where her grandfather, she knew, would already be busy with the horses, she thought: Rats desert a sinking ship. She walked down the alley of pawlonias, the wind rustling her skirts, repeating the phrase over and finding in it a melancholy satisfaction. And it seemed to her that the negroes, furtive and forever alien race, had got wind of some disaster which as yet was only approaching. "Yes," she thought, "we are sinking, sinking; and they know it and have deserted us."

11

LUCY was out on the little brick porch washing the morning milk vessels. The weather had changed overnight and the air had the balminess of summer. No green could be seen anywhere in the landscape but in the woods beyond the stable lot the Judas tree was already flowering. Lucy, as she worked, raised her eyes now and then to the woods and each time she did so the expression of her stern young face softened. The "red-bud" was the first harbinger of spring, eagerly awaited, and to see the black boughs clouded with its pink gave her some of the old stirring of delight.

She had finished drying the rows of bright vessels and was about to go back into the kitchen when a noise in the shrubbery made her aware that she was not—had not been for some minutes—alone. Lucy's first impulse was to run into the house but she resisted it and stood still, her hands clenched at her sides.

"Who's there?" she called sharply.

There was a faint giggle and a young negro girl came out from the syringa bushes and stood with her hands wrapped in her apron. Lucy recognized her as Julia, granddaughter to the old cook, Mimy. In her first quick glance she noted that the girl's eyes were deeply ringed with fatigue and that her linsey woollen frock was sodden and crumpled as if she had slept in it.

The girl did not speak, merely stood, smiling shyly. After a minute Lucy caught up her cup towel and hung it on one of the boughs of the pine tree. "Well, Julia," she said, "what is it?"

The girl, encouraged, came out from behind the shrubbery. Withdrawing her hand from her apron she held out a little pasteboard box. "Mama say ask Ole Miss to send her some quinine. Robert T., he got bad chills."

Robert T., Julia's little brother, had been born in August. He had been a particularly engaging little creature and Lucy had made him a frilled cap which she thought set off to great advantage his dark, round little features. A sharp rejoinder sprang to her lips now as she imagined the six months' old baby dragged about over the river front, exposed doubtless to the inclement weather of the last few days. She repressed it, however, and said dryly: "You'd better come and see Ole Miss yourself," and turning led the way into the house.

In the chamber Mrs. Allard sat knitting in her great chair by the window. She raised her head as the door opened and her glance rested for a moment on the two young women, then she bent her head to her work. "What is it, Julia?" she asked without looking up again.

Julia repeated her request for some quinine. "Robert T. was took bad, right after they got in last night. Maum Dep she come and look at him and she say . . ."

Mrs. Allard laid her stocking down. "What time did you get in last night?"

Julia replied that it was before daylight. "Must a been cause warn't no pink showin' anywhere in the sky. . . . Maum Dep say it's chills and fevers and ain't nothin gwine kill um but quinine . . ."

Mrs. Allard's eyes rested absently on the girl's face. "He'll die," she said coldly, "if he's having spasms already. He's too little to take quinine." She rose and went to the tall secretary that stood in the corner. "Julia, how many of you all are back?"

The girl, relieved to be free of her mistress' scrutiny, was voluble. Was Doc and Trip Butler and old Unc' Ben. Aunt Mimy had been took bad with rheumatism right after they started home. She and Lissy was laying up now in Mr. Gill's summer kitchen. Mr. Gill there by the bridge. He said he knew Aunt Mimy was Mister Fount's cook and he gwine let 'em stay there till some of the Brackets folks could come get 'em. Aunt Mimy say tell Ole Miss to hurry up. Lissy was having them coughing spells and spitting blood and she cain't do nothin' with her . . ."

Mrs. Allard stood in front of the secretary filling a small basket with medicines. She turned now and spoke to Lucy:

"I'll tell Uncle Winston to put a mattress in the spring wagon. And he better start right away. We can't leave Lissy there sick on Mr. Gill."

Lucy silently stepped out into the hall, closing the door behind her. The hall door was open and the spring sunlight lay in bright squares on the dark floor that was everywhere covered lightly with dust. Lucy stepped over the checkers of sunshine out onto the porch. Half-kneeling on one of the benches that ran on either side of the little gallery she folded her arms and stared off at the distant woods, noting mechanically the tracery of pink red-bud bloom that a few minutes before had given her such pleasure. "They've come back because they're sick," she thought, "all of them sick and now she'll work herself to death waiting on them." It seemed to her, inured during the past week to performing household tasks, that she and the rest of the family would be better off without the negroes and it angered her to think of them complacently settling down in their quarters as if they had never gone away. She gazed out on the landscape unseeing, muttering angrily to herself until the sound of light breathing beside her made her turn. The negro girl was standing beside her.

"Why don't you go back to the quarters, Julia?" she asked.

The girl gave a soft, deprecatory laugh. "I'm waiting to carry Ole Miss' basket. She huntin' up bandages for Aaron's little girl what got her head cut."

Lucy folded her arms on the railing and resumed her contemplation of the landscape, but the consciousness of the girl's presence beside her was disturbing. Half-turning, she said coldly, "Is Aaron's little girl hurt bad? I suppose you're all hurt or sick or you wouldn't have come home."

The girl who was still under the stress of great excitement seemed to accept this remark as an evidence of sympathy rather than a reprimand. She laughed on a high, excited note. "Miss Lucy, you ought to seen 'em last night! They was niggers leaving town, so fast they like to tore the Red River bridge down gittin through. One old man, old Unc' Aaron Dudley, he got caught twixt the j'ists of that bridge and looked like they was going to trample him to death."

Lucy looked down into the upturned eyes that were as restless and as shallow as an animal's. "Uncle Aaron Dudley," she cried harshly. "A good old man. Nearly ninety years old. And you trample him to death."

"Old man like that didn't have no business out larkin'. . ." The girl broke off, laughing nervously at the expression in Lucy's face, then shrank away before the upraised hand. *"Miss Lucy!* Don't hit me. I ain't done nothing." There was the patter of feet over the veranda floor and a whish of skirts. She had disappeared around one of the columns of the portico.

Lucy stood still beside the railing. Her hand was still drawn back as it had been when she moved forward to strike the girl. She watched it sink slowly to her side as if it had been the hand of another person, then went into the house and shut the door.

At twelve o'clock Mr. Allard, and Jim, Belle, and Love came back from Babylon where they had ridden that morning to oversee some plantation affairs. They reported that the Trenton road was black with negroes, some moving toward home, some forlornly milling up and down the road. Colonel Miles' negroes were camped half a mile from his gate, waiting while a white man of the community acted as intermediary between them and their master.

Love, taking off her bonnet in the hall, chattered nervously of what she had seen. "The poor things. Lucy, if you saw them you couldn't stay mad. You know Uncle John's old Cider? He'd hobbled all the way from town on those crooked legs and when we passed him he was just doubled up in a knot there by the road. He thinks the end of the world has come. When he saw who we were he cried, 'Marse Fount, I done been down into hell,' and he kept talking about sights he'd seen down on that river front. White folks stealing from negroes and negroes stealing from white folks and one woman he said had her apron full of salt meat and was trying to eat it raw. After the soldiers got there they fired into the crowd to get them away from the warehouse. They wanted to use it themselves for something. Unc' Cider said there were people sitting on the kerb who walked twenty miles from up in Kentucky and then had to sit out in the rain all night. . . ."

Belle had less to say of what went on on the road and she replied laconically to questions about affairs at Babylon. Yes, they had found everything going on as well as could be expected. The negroes had all run off to town, of course, like everybody else's, but they were beginning to come back. Joe Green, the overseer, thought they would all be back in a day or two and he hoped to get them to work. She drew the silk strings of her bonnet through her fingers, her expression abstracted and secret. "It might be better," she said suddenly, "if they didn't come back—ever."

When she went upstairs the two girls and Cally followed her. Lucy, awed by Belle's manner, went over and stood looking out of the window. Cally kept her place by the door. "Well, Belle," she asked bluntly, "what is it?"

Belle would not speak till the door was closed. "I don't want Mother Allard to know this. She has enough on her mind already."

She told them then what had been in the minds of everybody they had met on the road that morning. Mrs. Crawley, a widow, lived with her daughter, Flora, on a farm ten miles away in Trigg County. The farm had always been managed by a competent negro overseer. There were no white people on the place except Mrs. Crawley and her daughter. At daybreak this morning she had come in a state of distraction to the house of a neighbor five miles away. Flora had been missing since early afternoon of the day before. Her mother had run all over the fields and through the woods all night, searching for her, and had found her at daylight in an abandoned outhouse not far from the house. She had been kept there, gagged and bound, since the very time she had disappeared, the day before. Yes, it was Albert Jennings. Flora had been able to tell them that. He had escaped but Cousin Edmund and some other men were hunting him, in the Big Pond swamp. Mrs. Spencer was staying with Mrs. Crawley who was worse off than Flora almost, completely out of her head.

Cally, while Belle was speaking, had opened her mouth as if to say she didn't believe a word of this story, but at the mention of Edmund Rowan's name she fell silent, only giving Belle a glance out of shrewd gray eyes before she left the room. Downstairs she called Lucy and Love into her own room for a private conference. When they came in she was sitting on a hassock. A foot bath full of hot water stood before her into which she had plunged her feet swollen from too much standing. She spoke plainly and practically, laving her feet the while. This terrible thing that Belle had told of, doubtless it had happened, or Cousin Edmund and those other men would not have gone off to hunt that negro. Some people might think that the mother and daughter, living on that remote place without any other white people, had laid themselves liable to just such a happening. Be that as it may. It had happened. But terrible things were happening every day now—men that they knew were being killed in battle or suffering tortures in prison. The chief thing was to keep your head, not to forget the duty that you owed to others. Love and Lucy, if they did not allow themselves to be frightened by idle talk or by brooding on things that had actually happened, could be useful to their grandfather and grandmother, to everybody on the place. The negroes were coming back—soon they would probably all be at home. The problem was to keep them in order. The best way to do that was by disciplining your own thoughts. Love and Lucy must not only never show any fear before the servants, they must actually for the sake of their own safety never have any fear of them. As for Belle, they were all agreed that the best thing was to keep her away from the negroes as much as possible. They must remember, she concluded, that a servile insurrection—the girls started and looked at each other at the unfamiliar and frightening words—a servile insurrection was like cattle milling. They had heard Cousin Frank tell of such things in the West. Once one got started all followed. The thing was never, even for a moment, to give way to panic yourself.

The girls promised they would do as she said and left her sitting in her deep chair, her stout legs in their woollen stockings propped for ease on a hassock, her plain face anxious and brooding.

Mrs. Allard was busy in the quarters most of the day. Toward dusk she came in, reporting that Sally's baby, in spite of hot fomentations and doses of paregoric, had died an hour ago. It was not chills and fever, but acute indigestion. Sally, moaning, had finally confessed to having given the little thing some sort of strange meat, two whole sausages of it, during that first night when they had been down on the river front waiting for the Yankee soldiers.

The family ate an early supper, then went to sit on the gallery in the air which was as balmy and soft as summer. As they sat there they talked of the events of the day. The routine of work was already partially established. The two able-bodied men who had returned the night before had gone quietly about the tasks of milking, feeding and watering the stock, bringing up grain for poultry, but none of the women so far had reported to the house.

"They're too demoralized," Mrs. Allard said, leaning back in her chair with a sigh.

"It's because they've had you down there all day waiting on them, Mama," Cally declared. "When I think of all the work and nursing from that fool trip into Clarksville! What do you suppose they thought they'd get? I asked Unc' Yellow Ben if he got any of that salt pork they were looting from the warehouse and he laughed and said he left that for the poor white folks. Plenty of meat at home."

"They're like children," Mr. Allard said. "There was a circus in town and they had to go." He spoke in his customary formal and benevolent tones but his voice was weary. He had been up since dawn and had cared for a hundred head of stock during the day.

Cally was silent, then burst out again. For some reason Aunt Mimy's defection seemed to annoy her more than the others. "The rest have all come and taken their medicine," she said. "I gave some of the young ones what-for, I tell you, and they stood and took it. They had to. But Madam," she spoke in high, finicking tones, "she's too high and mighty to acknowledge she made a fool of herself. Pretends to be sick so we have to send and get her. *We* have to make the first move. I suppose you sent the carriage, Mama."

"The spring wagon," Mrs. Allard said wearily. "And I wouldn't have sent for Mimy by herself but Lissy had to be got home. We couldn't leave a consumptive negro there for Mrs. Gill to take care of."

Cally made a little explosive sound of protest and then was silent. The others, weary from the long day's work, sat quiet, Mr. and Mrs. Allard in the big hickory rockers, and the three young women dropped down on the steps. Lucy was watching the shadows creep slowly over the lawn and thinking that except for the bare branches you could fancy yourself sitting on the porch of a summer evening when she heard a sibilant, "Shh," and was aware of Cally's fingers tightly clutching her arm. Lucy, looking in the direction in which Cally's head was turned, at first saw nothing. Then she realized that a dark mass had detached itself from the low-hanging cedar boughs and was moving slowly toward the house. The scream died in her throat under the fierce pressure of Cally's fingers on her arm. The two sat silent watching the dark mass move slowly over the lawn. Then Cally on her feet was whispering: "Get in the house. Quick. We must all get in the house."

The others had risen. In the light from the open doorway their faces were turned upon her in bewilderment. It was at that moment that the moving mass resolved itself into figures that ran, like dogs, over the lawn. As they gained the gallery in one swift bound, Lucy caught the gleam of eyeballs, saw the gaunt faces under the drooping hat brims. She beat on the railing with her hand and cried hysterically: "They're white, Aunt Cally! They're *white!*"

12

IN the hall the two young men smiling, weary, clutching their sodden hats, turned from one to the other, trying to answer all the questions at once. Yes, they had come in from Hopkinsville that morning. Ned had thought he knew a short-cut through the woods that took off five miles, but they had got lost and wandered for an hour. After that they were afraid to ride, even on by-roads. They had left their horses with an old negro man Ned knew and had made the rest of the way on foot. They had got into the Brackets woods long before dark and had wanted to come to the house then but had been afraid of being seen. They had lain there actually in sight of the house for two hours. It was pretty hard, that time Lucy came out on the porch with an apple and they had to lie there and watch her eat it.

Mrs. Allard gave a cry at this and rushed toward the dining room. Cally went over and put out the single candle on the hall stand, then looked to see if the front and back doors were securely fastened. There were no servants in the house now, none had been in it for several days, except old Uncle Winston. Still one must be careful.

They tiptoed into the dining room where Rives and Ned, washing down cold ham and biscuits and preserves with hot coffee, told the rest of their story.

They had escaped with Colonel Forrest from Fort Donelson, had heard at daybreak shortly after they came out of the fort the sound of the bugle announcing surrender. They had expected pursuit but there had been none. The first night they had camped twenty miles from the fort and had reached Nashville the next day at ten o'clock. The city was in a panic, the whole citizenry demoralized. Government stores were being broken into and pillaged by broad daylight. Wagonloads of material had been carted off into the country for private use. The president of one of the railroads had appropriated an engine and train of cars for the removal of his property and had steamed away south.

Colonel Forrest—"the same officer that came here to see you that night," Ned said with a flash of his white teeth at his father—had been a magnificent sight. The rabble about the public commissary had refused to disperse. Forrest had led his troopers into the plunging crowd, had belabored the more obstinate over their heads and shoulders with the flat of his sabre. A fire engine was brought up and a stream of cold water played upon the mob. Ned, his spirits restored by food and drink, rose from the table and enacted the role of the gallant Colonel directing the playing of the hose with one hand while, with the other, he made reassuring gestures to a group of ladies who, clad, some of them, only in their nightgowns with shawls over their heads, had suddenly appeared on the street. "We'll have them out of here in a minute, Madam, the filthy scoundrels," and Ned bowed grandly from the waist while with one hand he went through the motions of a man playing a hose pipe on the recalcitrant mob.

Mrs. Allard had risen and was putting the dishes and food away. "I don't see that you two boys are in a much better fix now," she said. "The Yankees were out here the other day and they'll probably come again. The whole town is in their hands and they've begun to ravage the country."

Ned replied that, on the contrary, he and Rives considered themselves to be in an excellent situation. They could surely stay hid at Brackets a few days. They had come only because Colonel Forrest on reaching Murfreesboro had been ordered to disband his men. The entire command was disbanded on furlough to reassemble on March 10. "Only," he added, "we need new equipment. I've got to have a fresh horse. And Ma," he held out his arm from which the sleeve was dropping in rags, "can't you do something about this? It was cold last night sleeping in these things. Rives said he felt like he was pinned on the clothes line. Every time the wind blew it set his rags to flying."

There was a noise in the pantry. Cally got up quickly and went out. In a minute she came back with a grave face. Uncle Winston had just brought the milk and was straining it on the kitchen table. She hoped he hadn't heard any talk in the dining room, in fact she was sure he hadn't. But he had noticed the light. She had seen him glance toward the door. The question now was what were they going to do?

Mrs. Allard at the first sound of the disturbance had approached Ned and was standing, her hand on his arm. She let it sink slowly to her side now. Her eyes went to her husband's face.

He appeared to ponder for a moment, then he said quietly that Uncle Winston, of course, must know of all their plans.

Cally nodded and slipped back through the door. A few minutes later Uncle Winston, gravely smiling, entered the room. It was decided that the two young men should sleep in one of the small bedrooms in the company wing. There was an outer stairway leading to the ground from this room. Cally announced that she would occupy the room directly across the hall and would leave her door open. She would keep a good fire going and would sit up all night. "Stand guard," she put it, striking a military attitude.

Uncle Winston who had gone to lay a fire in the bedroom came back reporting that all was ready. As he went out Mr. Allard observed that the old man had volunteered to stand guard too, in the quarters. They had arranged a signal. Uncle Winston if he heard the slightest disturbance during the night was to go out on his porch and call to his hound. With two such intrepid individuals as Cally and Uncle Winston on guard and with the added protection of the set signals, he felt they were reasonably safe against alarms, for this one night at least. Tomorrow they could decide what to do. In the meantime the boys must take advantage of a good night's sleep in a comfortable bed.

13

LUCY awoke early the next morning, dressed quickly and went downstairs. She was about to go into the kitchen to help prepare breakfast as she had been doing now for several days when her grandmother stepped out of her bedroom and stood looking at her significantly, her finger on her lips. Lucy understood the warning gesture to mean that the old cook was back in the kitchen, with perhaps one of the young maids and that her grandmother wished the return to pass unnoticed. She turned back into the main hall. The front door was still closed. Lucy flung it open and going out on the gallery breathed the fresh morning air that was already touched with the odor of spring.

The very air seemed fresher and she saw buds on the sugar trees that had not been there yesterday. Lucy, like most people of sanguine temperament, often went through long periods of depression when she seemed to herself to be hardly alive. It was the more terrible because she had been forced to endure the close companionship of Love, to watch her blush when George Rowan's name was mentioned, to listen while carefully selected passages from his many letters—he had been transferred and was in a different regiment from the other boys—were read aloud.

Sometimes walking alone up and down the garden paths, among the dead, withered stalks of last year's flowers, she had asked herself why she was so different from Love, so different, she told herself, from all the other girls she knew. She mused on the engagement between Love and George: though they now seemed to love each other, each could just as easily have fallen in love with some one else. "Why am I not like that?" she asked herself. "Why am I different from all the rest? Am I going to be like Aunt Cally and end my days dosing out quinine and sewing flannel petticoats for negro women?" And her aunt's face would rise before her and she would hear with a kind of terror the dry, kindly voice that to Lucy's ear always seemed to come from a distance.

The advent of the two soldiers which ordinarily would have seemed an important happening became even more important viewed in the light of what was going on in her own being. She had been alert all day to execute her grandmother's orders. Nothing seemed too much trouble, no exertion too great. She flew up and down stairs all day, mended the fire to save Uncle Winston, cut out garments to help her aunt.

In the late afternoon the same mood held her as she sat at the sewing machine. She was working on new uniforms for the soldiers. Cally, rising a few minutes ago, had said, frowning, that she did not know whether they would be able to finish the uniforms tonight after all. Lucy, taking the cloth into her own hands, had laughed. "Of course we can. We can sit up all night, if necessary." And indeed she would have been able to sit up and work all night, such was the energy that possessed her.

Now bending over the machine she pedalled rapidly while her fingers flying in and out of the folds of cloth arranged them before the advancing needle. There was no one in the room now but herself and Rives. Cally and Love were walking in the shrubbery and Ned had got up a few minutes ago saying that he would go downstairs and sit with his father. Before he went he had been singing a camp song, imitating the accents of an Irishman who was a favorite in the regiment. Ned was gone but his song still lingered in the air. It seemed to Lucy that the machine ran to its rhythms. As she pedalled she sang, imitating Ned's rendition of the Irishman's accent:

When Johnny comes marching home again . . .
Ta Ra . . . Ta Ra!
When Johnny comes marching home again
Ta Ra . . . Ta Ra. . . .

When she came to the last verse she threw her head back, laughing, as if she expected Rives to join her. He had risen and was standing with his back to the fire. She was suddenly aware that for minutes he had been gazing at her as she sewed. She was embarrassed and rose and came to the fire.

She was not cold but she found herself bending over and shivering a little. Rives at once went out into the hall to fetch more logs. Lucy sank down in one of the deep armchairs drawn up to the hearth. She watched Rives as he brought the wood in and, kneeling down, skilfully arranged the new back-log in its place. She noticed for the first time his muscular hands and how his broad back strained at the seams of his ragged jacket. It seemed to her that he had actually increased in stature in the few months he had been away. Or perhaps it was that he stood straighter. There was an assurance in his bearing that had not been there before.

He had not resumed his own chair but stood, one arm leaning against the mantel. He was looking down into the flames, his lips a little touched by a smile.

Leaning back in her chair—she had not Rives' capacity for silence—Lucy began to talk. She recalled the summer with its pleasures, the summer that seemed so long ago. Did he remember the night of the dance, the night they first met, when that strange man who turned out later to be his own colonel, came? Did he, perhaps, remember the first time she ever spoke to him? She did, very well. And did he remember the dance at Music Hall and how they had ridden over in the late afternoon through the woods?

Rives standing beside the mantel smiled assent to her questions, looking at her, then looking away into the flames.

A feeling, that he was occupied with his own thoughts rather than with what she was saying, came over Lucy so strongly that she fell abruptly silent. He had been gazing into the fire but he looked up as if startled by the cessation of sound. He did not speak for a moment, then he strode to the window. "It's almost dark," he said. "Let's go out and walk in the garden."

Lucy was about to make some objection. She did not think her grandmother would approve. Some of the servants might see him. He seemed to read her mind, for he shook his head and smiled at her, a smile so sweet and so compelling that she went silently from the room and getting her bonnet and shawl met him on the stairs.

14

UNCLE WINSTON came in the next morning just as the family was finishing breakfast and informed his master that the pen in the woods was finished. Fontaine Allard made no comment. Mrs. Allard, glancing at her husband, said that she thought it would be a good plan for the girls to go along and help Uncle Winston drive the horses over into the woods. It had been decided some days ago that they were to be hid in there. It had been decided also that none of the servants except Uncle Winston should know of their hiding place.

Immediately after breakfast Aaron and Trip Butler, the only two able-bodied negro men who had returned, were sent on errands to a neighboring farm. As soon as they had left the cavalcade started off, Uncle Winston carrying a sack of nubbins, the two older girls each leading a horse and driving one before them while little Jenny Morris proudly led the gentle old mare.

It was a beautiful day, misty but with a balminess in the air. The woods were still dark except for the pink blossom of red-bud here and there, but the earth under last year's leaves was moist and steaming. Birds, returned since the last snow, sang from the black boughs. Everywhere there was the feeling of awakening life. The young people walked briskly, with colt-like jumps, intent on discerning every sign of spring. Once Jenny Morris, who had run on ahead, summoned everybody to a low hanging oak bough where a spray of mistletoe rose, starred with white wax-like berries. Lucy held the child up so that she could pluck the mistletoe for herself, then with Love's help hoisted her up on Dolly's back. Jenny Morris rode, holding her clump of mistletoe to her as if it had been a bouquet, bending to lay her face lovingly against it.

"It's the prettiest thing in the woods, isn't it, Cousin Lucy?" she chanted.

Lucy, walking along, one arm over the old mare's back, looked at the mistletoe. The dark leaves and white berries affected her disagreeably, reminding her of the year just gone and of seasons that had not fulfilled their promise. It seemed to her that the misty black boughs of the trees showed more life than the green and white mistletoe. She pulled a dogwood branch to her and showed Jenny Morris how, though it was still dark, it was swollen at the tip with this year's leaves. "I'd rather look at this," she said, smiling.

Uncle Winston, laden down with his sacks of corn, had fallen behind. Love, who had been leading the procession, suddenly stopped still.

"I'm perfectly certain I saw somebody around that bend there," she said in a low voice.

They walked on without saying anything to Uncle Winston. In a few seconds they discerned the figures of two men approaching. Lucy burst out laughing when she saw that it was Rives and Ned.

The young men came up laughing. "We sneaked down the back stairs," Ned explained. "We knew what you were going to do and we thought you might need some help. Expert help," he added with a sly glance at Uncle Winston.

"Well, we better get further on in the woods," Love said nervously. "We better get these horses where they're going. Don't you think so, Uncle Winston?"

Uncle Winston who had been looking from one to the other uncertainly said dryly that that was what Ole Marster sont them over here for and they proceeded along the road.

Ned, who had not seen Crevasse since he came back, took her halter from Uncle Winston and fondling the mare called to Rives to notice her beautiful conformation and proud carriage.

Suddenly he got up on her back and looked down at Rives, smiling. "Want to race?" he asked.

Rives at once leaped astride the gray horse. "Come on," he said.

The others stood still and, fascinated, watched the two horses, furry in their winter coats, disappear with flying hooves down the narrow road.

Jenny Morris in her excitement slid off Dolly's back. She shrieked and jumped up and down calling shrilly, "Rives! Rives! Beat him, Rives!"

Lucy, in the midst of her excitement, could not help but think of the dangers of such a race. "They'll kill themselves," she said, "or break that mare's neck. And what'll Grandpa say?"

Uncle Winston watched Ned dexterously manœuvre the mare around a clump of trees. "Naw, he won't," he said. "That boy, Ned, he don't need no bridle." He cackled out suddenly, "That boy he warn't born like us'ns. He uz foaled. I remember. Marster he kept begging Mistis to quit riding old Prince. Mistis say she ain't gwine do it. Prince just like a rocking chair and ain't nothing make her feel better'n a ride every evening. Well, that day she got far as the gate and she turned around and come back mighty quick, I tell you. Marster was standing on the steps. He took one look at her and was hopping mad. 'My God, Charlotte,' he say, 'way you act anybody'd think you was a mar. I'm surprised you didn't go on round to the stable to foal.' "

The old man bent double, cackling, but the girls who had heard this story often before hardly listened, keeping their eyes on the horses.

"Rives rides just as good as Ned," Jenny Morris said. "Look. He's up with him now. He's going to beat him."

The two horses had emerged on a comparatively straight stretch of road. The gelding, more powerfully built than the mare, had been slow in starting but he was gaining on her steadily. Ned, who at first had ridden carelessly, certain of winning the race, was now bending low, gripping the mare's barrel with his knees and urging her on to her top speed. The gelding gained a little more. For a moment they were neck and neck.

Jenny Morris who had constituted herself Rives' champion had to be restrained from yelling her joy, when suddenly the mare shot forward, almost sending Ned over her head. He recovered himself, rode her two or three hundred yards beyond the beech tree, then turning around with the motion of a jockey turning a horse on a race track he rode the beautiful, foaming animal back toward the others. Sweeping his hat off and sliding to the ground he put his arm about the mare's neck. "Couldn't beat you, Old Girl, could he?" he asked fondly.

Rives, coming up, grinned. "Trade horses and race again," he offered.

Uncle Winston, recalled to a sense of duty, intervened. "Naw, you won't. Marster say for us to git these horses in that pen. Somebody going along the road'll hear all this racket and be in here on you first thing you know."

"That's right," Lucy said. "We better go on."

They drove the horses off the main road and made their way through the underbrush to the little clearing where Uncle Winston had contrived a pen of white oak saplings. Jenny Morris, when she saw the small space the horses were to be confined in, protested: "Uncle Winston, they can't hardly turn around in there."

The old man throwing down the nubbins of corn to toll the horses inside frowned at the child. "I reckon you know more about it than I do, Miss," he said crossly. "These horses mighty lucky to have this good a place to stay. Yankees come yesterday and made off with three of Colonel Miles' four-year-olds."

Ned looked up with interest. "The thieving devils!" He walked over and laid his arm along Crevasse's back. "Ladybird! Well, she won't have to stay here long. I'll be riding her off in a day or two."

Uncle Winston tied the old brood mare, Dolly, to a stout sapling in the center of the pen, fastened his rough but substantial gate, then looked about him with satisfaction. "Won't any of 'em try to git out long as Dolly stay," he said. "Everything on the place follow her." He turned to Ned, the momentary glow obscured by the austerity which was natural to him in addressing young people. "Ned, you better be riding Shanks mar' back to that house. Ole Miss gwine give you what-for when you git thar."

Ned had dropped down on a log and taking out his knife began whittling a green bough. "Then we better stay out as long as we can, Winston," he said nonchalantly. Jenny Morris who had never heard the old negro addressed without the prefix of Uncle was pleased with this turn of affairs. She took her place on the log beside Ned. "Yes," she said, "once you git back to the house, they won't let you git out again."

"Get," Love said mechanically. "What *makes* you talk that way, child?"

"Hi!" Rives cried excitedly. "Hi!" He had seized the knife from Ned and had thrown it at a rabbit which had suddenly emerged from some buckberry bushes a few feet away. The clumsy knife fell short of its aim. The rabbit with a flirt of its white tail disappeared in another clump of bushes. Ned retrieved the knife and stood holding it in his hand. "It ain't right to throw," he said. "Don't turn right in the hand." He looked up at Rives. "Did you ever hit one that way?"

Rives nodded. "We used to do it all the time at home. When I was a boy I had a little knife that was just right for it."

Ned shook his head admiringly. "Used to be an old man lived here at Brackets could hit every time. But he was an old settler. They said he was raised with the Shawnee Indians."

Jenny Morris' eyes grew large. "Did he *live* with the Indians?"

"That's what they said. He was living here in a cabin when old Grandpa Allard came out from Virginia. Made his living hunting."

Lucy had dropped down on the log and was gazing at the ground. "I remember," she cried suddenly. "Old Mr. Powhatan. He slept in the woods. And he was dirty and smelled like snuff. Once Grandma made me take him out a bucket of soup. I remember. He was sitting over there"—she gestured to the right—"in a little sort of cave. And I gave him the soup and he reached down and picked up something that was lying by his chair and gave it to me, for Grandma he said. It was a squirrel. And it had blood all down the front. And I didn't see it till I'd got out of the cave and started home. Ugh!" and she shivered, yet glanced around at the others with bright eyes, pleased to have recaptured so clearly an incident from the past.

"There was another one too," Ned said meditatively. "Old Cousin Aleck. Used to live in the office. I bet you don't remember him."

"I do too," Lucy cried. "He had a long white beard and he said, "Switches for boys and kisses for girls, and he used to swing me 'way up high."

"And he used to take you and Love for walks and always kept a switch to hit at me with if I tried to go along," Ned said. "Looks like there used to be funnier people then than there are now," he added reflectively. "That old nigger Uncle Ben, used to ride for Pa. Thought everybody was trying to poison him."

Lucy glanced at Rives and blushed. "He's seen him," she told Ned. "Last summer."

"Uncle Winston's going," Jenny Morris observed. "He's going off and leave y'all."

"Let him go 'long," Lucy said carelessly. "He can take a turn up and down the road and watch and then he won't be so nervous."

As she spoke she glanced up and saw the chimneys of the house, only partly obscured by the boughs of trees. She looked quickly away. The house, the trees, all the surroundings of Brackets were to her at this moment less real than the scenes she and Ned were calling up from their childhood. Indeed it seemed to her that she had been away from Brackets for a long time and that only here in the woods, which this morning seemed an enchanted place, was she recapturing the old feeling for home. So now, anxious to prolong the spell, she looked away from the tall chimneys and the black trees and leaning toward Ned and smiling, asked: "Do you remember, Mademoiselle?"

Ned burst out laughing and hummed a tune: *"'Sur le pont, d'*

Avignon.' She was always trying to make you dance to that and Old Cousin Lydia just for meanness would sing, *'Ca'line, Ca'line, can't you dance the pea-vine?'* "

Ned rose and began brushing the shavings of green wood from his trousers. "We better be going along," he said. "Ma'll be worrying about us."

"All right," Lucy said. She rose with the others and walked a little way, then paused involuntarily where a path edged with buckberry bushes diverged from the main road. "Let's don't go in yet," she said. "Let's go down this a little way."

Ned shook his head. "I'm going on. And you better come too."

Lucy did not answer. She had run on down the path and stopped now before a great tangle of vines which, using a sapling to climb by, had flung their tendrils to the topmost limbs of a poplar tree. Lucy standing under this natural canopy was exclaiming in delight over the red berries that clustered among the green leaves.

"I wish we could get some to put in the blue vases on the mantel," she cried.

"You'd have to be a monkey to reach them," Ned said, not advancing further on the path.

Lucy, her lip trembling as it often did when she was perplexed or hurt, measured the distance from the ground with her eye. "No, I suppose we can't," she said and was turning away when she saw that Rives was taking off his new jacket and laying it carefully on the ground.

He then advanced to the tree and wrapping his legs about the trunk began hoisting himself with the aid of his arms slowly along the trunk. Love, as if disdaining to have anything to do with the procedure, had gone on along the road and was now out of sight. Lucy stood still watching Rives. The girl's eyes sparkled as the sturdy, active young man drew himself skillfully up the tree. At the same time she cried out, as if in alarm. "Don't, please. You'll break your neck."

Rives turned his head a little so that he could look down on her. His swarthy face was illuminated by a smile. "Don't you know I've got squirrel blood in me?" he asked and proceeded to crawl along on the limb on which the vines were climbing.

The limb was fragile. Lucy cried out again in alarm when she saw it bend perilously under his weight. He managed, however, by swinging himself along it, to reach the place where the berries clustered. The bough cracked and splintered slowly. He hung on until he had torn off a great cluster of the vines and flung them at Lucy's feet. Then he dropped to the ground.

Lucy caught up the cluster and began to arrange it so that she could carry it more easily. Rives, breathing hard from his exertions, was putting on his jacket and buttoning it. He glanced over his shoulder as if to assure himself that the others were still out of sight, then came toward her. His face wore the same determined expression that it had had when he began to climb the tree. He took her hand and then as she made no resistance drew her swiftly to him.

They had kissed each other when he became aware that Lucy, her head pressed against his shoulder, was crying. He put his hand under her chin, slowly forced her face upward. Lucy met his eyes, her lips trembling. "Oh," she cried, "I never thought I'd be happy again."

15

TWO afternoons later Fontaine Allard was sitting on the front gallery, reading, when three squads of Yankee soldiers came into the yard. They rode up the avenue of cedars, then suddenly broke across the lawn and made for the house. Allard shut his book, a finger held in it to mark the place, and stood up.

The officer in charge, a heavy-set blond man of forty, had ridden his horse up to the very steps of the porch. "Is this place called Brackets?" he demanded.

Back in the hall there was the rustle of skirts, the sound of a quick, intaken breath. Allard knew that his wife had come up behind him. He knew, too, what was in her mind. The two boys and the two girls had been over in the woods all afternoon, might be coming back now at any minute. He looked down into the officer's face.

"It is, sir," he said formally. "Can I do anything for you?"

The blue eyes hardened. "We understand there's three barrels of shot concealed here." The officer hesitated, compressed his lips. "We'll have to search the place," he added bluntly.

There was the sound of quick steps down the stairs. Cally's voice rang out passionately. "I know who told you that. Those negroes of ours that ran away the other night." She pushed past her mother and confronted the officer angrily. "You Yankees believe everything niggers tell you, don't you?"

Fontaine Allard motioned her back peremptorily. His face was crimson but his voice was composed. "There is no shot concealed here. If it will reassure you I will give you my word to that effect."

The officer's voice was one of strained patience. "Mr. Allard, three of the Confederate generals who escaped from Fort Donelson were mounted on your horses. You have a son in the Rebel army. I understand that you have already furnished a considerable number of arms to the Confederacy." He looked past Allard at the women in the doorway. "The complaint comes from two colored men on Colonel Miles' place," he said wearily.

"*Colored* men!" Allard said. "Colored men on Colonel Miles' place!" His voice broke; he laughed harshly.

A rough good-humored Irishman pushed his horse forward out of the crowd of mounted men. "That shot ain't likely to be in the house, Major. More'n likely the out buildings. What say we start there?"

The Major hesitated, then nodded. "All right, Sabin. You take a squad and go around to the back. Lieutenant Lewis," he turned to a blond boy who could not have been more than eighteen, "you will take the rest of the men and begin the search of the house. Better start upstairs."

Fontaine Allard stood looking at the officer. The red had died out of his face, leaving it a deathly white on which the engorged, thick-spreading veins shone purple. His wife gave a cry of alarm and rushed to him. He looked at her and the expression of his face was such that she recoiled.

"Don't," she cried. "Oh, Mr. Allard, don't!"

He made a gesture as if to push her away, then turned through the hall into the parlor. He walked the length of the long room once, then sat down on a little sofa. He sat, leaning the upper part of his body back stiffly. His legs were stretched straight out in front of him, knees unbent. After a little his wife saw that he had picked up a book from the table and was turning its pages.

She stood in the doorway between the hall and the parlor. The Major was standing at the foot of the stairs, one arm slung about the newel post. The men, twelve or fifteen of them, were filing past him up the stairs. He called out sharply to one of them as he went by. "See that you don't do any damage up there," then turned to Mrs. Allard. "Would you like to go up and watch them, Lady?"

Without answering she started up the steps. Above her she could hear the soldiers tramping from room to room. A bed was being taken to pieces. She heard the slats thud on the floor, then the creak of a wardrobe door being flung back on its hinges. There was a shrill, protesting cry from Cally, a laugh from one of the soldiers. "Just carrying out my orders, ma'am. Got to make sure." More tramping steps, this time out to the upper gallery. The acrid smell of burning feathers rose on the air. Cally looked down wildly from the head of the steps. "They're throwing the feather beds over the gallery and burning them. Say the shot may be in them." She turned and flew back into the upper hall.

Mrs. Allard stood where she had stopped, with her hand on the stair rail. The woods across the road were framed in the open doorway. Something had moved there for a second, moved beside a tree, then vanished. A gray head or was it just the sun slanting on a moss tree? Winston! She remembered that she had not seen him since the soldiers came. She released a long breath, came back down the stairs.

The officer still stood with his hand on the newel post. He was looking straight in front of him but fixedly as if he viewed imaginary rather than actual scenes. She came around the corner of the stairs, took up her position midway between him and the parlor. His eyes came reluctantly away from the green vistas of the wood, met hers. She thought: "I have made him look at me, made him look away!" Her hand—the one farthest from him, clenched in the folds of her skirt. She felt her lips drawing back in a wide grin. "Where are you from, Major?"

"Illinois."

"You are a farmer?"

He smiled suddenly. His eyes were candid and blue, like a child's. "My father settled on three hundred acres of Cook County land. It's rich as cream. They call it Egypt around there."

She tried to keep the words back but they came: "Why didn't you stay—on your rich land?"

He said stiffly: "I don't hold with slavery."

In the hall above the soldiers were laughing noisily. One came to the head of the stairwell with an eiderdown quilt in his arms, then fell back before the officer's hard, upward stare.

She said, almost mildly: "I don't imagine they'll take anything but what they can stuff in their pockets . . . jewelry . . . money, though I don't believe there's any money up there. . . ."

A muscle flickered in his cheek but he made no reply.

There were rapid steps down the back stairs and then the hall was full of clamor. Cally had rushed in with Jenny Morris clinging to her skirts. "They've taken all the hay and put it in their wagons and they're driving the horses out. One of 'em went into Old Beck's stall." She wrung her hands fiercely. "I hope to God she kicks him to death."

Jenny Morris stared up at her mother. Cally returned the gaze. "God," she reiterated. "I said God. It's time to call on him."

"God!" Jenny Morris shrilled. "God, less all call on God," and she ran and hid her face in her grandmother's skirts.

The Major turned and called up the stair well. "Lewis, aren't you about through up there?" Then he walked out on to the porch.

Mrs. Allard watched the soldiers come down the stairs. Their spurs jingled on the polished boards. One as he came played a tune on the banisters with his sabre, the way a child might have done with a stick. When he came opposite her he gave her a bold stare, then grinned. They hesitated a moment in the hall, then made for the dining room, all except the one who had grinned. He pushed suddenly past her and went out the back way. It came to her that he had gone to receive the silver that the others would dump out of the window to him. The young lieutenant, frowning, was on the last step. She turned to him.

"Does it interest you to know that your men are in the dining room stealing my silver?" she asked, then went out on to the porch.

The yard was black with negroes. Her first thought was, "But we haven't that many," and then she recognized a face here and there. Half a dozen from Colonel Miles' place, one or two from Bro' John's, Old Unc' Cripple Dan from Sycamore. . . .

She walked to the gallery rail, looked over their heads. There was nobody in sight there on the edge of the woods. Nobody. . . . She turned her attention to the scene before her.

In the drive three or four wagons were loaded with corn and hay. Soldiers were coming around the corner of the house, leading or riding half a dozen horses. There were one or two she recognized: Fraxinella, the old blood mare, "Tom" a tricky three-year-old whom nobody had ever been able to break, some young mules. . . .

The sergeant who was herding the horses and mules had come up to the edge of the porch. He was perspiring, breathing hard. "Major, they ain't much here that's worth taking." He shook his head. "And they told me this old feller had the best horses of anybody around here."

The Major had taken a note book out of his pocket. Using the railing as a rest he was writing something on pale, ruled, blue paper. He looked at the horses, "Six?" he asked. "Right, Tom?" He rapidly noted down a number, then handed the paper to her.

She would not take it. She had put her hands behind her. Her eyes were glittering. "Maybe he's given them all away," she said, "to the Confederate generals."

Cally came out of the front door. She had a hickory split basket in her arms piled high with objects. The major was not looking at her. He was staring at the roof. "Is that smoke?" he said.

Mrs. Allard watched the thin plume curl along the ceiling, like a feather on a lady's hat. "The gallery," she said dully, "they set it on fire when they burned those feather beds."

He was gone into the house, shouting. She ran after him. In the front parlor Fontaine Allard still sat stiffly on the sofa. She ran up to him, shook his arm. "Fount, come. I think the house is on fire." He rose. In the instant's glimpse she had of his face she thought that his eyes looked fixed, but he walked obediently into the hall. She looked about her wildly, took up a book from a table, snatched a picture from the wall, then she saw him standing uncertainly in the hall. She went to him, caught his arm and pressed with him through the throng of negroes and soldiers out into the yard.

The Major came out of the house. His hat was off and his face was smudged with smoke. "They've gone around to the back," he said, "and started a chain of buckets. I think they've got it under control, on the gallery, but it's got into that big room. . . ." He broke off to shout directions to a man who came up with a ladder. "We must start getting things out. From the lower floor, that is. No use fooling with upstairs." He gestured at the negroes moiling over the lawn. "These blacks here. Have you any you can trust?"

She shook her head, unable to speak because of the tears that had come into her eyes. "Not now," she whispered.

He bent toward her—she was ever afterward to remember him as one she had known long and intimately. He said, "Scum . . . of the cities. I can't control them. Nobody can. Colonel Bruce said. . . ." He broke off, dashed in among the milling men. "Here, you, Crooks, Slayden, take these men. Get everything you can out of the house."

They started up the steps, soldiers and negroes in an indiscriminate mass. Articles of furniture began to appear. A sofa heaved through the tall parlor windows. Grandfather Crenfew's picture. From the dining room, silver tankards, platters—they hadn't stolen them after all—china tied up in a table cloth and dumped crashing on the ground.

The flames had soared up from the back now and were creeping over the front of the house. The heat had grown intense. It was necessary to start dragging some of the things already brought out farther back into the yard. Jenny Morris ran shrieking beside each piece of furniture as it was moved. A little colored boy from the quarters had appeared and ran beside her. They seemed to play a game, touching each article and claiming it for their own as it was brought out.

Mrs. Allard realized that her husband had moved a little way off. She went and stood beside him. Cally had stopped trying to save anything and stood with them. A little while ago she had been wringing her hands but she stood quiet now, occasionally calling out the name of some article as the men brought it out.

They had stopped bringing things out and all stood watching the burning house. The smoke rolled low so that sometimes they saw nothing, and then licked by the wind a great flame would rise and tower. Mrs. Allard saw one, a fiery mass that seemed to have fingers to tear the house apart. She watched the dividing walls melt away and suddenly saw revealed in the burning mass a rectangle of glowing logs, a cabin, it seemed, burning inside the house. She touched Cally's arm. "The old house," she said quietly, "the original old log house. See it burn."

Cally did not answer. She was looking at her father. One of the men had taken hold of a marble-topped table and was dragging it farther away from the heat. Fontaine Allard saw him and went forward. He had picked up one end of the table when he turned a bewildered face, said something indistinct that sounded like "My child," then fell face downward. His wife heard his head strike the marble slab and ran toward him.

16

THE house was in ashes when Love and Lucy, accompanied by Uncle Winston, stole back by a circuitous way. They had crossed over into the woods at four o'clock that afternoon, had spent an hour wandering about and were on the edge of the woods, about to cross the road when they heard the sound of hoofs. The two soldiers at once retreated farther into the woods. The girls were afraid of drawing attention to the soldiers if they tried to cross the road, so they lay hidden for a long time in a buckberry thicket a hundred yards from the road. Uncle Winston, walking cautiously up and down, found them there and told them that Yankee soldiers had come and were searching the house. The two girls looked at him, trembling.

"Are they looking for Ned and Rives?" Love asked.

He shook his head. "They ain't studying 'bout nothing but plunderin' as yit, but they might be coming 'cross the road any minute." He sat down on a stump and reflected. "I'm going to slip back 'cross the road," he said finally. "I'm goin' to work in 'mongst them soldiers and find out if they's any danger of 'em crossing the road. And if they is," he glared at the girls from under drawn, bushy brows, "if they is, I'm going to raise my voice like we does in meetin'. I'm going to sing out 'Oh, my Lord. Oh, my sweet Saviour!' If you gals hears that you git back in the woods as fast as you can and tell them sojers to make tracks away from here."

The two girls stared at him. "You reckon they'll come get 'em?" Love whispered.

"Not if you does like I say," Uncle Winston returned shortly. He got up and began working his circuitous way through the bushes. The girls lay hidden in the thicket for a while, then tiring of the confinement got up and paced about in the little glade, listening for sounds from the house. They could hear all the time a confused shouting. Occasionally a single voice would rise above the din. Once Love clutched Lucy's arm. "That's Aunt Cally," she cried excitedly. "I know her voice. Do you suppose they're doing anything to her?"

Lucy was frowning. "It's not Aunt Cally," she said. "It's some negro. And we're going to stay here just like Uncle Winston said."

Love stole back some distance into the woods and signalled to the two boys who were waiting at the tree they had appointed as a meeting place. But Lucy would not move from the thicket.

At six o'clock the din across the road rose to a babel of sounds. A little later they saw the smoke curling high over the trees and then the great tower of flames. Love had come back up the path. She and Lucy stood there and watched the flames mount higher until finally the whole eastern sky was red.

It seemed a long time before Uncle Winston came stumbling back through the bushes. Love ran to meet him. "Uncle Winston, is the house burned down? Is anybody hurt? Are the soldiers gone?"

"Hit's *ashes,*" he said. He reeled as if he were drunk, then collected himself. "Come on, you gals. I got to git back and help my mistress."

The soldiers were gone when they reached the house. The blaze had died down but embers smouldered and now and then the wind would fan them into brief flames. There was a heavy smell of smoke on the air and contending with it and biting into the nostrils was the reek of whiskey and wine. As Winston and the two girls came up they saw two negroes making off across the lawn kicking a wine cask ahead of them.

Two or three Federal soldiers stood on guard over the ruined house and two paced up and down in the little alley of crape myrtle that separated the "office" from the main lawn. The family during the last hour had established themselves in this three-room building. Mr. Allard had been carried in on a mattress and lay breathing heavily, still unconscious. Mrs. Allard sat at the head of the bed fanning him and applying cloths that had been steeped in vinegar to his forehead. Jenny Morris had at last gone to sleep. She was afraid to stay by herself so they made her a pallet at the foot of Mr. Allard's bed. She lay there, her stout little legs and arms sprawled wide. Occasionally she muttered in her sleep. Cally stopping once to lay a hand on her forehead found it burning hot.

Nobody had thought to save candles from the burning house. They were in the dark until Winston brought a lamp from one of the cabins. They kept it burning all night in the room adjoining Mr. Allard's. The two girls lay in there side by side on the same bed. Cally came in occasionally and lay down on the other bed but for most of the night she sat up, assisting her mother or changing the cold cloths on Jenny Morris' forehead. The two girls, lying wakeful on the bed, heard the soldiers pacing up and down, the occasional sleepy murmur of their talk. For a while there had been the sound of shouting and singing in the quarters but the guard had quieted the negroes down.

About eleven o'clock Uncle Winston came back. They knew that he must have been across the road again, perhaps to take what food he could find to the boys. But they did not dare question him even in whispers. Silently they watched him settle down in the doorway of his mistress' room. He had found an axe somewhere and he held it cradled in his arms, even after his head drooped forward in sleep. The light was finally put out and silence settled on the little house. The smell of vinegar was acrid in the rooms. After a little it was mingled with a heavier smell, the body odor of the negro mixed with sweat.

Mrs. Allard sitting motionless at the foot of the bed, absorbed in her thoughts, had not realized that Winston was there until that moment. She raised her head quickly in the dark. Hei nostrils widened. She thought that if she lived through all this, lived to be an old woman, they could never be assailed by a more grateful odor.

17

EDMUND ROWAN arrived early the next morning. He had seen the blaze rising high over the woods last night, he said, had watched it from his porch. But he had no idea it was the Brackets house burning until a wandering negro brought the news to old Uncle Simms, his body servant. He came over at once, with Uncle Simms and two young negroes who he said he could trust. After conferring with Mrs. Allard he approached the Federal sergeant and asked him to take the soldiers away. The sergeant hesitated but his orders had not been definite. He was to stay at the place only as long as there seemed to be any danger from the negroes. The sergeant was from Maryland. He knew, he flattered himself, a thing or two that his major would go to the grave without learning. He looked shrewdly at Rowan:

"Them niggers made off with a lot of liquor last night. I ain't sure they've drunk it all up."

Edmund Rowan looked hard into the man's eyes then let his hand stray for a second toward his hip. "I'm an old widower," he said good-humoredly. "Nothing to keep me at home. I can stay here and take care of this place long as they need me."

The sergeant nodded, called his men and a few minutes later they rode out of the yard. Cally, standing beside the still smoking ruins of the house, watched them go. She had been up since before daylight, trying frenziedly to bring things into some sort of order. The summer kitchen had escaped the flames. Aunt Mimy was to cook there. The small back room of the office was to be the dining room. A deal table and some kitchen chairs had already been installed theme. Cally was not satisfied with putting the small office domain in order. She put on her bonnet and went up to the ruins to see if there were anything she could salvage. Some negroes were wandering about there. They poked the smoking ashes with sticks, laughed childishly when a flame would break out. Sometimes one would pounce on an object, rub the ashes off of it and put it in his pocket. Cally watched them, a bitter look on her face. Finally she called sharply: "Here, Reuben. You, Ed, I want you to help me take these things down to the office," and she pointed to a trunk that had been thrown over the end of the gallery.

Two of them came, running clumsily. The third, Ed, a field hand, sat down suddenly and gave her a wide drunken smile. "Yes, ma'am, Miss Cally, I be there in a minute."

The fumes of whiskey on the other two made her wrinkle her nose but she marched beside them as with many halts they carried the trunk to the office. "Set it down here," she said sternly, "and begone with you." She gave her hands a smart slap together in dismissal. That, she told herself, was the way to treat them, the customary manner, only perhaps a little sharper. . . . She crossed the floor, sat down in a kitchen chair and found that her heart was beating like a trip-hammer.

Lucy was in the room, moving around uncertainly in the small floor space. In the next room Mr. Allard still lay, not unconscious now, but wandering in his mind. The doctor had said that he might be like that for weeks, or he might have another stroke any day. Cally got up, quietly closed the door between the two rooms and came back to her seat.

Lucy paused before the one dresser that had been saved. She looked at the two beds, the small cot, and shook her head. "Love and I over there and you and Jenny Morris in the big bed. . . . I've figured out a place for everybody to sleep but Cousin Edmund. Where *can* he sleep, Aunt Cally?"

Cally shook her head. The girl, not looking at her, talked on. "We'll have to build an addition, I suppose." The prospect of any activity fired her. She looked up eagerly. "We could do that, couldn't we? An ell, here in the back."

Cally stared at her. As she passed the open doorway of the

other room she had heard her father's stertorous breathing, caught a glimpse of her mother's despairing face. She felt that she hated Lucy for her youth, her eagerness.

"How would you go about building an addition to this house?" she asked in a dry, hard voice.

Lucy returned her gaze wonderingly. "With logs. You could get logs out of the woods."

Cally stood up. "Yes," she said and her voice that had been icy was shaking. "And it takes axes to fell trees. You saw those drunken negroes stumbling around on the lawn. You'd like to arm them all with axes, I suppose, so they could come here and kill us in the night."

Her voice broke. She sank back in her chair, her cupped hands before her face. Lucy came swiftly and knelt beside her. "Aunt Cally, darling. Please. I'll do everything you say just the way you want it done. . . . Please. . . ."

Cally still held her hands in front of her face. Tears trickled down between her fingers. "You don't know how to do anything and neither does Love. There's nobody. Nobody but me!"

When she let her hands fall a few seconds later and rose to bathe her swollen face, she was alone in the room.

At supper that night Lucy too was red-eyed and constrained in manner. After supper she took her aunt aside and told her that she and Rives had decided to be married. They were going to ride tonight to Hopkinsville—by the back road—and would be married in old Dr. Andrews' study and set out the next morning for Rives' home in northern Georgia.

Cally flung her arms about the girl's neck and they cried together. Then Lucy went into the bedroom and gathered up the few garments she could muster for the journey.

18

IT was late in the afternoon. Lucy and Rives, now married more than a week, were riding along a sandy road in northern Georgia. Rives suddenly put his tired horse to the gallop. Surmounting a little rise he stood in his stirrups, pointing. "There it is. You can see the house from here."

Lucy looked but could see no break in the pine woods that stretched, seemingly interminable, on either side of the sandy track. He pushed his horse close to hers and slipping his arm around her made her look in the direction in which he pointed. "See? That black something there over the tallest pine. That's the house."

Lucy could not see what he was pointing at. "The pines are so dark," she said. "It makes the woods all look alike, Rives."

"You'll get used to that," he said. "It always seems that way to me too after I've been away for awhile."

They turned off the highway into another sandy winding road. Rives, riding a little ahead of Lucy, called out as he recognized landmarks. "Lucy, the mill where we have our corn ground is right down that road. And there's Fowler's. Two of the Fowler boys were at Fort Donelson."

He talked on, forgetting fatigue in the excitement of getting home. Lucy rode beside him, turning her head obediently each time he spoke, but in reality staring blindly before her. The house which he had pointed out was a black oblong with one murky light showing, the road to the old mill only a faint track in the gathering gloom. It did not seem possible that people could live in the depths of these pine woods and she had for a moment the fantastic notion that Rives might have taken the wrong road and that in a little while they would have to turn back to the main highway.

But he had ridden on ahead and was letting down some pasture bars. "It's not a quarter of a mile now," he said. "You can see the light from the house."

Lucy saw before her a broad slope of cleared land dotted with the stumps of pine trees. At the farther end of this clearing a paling fence glimmered white and she could make out the outline of a house crowning the hill.

The horses, scenting rest and food, increased their pace. The travellers took the slope at a gallop, stopped where a huge crape myrtle bush dropped its branches over the fence. Rives swept his hat off and sent forth a loud halloo then helped her to dismount. The baying of hounds had announced their approach. The door of the house opened. Steps clattered on the brick walk. A fourteen-year-old boy burst through the gate followed by half a dozen hounds. Rives motioned the dogs down with one hand while he embraced the boy, at the same time calling loudly to the dogs. "Down, Rattler, Muse. . . . You scoundrel beasts." He turned to Lucy. "They remember me, all right. . . . Miles, here's your new sister."

The boy put out a shy hand, mumbled. "I'll take the horses, Rives," he said and slinging the horses' bridles over his arm went through the side gate to the stable lot.

Rives caught Lucy's arm. "Come on. Let's get to the fire." They went up the brick walk which was arched over in several places with boughs of crape myrtle and lilac, the yellow light still streaming before them. Lucy had thought that they were approaching a doorway but as they stepped up on the porch she saw to her surprise that the wide hall before them was unroofed and without a door at either end. The light which had guided them came from a door in one of its side walls. In the open doorway a woman stood. Her head and shoulders were muffled in a shawl. She stood peering out near-sightedly, one thin, veined hand holding the shawl close about her throat. "Rives!" she cried, not seeming to see him until he was almost upon her.

Rives caught her to him so roughly that she was suspended for a moment in the embrace. She looked down at Lucy shyly over his shoulder. He set her on her feet. She sprang to the door and shut it hastily. "We don't leave the front door open now after dark," she said. She turned to Lucy, "I'm Sister Mitty."

As she crossed the floor Lucy saw that she was not a middle-aged woman as she had at first supposed, but young and slender with light hair strained back from a high forehead and large, clear gray eyes. Little wrinkles radiated from the corners of these eyes when she narrowed them near-sightedly to look closelv at anything.

"Come up closer. You must be frozen," she said and laying a timid hand on Lucy's shoulder moved her nearer to the fire. Lucy, standing in front of a blazing fire of logs, allowed her sodden travelling cloak to fall from her shoulders, drew off her gloves, and slowly raising her hands, unpinned her small hat with the curling ostrich plume. Weary as she was—so weary that it seemed to her she could have dropped down on the hearth to sleep—her eyes yet mechanically took in some of the details of the room. A huge four-poster bed in one corner, the trundle bed under it, and a tall secretary were the only furnishings except for the circle of chairs about the hearth. Lucy noted with most surprise the absence of a carpet from the wide oak planks. It was the first time she had ever seen a chamber in gentle people's houses uncarpeted, unless, she thought with a flicker of amusement, in Music Hall.

Mitty had picked Lucy's hat up and was running her hand over the length of the curling plume. "I expect you brought lots of pretty clothes," she said with her shy smile.

Lucy, remembering the ruin of her wardrobe and all her other possessions, would have spoken but Rives laid his hand suddenly on her shoulder. "We've ridden all day, Sister," he said. "Lucy's tired. You'd better let her go up to her room. Which is it?"

"The boy's room. Your old room," Mitty said eagerly and taking up the lamp led them from the warmth of the big chamber out on to a dark gallery. Before them a flight of stairs led to another storey. At the head of this stairway Mitty paused and flung open a door. "Here we are," she said, and stooping to pass through the low doorway, preceded the others into the bedroom. Mitty set the lamp on a small center table and went over to make the fire up still higher. Rives took the poker from her and shifted the back log to his own liking. Lucy, remembering that this was the room in which Rives had spent a great part of his boyhood, stood looking about her.

The room she thought, was more like a dormitory for boys than a lady's bedroom. Two big four-posters occupied the west and east corners, a trundle bed visible under each one. The few chairs in the room were scarred as if by generations of heels, and the screen that stood in front of the washstand was so worn that only a few of its original bright colors showed. Some effort, however, had been expended to make the room as attractive as possible. A rag rug woven in soft blues and reds covered a greater part of the floor and antimacassars had been fastened on the backs of the chairs. Approaching the center table Lucy saw a small flowering plant in a little pot and thought that that, as well as the other knick-knacks, must have been brought there by Mitty. "She's doing everything she can to make me feel at home," she told herself.

Rives was holding the lamp so that Mitty could see her way down the stairs. When her heels sounded on the bare floor of the gallery below he shut the door and coming swiftly across the room set the lamp down on the table. He put both his hands on Lucy's shoulders and stood looking down into her eyes. She returned his gaze for a moment, then suddenly locked her arms about his neck, pressing her face against his breast. The rough wool of his shirt rasped her face. She could smell the tobacco which he kept loose in the pocket of his shirt. She pressed her face closer, her eyes tightly closed as if to shut out the room.

After a little she stirred, drew away. "Are you happy?" he asked.

"Yes," she whispered passionately, and clasped her arms about his neck. They stood like this for some seconds when there was the sound of a door opening below stairs, and Miles' voice called: "Rives, how many ears of corn must I give these horses?"

Rives frowned. "That boy is as likely as not to water those horses while they're hot." He left the room, ran down the stairway.

She stood gazing out of the window for a few minutes, then set about unpacking her few belongings. She had hung her gowns up in the closet and was unfastening her riding habit when the door opened softly and an old negro woman came into the room. She advanced a few paces and stood with her broad, good-humored face bent thoughtfully upon the girl. "Which one is you?" she demanded after a moment.

Lucy had recoiled at the woman's entrance, but she realized now that the intruder must be a privileged person. Accustomed all her life to demonstrations of affection from the family ser vants, she smiled good-humoredly. "Miss Honoria's daughter. You know—the one that died."

The woman still stood with her head to one side, a contemplative expression on her face. "Miss Honoria," she said, "and Miss Ca'line. And that Jim. I know'd 'em. I knowed 'em all. And when they told me Marse Rives done gone up in the old neighborhood and got him a wife I says to myself, Rivanna, you just step upstairs and see what she look like."

Lucy had gone over to the washstand and was laving her face and hands. She turned with an expression of childlike interest. "And who do I look like?"

The woman laughed. "You don't favor these folks down here. You favor them other Allards."

"Did you used to live in the neighborhood?"

Rivanna moved her head slowly from side to side. "I lived thar till they sont me away. They sont me down here to look after Miss Sue. They knowed she didn't have sense enough to do it herself." She sighed. "But it come hard, child. I don't like these piny woods." She came over and with swift fingers buttoned

Lucy's gown. "Hurry up, chile, Miss Sue done come and supper ready to go on the table."

Lucy twisted around to look into the woman's face. "Where's Miss Sue been?"

A malicious flicker came into the old negress' eyes. "Sashaying around," she said. "Miss Sue just like a free nigger. Don't know when it's time to come home."

Lucy was curious about her mother-in-law. "What does she do when she's sashaying around?" she asked.

The woman gave a light groan. "She like de prophet, Job," she said. "She goes up and down the yearth. Half the time she don't know whar she gwine. She just gits on her horse and waits till the spirit move her. She sits thar till the spirit moves her and then she say, 'Rivanna, them Thompsons down the road got a poor little baby what's bowels is runnin' off,' and off she goes. Half the time the pot would bile over at home if 'twarn't for Miss Mitty and me."

Lucy turned from smoothing her hair at the cracked mirror of the old walnut dresser. "You look like you were smart," she said simply.

The woman laughed, a high, delighted chuckle. Her knotted fingers rested a moment on the girl's shoulder. "Go on, chile," she said, "go on, git down them stairs. Supper ready to go on the table."

The family were still gathered in front of the fire in the big chamber when Lucy went downstairs. Mitty had drawn her chair up to the table and was sewing. In the chimney nook Rives and Miles sat side by side on a bench, talking. At the other end of the hearth a small, gray-haired woman sat erect in a big chair, staring into the flames.

Lucy realized that this must be her mother-in-law and was advancing to meet her when the woman, hearing the noise of the opening door, turned suddenly. Lucy found herself looking into a pair of very large gray eyes. The gray-haired woman was on her feet and coming toward Lucy. She kissed the girl on the mouth with lips that seemed dry and cold, then held her off for a moment examining her features. "You have Honoria's chin and eyes," she said abruptly, "but I suppose that's your father's mouth."

Lucy had endured such scrutinies at the hands of relatives many times and was quite used to having her features attributed to this or that ancestor, but there was something in Mrs. Allard's gaze that disquieted her. She was relieved when Mitty announced that supper was on the table.

The dining room was an ell, built of logs, daubed and chinked with white clay. Rough wooden benches ran alongside the table and at either end stood a great chair of carved rosewood. Mrs. Allard sat in one of these and Rives, after a glance at his mother, took the other. Mitty sat on her mother's right. Occasionally she cut up some morsel from her own plate and reaching over placed it on her mother's. Mrs. Allard would obediently take the morsel up on her fork. When she had eaten it she would relapse again into a reverie. The old negro woman, Rivanna, stood behind Mrs. Allard's chair, her huge silver salver clasped before her like a buckler. In the intervals of serving she nodded and once went fast asleep, letting the tray fall to the floor with a great clatter.

The supper, to Lucy, accustomed to the lavishness of Brackets, seemed frugal. But the dishes, though few, were well cooked. Lucy thought that that must be attributed to Mitty who evidently did most of the housekeeping. She sat now almost forgetting to eat in her anxiety to see that everybody was well served. When a floating island pudding was brought in in a great blue bowl, Miles cried out, "Rives, I wish you'd get married every day."

Rives finished his portion and held out his saucer for another helping. Miles did likewise. The old negress served Rives without hesitation but delayed over bringing Miles' saucer back.

Susan Allard, seeing her whisper in Mitty's ear gave a start. "I'm sorry, daughter. I'm afraid there's no more pudding."

Mitty looked at her despairingly. Susan's pale cheeks flushed. "I was in the milk room getting some milk for old Mr. Bascomb and I saw that big bowl of pudding. I thought it was so much more than we could eat." She looked at Lucy apologetically. "He's such a thin old man, nearly ninety years old and with a delicate digestion."

Rives broke out in a laugh. "Now I feel like I'm home again. Ma, where's the old bell?" He turned to Lucy. "When we were little there were eleven of us to sit down to the table, seven of us and four orphans Ma'd taken to raise. There were eight boys in all and you know it's hard to get enough food on one table for eight boys. The old cook used to cry sometimes. 'Miss Sue, make them boys leave something for us poor niggers.' Finally Ma hit on the idea of ringing a bell toward the end of the meal. You could eat right up to the time the bell rang but you couldn't take a mouthful after that. We used to call that old bell 'Poor Niggers.' "

Mrs. Allard was rising from the table. The others followed her into the chamber. The fire had died down and the room seemed dark. Rives brought in fresh logs and made the fire up, then sitting down on the bench in the chimney nook beckoned to Lucy to come beside him. An old hound took advantage of the open door to slip in and establish himself on the hearth rug. The boy, Miles, lay down beside him. Mrs. Allard was in her customary great chair at the other end of the hearth, Mitty in her low rocker by the table, sewing. She kept the conversation going, recalling incidents of childhood days. Lucy raised her head to look about the room. It had struck her as harsh and bare when she first entered it, but now, illuminated by the leaping flames, it seemed cheerful and homelike. They were talking of the absent members of the family: Tom, now a second lieutenant with the Third Georgia, Valentine the absent-minded one, Nicholas who they all said was most like Rives, the three foster brothers, Robert, Nathan, and Samuel, red-headed and freckled, the two married sisters who lived in Louisiana. Lucy pictured them all as grouped around this fire. Once she stole a glance at her mother-in-law sitting bent a little forward in her great chair. A few minutes ago Mrs. Allard had been leaning forward to listen to the talk, a smile on her lips, but now she sat, her hands linked in her lap, staring into the flames. Aware of Lucy's glance, she looked up. Lucy saw the gray eyes which seemed too large for the small, pale face. It occurred to her suddenly that Rives had his mother's eyes.

19

TOWARD dawn Lucy awoke but Rives' arms were no longer about her. She sat up, then fell back when she saw the wall over her head. The ceiling sloped menacingly low on two sides of the room. In her dreams a huge box—a coffin—had hovered over her, had been at times ready to descend, And then this dream would merge into an image of the wall of the Brackets house flaming higher and higher, and falling with a crash into the blackened wistaria vine.

She drew the covers tight under her chin. She looked out into the room. She had been wakened, she realized now, by Rives' getting out of bed. He was kneeling on the hearth, raking last night's embers together. As she watched he threw a handful of chips on the embers, then getting a log from the wood-box laid it on the smoking chips. He stood with his legs spread apart, looking meditatively down, until the logs caught fire from the flaming chips. His hairy, muscular leg showed through the V-shaped slit at the side of his long night shirt.

She lay silent, staring before her with bright eyes. This man who a few weeks ago had been only one of her numerous family connection, less known to her, really, than George Rowan, Edward Sumner, any of the boys she had grown up with, was now closer to her than anybody in the world, shared the same room, the same bed. It was incomprehensible how this had happened, and then she remembered the evening when she had run over into the woods, stumbling ahead of Uncle Winston who was bringing the soldiers' supper. Rives had been sitting there by the spring, had not seen her till she was almost upon him. She was crying out, really, the things she had wanted to say to her aunt

Cally. "They don't want me . . . I haven't anywhere to go . . . They don't want me. . . ." He said, "I want you, more than anything in the world." He said that, even before he put his arms about her. Ned, seeing how it was, had walked off toward the edge of the woods. They had sat there together till Uncle Winston came back grumbling. Rives stood up then and said they would ride to Hopkinsville that night and be married. . . .

He was at the side of the bed, slipping in under the covers. She slid forward into his embrace. His arms moved down her body. He was spanning her waist with rough, tender hands. She moved closer to him. "I love you," she murmured.

The fire burned brighter. One of the logs that Rives had just laid on was green. From one end of it little drops of moisture formed and fell hissing into the ashes.

Rives stirred, ran his hand over her hair. "I have to go away today," he said in a low voice.

"When?" she asked.

"This afternoon."

She was silent. Downstairs a bell pealed, faint at first then growing louder as the little negro boy who was ringing it walked from the out-kitchen toward the house. Rives raised up in bed. "Let's get up. There are a lot of things to do today."

She rose, bathed her face and hands in cold water, dressed hurriedly, and went downstairs. Miles and Mitty had already breakfasted. Mrs. Allard sat alone in the dining room. She lingered a few minutes after their arrival to tell of the plans for the day. There was to be a dining. The ladies of the party would arrive early in the morning and spend the day at the loom. The ladies met three times a week now at different houses and spun and wove cloth for uniforms. The meeting was to have been at Mrs. Pilcher's but Mrs. Allard had not wanted to be away while Rives was here so she had dispatched a negro boy on a horse to notify members of the ladies' association of the change in plans.

She gathered up her keys and left the room. Aunt Rivanna came in with her heavy tread to bring hot batter cakes or refill the syrup pitcher. Rives was putting his napkin down, "Run get your cloak," he said.

Lucy found her travelling cloak, brushed free of mud, neatly folded and hanging on the back of a chair. She put it on and fastening a woollen fascinator over her head followed him outdoors.

They went through the back lot and took a path that wound up over a slope toward some woods. The field they traversed was rank with coarse grass. Last year's cotton stalks were still standing in the rows. Lucy stooped and broke off a dead stalk. "I never saw cotton growing before," she said.

Rives did not answer. She put her hand on his arm and because she wanted to hear his voice repeated the remark. He looked down at the stalk she was still holding in her hand. "This is my land," he said.

She was looking at him, not understanding. He raised a finger and slowly sketched in the air a rough rectangle. "This is my field and the one next to it. Half of those woods are mine and half Tom's. Nick's begins on the other side of the woods."

"You mean your mother has already given you all your land?"

"When Tom was twenty-one. She parcelled it all out between us." He guided her to the right. "See that grove over there? I've always thought it was a nice place for a house. Nice spring at the foot of the hill."

They approached a little hill that had on it a grove of trees. There were oaks and silver poplars and down the farther slope a line of weeping willows marked the spring. They went down to the spring and got a drink. They stayed there a long while then they came up the slope again. Far off on the horizon the mountains rose cloud-like and blue. At their feet lay the green valley. There was the field through which they had ridden last night and beyond that the pine forest. It had seemed interminable then but now it was only a darker band encircling the brighter green of the fields.

Rives walked off a little way and paused beside a great twisted poplar. "We could have the house here," he said. He stepped off the paces in a great rectangle then walked into the center of it, laid his hand on a tall oak. "This fellow would have to go," he said, "and those three young maples but you wouldn't have to cut down any more of the big trees."

Lucy was still following with her eyes the rectangle he had paced off. She went now and stood a little distance from the oak tree. "The front gallery would be here," she said. She shut her eyes. It seemed to her that she was standing on the gallery. She opened her eyes upon the white trunk of a young poplar. "We could leave that one standing," she said. "We wouldn't need to cut that one down, Rives."

He came and stood beside her, measuring the distance with his eye. "It would be right near the gallery. Trees rot a house."

"You could see it from the front windows," she said. "It would be nice in spring."

He did not answer. He was listening for something. After a second the call came again. They could see a woman's figure framed in the doorway of the house below. She was making a trumpet of her hands to call "Rives! Rives!"

"We'll have to go," Rives said.

They went back down the hill. Once Lucy looked back. She could almost see the house standing there.

Part Three

1

RIVES had expected to rejoin Colonel Forrest's command at Huntsville where he had been furloughed but on his way up from Dalton he heard that the colonel had been incapacitated by a wound in the thigh and his command disbanded. Rives therefore went straight to Chattanooga. There he met Colonel Lawton, a friend of the family, who arranged to have him enrolled in his regiment, the Second Georgia. In the office where the men were mustered in, he met a man whom he had known at Donelson, Joe Troup. The two soldiers, after their papers were made out, set off on a stroll about the town.

They walked along Market Street but progress was difficult. The street was crowded with citizens who had gathered to watch the parade of some incoming regiments. Brass bands blared. The military police kept soldiers and citizens alike moving on constantly. Joe was disgusted. "Come in," he said, "less get out of here."

The place to which he led Rives—"Hell's Half Acre" it was called by the citizens of the town—was the favorite rendezvous of soldiers off duty. It was crowded tonight. Lanterns swung from the boughs of trees and pine knot torches flared. The crowd, which included women in frayed finery, oscillated between the sutlers' wagons drawn up in rows on the edge of the field and the roulette wheels and faro and chuckaluck spreads.

Rives and Joe, too restless to settle down to any particular pleasure, passed by a roulette wheel operating under the light of a pine knot torch. A crowd surrounded it, those on the outside reaching over the shoulders of those nearest the wheel to lay their bundles of Confederate currency on their favorite color. A little way off a ragged, Ishmaelitish-looking man was preaching.

Rives and Joe passed on to where a group of men were gathered under an oak tree. There was a tall man in the center whom Rives recognized as one of the men who had come out from Fort Donelson with Forrest. Rives knew this man by reputation as an experienced scout. He was a man who knew his own value but tonight his bearing was more assured than usual, perhaps because he was telling the assembled men something that seemed to interest them greatly.

"Yes, sir," he said, "it was the middle of the night when the message come but it was all over camp before morning. There was a hot time around there for awhile, I tell you."

Rives pressed nearer. "What's he talking about?" he asked of the man next him.

The man clicked shut the blade of an enormous knife. "He's talking about General Forrest," he said, "when he come up from Corinth."

"What?" Rives said. "Have they made him a general?"

The man nodded. "They done put him in command of all the cavalry round here. But they wouldn't let him take his old regiment with him, just let him pick out ten men for his escort. Tom Miles there, he was one of 'em. He's my brother."

Something in the man's face made Rives ask, "Were you one of 'em too?"

The man's face had been alert and shining as he talked. It composed itself now into more decorous lines. He spat onto the root of a tree. "Yep," he said. "Me and my brother, Tom, we was in the old Forrest regiment. But we're in the escort now."

The narrator had come to the end of his tale. There was a great burst of laughter. The man who had been talking to Rives got up and edged into the circle. "Come on, Tom," he said, "less go spin that wheel."

The tall man said he didn't care if he did. The two brothers walked off together across the hard, trampled ground. The crowd had been held together by the story. It broke into smaller circles, merged into other crowds. Joe Troup had been watching a group of men who sat around a stump playing poker. He said he believed he would sit in the game awhile. Rives went over with him, bought some chips and sat in a few hands then rose saying a man had just gone by whom he had to see.

He walked away from the poker table but soon began to drift aimlessly with the crowd. No game of chance just then could be as exciting as just walking around, seeing old and new faces and drawing into his nostrils the well-remembered odors of camp life. He found himself speaking amiably to a gambler whom he had once rejoiced to see run out of his regiment, then got away from the man to find a woman's hand clutching his arm, a doll-like face turned up to his. He disengaged his arm and, smiling and shaking his head, walked over to where a great tree root arched up, and sat down. He had been sitting there for a long while watching the crowd when a man came up and touched him on the shoulder.

"Allard," he said, "I been looking for you everywhere. Ben Bigstaff wants to see you."

"Where is he?" Rives asked.

"He's been in the guard house. But they took him out. Got him over at headquarters now." The newcomer grinned. "You better start. They might court-martial old Ben before you git there."

"All right," Rives said.

Rives' guide conducted him to within a few yards of the head-quarters' tent and left him. Rives had started on alone when a voice hailed him:

"Well, boy, where you been?"

Rives stopped, grinning: "Where *you* been?"

Ben Bigstaff looked up at his tall guard, shrugged his fat shoulders. "Boarding," he said.

The guard clapped him on the back. "Well, Ben, here's where I leave you. Don't do nothing rash."

When the soldier had walked away Ben turned to Rives. "It was old Jackson's brandy," he whispered. "Coming up from Corinth. I found out which wagon it was in and I just couldn't stay out of it. Got me an auger and bored through. Put a pipe to it." He rolled his eyes and smacked his lips. "Boy, it warn't none of this pine top!"

They had been walking rapidly while this conversation was going on and were now at the entrance to the General's tent. A burly, fair-haired officer whom Rives recognized as Captain Anderson was sitting at a table just inside the tent, writing. He looked up and acknowledged the two soldiers' salute.

"Well, Ben," he said mildly, "hear you been in a little trouble."

Bigstaff stood stiffly as if on parade. "Yes, Captain," he said. At the same time he let the lid of his left eye droop toward Rives as if to say that a man might find himself in stranger places than the guard house before he was through.

Rives, trying to stand at attention as rigidly as Bigstaff, looked past the Captain to the rear of the tent. The big man standing there with his back turned was the General. A black-haired, long-legged young officer beside him was bending over packing some saddlebags. The General was directing him what to put in.

In a few minutes they came forward. The General greeted Bigstaff, then passed out of the tent with the young officer. They stood a little way off under the trees and conversed in low tones. At last the young officer turned to go. The General leaned forward, laid his hand on his shoulder. Rives could see the expression on the General's face, could hear his suddenly gentle voice: "Now, boy, you take good care of yourself."

He came back into the tent. He was sitting down in a chair beside the table, a big man with towering shoulders and black hair streaked with gray. His eyes had been soft as he gazed at his young brother. They hardened as he turned to Bigstaff. "This the man you want to take with you, Ben?"

"Yes, sir."

The General turned to Rives. "What's your name?"

"Allard."

"I've seen you before. Were you at Donelson?"

Rives said again, "Yes, sir." He wanted to add that he had been among the men disbanded at Huntsville and that he had expected to rejoin Forrest's command but Forrest was speaking before he had collected himself.

"You came out of Donelson with my boys, eh? . . . But I've seen you before. In Kentucky?"

"Yes, sir. At old Mr. Fontaine Allard's."

The General nodded. "My men camped in his yard one night. The old gentleman gave me a fine horse. Killed at Donelson. . . ." He nodded again and as if the colloquy were ended he turned to Bigstaff. "Ben, you sure you want to take this boy with you?"

"He knows the country," Ben said.

The scout and the General exchanged a look. Whatever other questions the General might have asked seemed to be answered in that look for he suddenly turned away, to Anderson. "Charley, where's that stuff?"

Anderson hauled up a saddlebag and spilled its contents out onto the table. A stack of blank paper sheets, pale blue, heavily embossed at the top. Ben walked over to the table, picked up a sheet. He gave a whistle. "Provo' marshal of Kentucky, hunh?"

Anderson was grinning. "Captain Jeffrey Forrest was going by and he thought this stuff might come in handy." He picked up a sheet and handed it to Bigstaff. "How's it look?"

Bigstaff studied it a moment then handed it back. "Captain, you write mighty pretty."

The Captain was modest. "I worked an hour before I set my hand to the first sheet. Look all right?"

"It looks all right," Ben said.

The General had been sitting, head bent down, evidently in deep thought. He looked up, spoke brusquely. "Ben, I've got to get somebody over into Tennessee, as far as Murfreesboro. Here's the way we've got it figured. You take your papers signed by the provost marshal and work your way through. The Yankees have got home guards in most of those towns. Well, you've got a message for the captain of every one, from Jere Boyle. . . . How does it look to you?"

Ben turned his head slowly to one side, studied the lantern

flame. "I don't see nothing wrong with it," he said. "Of course I couldn't hit nothing but the high spots with those papers and I'd have to come back another way. . . . Me and this boy'd travel in Yankee uniform, of course."

"You'd have to," Forrest said, "to work this dodge. Can you think of anything better?"

"Naw," Ben said, "I can't think of anything better." He stood, reflecting, one stout leg advanced, his plump hands weaving before him an imaginary cat's cradle. "Naw," he said again, "it sounds all right, for that kind of trip."

"Well, what about it then?" the General asked at length.

Ben raised his head. His curious, light-colored eyes dwelt calmly on Forrest's face. "General," he said, "I ain't going to volunteer for nothing. Course anything you tell me to do I'm going to do it best I can."

The blood had surged into Forrest's face. He knit his thick brows. An angry retort was evidently on his lips but he checked himself, took two or three quick paces to the side then turned to Bigstaff. "All right," he said curtly. "When can you start?"

Ben's face had changed in the last few seconds. It now wore its customary look of good humor. His voice was bland and cheerful. "Right away," he said. "This boy's papers ready?"

Forrest had sat down at the table beside Captain Anderson. "They're over at the quartermaster's," he said, "and the uniforms." He stood up. His voice softened suddenly. "Good-by, boys."

They left the tent, crossed the enclosure to the quartermaster's tent. When they were out of sight of the General Ben slapped his leg and chuckled. "I got him that time, didn't I?"

Rives was bewildered. "How you mean, Ben?"

"Didn't you see him stand up there and take his medicine?" He hates to order a man out on a trip like this. But he made me mad, about that brandy. I made up my mind then I warn't going to volunteer for awhile."

They walked on. Ben was talking about Jeffrey Forrest, the General's young brother whom he loved, Ben said, better than his own son. Jeffrey was a long-legged rapscallion in Ben's opinion. "Warn't that just like him now, to capture a lot of that provo's stationery just so some poor devil'd have to risk his neck using it!"

They arrived at the station. Blue uniforms were handed them, one with a corporal's chevrons, the other plain. They stripped and put them on. Ben, who seemed in high feather now, was explaining the way they would work it. The first thing, he said, was to discard the horses furnished by the government. He knew one of them, an old side wheeler, and the other probably just like him. He knew where there were two good horses, though, just what they needed, in a man's stable down by the river. He passed one day and saw them horses and he'd been keeping his eye on them ever since, knowing he might be needing a horse any day. Soon as they finished dressing and had a snack to eat they'd slip down to the river and get the horses. Lucky it was such a dark night.

Rives listened. He hardly realized that he was about to set out to steal a man's horses, dressed in a Yankee uniform. He was still thinking of the young captain, Jeffrey Forrest, and of the General who had laid his hand on Jeffrey's arm and told him to take good care of himself.

2

THEY were sitting at dinner when the little negro boy brought Rives' letter in. Lucy read snatches of it to the others. When she had finished Mitty gave a long sigh. "I'm glad he's with Coloned Lawton," she said. "I'm glad he's with him instead of that Colonel Forrest."

"Why, pray?" Susan demanded.

"I don't know," Mitty said, confused as she always was when any notice was taken of anything she said, "I thought—well, you didn't like him so much when you saw him at Brackets, did you, Lucy?"

"I only said I thought he looked stern."

Susan helped herself to black-eyed peas. "Sternness is a virtue in a military man," she said. She handed the sparse dish of peas to Lucy. "Eat, child. You and Mitty need to keep up your strength when you're spinning half the day."

"I believe Lucy's mastered it, Mama," Mitty said enthusiastically. "This morning she ran the thread on the broach without a tangle."

Susan glanced at Lucy. "Yes," she said kindly, "but she mustn't stay at it too steady. Whyn't you go lie down a while after dinner, child?"

"I believe I will," Lucy said and got up and left the dining room. She mounted the stairs quietly but the fingers that clutched her letter were tense. The door of her own room shut behind her. She went quickly to the window and began reading the two closely written pages over again. Downstairs before the others she had read the news in the letter. Now her eyes skimmed eagerly over those sentences to find the phrases that were meant for her alone. "Last night before I went to sleep I thought of you for a long time. . . . Joe Troup is here. He says. . . ." No, that could wait for a second reading. Her eyes flew on, to the end: "I can't believe that you love me as much as I love you. Write and tell me so. I won't believe it but I will love to hear you say it. Yes, I will write every day that I can and you do the same but, darling, if a day should pass when I can't write don't let that stop you. . . ."

She gave a long sigh and, still holding the letter in her hand, walked over to the deal table that she used as a desk. She got out a sheet of paper and dipping her pen in the ink—red ink that they had made from oak galls—began to write: "Dearest, dearest Rives. . . ." Then she laid the pen down. If she wrote now she would have to do it hurriedly. In a half-hour or at most an hour they would expect her back in the loom room. It would be better to wait until tonight when alone in her own room she could think of what she wanted to say.

She lay down on the bed. Lying there staring at the ceiling she re-lived the morning of Rives' departure. In imagination she traversed the path up over the slope and then down the steep descent to the spring. She had drunk cold water from his cupped hands and then they had flung themselves down on last year's leaves under the oak tree. The sun had been hot coming through the field but the woods still kept some of their winter chill. He said, "Love, your hands are cold," as he drew her to him. They had stayed there a long while. It seemed to her that she could *hear* time, hear it running through the woods. Or no, you could stop it, hold it at bay for a little then some bird would call or the woods about them would stir and time would begin again. Once some small animal ran through a near-by thicket and she started up. He laughed, pulling her down beside him. "You remind me of a little mare I had once named Kitty." "Why?" she asked. "I don't know. The way she turned her head, I reckon."

She knew that he meant that she was wild and restless and that as Mammy once said she had eyes like a nervous colt. She got up on her knees and faced him. "I wish I was different," she said. "I wish I was the best person in the world."

He was smiling. He put his hand up and traced an imaginary line above one of her eyebrows. "I wouldn't have it go this way, even that much," he said and then he brushed the palms of his hands over her cheeks. "I wouldn't have anything about you different."

She showed him how on one hand the little finger grew out crooked from the others and she showed him how plain she looked with her hair drawn back tight from her face. They laughed together. "You don't know how bad I am," she said, and she told him how she had flirted with Spencer Rowe and how once years ago she had stolen some tarts from the pantry shelf and let Aunt Mimy give Della a beating for it. "I wanted to tell," she said, "but something kept saying 'no.' "

"You were scared," he said. "Children will do anything when they're scared."

He told her how he had felt about his father's death, how as a child he had thought that it was through some fault of his father's that he got killed and how it was only after he was grown that he realized that his father was a good and brave man.

All the time they were talking she had kept looking at him, telling herself that if she didn't she would be sorry tomorrow. She reached up and touched his cheeks, pressing her finger tips into the hollow about his eyes. "I tell myself you won't be here tomorrow," she said wildly. "I keep telling myself but I can't make it seem true. How can you leave me? How can they take you away?"

After she had said that she was sorry. Time came back then and didn't go away. He said, "It isn't they," and kissed her, oh, a dozen times. But his face, even his eyes when he looked at her had changed. After a little he got to his feet and drew her up beside him. "We ought to go," he said.

She looked around, at the little branch, at the new leaves. She was going to say "No, let's stay another five minutes, another ten. . . ." But she knew that it would be the same at the end of those minutes. "Yes," she said, "we ought to have gone a good while ago," and she stepped up the path so fast that he had to hurry to catch up with her.

They stayed in the grove on the top of the hill a little while and then they went back to the house. She got up now and going to the window pushed the blind aside. She had gone back to the spring since then, she had descended the same path and had sat down on the very spot where they had been that day. She had thought she could tell by the way the leaves were pressed down the place where Rives' body had lain and she had pressed her hand upon it. But she could feel the chill of the earth under the dry leaves and the whole hollow seemed darker now that the leaves were out full. After a little she got up and came back up the hill.

She turned from the window. Going to the bed she took Rives' letter up and thrust it inside the bosom of her dress. Then she went to the washstand and bathed her face and hands and rearranged her hair. The face she saw in the mirror was pale. Her eyes showed that she had been crying. "I look plain," she thought. "I look almost as plain as Mitty."

There was a tap on the door. She opened it. A little negress looked up shyly, wrapping her hands in her apron. "Miss Sue out in the loom room. She say if you come down now she show you about that twist."

Lucy stood looking down at the child a moment then she said, "All right," and followed her down the stairs.

3

IT was almost dark when Rives and Ben came up over the rise and stopped. Off to the left was the sound of water plashing over stones. Ben cocked his ear at the sound. "What crick's that?"

"That's Double Springs," Rives told him.

Ben grunted. "I ain't anxious to get into that town too soon. I reckon this is as good a place to stop as any."

Rives did not answer. He was out of breath. And he still did not know why they had left the road so suddenly. They had came out of Woodbury with a squad of Yankee cavalry. Rives, riding along silently, had admired the ease with which Ben sustained conversation with the Yankee corporal, a regular who had seen service in Mexico. He remembered hearing long ago that Ben had once been in the United States army. His experience was evidently of great service to him. Adroitly during the afternoon he had introduced references to places he had been stationed, bits of information about certain regiments, finally the names of one or two officers he had served under.

Then suddenly, a few miles out of Murfreesboro he had stopped, snapping his fingers as if he had just remembered something. "Allen," he said, Allen was the name Rives travelled under and Ben called himself Higgins, "Allen, what in the devil did you let me forget that letter for?"

"What letter?" Rives asked before he thought.

Ben's voice was sarcastic. "Allen, you'll go far." He turned to the red-faced corporal. "Our colonel's sweet on a lady back there in Woodbury and here we've done rode by and forgot to give her the letter."

The corporal had looked surprised and, Rives thought, suspicious. He had opened his mouth to say something. Nobody ever knew what, for Ben grasped his hand, shook it, told him what a pleasure it had been to travel with him and was riding back up the road before anybody concerned had had time to get his breath. Rives followed. They had ridden on in silence—not too fast. Rives remembered now the prickling sensation he had had in his back. The corporal and his troop might be after them any minute. But they had not come. Finally at a cross-roads Ben stopped, glanced swiftly around and then without a word to Rives dove into a little used trail that led back toward the town. They had progressed along this until it came to an end when they had left the horses in a thicket and made the rest of the distance on foot.

They went down to the water's edge now and fell on their knees to drink out of their cupped hands. Ben sat down on a rock. He was panting. "Lord," he said, "I ain't made for briar jumping." He looked at Rives. "It ain't so hard on a lean feller like you."

Rives, still kneeling at the water's edge, splashed the water on his dusty face. "Well, what'd we leave the road for?" he asked. "Seemed to me we were getting along all right."

Ben shook his head irritably. "Yeah, you was so busy thinking about how smart we was you didn't look at that feller. I tell you he was on to us."

"How do you know?"

"My fault," Ben said wearily. "I was too smart too. Talked too much. I made a slip back there, about that Captain Renshaw. I thought the damn fool was dead or kicked out of the army by this time. But he must be somewhere right around here. Didn't you see that feller look at me kind of surprised? I knew then it was up to us to move."

Rives remembered hearing the corporal repeat the name: "Captain Renshaw . . ." He remembered too that the man had been quiet for some minutes after that but he had thought nothing of it. He realized now, however, that Ben was probably right.

"Well, what we going to do now?" he asked.

"Oh, I don't know," Ben said irritably. "I got to study it out." He twisted around and looked over the meadow behind him. "If I was you I'd go out and gather up some of this here wild hay for those horses. We may have to leave here in a hurry tonight."

Rives gathered the hay and put it down before the two horses. He did not have to bring them down to drink; they had watered them at Cripple Creek a half an hour ago. When he got back, Ben had taken a can of sardines out of his haversack and was struggling to open it with his clasp knife. He was curiously unskilful at any mechanical operation. Rives took the can from him, opened it and set it down on a rock. He brought some hard-tack out of his pocket and they ate it with the sardines. Ben's irritation seemed to have disappeared. He talked of desultory matters as they ate. As they got out a second can of sardines—they were plentifully supplied with this delicacy—he laughed. "I was thinking about when I was with Morgan," he explained. "One thing when I start out on a trip like this I got to eat. The best they got is none too good for me. One time I was going out for Morgan and one of them rapscallion cooks packed my lunch. They wasn't anything in it but sow-belly and cold hoe cake. Well, I come in about midnight. The General was waiting up for me. 'Well, Bigstaff,' he says, 'what you got to tell me?' I looked him right in the eye. 'General,' I says, 'they's one thing I got to tell you. You know what them trips are. A man lays on his belly all night on the cold ground he wants to have something in it.'

"He laughs and says 'What do you like to eat?'

" 'Well,' I says, 'I ain't got nothing against cheese but if you give me my pick I'll take sardines.'

" 'All right,' he says, 'you shall have sardines. And now what you got to tell me?'

"Well, they was a whole gang of Yankees coming in. I'd found out which road they was on and when they was coming. He was tickled because he knew he could go right down and scoop 'em in. 'Bigstaff,' he says, 'you can have all the sardines you want. I only wisht I had some whale to give you. I'd like to see what you could do on a whale.' "

Rives laughed. "I didn't know you'd been with Morgan, Ben. When was that?"

"A good while ago," Ben said evasively. "I got myself transferred. It ain't every one of them generals I can git along with."

"Which'd you rather be with, Morgan or Forrest?"

Ben considered. "I reckon I'd take Forrest."

"Why?" Rives persisted.

Ben shook his head. "I don't know. Just something about him suits me better. Morgan's all hell for leather. The General he rides hard, too, but he don't never forget where he's going."

He stood up, brushing the crumbs from his pants. "Them sardines tasted all right. Now, boy, we got to get started. How far you reckon it is into that town?"

Rives looked at the lights of the little town glimmering through the mist. "It's about two miles from here, I reckon."

Ben nodded reflectively. "And the pickets'll be pushed out a mile or so outside town. Well, we'll just have to work across this field till we strike one."

"I thought we were going to ride into town," Rives said. "We got Yankee uniforms and we got papers. Why can't we just ride into town?"

Ben looked at him contemptuously. "We can't do that, now I made that slip. They'd be laying for us, sure. Naw, the only thing to do now is to catch us a picket and shake him till he spits. If he don't know what we want to know we'll have to try some other way."

He waded across the shallow stream, then stopped. "I'll tell you something else," he said, "it's a thing mighty few people seem to know, about how to work up on a picket."

Rives looked at him intently. "How do you do it, Ben?"

"Don't fool with the man. Slip up on the horse. Slip up and cut the horse's tether then get back to cover. They'll hear the noise and raise up, maybe, but when they find out it's just a horse they'll go back to sleep. And any noise they hear after that they'll say that's just that old loose horse. Gives you a chance to turn around. See?"

Rives nodded. "I'll do just like you say, Ben."

Ben laughed shortly. "You better."

They walked up the slope, climbed a fence and struck a field full of corn. Ben worked across it by slipping down first one row after another and Rives followed his example.

Late in the night they came out on a high meadow overlooking the town. Most of the lamps in the houses had been put out but lights still showed in the military encampment. The two men crouched in the shadow of a clump of bushes. From the road, a quarter of a mile away, came the measured beat of hoofs: a body of cavalry was evidently moving out of the town. Ben was silent for a while, listening, then he stiffened like a dog on a point. "What's that?"

Rives heard voices. Thev were some distance off yet but they seemed to be approaching. Ben had relaxed. "It's all right," he whispered. "They're changing the pickets."

They sat quiet. The voices were closer now. They heard a man's laugh and then another man's voice answering. There was a rustling of bushes, probably a horse being tethered and then retreating footsteps.

Ben sighed. "Them Yankees! Why don't they change their pickets earlier? Now we got to wait till they settle down."

He sank back on the ground. His breathing became heavy. He was asleep. Rives stretched himself out too. But he was too excited to sleep and after a little he sat up. There was still a moon but it was veiled with mist. Mist was everywhere. It had been creeping up slowly from the creek bed in the last hour and now it was drifting as high as a man's head in the field before him. The whole landscape had changed in the last few minutes. He was shut in with his thoughts. He took a plug of tobacco out of his pocket and bit off a chew. His mind went back over the events of the last ten days. It had been ten days since they left Chattanooga. It seemed years. He thought of the different towns they had been in, of the Yankees they had encountered. It seemed impossible that you could slip in among them, sit around, talk, swap stories and not be discovered. Ben had a theory about that. "Don't let your mind run on yourself and you're all right." Another of his maxims was "Get 'em tickled." Rives grinned, thinking of a story Ben had told the corporal. He had a fund of lewd stories which he said came in handy on trips like these. A few minutes after he met a man he would give him a quizzical look; "Ever hear the one about the old maid and the parson?" The captain of the Woodbury home guard had had tears streaming down his face as he examined or pretended to examine their papers.

He thought of Lucy. He had written to her just before he met Joe Troup that night. And an hour later, involuntarily he straightened his shoulders, he had been picked as one of Forrest's scouts. He had had plenty of opportunities to write to her on the way over here but Ben had cautioned him against putting anything down on paper. He wondered what she would think when she didn't hear from him, for ten days, maybe even two weeks. Mentally he began a letter to her, a mild but he thought humorous version of Ben Bigstaff's character and eccentricities and then his thoughts stopped short. He remembered something Ben had said to him, looking up suddenly as they rode along a dusty by-road. "See here. One thing to remember. When we get back from this trip you don't know me and I don't know you." He grinned after saying that and shook his head. "You a married man, ain't you? Well, now you started on this kind of work you better not write home so often. If you do tell her about the little birdies in the woods, how sweet they sing."

He would not be able to give Lucy any real explanation of his ten-day silence. He would just have to say that his duties had prevented him from writing. Perhaps he could give her some intimation of the nature of the service he was engaged in but if he kept on being a scout he would never again be able to write her the kind of letters he had written before—the kind of letters he knew she expected him to write.

The footfalls he had been hearing ceased. The pickets had evidently settled down for the night. There were no sounds at all except field rustlings and the occasional twitter of some bird. He knew now why Ben Bigstaff and Tom Miles were different from the others. They were alone so much, nobody to talk to but themselves, in the dark half the time, waiting. But he wanted to go on with it. He wanted to be sent out again. . . .

Ben sat up suddenly as if awakened by the silence. He touched Rives on the arm. "Let's start now," he whispered. "Work that horse trick."

They moved off, lifting their feet almost in unison, making the same stops. They could not see the man they were creeping up on but they could make out the ears of his horse jutting through the mist. "Half them horses got more sense than the pickets," Ben had said. This horse had got wind of their approach already. He was moving restlessly. They waited. He got quiet. They still could not see the man but they could hear him breathing. Ben touched Rives peremptorily on the arm and went forward alone. Rives could hear his foot fall softly on the ground each time, hear the horse move suddenly as he came up and then the rasp of the rope as it was cut.

The horse took two or three rapid steps forward. Then a shape rose up out of the mist. A man's voice rang out. "Joe, git up!"

The man who had called was coming toward Rives. He dodged, but the man dodged too, and caught him by the shoulders. Rives' arms were pinioned to his sides by powerful hands. There was hot breath on his neck. "Oh, you would, would you?" the voice said.

Rives walked slowly forward beside his captor. The picket was just rising up. He struck a match. His blanket trailing off over his shoulders gave him an old womanish look. He said: "Steve! Thank the Lord it's you."

Steve laughed. "You better be thankful," he said.

The picket bent and lit the lantern he had set down beside a bush. "I just dropped off," he said; "warn't more'n two minutes."

Steve said that it was lucky he had come over to borrow a

chew of tobacco. He turned to Rives: "Well, my bucko, less see." Rives stood still while they searched him. He strained his ears and then an excited grin came on his face. He was certain now that he had heard footsteps making off over the rise. It was all right. Ben had got away!

4

THE Federal soldiers took Rives through the streets to the brick jail on the public square. Its halls were full of soldiers, some on guard, some lounging about and talking. In the upper hall to which Rives was taken a group of civilians under guard awaited their trial in one of various "courts" set up in the building. One of these prisoners, a portly man of fifty-five or sixty, had evidently just been brought in for he was still protesting against his arrest, volubly and with ineffectual jerkings of his hands and feet. Rives recognized this man as a Mr. Galloway, whose farm adjoined his uncle's. As he passed, so close that his sleeve brushed the other man's, he spoke to him in a low voice, calling him by name. Hearing a friendly voice, Galloway turned quickly. He stared at Rives a moment with drawn brows and open mouth, and then, as if the effort to identify this strange face were too much for him, he buried his face with its working features on his arm while angry sobs shook his body.

The soldiers took Rives swiftly down the hall and, unlocking the door of a cell, thrust him inside. The cell had two occupants. One, a handsome young man with curling chestnut hair and fine brown eyes, sat on the edge of a cot, gazing fixedly at the wall. He did not turn his head when Rives entered or give any recognition of his presence. The other man, heavier set and some ten or twelve years older, was pacing up and down the room. He wheeled when Rives came in, looked him over, then, nodding curtly, went on with his restless walking.

Rives sat down on the only chair in the room. The guard had not taken away his pipe or tobacco, for which he was thankful, and now, lighting up, he reviewed his situation. His excitement had died down. He began to realize that he lacked the peculiar talents necessary to extricate himself from such a situation. He was badly frightened.

His meditations were interrupted by the jailer, who brought a tray of food and set it inside the door. He had evidently heard that Rives was a deserter, for, as he set the tray down, he winked, observing: "Well, Bud, you'll get a square meal now."

The older of Rives' two companions wheeled. He stood looking at Rives as if trying to make up his mind about him, and then a peculiar glancing light came in his eye. "Couldn't bring it off, eh?" he asked.

Rives had determined that even before these Confederates he would continue to play the deserter, so he answered sullenly that he hadn't had a square meal now in some weeks and would be glad to get one, even if it had to be in jail.

The three men ate the food, which was coarse but plentiful. The young man ate in silence for some minutes, then seeming to recollect himself, he turned to Rives and courteously asked him his name and regiment. He himself, he said, was Captain Robert Williams of the Eighth Alabama. He had been taken prisoner at the Battle of Shiloh and forwarded to a Federal prison in Indiana. He had made his escape and got back to Nashville to find it in possession of the Federals. Friends in that city had placed him in company with "Mister Paul"—here he bowed slightly—who was familiar with the routes leading out of the city between the Federal pickets. At Black's shop, on the Murfreesboro turnpike, he and his companion had run into some Federal pickets. "And," he concluded with a charming, melancholy smile, "being in citizens' clothes it has gone hard with me."

The older man listened to his recital with a noncommittal expression. Once or twice he shook his head as if baffled by the inscrutable ways of Providence. "They know my face. That's the trouble," he said. "I told 'em," he jerked his finger toward the young officer, "I told 'em he didn't know any more about the stuff they found on me than a babe unborn. But they didn't listen. They don't never listen. After they take you up. Yep. It's all over, once they take you up."

The door opened. A tall man in clergyman's dress entered. He at once went up to Captain Williams and half embraced him, addressing him as "Robert" in a voice shaken by emotion. After a little he and the young officer withdrew to a corner of the room, where they could be heard conversing in low tones.

The spy, James Paul, seemed to be made more restless by this low-voiced, earnest conversation. He walked up and down the room, taking shorter and shorter turns and finally coming to stand by the window. There had been a great commotion in the street a while ago. A little girl playing in the yard of a house opposite the jail building had been fired upon by a soldier. The bullet struck the child in the throat, wounding her severely. The soldier, a poor, half-crazed creature, got on his horse and fled from town before he could be apprehended. The parents of the child, ardent Secessionists, had not, however, been allowed to take her into the house, which was occupied by Union officers, and she had lain now for an hour upon a hastily improvised bed in the yard. During this time she had been almost constantly surrounded by a curious throng, composed mainly of soldiers. These men, accustomed to bloodshed in battle, had never before seen a child wounded and for an hour they filed by staring down at the little girl as she lay supported in the arms of her mother. The spy, Paul, was as deeply interested in this scene as the soldiers outside were, and as he stood at the window he called out to Rives whenever he got a glimpse of the child.

Rives, sitting on the cot, gazed straight before him. He hardly heard the man's voice and did not trouble himself to respond. Up to this minute he had supposed that these men were in the same plight as himself and had given them little thought, being occupied with revolving in his mind his own situation. But something, some note in the clergyman's voice, or expression on the face of the young kneeling officer had suddenly arrested his attention. He had suddenly realized that these men had already appeared before a court martial, had been condemned, and doubtless would be executed within a few hours.

The spy, Paul, meanwhile, continued with rising excitement to report on the scene outside: "The old man must have taken the oath of allegiance. They're bringing the doctor. Yep. That's the doctor. Black bag and everything." He was silent for a moment, then, as the crowd fell back under the doctor's peremptory gestures, he was able to get a full view of the child lying on the pallet with the bloody bandages about her throat. He craned his neck out of the window until the crowd, surging in again, shut off his view of the scene; then he turned to Rives, shaking his head and laying his hand on his throat, "Must have clipped the jugular," he said. "I knew a fellow once got hit like that. They sewed him up all right, but all he could ever say after that was 'Hobble Gobble.' Yep, if that kid over there comes through, expect she'll be in the same fix. Hobble Gobble." He laid his hand again on his throat and laughed not unkindly and yet with real mirth.

The clergyman and the young officer had concluded their conversation and the clergyman now approached the spy. The latter suffered himself to be drawn aside, but his colloquy with the minister was short and he was evidently relieved when it was finished.

The young officer, on the contrary, seemed in better spirits and less abstracted than he had been before. Seated on the edge of the cot and looking from one to the other with bright eyes he talked vivaciously and cheerfully of his situation. His chief concern now seemed to be whether his mother and sister and a young lady, "a friend of the family," who had set out to ride from Huntsville to Murfreesboro would arrive there before dawn. The message sent shortly after he had been captured had surely reached Huntsville. There were still good horses available in the town. If they had started at once they might arrive in Murfreesboro by three o'clock, possibly earlier.

Rives listened. Everything the young officer said or did was now of the greatest interest to him and yet all the time there was in the back of his mind the half-angry thought that this man, whose every movement and speech were to him so strange, so fascinating, would soon be dead and would never speak or move again.

The spy's restlessness, on the contrary, seemed to be increased by the young officer's conversation. He rose and began pacing the floor again. Once he turned to Rives and asked if he had a deck of cards. Rives said that he hadn't. The spy frowned. "That's too bad," he said.

He resumed his pacing, then suddenly came up to Rives again. "You got any money?"

Rives nodded and drew a bill from a pocket of his shirt. A smile of childlike happiness came on the spy's face. He snatched the money from Rives and, running to the door, knocked until the guard came and sold him a deck of cards.

He now proposed a three-handed game of Set Back. The young officer declined, saying that he had one or two more letters to write. Rives and the spy, seated on the cot, began to play.

The night wore on. The young officer, his letters written, was lying in a corner of the cell on a folded blanket, his head pillowed on his arm. When his eyes fell on his companions he smiled abstractedly like a man whose mind is taken up with weighty matters. Occasionally his lips were seen to move.

The game of Set Back ended—the spy had won all of Rives' money. He leaned back against the wall, weary, and yet he seemed not to be able to go to sleep. Finally he began to speak almost like a man talking to himself and yet turning to Rives now and then as if to assure himself that he had a listener. His speech concerned his experiences in the army. Early in the war he had developed peculiar talents and, these talents being recognizd, he had been shunted first from regiment to regiment, then from brigade to brigade, division to division. Like an old man who will not spare the listener any minutiæ, however tedious, he recited details of the positions of the two armies in half a dozen encounters, occasionally interrupting himself with a glance at Rives as if to say as old men do, "Where was I? I forgot what I was talking about." And then in the midst of the circumstantial detail, the effort to recall some under-officer's name, came the story of a comrade, taken as he himself had almost been taken between the lines at Corinth. The man stepping into the Federal pickets' traps had turned around, thinking that he, Paul, had betrayed him, had given him one look before he was led off. "I didn't have time to tell him," he said heavily, looking down at his hands swinging between his spread knees. "They didn't give me time to tell him . . ."

It was in the midst of this long drawn-out, monotonous and terrible story that Rives heard, at first from far away and then coming rapidly nearer, the hoof-beats of horses on the hard turnpike and the yell of oncoming cavalrymen.

He leaped to his feet. The other two were already at the window. They hung out, staring. The streets were full of cavalrymen and fleeing citizens. The spy turned around. He was laughing till his eyes were mere slits in his fat face.

"It's old Forrest," he said. "He's done captured the town!"

5

WILLIAMS turned around. "It can't be," he cried, "Forrest isn't anywhere near this town."

"Yes he is," Rives told him. "He was on his way here when I left his command at Chattanooga."

The young officer came toward Rives. "Are you sure of that?" he asked in a trembling voice. "Are you one of Forrest's men?"

"I'm one of his scouts," Rives said.

The spy, Paul, had been straining out of the window, oblivious to the conversation going on behind him but now he turned. "He's right, Williams. I could tell he was up to something way he looked when he came in here."

The young officer looked from one to the other. His eyes were blazing. "We'll get out then," he cried. "They'll get us out!" and he rushed to the window.

The noise out grew louder. The Confederate cavalry was inside the prison yard now. The Rebel yell rose, sudden and fierce. There was the sound of firing. The spy pounded Williams on the back. "The Yanks are running!" he shouted.

The sounds without were obscured by the trampling of feet on the stairs. Rives got away from the window, stood with his hand cupped over his ear. "They're getting out through the prison," he said.

"Somebody's coming up here," Williams said.

The three prisoners stood, listening, while the trampling feet came nearer. Suddenly the door was unlocked and two guards burst in. They had muskets which they levelled upon the prisoners. But before they could shoot the three prisoners had scuttled across the boards like rats and were crouching behind the door.

The man with the musket whirled and was taking aim at them when the door banged to, hiding the bodies of the crouching men. He called to his comrade: "Bill, hold that door open," but the other man laughed. "I ain't goin' to do it. You'd shoot my blamed hand off." As he spoke he was taking something from his pocket then he dodged into the hall, stooped a moment and was gone down the corridor. His voice floated back. "Better hurry. They're battering the door down."

The man with the musket lunged after him out of the room. They heard the lock click to and then there was silence except for the battering sounds below. Rives tasted wet wool. His open mouth for some minutes had been pressed against the spy's fat back. He heaved his shoulders furiously upward. The spy tumbled out onto the floor and the other two crawled after him.

They remained on all fours for a minute glaring about them then got cautiously to their feet. Rives was shaking with rage and fright. In the effort to control himself he began mechanically picking dust and lint from his clothes. The spy had sat down beside the table and was cursing softly and monotonously. Suddenly he fell silent. His head was tilted toward the ceiling. His light-colored eyes were intent. Rives saw his nostrils slowly lift and widen. "They've set fire to the place, boys," he said.

Williams raised his head, sniffed until he, too, caught the smell. "That's what he was doing in the hall," he said calmly.

He stepped quickly to the door, looked through the grating. "Those loose planks," he said. "He stuck a bunch of papers under them."

The spy stood up. He was trembling all over. "We better try to break the door down," he said.

The three men hurled themselves against the door but it was made of iron with hinges sunk deep in an oak jamb and it held. They tried it again and again until their shoulders were bruised and the breath knocked from their bodies. The spy gave the word to stop. "My heart's bad," he groaned. "I can't stand much of that."

Rives, himself exhausted and drenched with sweat, was about to stagger to a seat when he met Williams' blazing eyes. "Come on," Williams sobbed, "I'm not going to die like a rat in a trap," and he hurled himself at the door again.

Rives found himself wasting precious, angry breath. "Stop that, man. You can't do any good by yourself." He had Williams by the shoulder, was drawing him away from the door when he heard footsteps rushing down the hall and stepped back.

The spy, still groaning in his chair, looked up. "Our men?"

Williams rushed to the grating. "Our men," he yelled, "and they've got a chain of buckets."

There were rapid steps down the hall. A face appeared at the grating. "Stand aside, boys," a voice called. A few minutes later the hinges tore from the oak and the heavy door clattered inward and fell.

The prisoners stepped over it and were out in the hall. It was full of soldiers. Some of them were laughing. One gave Rives a slap on the back as he staggered toward the stairs. "Tried to burn you up, did they? Reckon you're glad old Forrest made it in time."

Prisoners were being released from cells all along the passage way. A sergeant herded them down the stairs and out into the open. The prison yard was full of dismounted cavalrymen. Rives, with some of the released prisoners, went over to a bench at the side of the yard and sat down. Presently he was aware that Williams and Paul were no longer with him. At the same time he realized that most of the cavalrymen were mounting to ride away. "What is it?" he asked dully. "Where are they going?"

The man next to him, a tall, lean countryman, answered. "Over to the square. They've done took this place and the depot and now they're going over to the courthouse to git the garrison."

"Who took the jail?" Rives asked.

"Lawton's Georgians. And now they're going to take the courthouse."

The man rose as he spoke. Rives rose too and walked beside him. The mention of Lawton's Georgians, the regiment in which he had so lately enrolled, recalled him to a sense of duty. He wanted to rejoin his regiment as soon as he could but he did not know how to go about it. It seemed easier to walk beside the stranger through the streets which were lighted now with torches and thronged with civilians.

Once the people fell aside to make way for a detail of galloping soldiers and then yelled wildly as the ruddy torchlight revealed the horseman in the center of the group, a man wearing only a nightshirt who rode stiffly, his arms bound to his sides.

Rives' companion laughed loudly and threw his hat in the air. "Yankee provost marshal," he gasped when he was able to walk on. "Don't them shirt tails make pretty flags?"

Later he explained that the provost marshal, Oliver Cromwell Rounds, had incurred the hatred of the whole countryside because of his tyranny. People were already delighting in the rumor that the Confederate soldiers when making his arrest had pulled him out from between two feather beds. "In a young lady's room," the countryman added with a wink. "I ain't telling who it was."

They arrived on the outskirts of the square and found that the besieged garrison had already surrendered. The crowd of civilians fell back as the prisoners, men of a Michigan regiment, were brought into the yard and lined up. With them were some of the guards who had fled from the jail. Rives saw Williams. He was walking with an officer in front of the line of prisoners. Rives saw him stop before a man, give him a long look then raise his finger and knew that he was identifying the guard who had set fire to the prison.

He watched the cavalrymen lead the guard off. He wondered whether the orders were to shoot him now or whether he would be given any sort of trial. The officer with Williams turned around. It was General Forrest. He was walking over to the side of the courthouse to mount his horse. Rives saw the gigantic figure of Captain Boone, commander of the escort, among the men waiting there. He was about to go over to Boone, to ask him whether he should report back to the Georgia regiment or whether he should consider himself attached to the escort when he was aware that Boone and the men around him were all looking in one direction.

Rives looked and saw that the door of one of the red-brick houses on the square had opened. A slender woman dressed in black was coming down the path. She had a handkerchief in one hand. A silver spoon glinted in the other. She was coming straight up to the General. Rives heard her voice, low but distinct: "General Forrest, will you back your horse for me?"

The cavalry commander looked down, startled, then lifted his hat and obediently pulled on the reins. The horse, a powerful gray, took two steps backward. The woman bent over and with the silver spoon scooped up some of the earth on which the charger's hoof had rested and put it in the handkerchief, then without a word to the General she walked back up the path, the laden handkerchief clutched in her hand.

The crowd cheered tumultuously and cried, "Forrest! Forrest!"

Forrest was riding toward them. His hat was still off, a lock of black hair had fallen across his forehead. His expression was stern then as if he had just realized what the woman's action meant, he smiled and held up his hand for quiet. The people, he said, must go to their homes. The town was safe, the Yankees would not get it again but the soldiers still had work to do; the detachment of infantry across Stone's River was yet to be dealt with. He let his hand sink to his side. His face resumed its usual stern expression. He was riding off through the crowd, his escort pressing close behind.

The crowd began to disperse. Here and there torches were extinguished. Those that were left flickered palely as the morning light grew. People started and looked at one another when from behind the courthouse a single shot rang out.

Rives, standing with the others, drew in deep breaths of the cool air. He had seen a man led off to die, had just heard the shot that killed him. He knew that he himself would not be standing here in this fresh morning light if the Confederates had not captured the town and his eyes followed the towering figure on the gray horse till it was lost in the crowd.

6

LUCY came out of the house and walked slowly across the back yard. In front of the smokehouse Susan Allard and old Rivanna were at work. They had brought in armfuls of the wild castor bean plants late yesterday afternoon and now they were expressing the oil in the great scalding kettle. Susan stood beside it now, stirring the contents with a stick. Old Rivanna was squatting on the ground a little way off, pounding more beans in a mortar.

She looked up as Lucy approached. "Going over to the swamp now, honey? I'd go with you if I didn't have to stay here and help Miss Sue."

Susan stepped back from the steaming pot. She wore a faded calico blouse. Her heavy homespun skirt—it had been made too big for her or she had got thinner in the last few months—sagged at the waist and showed a little strip of pale flesh. She seemed unconscious of her appearance, however, as she lifted her hand and pushed gray strands of hair back from her heated forehead. "What's there to be afraid of, Rivanna?" she asked coldly.

The negress got to her feet, yawning. "Your meat's showing, Miss Sue," she said matter-of-factly. "You ain't afraid of the devil and high water, but it ain't natural for a young gal to go traipsin off in them swamps by herself." She leaned over and ladled up a little of the liquid from the pot. "Smell it, honey."

Lucy drew back, wrinkling her nose. "I wouldn't take a dose of castor oil if I were to die for it."

"Humph," Susan said, "you might be glad to get it, Miss." She took up the ladle where Rivanna had let it fall, tilted it so that a few heavy drops fell out. "See, almost transparent. I believe this is going to be as fine as that Mr. Gossett showed us."

She was looking at her daughter-in-law, her strange bright eyes shining. Lucy's face softened. "I believe it is," she said. "Well, you ought to get nearly a gallon out of this boiling."

Molly, the fourteen-year-old negro girl, came up, leading the horse, "Yankee." Lucy took the halter from her and they went out of the yard and up over the field. They walked in the shade of the fence row, the horse ranging out beside them. The ground —it had not had any crops on it for two years now—was bare or covered with short, harsh grass. Still the horse managed to find a bite here and there. Lucy let him stop and browse where he would. He would need all the strength he could muster for the trip to the cane brake and back. She herself was glad to walk along slowly in the sparse shade. If she were not taking the horse to get fodder she would be in the office with Mitty, tramping back and forth beside the spinning wheel or, worse, reeling the thread she had spun.

They came to the wagon road that bisected this field. Molly was pointing. " 'Long about here, Miss Lucy, warn't it?"

Lucy said "Yes," her voice sounding harsh in her own ears. It seemed a long time ago. She and Mitty and Cousin Susan had been sitting down to an early supper when Molly came into the dining room, screaming: "Miss Sue, yard's done full of soldiers."

The three of them had run out into the hall. A Yankee officer was coming in the door. He said, "Madam, I want to use your roof for observation," pushed past Susan, and was up the steps when a voice sang out from the porch: "No use, Schofield. Here they come now." The Yankee officer was out of the house and up on his horse in two seconds. Men were crowding up around him. He pointed to the road across the field, jumped his horse over the low-paling fence. They were all after him in a minute.

The women watched them tearing over the field, saw them disappear in a grove of trees, and then the Confederate cavalry was in the yard. Mitty and Lucy ran to meet them. Lucy remembered that she had run up to the brown-bearded captain, panting: "Take me. I'll show you." But he shook his head and went on through the gate, his men following. They went slowly, compared to the Yankees. It seemed a long time before they heard any sounds of fighting, and then all of a sudden bullets whined and smoke was drifting up over the silver poplar trees.

They went inside the house. Mitty sat down at her place at the table. The girl Molly got in that corner between the sideboard and the wall and kept moaning. Susan and Lucy went back out on the porch, but they couldn't see much. After a little, bullets did not come so often, then they stopped. Susan turned to Lucy. "We'd better go down now," she said. She walked into the dining room. The girl was still crying. Susan fetched her a clip on the head. "Aren't you ashamed of yourself, crying like that, when men are over there wounded and dying?"

She had been snatching old tablecloths out of the sideboard drawer as she spoke, took down from somewhere a basket of lint. They ran over the field and down into the road. Soldiers were there. All gray now except for one or two blue on the ground. The brown-bearded officer had stood beside this tree, a bitter, school-teacherish-looking man with the smell of sweat and blood upon him. He did not seem to know that one of his arms was hurt, tried to raise it to the felt hat that clung to the back of his head, then winced. His mouth was wry with the pain, but he spoke formally to Susan: "Most kind, Madam . . . yes, one or two of our boys. . . ." His face went soft suddenly in the middle. He passed his good hand before his mouth. "Captain Linton," he said in a different voice, "if you would just . . . Captain Linton . . ."

Captain Linton was lying on his back in a clump of ironweed. Blood was all over the front of him. She bent over, said, "Can you walk?" He looked at her and his fair eyebrows met. A whistling sound came from him. He got to his feet. She thrust her shoulder under his—he was not tall—and they went slowly up the slope. Mitty saw them and came running. Together they dragged him into the house, laid him down on the parlor sofa. She did not know what to do and neither did Mitty. His face was pasty green and the whistling sound had started again. Mitty went to the kitchen to get some water. She stood over him. He was lying back, his eyes closed and suddenly he sat up. He put his hands to his chest. Something was inside, trying to get out. It was tearing him to pieces. His eyes rolled back in his head, but he was still looking at her. She ran out of the room, through the hall, out on to the porch. She stared at the trees, the sky. But they looked strange. She put her head down on the wooden railing.

Susan was beside her. She said: "That man in the parlor has to be moved to a bed."

Lucy got up and went back into the house. Uncle Mack was waiting there to help move the wounded man. They got him on to the bed in the spare room by the hardest. He lay back, cocked one eyebrow and fainted. As soon as he came to, Susan hurried out into the other room. There were three other wounded soldiers, two lying on her big bed and one who would not sit or lie down but stood with his right arm dangling at his side. Susan said his arm was broken and she sent Molly on the horse for the doctor.

It was three miles there and back. The doctor arrived at five o'clock. Lucy heard him step up on the front porch, then go through the hall into the chamber. He stayed in there a while, then came out, closing the door behind him. He and Susan talked. She heard him say, "Better now than later," and then bawl out for somebody to be heating water, quick. A few minutes later Susan came into the little bedroom. She had her sleeves rolled high, her blue, checked apron was spotted with blood. She went to the cabinet and took down several bottles. One was the chloroform bottle. Lucy knew then that they were going to cut the man's arm off.

She thought she could not stand it. She walked up and down the room, her shoulders hunched over, her hands pressed tight against her eyeballs. Then she heard a strangled cry from the bed. Captain Linton was sitting up. His head shook from side to side. His poor hands kept tearing at his throat. She went and sat on the edge of the bed and put her arms around him and caught both his hands and held them down. When he managed to get his right hand away from hers she caught it and held it in the vise of her knees until the spasm passed and he lay weakly back on his pillow. This hemorrhage had been worse than the last one. Her hands and her gown were sticky with blood and blood was still oozing from his mouth on to the pillow. She went out and got a basin of water and fresh linen and sponged his face—she did not dare touch his throat—and then as gently as she could slipped a fresh pillow case under his head. His neck as she lifted his head felt limp. She thought that perhaps he was dying and drew back with the wet cloth in her hand and then suddenly he opened his eyes and caught her hand and pressed it. When she would have taken her hand away it seemed to her that the limp fingers held on to it so she drew a chair close to the bed and sat beside him, holding his hand.

In the other room the terrible loud groaning kept on. Once a man's high voice cut across it. "Shut up, Joe! They got to do it." There was a cry after that more bestial than any of the others and then that too died away into a faint whimpering that might have been made by an injured dog trying to go to sleep.

The light faded from the room. She still sat there holding the man's hand. After a while Molly came, bringing a candle and after her, walking heavily, the doctor. He knelt beside the bed but he did not touch the wounded man; merely leaned forward and peered out of his bloodshot eyes that had heavy pouches under them. Once he put out a stubby forefinger, seemed about to touch the man's throat, but the finger came back and he got to his feet, shaking his head. "In a coma now," he said. "Morphine won't do any harm," and he got out his hypodermic syringe and showed Lucy how to give the injection in the fleshy part of the forearm. "You might have to do it again and you might not," he said wearily and was gone from the room.

Mitty came. She said that she had already eaten and would stay with the captain while Lucy ate. Lucy went into the dining room and got a piece of cold cornbread and a glass of milk. She drank the milk but when she swallowed a piece of the cornbread it felt harsh in her throat and she put the rest of the pone down and went back into the bedroom.

Mitty had lit a candle on the mantel shelf. She was standing beside the bed, looking down at the soldier. He was lying as Lucy had left him on his back. His wide-open eyes appeared to contemplate the ceiling, but the lower part of his face was contorted and blood oozed from the gaping mouth down on to the pillow.

Lucy bent over him a moment then looked up at Mitty. "He's dead, isn't he?"

"I don't know," Mitty said helplessly. "I was just standing by the window and I heard a little sound, not anything like he made at first and I turned around and saw all that blood. . . . Lucy, what ought we to do?"

"Nothing," Lucy said. She looked abstractedly at the candle flame, then as if with an effort withdrew her gaze. Her eyes fell on the negro girl, staring in the doorway. "Molly, bring me a basin of water."

Mitty held the candle and Lucy washed the soldier's face and hands. She would have turned away when she had finished but Mitty still stood irresolute. "We ought to shut his eyes," she whispered.

"I can't," Lucy said harshly, then she knelt down beside the bed and with her finger tips stroked the eyelids shut. One of the soldier's hands was clenched at his side. She straightened the fingers and then brought both hands up and crossed them on his chest. Mitty would have pulled the sheet up over his face but Lucy stopped her. "Let's don't do that now."

"All right," Mitty said.

Lucy looked at her and saw that she was trembling all over. "You'd better go to bed," she told her.

They left the room. Mitty went upstairs to bed. Lucy said that she wanted a breath of air and stepped out on the porch. Behind her the house was quiet except for an occasional footfall on the stair or in the hall. Old Rivanna had finished washing up in the kitchen and she and Molly were moving slowly along the path to the quarter. Lucy could hear old Rivanna's weary grunt as she stepped over a stick of stovewood that somebody had left in the path and then their voices died away and everything was quiet again.

She sat down on one of the benches that ran along either side of the porch. Now that she was still she realized that her feet and legs, even her arms ached. There was a dull ache too at the base of her neck. She laid her head down on her folded arms but when she shut her eyes she kept seeing pictures: a man jumping his horse across a gulley, the first spiral of smoke over the poplars, a stern face under a black felt hat. . . . She raised her eyes. The three days' old moon rode high over the pine trees, spilling its silver light. The field that stretched away on this side of the house was bathed in light. There was a place on the nearer edge where the pearly blades of grass were all trampled. The Confederate soldiers jumping their horses over the fence had landed there. Somewhere, not many miles from here, the stern-faced major, father to the boy in there on the bed dead, was still riding. Her lips trembled. If she thought of him she would cry. But she had no tears for the young captain. It seemed to her that he had died a long time ago. It seemed to her too that she had known him a long time. There was something about him that reminded her of George Rowan. Or was it that the night itself reminded her of George? She remembered a night—it was long ago before George had ever thought of falling in love with her—when he and she had ridden home from Sycamore by moonlight. In late summer—it must have been because you could smell new-mown hay in the fields along the road—and a moon so full that every little leaf on the roadside bushes was picked out in silver light.

George had ridden in silence a while, his eyes roving the

fields as if he did not want to miss any of it. Then he turned to her and began reciting:

"On such a night as this . . ."

She laughed to cover her embarrassment but he went on:

" . . . . When the sweet wind did gently woo the trees
And they did make no noise
Troilus, methinks, mounted the Trojan wall
And sighed his soul toward the Grecian tents
Where Cressid lay . . ."

She laughed again—pert child of fifteen—and asked him who Cressid was this summer. He looked at her. His eyes were dark under the shadow of his broad-brimmed hat. There was an expression on his mobile lips she had never seen before. He said gently: "Little Lucy. You don't know anything about that, do you? Well, you will some day . . ."

She got up and walked to the edge of the porch. As she rose she felt the sharp edge of Rives' letter which she had folded and thrust into the bosom of her gown. This one had come yesterday: ". . . I went out reconnoitering this morning and saw the enemy's position. Tomorrow we cross Lookout mountain and will, I suppose, make directly for the Tennessee River. It will be strange to be so near home and yet so far away. I have no expectation of any leave nor would I feel entitled to one at this juncture . . ."

She laid her head down on the railing. Her body shook with sobs so that she had to put her hands out and grasp the wood to steady herself. There were steps in the hall. Susan came out on to the porch. She stood there and sighed, the deep sigh of physical exhaustion. Lucy moved on the bench. Susan heard her and turned.

"Is Captain Linton dead?" she asked in a low voice.

Lucy nodded without raising her head from the railing.

Susan hesitated a moment then came and stood beside her. She put out an awkward hand, touched her shoulder. "Don't cry, child. He's better off."

Lucy raised her head and looked at her mother-in-law out of eyes heavy with unshed tears. She cried out wildly: "I'm not crying for him!" and again as Susan fell back, startled, "I'm not crying for him!"

7

THE horse shambled on through the dust then came to a stop where a post oak threw its shadow across the road. The negro girl stepped up with her stick, then seeing how low he held his head, turned back to Lucy. "We better let him rest a while," she said; "it ain't on the cyards he gwine git to that cane brake."

"All right," Lucy said. She sat down on the bank. The horse, as if knowing that he had been the subject of conversation, moved deeper into the shade. He stood with his head lowered. His hind legs caved in until they almost locked together. Rumblings came from his gaunt belly. Lucy looked at him and looked away. She had come in the last few weeks almost to hate him. He was starving. The Yankees had taken all the corn long ago, of course. There had been pasture in the early summer, but that was gone too, a month ago. This beast—Cousin Susan had found him one day strayed on the road, a great sore half hiding the letters US branded on his hip—this horse and Uncle Mack's mule were the only two work animals on the place now. They had subsisted for weeks on the sparse grass and the clover found in fence corners. Uncle Mack's mule had died a few days ago of blind staggers. There was only this horse left.

She thought of horses she had known long ago. Cholera and Crevasse had been brought to the same pass as this wretched creature. The Yankees had stolen them. They had stayed away for months and then somehow had got back home. Jenny Morris looked out and saw them standing, their heads hanging over the gate. She went screaming into the house: "Mama, two old horses out here." Fontaine Allard went out, looked at the pitiful creatures, then with a glance over his shoulder for spying negroes, said: "Drive these old horses off. No telling what diseases they've got." Uncle Winston had driven them off to the pen in the woods. They had been there for two months, had got fat and sleek again, but had never got over being wary. Cally wrote that they would stand without moving a muscle if any alien step came near, but that they knew Grandpa's and Winston's step and whinnied when they heard them coming.

No, it was Grandma who had written that. Cally, when she wrote, always pretended that Grandpa was the same as ever. But Grandma was kind and wrote more frankly, "I am so glad the horses are back. Your Pa is more like himself when he is fooling with them. . . . That was in the next to the last letter. She had not had any letters from anybody at Brackets now for over a month.

She got up. Molly had shooed the horse on and they moved forward a little faster. They were approaching the swamp and the shade along here was dense. Even the dust of the road was cool. Lucy felt the gritty particles sifting in through the loose fastenings of her brogans. She looked down at her own feet contemptuously. She walked like a field hand and a slew-footed one at that. But it was necessary to fling her foot out each time she raised it. Keeping these brogans on was a task in itself. Uncle Mack had made them for her out of hog-skin when the hogs all died of the cholera. They had all been very excited when the first supply of homemade hides was brought to the house. Uncle Mack had showed great resourcefulness in the tanning. He made a vat by digging a hole in the ground near the spring. The hole was lined with oak boards, the seams caulked with lint cotton to keep the tan-ooze from escaping. Then the long strips of red oak bark had been put in, a layer of bark and then a layer of hide. It took three months but the leather on first inspection was as soft and pliable as any you had bought before the blockade. The swine leather, however, turned out to be too large pored. The shoes started out all right, but after you had worn them a day or two they spread out flat, like the ones she had on.

They had come to the edge of the swamp. The odor of cool, festering vegetation was heavy in the air. The horse smelled it and went forward at an awkward run. Molly let her stick fall. "We'll jest let him go," she said. "He can be filling hisself up whilst we're picking."

She handed Lucy one of the tow sacks she had folded under her arm and the two women began stripping the leaves off the cane and stowing them in the sacks that they had swung from their shoulders. When they had stripped all the cane on the edge they moved farther into the brake, stepping from one tussock to another. Once Lucy made a misstep and her foot slipped into the black slimy water. She took her shoes off after that and went barefoot thinking that in this way her footing would be surer.

Molly was adventurous and penetrated farther and farther into the swamp. Lucy tried to keep up with her but she could not pick as fast. Her great sack was only three-quarters full.

They reached a place where the cane was thick as grass. Molly exclaimed in pleasure. They set to work picking as fast as they could. Molly's sack and the sack they would put on the horse's back were full. She had come to stand near Lucy and was reaching over and putting handfuls of cane into her sack when they heard something moving in the brake. The negro girl began to jump clumsily from one clump of grass to the other. Lucy stood her ground for a few seconds then she followed. On the outside of the brake they stood breathless waiting for the sound to come again.

It did not come, but the negro girl had already started walking rapidly away over the field. Lucy started after her then turned. She could see the road stretching away, a good two miles home. They could not go back without as much fodder as they could carry. They would have to come back soon enough as it was.

She called: "Molly!" The girl paused and stood looking at her. Lucy called again peremptorily. The girl came sullenly and they went back into the swamp. They stood on adjoining tussocks and picked as fast as they could. They did not hear the sound again but they were expecting to hear it any minute. Lucy told herself that it was not a wandering negro or marauding cavalry, only some wild animal or perhaps a horse, strayed just as "Yankee" had been straying when they found him. She told herself that and yet all the time she could feel the Yankee's or the negro's eyes looking out at her from the thicket. She stripped the stalks with nervous, fumbling fingers. Sweat stood on her forehead. She felt faint inside.

Molly gave a grunt of satisfaction. Lucy's sack was full. They made their way out of the brake. In the field Lucy bent to pick up her shoes where she had left them. In the effort to put them on she lost her balance and, struggling to regain it, slipped and fell on her back. She tried to rise but the great sack was stuffed so tight with cane that it would not bend. The negro girl was coming to assist her. Her face had been sullen with fear but a grin broke across it now. Lucy, lying on her back as if strapped to a mattress, her feet kicking in the clumsy shoes, laughed too, not merrily, but grimly, as she fancied a hyena would laugh.

8

GENERAL HILL dismounted at the gate and threw his horse's reins to an orderly. As he went up the walk he looked about him. The path to the little house was neatly kept, edged with broken bottles, and over to the right was a round bed of larkspurs and bleeding hearts. He had noticed that all these mountain cabins had about them some attempt at adornment. The region was not so wild as he had expected to find it.

A woman in black, who was weeding one of the borders in the corner of the yard, rose up suddenly and turned a startled face upon him. The widow, doubtless, to whom the house belonged. The General bowed formally and touched his hat to her before she scuttled around a corner of the house. When the young staff officer behind him laughed he shook his head reprovingly. "I pity these poor people, Faulkner. It is a terrible thing to be invaded by the military."

He went slowly on up the path. He was thinking of the last time he had sat in the yard of a domestic dwelling. It had been a house in the suburbs of Richmond, his host a Mr. Poe, a relative of the poet. They had been sitting there, three or four gentlemen on a hot day, glasses in hand, when President Davis, in a suit of plain gray and attended by a small escort in brilliant uniform galloped up. His Excellency would not get off his horse. He called Hill over to the fence, began speaking, rapidy:

"Rosecrans is about to advance upon Bragg. I have found it necessary to detail Hardee to defend Mississippi. Bragg's old corps is without a commander. I wish you to command it."

Hill was startled. He thought: *"I cannot leave Virginia."*

Aloud he sparred for time. "How can I do that? General Alexander Stewart ranks me."

There was a curious smile on the President's face. "I can cure that by making you a lieutenant-general. Your papers will be ready tomorrow. When can you start?"

That was on the thirteenth of July and on the nineteenth he had reported to General Braxton Bragg, in Chattanooga.

General Bragg! It seemed strange to address his old messmate as "General." He had not seen Braxton since the old days together in Texas. In 1845 that was. He had been the junior lieutenant of Bragg's battery. The other two lieutenants were John Reynolds—and a damned good man he turned out to be—and George Thomas. Reynolds had been killed at Gettysburg. Thomas was Rosecrans' corps commander in the battle which would certainly take place within the next few days. Strange for him to have taken the Yankee side. In the old days he had been the most ardent, the most pronounced Southerner of the lot.

He had arrived at the steps. Two or three officers fell aside to let him pass. He went through the narrow hall and entered the room to the right. It was crowded. The commanding general sat at a small table, writing. McCall, his chief of staff, bent over him. The other commanders, Buckner, Walker, Johnson and Bishop Polk sat in a ring around the table. There were not enough chairs to go around. Half a dozen staff officers were backed up against the wall.

A young officer was bringing a chair. Hill, smiling, indicated that it should be placed next that of General Polk. He sat down. The bishop shook hands with him cordially and included him in the conversation he was having with Buckner. "General, we have been talking of your great brother-in-law, Stonewall Jackson, of his habit of sucking lemons when he wanted to do some hard thinking."

Hill laughed. "Jackson was a man of many idiosyncrasies. I remember once he told me he never ate black pepper; it made his left leg ache."

The bishop laughed too. "I know a man, Colonel Cyrus Sugg, who always goes into battle smoking his pipe. I asked him once if it wasn't inconvenient. He said it would be more inconvenient to be without it. His mind, he says, does not function when there is no tobacco in his system. Well, you yourself are addicted to Lady Nicotine, eh, General Buckner?"

Buckner smiled but only with his lips. On the other side of him Walker and Johnson were conversing in tones that they kept almost too low. There was tension in the atmosphere. Buckner felt it and so did Polk for all his casual talk.

Hill looked at Buckner. The four men sitting there in those chairs would be corps commanders in the battle that impended and two of them had already experienced a perplexing, if not an ignoble defeat. Buckner and Bushrod Johnson had both been in high command at the siege of Fort Donelson. Johnson, he had heard, had conducted himself admirably. Floyd, the senior commander, had undoubtedly been most to blame. He was in a hurry to get away because, being under indictment by the Yankee government, he feared capture. Buckner had behaved better than either Floyd or Pillow. He had at least been willing to assume the command they were in a hurry to get rid of. Hill studied the man's handsome, dogged face. He looked a fighter, every inch of him. Why had he given up the fort? By all accounts a victory had been won, almost a great victory. No telling what turn affairs might have taken if Fort Donelson had been held against the enemy.

Bragg raised his head from the papers he was studying. The young staff officers stood suddenly aside as if to disclose him to the other generals. He had not seen Hill until that moment and he rose at once, came forward and shook hands. Hill was about to make some reference to their young days together but something in Braxton's expression deterred him. He took his seat silently. Bragg was bending over his papers again.

Hill's eyes were held by the gloomy face. A foreboding ran through him. This was the man whose appointment to command had sent the South wild with hope. Well, Bragg's invasion of Kentucky had been a failure. He had not been able to drive Buell from the country. Worse than that he had allowed him to take possession of Louisville where he could draw on the northwest for both men and supplies. The battle of Stone's River had been a barren victory. Bragg's retreat after the battle, his subsequent falling back to Chattanooga had seemed, when viewed from Richmond, the advisable, the military procedure. "Chattanooga," as he had informed the war office in many dispatches, "was the natural stronghold and storehouse of the South." But Bragg had not been able to hold Chattanooga. Rosecrans had cleverly manœuvered him out of the town and now here he was with his army strung out all the way from here to Lafayette, Georgia.

It would not be so bad if you only knew what Rosecrans was doing. But there was a depressing lack of information at Bragg's headquarters. He had no well-organized system of independent scouts such as Lee had. For information in regard to the enemy he evidently trusted alone to his efficient cavalry. The failure to attack Negley's division in the cove on September 10th had been due to his ignorance of the position of the enemy. He attributed the failure to attack on the eleventh to Hindman, but it was possible that Hindman knew his commander and realized that Bragg did not really intend him to attack. All day on the eleventh Hill's own signal corps and scouts had reported the march of a heavy column to the left and up the cove, but Bragg would not credit the reports.

He remembered something that Bragg had said to him when they first met—after fifteen years separation—in Chattanooga earlier in the summer. "They say it's easy to defend a mountainous country, but give me fighting in the open every time. A mountain is like a wall full of rats. They lie at the holes and pop out when you are not watching. Who can tell what lies behind that wall?" And he had pointed to the blue Cumberland range across the river.

His lack of information about the enemy's movements had kept him in a nightmare of indecision for a week now. Well, he seemed to have come to a decision at last. He was on his feet. His dark eyes that always looked too large for his gaunt head, went for a second from face to face as if he were asking himself whether the man before him were friend or enemy. "The plan of battle," he said impressively and began to read in a jerky, excited voice.

"1. (Bushrod) Johnson's column (Hood's), on crossing at or near Reed's Bridge, will turn to the left by the most practicable route, and sweep up the Chickamauga toward Lee and Gordon's Mills.

"2. Walker, crossing at Alexander's Bridge, will unite in this move and push vigorously on the enemy's flank and rear in the same direction.

"3. Buckner, crossing at Tedford's Ford, will join in the movement to the left, and press the enemy up the stream from Polk's front at Lee and Gordon's.

"4. Polk will press his forces to the front of Lee and Gordon's Mills, and if met by too much resistance to cross will bear to the right and cross at Dalton's Ford or at Tedford's, as may be necessary, and join the attack wherever the enemy may be.

"5. Hill will cover our left flank from an advance of the enemy from the cove, and, by pressing the cavalry in his front, ascertain if the enemy is reenforcing at Lee and Gordon's Mills, in which event he will attack them in flank.

"6. Wheeler's cavalry will hold the gaps in Pigeon Mountain, and cover our rear and left, and bring up stragglers.

"7. All teams, etc., not with troops should go toward Ringgold and Dalton beyond Taylor's Ridge. All cooking should be done at the trains; rations when cooked will be forwarded to the troops.

"8. The above movements will be executed with the utmost promptness, vigor and persistence."

The aides came forward, put a copy of the battle order before each commander. They studied it in silence. Bragg, leaning back in his chair, tapped on the table with a pencil, spoke finally:

"General Hill, what do you think of it?"

"Admirable—and practicable," Hill said slowly. He was thinking that if this order had been issued on any of the four preceding days it might have found Rosecrans wholly unprepared. Now there was no telling.

The same thought was evidently in Buckner's mind. He said: "All right, provided the enemy doesn't get in our rear."

Bragg eyed him coldly. "Have you any reason to believe that the enemy is in our rear?"

Buckner was looking at Hill. Hill spoke up. "General Buckner is referring, I think, to reports received by my signal corps."

Buckner nodded. "Lieutenant Baylor reported three nights ago that McCook was encamped at Alpine."

Bragg was enraged. "Lieutenant Baylor lies!" he cried excitedly. "There is not an infantry soldier of the enemy anywhere to the south of us."

Buckner stared at him, then shrugged his broad shoulders. "Perhaps Lieutenant Baylor is mistaken," he said finally. "At any rate I see nothing for it but to attack."

Bishop Polk was on his feet, evidently anxious to quit the conference as soon as possible. "General Buckner is quite right. An engagement is called for." He advanced to Bragg, extended his hand. "An admirable plan, General. I feel convinced of victory. . . . When does General Longstreet arrive?"

"Tomorrow night," Bragg said.

They were all rising. Walker lingered to ask the commanding general some question. The others, handshakes exchanged, were filing out on to the porch. Hill found himself moving down the walk beside Bishop Polk.

The "fighting bishop" gave a long sigh then turned to Hill. "The temper of the troops has demanded a battle for some time now. General Bragg is quite right, in my opinion, to precipitate the engagement."

Hill did not answer. He was thinking of Sharpsburg. The bitterness of death had passed with him long ago, even before the great reverses. Yet it seemed strange that a man could live through that and fight again. He concentrated his gaze on the scene in front of him: a wooded slope reaching down to a little river. Those wooded slopes stretched for miles around to form the great shallow basin of the Chickamauga. An arena, as Sharpsburg had been, only it was dark woods instead of fields of grain.

They had reached the gate. The water of the river could be seen glinting through the black tree trunks. The bishop waved his hand. "Beautiful country, General. It once belonged to the Cherokees. There is a legend that they made their last stand here in this valley."

Hill inclined his head courteously. "Indeed? Chickamauga, I presume, is an Indian name."

The bishop was gathering up his reins. "Yes, it means the 'river of blood.' "

9

HENRY DUNBAR was thirteen years old on the nineteenth of September, 1863. On the night before his birthday he slept as usual in the loft of his father's cabin on the banks of Chicamauga Creek. Toward dawn he was aroused by his mother's shrill cry:

"Hen*ree!* Batter bread!"

Henry rolled over in bed, stretched, opened one eye and gazed at the rafters. He knew that it took batter bread twenty minutes to bake. He knew also from long experience that it would take him all but two of those twenty minutes to milk the three cows waiting for him in the stable lot. But this morning he would have a helper. His cousin, Bud, from over on Long Branch, was spending the night. Bud expected to share in the pleasures of the day; he couldn't in decency refuse to help milk. Henry made another swift calculation, rolled over on his side and went back to sleep.

A few minutes later the call came again. Years ago Mrs. Dunbar had called, "Batter bread's in the oven." Now she simply shrieked the word "Bread!" as she passed from back porch to kitchen.

Henry, subconsciously on the alert, heard her. He got up, this time without stretching, drew on his pants. As he started for the ladder he passed the cot where Bud lay swathed in quilts like a cocoon. Bud's big toe was protruding from the quilts. Henry leaned over, swiftly gave it a vicious jerk. "Ain't you going to help me milk?" he called plaintively from the head of the ladder.

Bud gave no answer save a groan, but the question lingered in the air, brought him finally upright in bed. "Hey?" he muttered, then seeing Henry's pallet empty he got up, dressed, and after a dash at the washbasin on the back porch went out to the cow-pen. His mind, too, was busy with arithmetical calculation. It was ten miles to Porter's Ford where the boys intended to spend the day fishing, and there was only one horse. Be just like Henry to make him walk if he didn't help milk.

In the cow-pen Henry squatted on his haunches. His head was nudged into Old Bell's ample flank. His lean, dirty hands moving rhythmically brought the milk down in an even white flow into the bucket. Bud, rubbing his eyes and yawning, looked at the cow next to Bell. A little, hardly grown heifer with a bag that he mentally likened to a dried apple. It occurred to him that a person looking at the little old dried-up thing couldn't tell whether she'd been milked or not. He looked away. "Want me to let down the bars?" he asked with false geniality.

Henry turned his head so that one irate eye had Bud in its field of vision. He met deceit with sarcasm. "That's right," he ejaculated. "Let the bars down. Git 'em all stompeded before I'm through milking. . . ." He broke off, realizing that he did not have an audience.

Bud, unruly for once, had already started to the corner of the lot where movable bars served as a rude gate. His hand was on the top bar. He had slid it back and was about to lay it on the ground when he stopped and stood erect, his hand cupped to his ear in a gesture which Henry considered ludicrously imitative of a grown person.

Henry picked his bucket up, squatted down beside the cow he had hoped to get out of milking. "What's the matter?" he enquired as he dug his head into her flank. "Hear the sap running?"

Bud did not answer. The bar had fallen from his hand. He stepped around it and going out into the road, disappeared behind some bushes. The next minute he was coming back around the clump of sumac, on the dead run. "Soldiers!" he gasped. "Millions of 'em!"

Henry upset his milk bucket, rising, but he reached the fence at the same time Bud did. They hung there, staring as the noise emerged from the mist.

A big man rode first on a gray horse. He looked queer to be at the head of such a parade. Black hair curled stiffly to his coat collar from under a black slouch hat. A linen duster, such as Henry's father wore to protect his Sunday clothes on long rides, was buttoned under his chin. The boys' eyes passed swiftly over him. It was the man riding next who roused their astonishment, a great hawk with swinging beard who balanced ponderously in his saddle and beyond him a burly, fair man who rode with his legs dangling out of the stirrups.

Behind these leaders rode four or five hundred men. The boys' eyes slid over the long line, trying to pick out a face. They would have whispered to each other if they could have found breath. They would have said: these men are not soldiers. Both Henry and Bud had seen bodies of armed men. A regiment had come marching down the road through the dust a week ago, had broken ranks at the gate to spill over into the yard and to drink the cistern dry. One of them had gibed at little Laura Belle, staring from the doorway: "Yes, ma'am, I'm a Yankee and I eat little children. Gal babies mostly, fried." Somebody had yelled to him then, "Come on here, you fool," and he had scurried off over the yard, turning to make the immemorial gesture of greasing the head, pinning the ears back, swallowing whole. . . . And there had been the impressive figure on the Widow Glenn's front gallery just a few days ago. Stout legs in fine blue cloth were stretched out beneath the newspaper he was reading, and when he laid the paper down to stare off into the woods gold braid had showed, gold straps on his shoulders and splendid twisted snakes on his sleeves. "The head Yankee general," their cousin Roswell had whispered before he pattered off down the road.

But these men, moving secretly through the woods, were not soldiers. They were hunters, hunters who had chased the same quarry so long that they had come, all of them, to look alike. Their horses, bay, roan, chesnut were all plastered dun color with mud, all kept the same gait. The men, boys of nineteen or burly majors, had the rigid slouch of the seasoned horseman. In their drawn, impassive faces only the eyes managed to be alert.

A pair of those eyes, flat and black in a yellow face, seemed to be fixed on Henry now. Something squirmed coldly in the pit of his stomach. He put his hand down, softly felt the cool, hard rail that was between him and the cavalcade. But the eyes had moved on, were fixed on a point to the left of his shoulder. Henry staring into them saw a spark of light grow in the flat pupil. The man leaned over, said something to a comrade, who immediately turned a sharp face, muttered. But it was as if they had spoken to the horses, not each other. All along the line gaunt heads came up, tails flirted. They were suddenly moving down the road in a swinging trot.

The last one had come up, a skeleton roan with silver mane. As the boys watched, his lean, burred tail rose, stretched out horizontally long enough to let three or four balls of manure drop down into the road. Then he, too, vanished into the cloud of dust.

The boys looked at each other, sighed, slipped down from the fence. Bud was turning back toward the milking place but Henry had run around through the down pasture bars and was in the road and after a second Bud cautiously followed him.

In the road the globes of manure lay, a greenish, disconnected snake that trailed through the dust. Henry put out his toe, poked one of the globes slyly. It was warm.

"Them old horses," he said mechanically, "been on grass too long."

He raised his face. There was a look on it with which Bud was familiar. That look had carried them into Bell's Cave, past the buzzard droppings, past the dark branch, a mile farther than anybody else had ever gone. "Come on," he said curtly.

They were off, pounding down the road almost as hard as the horses that had gone before them, raising, Henry thought proudly, almost as much dust. At the crest of the hill he veered, made for a wooded knob that swelled up suddenly at the side of the road. Bud scrambled up behind him. They dropped to the ground and lay panting, their eyes fixed on the road.

The cavalcade was still in sight. They had had to slow up for the hill and were moving slowly down the slope toward the ford. Henry and Bud could see beyond the black line of the creek the old sawmill, sedate in its hollow, the maple boughs making a scarlet lacework against its crumbling walls. The horsemen must be making for that. They would rest there, stable their horses. . . .

Henry was on his knees suddenly, his thin hand scrunching Bud's arm. "Hey," he breathed. "Look!"

The gray walls of the old mill were obscured by a cloud of black, hurrying figures. They rose up from behind, rushed out from inside, were suddenly everywhere, a monster swarm of bees that clouded the slope and hummed angrily.

The boys stared, then their eyes went to the road. The horsemen were behaving oddly, leaping off their horses to vanish into the woods on either side. Some of them as they leapt threw their bridles to others and these men, holding eight or ten bridles at a time hurriedly began shepherding the horses back up the road.

Shots began to ring out. The boys could see the cavalrymen moving up and down the slope or crouching behind trees to fire steadily. One of them was coming around the side of the knob. He wore a ragged straw hat and a canteen was slung over his shoulder. The upper part of his face was severe, expressionless, but his lips grinned away from yellow, parted teeth. He dropped to his knees behind the white trunk of a sycamore, rested the butt of his rifle on the ground while he drew out the ramrod. He had the cartridge paper in his mouth, was biting the end off when he heard Bud chattering in the grass like a doomed rabbit. His eyes looked amazedly into theirs for a second, then the lips drew away on each side of the greasy paper and one hand left the rifle, came up, thumb pointing imperiously over the shoulder.

The next moment he flung the gun from him and plunged forward. The hand that had been pointing dug into the ground, clutched and dug again. His body twisted around. The boys saw the dark, spreading bullet hole, and then he was on his feet, coming toward them. Blood trilled from his mouth and sprayed out on to his dusty front. He cried "Ulll!" and pitched forward on his face.

Henry sank his wiry fingers into Bud's shoulder, hauled him to his feet. They were over the side of the knob, pelting down through the dead leaves and brambles. It seemed a long time before their bare feet struck the cool dust of the road.

10

GENERAL BRECKINRIDGE stirred the sugar in the tin cup, tilted his head so that the last drops of coffee could run down his throat. His eyes were on the retreating back of the negro servant but he spoke to the young aide who had just come up to the fire. "That's a valuable man of yours, Rowan. Want to sell him?"

George Rowan smiled. "No, sir," he said respectfully and took advantage of the brief interchange to let his eyes rest on the General, taking in every detail of his appearance.

Breckinridge sat on a fallen log, leaning a little backwards so that he could stretch out his legs to the flames. His breeches were soaked to the knee with dew—he had been riding about through the undergrowth since early dawn—but above the waist he presented his usual, trim soldierly appearance, dark butternut blouse buttoned to the chin, his long moustaches sprightly, and the eyes in the swarthy face as bright and glancing as a squirrel's in a thicket. He turned back to General Deshler who stood on the other side of the fire, resumed his animated discussion of yesterday's fight.

"They were on the run then. Right after we drove Negley off. In my opinion that would have been the time to attack the right."

Deshler nodded. "At Lee and Gordon's Mills," he said thoughtfully. "You and Cleburne could have flanked them out of there in no time."

Breckinridge's remarkable eyes flashed assent. "The two handsomest, most soldierly-looking men in the army." George, watching the two, mentally added the words to the letter that reposed at that moment in his pocket. Since one of his letters had been published in the *Tobacco-Leaf* he wrote home often, now to this member of the family, now to that. The letters, which would be carefully preserved, contained in molded phrases his impressions of the great whom he had seen since he had become Deshler's aide. "Vignettes" he had come to call them: "Longstreet . . . has a broad face that at first glance seems dull, with elephant eyes. They say it takes three rounds of cannon to get him steamed up. . . . D. H. Hill, not so impressive as his great brother-in-law,* but soldier all through. . . . Cleburne, pugnosed, fiery yet kindly eyes, true Irish, one of the best tacticians in the army. . . ." He smiled, thinking of a phrase he had written in last night's letter about "one who threatens to become great also. They all say Zack makes the best coffee of any nigger in camp. I am afraid he is growing too big for his breeches. He says tell you all he is taking good care of me but we lives like jack rabbits out in the bushes. . . ."

General Breckinridge got to his feet and straightening his shoulders walked over to where an orderly was holding his horse. General Deshler still sat beside the fire. He had been gay enough a few minutes ago, laughing and joking with the young officers as was his custom, but his attitude now was that of a man engaged in deep thought. George, awed by his stern expression, suddenly recalled that this was his chief's first engagement as a general officer. He got up, walked off a little way through the trees.

As he went his mind was busy with more phrases that he would put in his next letter. " 'This morning,' yesterday morning it would be by the time he got a chance to write a letter, 'your humble servant was sitting around the fire in the company of four generals' . . ." Yes, Cleburne had been there too when Hill rode up. Hill's face was lined with fatigue, his scrubby beard hung in stiffened wisps. His deep-set eyes lightened when he caught sight of Breckinridge and Cleburne by the fire. He called out almost angrily that he had ridden half the night, that there

* Stonewall Jackson.

had been no couriers at the bridge to which he had been directed. Did either of them know where in the name of the Almighty the commanding general had moved his headquarters to? Captain Wheless had come up just then with the message. General Hill thought the order was for him and he put out his hand, but the courier said: "These orders are for General Breckinridge and General Cleburne." Breckinridge had read his order, then handed it to Hill. Hill read it, pulling savagely at his beard. "They can't go in now," he said, "there's been no proper reconnaissance made." He raised his head, glared at the other two. "Those lines will have to be adjusted. Cheatham's whole division is at right angles to my line now."

Breckinridge nodded. "My wagon trains aren't up yet," he said in his deep voice. "Some of my men haven't eaten in forty-eight hours."

George wished he could remember what else Hill had said before he swung up into his saddle, but the words of the great, he reflected, were surprisingly like those of ordinary mortals in the moment of utterance. Anyhow, the battle which had seemed imminent would be delayed for another half-hour or so. Unless the enemy made another surprise attack. They could not be far off. You could hear them felling trees for fortifications all night.

He had advanced to a place where the sound of axes was as sharp, as insistent as the chatter of squirrels. He stood very still and looked through the aisles of the trees. They said that an Indian tribe had waged its last desperate battle here and had given the river its name. Well, these woods, sombre even in autumn, looked as if they would always harbor an enemy. It was only strange that he remained so long hidden.

He stooped, picked up a stick and threw it at a squirrel. His mind left the impending conflict, went back to yesterday afternoon when he had seen his cousin, Rives Allard, for the first time in two years. He had been standing at the counter of a country store there by the bridge when somebody had called out, "Hey! Orderly out here looking for Lieutenant Rowan." He had gone out expecting a message from a member of Deshler's staff and there was Rives on a little bony yellow mare. He was on his way to Reed's bridge, he said, but had heard somebody say "Tenth Texas" and stopped. He had not even known that George was with the Tenth Texas until the week before when somebody at home had written him the news.

"Well, it's a damned good regiment," George said.

He had thought as they stood there grinning at each other that it was strange how things fell out. He and Rives and Ned Allard had all set out from the same camp and here he and Ned were under Deshler, and Rives with Forrest. He had enquired tactfully if Rives had had a promotion and Rives had replied, still grinning, that it looked as if he would stay an orderly for the duration of the war. George knew what that meant. Those fellows, the men down on the lists as "orderlies," were old Forrest's hand-picked scouts. One of their best tricks was deserting to the Federal lines with fake information. Rives, he had heard, had done that at Murfreesboro and would have paid with his neck if Forrest hadn't captured the town that same night.

Well, they were a dangerous lot, bold as the devil. They said old Forrest himself carried a sabre big enough for any two men and ground against all military regulations to a razor edge. A man in the Tenth had seen him whirl it in both hands and slice off a Yankee's head as if he'd been a gobbler on a block. Captain Bill Forrest, his brother, was no better than a guerrilla. They called his men "The Forty Thieves." The younger brother, Jeffrey, was said to have something of the manner of a gentleman. God knows where he had got it. Old Forrest himself had been a nigger trader before the war. . . . Well, Rives Allard had always been a queer cuss. It was only natural that he should land in a queer branch of the service. For it was a queer way of fighting. Some men's families thought they had been killed in action when they had met ignominious deaths. He had heard dark stories. They had bungled the hanging of the boy spy, David Dodds, so that he had been choked to death. Two men in line had fainted at the sight, and the Yankee officer in charge of the execution had wept. A man's country had the right to demand his life but had she the right to demand more—to demand that he be dishonored in death? He didn't know that he would have the stomach for it and yet—he suddenly saw himself as he must appear to his comrades—he was accounted a brave man.

He raised his head. "I am willing to give my life for my country," he said proudly. The words spoken in the quiet woods rang a little theatrically on his ear yet evoked a sudden, immediate sense of beauty. He recalled fox-hunting nights when still fresh at dawn he had ridden home through wet woods, recalled other softer nights. That peculiar, excited feeling that came when he was on the verge of making a conquest that most people would have said even he couldn't make. Love itself never had a moment to match that feeling. The last night riding home from Brackets with Lucy Churchill. . . . It was the first time a woman had ever refused him. And yet though he was in love with Lucy at the moment he had not suffered. It was as if he knew that he was soon to be caught up into greater affairs. . . .

Off to the right a bugle fluted silverly. *Ta-Ta-Ta-Ta!* There was the sound of trampling feet. He realized that he had been away five or ten minutes. As he ran back to the camp fire he was thinking that after the war was over and he had leisure he might collect his impressions into a book. "In Tent and Saddle" might do for a title or perhaps "Bugle and Bayonet" would be better. He might even look up the Indian legend, put in something about "the bloody river."

11

THE last wagon had lumbered up and the men had all got their ration of cooked beef and cold pone. They ate standing, in an irregular battle line. Some of them occupied the same ground on which they had slept last night. It was littered with empty cartridge boxes, belt buckles, playing cards, here and there a rifle that had not been gathered up. The fighting had been hot in this part of the field. There were other souvenirs of battle. The stiffened body of a fair-haired, blue-coated farm boy lay at the foot of a mound just back of the lines, and another dead Yankee was propped up against a tree a hundred yards away, his gun resting across his knees.

One of the men, still chewing, stepped out of line and absent-mindedly but expertly rifled the dead boy's pockets. They yielded nothing but a piece of string and he got to his feet with a shake of the head for his own foolishness. As he stepped back to his place he gave a glance at the other dead Yankee.

"That feller must be tired sitting down and here we been standing in line since daybreak."

The man next to him did not answer. He had long ago wolfed down his bread and meat and stood gazing straight ahead. You could not see far. A curious red fog enveloped all the trees and the smell of gunpowder was still in the air. The men, rising before daybreak, had expected to go straight into battle. Indeed it had seemed to them, moving in this red fog with the foul smoke thick in their nostrils, that they had only lain down long enough to rest between fights. But that had been several hours ago and the battle had not yet begun.

There were rumors afloat. General Bragg in a plain uniform had been seen galloping back of the lines an hour ago. It was said that he had gone to see why the battle had not begun, as he had ordered, at dawn. That was the interpretation some put on it. Others whispered that the plans for the battle had all gone wrong. The enemy had made a night march and had got in the rear. Two men were talking in undertones of these matters when the would-be looter stepped back into line. One of them as he talked kept his eyes fixed on a knot of officers a few feet away. The big man on the bay horse was his own colonel. The other, more impressive figure that had just galloped up he surmised to be General Breckinridge himself. He cut short his companion's complainings with a finger jerked over his shoulder and a laconic: "Well, looks like they going to do something now."

A moment later the captain of the company was in front of the line waving his sword and shouting, "Move forward, men!" The lieutenants bustled about, straightening the line with parrot cries of "Dress on the right. Dress on the right!"

The regiment on the instant was transformed. Men straightened up, gripped their rifles, went forward at a quick march. Eyes that had been vacant and staring glinted in grimy faces as stepping faster and faster they looked down the line, saw the whole division unroll like mist moving over a field.

They had progressed not a hundred yards into the woods when the command came to double-quick. A fool race it seemed, jumping over stumps and gullies and crashing through brambles and all the time no enemy in sight.

They came to a little glade, a pretty spot where in a happier time a man might have stopped to rest. Much clearing had gone on here and only the nobler trees were left. The space between them was filled with blackberry thickets. In the deep shade the leaves were still green. A lank Tennesseean, an inveterate blackberry straggler, saw a bunch of late berries hanging heavily, put out his hand as he ran and was cramming some into his mouth when the ground at his feet suddenly dislodged itself and broke into a million flying particles.

The blackberries fell from the man's hand. He stood, staring. Figures that a moment before had been running now lay on the ground in a variety of attitudes, as if a hand carelessly shuffling a deck of cards had splayed them out upon a table. Some were perfectly quiet, some ceaselessly contorted their bodies and moaned. One man who had had his leg taken off at the knee lay and with bright, intelligent eyes regarded two officers who came riding upon the scene.

These officers, a captain and his colonel, rode slowly and with apparent indifference among the bodies of the dead and dying. The colonel was looking at the Yankee barricade, a stout line of breastworks crowning a low ridge, clearly visible now through the eddying smoke.

"Pretty well fixed up there," he said.

The captain's eyes were as bright, as intent as those of the dying man at his feet. "Send 'em right up, sir?" he asked cheerfully.

The colonel nodded and the captain rode in among the men and suddenly was bellowing. "All right, boys. Straight ahead now! Get into 'em!"

Men who had been looking at one another as if wondering what to do next bent their heads this way and that. There was hesitation, a slight surging backwards then loud, indignant voices were heard. A handful of men broke from the ranks and rushed forward. Others followed. Soon the whole line was in motion up the slope.

The Yankees greeted them with a storm of bullets. Some men fell under it, others dodged to the rear but most of them came on. One big corporal, running lightly ahead of the whole line, kept his head up like a man who finds exposure to the elements bracing and fired wildly into the air. They had reached the crest, were almost up to the breastworks. All along the Yankee line men were standing up or leaping on top of rails to fire down into blind, uplifted faces. One man who sat firing easily and steadily until the Confederates were upon him suddenly threw his rifle aside and quivering as if with rage hurled himself fifty feet down the slope.

The big corporal, still in the forefront, looked over his shoulder, saw his colors fluttering behind him. He lifted the standard from the bearer, bent over, and with clumsy intentness drove it into the interstices between two rails. He had straightened up, was looking about as if uncertain what to do next when a Yankee bashed his head in with a clubbed musket.

There had been all this time a demoniac yelling that rose even above the screech of shells. The young captain had not realized that it came from his own men until it ceased suddenly. He looked about, saw that they were falling back, some men doggedly, others making for the rear at top speed. His mouth opened to roar at them, then almost as if without his volition it closed. He stood perfectly still in the midst of flying, cursing men, his eyes seeming to be fixed on a tall tree of beautiful proportions that crowned the opposite hill. Suddenly he was flying down the slope as fast as any of his men. They were eddying about a big oak tree. He rushed in among them, slashing with his sword, howling, "You got to get back up that hill. Want to stay here and be mown down by canister?"

The men dodged backwards and forwards, melted away before him, sought the shelter of another tree. Two officers at the rear saw what he was about, bore down, grimacing and cursing. The men milled for a moment, then started up again. The first advance had been simultaneous, a wave of men that rolled up the slope. Now as they advanced more slowly individual posture and mental attitude was revealed. Some moved crouching like dogs that beaten know there is no turning back. Others as they went hitched up their pants, tightened their belts, futile gestures that served only to show that they washed their hands of the affair. Here and there was to be seen the wry grimace, the sightless eye of a man who knew that in an instant he would be killed.

They went up slowly, reached the height again. Dead Yankees lay thick but others had sprung up to take their places. The newcomers fired with ease and fury, running out, some of them, beyond the breastworks and down the slope.

The Confederates doggedly sustained the fire and were pushing on when a battery was seen just moving into position where the ridge turned. The arrogant gunners leaped from the still bouncing carriages, slid to their places and began sending round after round of grape into the surging mass of besiegers. Men fell thickly. Those who were left turned and ran at top speed for the foot of the slope. They passed the oak where they had been rallied for the second charge, pushed pell-mell through briar thickets and undergrowth to fall sobbing with exhaustion on the ground.

The captain was there, leaning against a tree, drawing rasping breaths. As the men rolled apprehensive eyes toward him he jerked himself to his feet, went forward to salute the colonel who just then galloped up. Those men who were lying near heard the colloquy between the two, heard the young captain sob out disgustedly the colonel's order:

"General Hill says to hold this position and await fresh troops."

12

GENERAL DESHLER'S heart, and the ribs that so stoutly enclosed it, were torn from his body by a shell that came ripping out of the woods at noon. George Rowan was with him when it happened.

The Tenth Texas arrived on the ground they were to occupy at ten o'clock. It was a wooded ridge two hundred yards from the Yankee breastworks. Colonel Mills had dismounted and was running alongside of his men when they came up to the crest. Semple's battery at the left of the ridge was still firing then. Mills swore savagely when he saw the gunners limber up and lash their horses to ride away.

"They want us to hold it without artillery, boys. Well, we God damn will!"

A shell bursting ten feet below threw up a black geyser that covered him from his men's sight. He emerged, wiping his face free of cinders and ordered the men to fall back a little and fire lying down. Then he went down the hill, still swearing, to see if he could get Douglas' battery up.

The Yankee fire got hotter instead of decreasing. The ridge was just within range of canister. But the grape was the worst. Under it men dodged backward and forward like jack-in-the boxes, or plastered themselves to the hill so tight that only the upward reaching of the arm told the living from the dead. Toward noon the Texans' supply of ammunition ran low. George was lying behind a stump trying to pick off a Yankee gunner when he felt a hand on his shoulder, and Mills told him to go find General Deshler and tell him the ammunition was giving out.

George plunged down the hillside through a cloud of hot smoke just in time to see his little mare break her tether and go snorting off. He cut a horse loose from a captured gun, mounted, and using part of a rope trace as his riding whip rode off in search of Deshler.

The young brigadier was sitting his horse beside a clump of sumac bushes. Two of his staff officers were with him. Hearne was telling the General that the place was too exposed, when Rowan rode up. Deshler kept his eyes fixed on the ridge as Rowan was giving the message. It was perhaps the sight of a man who suddenly fell sidewise from behind a stump, spread-eagling as he fell that decided him not to ask a staff officer to risk his life up there. He had half turned to Hearne when he shook his head and murmuring something—George thought it was "Can't send that boy"—rode off at a gallop.

He went so fast that George on his winded horse had trouble in keeping up with him. It was hotter now than it had been a few minutes ago. And Mills did not seem to be in the place where he had left him. Or was it that the place itself had changed, with the black geysers springing up everywhere, keeping the very ground under your feet in motion? The fire and brimstone Aunt Charlotte's preacher talked so much about, he thought, and he dodged his horse desperately through the smoke, trying not to lose sight of Deshler.

Deshler's big back was just in front of him when the shell struck the oak a few feet away. George's horse danced and George swayed involuntarily far to the right. When he came up Deshler was out of the saddle and flat on the ground. George looked down, saw the red sponge that had been Deshler's chest. He got off his horse, put his hands to his face and cried out. It seemed a long time before men came running with stretchers.

Mills was standing there as they carried Deshler's body off. He would not look. His face was black as a fiend's with powder and he kept shouting to men who were so far up the hill that they could not hear him. "Ammunition out? Get up and bay'net 'em then!"

Rowan tethered his horse to a sapling and followed Mills back into the fight. The men were down to their last round now. George ran about over the field gathering up cartridge boxes from the dead and wounded. He had just taken a pistol from a dead Yankee when he heard his own name called. He looked up and saw Ned Allard in a hand-to-hand struggle with a Yankee. George ran a few steps forward then stopped. He passed a hand before his forehead to clear his sight. Ned's arm was locked around the Yankee's body but above that arm George could see blue cloth. He levelled the pistol barrel, took careful aim. The hammer clicked. George threw the pistol away and ran on. He was within a few feet of the combatants when a bullet from a sharpshooter's rifle hit him. He fell, then after a second got up and staggered forward. The Yankee soldier had hit Ned over the head with the butt of his musket and was dragging him off the field. Ed Johnson coming up saw only George staggering and ran forward to help him. George, who was suffering no pain, saw no sense to that and resisted, but he was suddenly unable to see and collapsed against his helper's shoulder. When he came to himself he was being carried on a stretcher through a grove of scrub oaks. They passed Mills, who was still roaring.

One of the bearers stumbled over a rock. The stretcher tilted forward. Mills' red face, with the mouth stretched to an O under the straggling moustache, was for a moment within George's field of vision. It seemed to him somehow not so red but he thought that was the smoke. He had forgotten about Ned. He did not know that he was dying. He was thinking of the captaincy that would be his tomorrow when he looked at his colonel and smiled before he was borne from the field.

13

RIVES rode to General Ector with a message at ten o'clock. When he got back they had dismounted Armstrong's men and were sending them in. He sat under a sycamore tree behind the lines and watched them stream past, a jostling mass of swinging arms and legs, faces that turned to grin, emit messages: "Tell him I'll see him at sundown. . . Where's Bill? . . . Tell him I was looking . . ." A tall Tennesseean had gone waving his hat over his head and whooping: "Well, boys, we'll all meet at the hatter's!" *

Major Anderson had told Rives to wait under this tree so that he could be found if wanted. Messages had been going back and forth all morning, mostly to General Ector who had been uneasy first about his right, then his left flank. Old Bedford had reared up on his hind legs when Rives came sweating up with the last message. "Tell General Ector that by God I am here and will take care of both his flanks." A private running by, hearing words not in his own vocabulary, had rolled white eyes admiringly over his shoulder.

Rives recalled the obscene phrase, grinned, turned his eyes to the front. The fog had come back, settled under the trees. The shells burst through it like something blooming. Armstrong's men must be catching hell, but from here you couldn't see a one of them. The battle existed only as sound. Riding back of the lines a while ago he had got his ears a little free of it. Now he knew what the sound was—planks that kept clattering down continually from some great height.

Armstrong's men had gone in far to the right, but they must

* Reference to a pioneer story, a dialogue between two coons pursued by hounds.

have worked over. They were bringing the wounded back on stretchers along this path. One man, strangely cocky, with his dead white face, had something red sticking out of his side. He waved his hand, shouted "Boys, when I left we were driving 'em," then collapsed on the canvas.

The bushes to the right parted. More wounded men taking the short-cut to the spring. The one coming now was on hands and knees, tongue lolling, a crawling dog with hanging what's-its-name. Rives got impatiently off his horse, went over and put his canteen to the lips that were freckled with little white blisters. The man drank with greedy, sucking noises then slithered over on his back. His features swam grayly with fatigue then his mouth puckered. He might have been going to cry, but produced instead a smile for his own astuteness. "You're Allard," he wheezed and when Rives nodded. "Your—pardner out there. . . . Better get him."

Rives dragged the man off the path into the bushes, went back to his mare. As he pulled a limb down, slip-noosed the bridle, he was thinking that she could stand or not just as she pleased. He knew whom the man meant: the scout, Ben Bigstaff. Ben had gone in at ten o'clock with Armstrong's men. He had known earlier in the day that he was going to be put in the line and had fumed while he cooked breakfast. "I don't like this close work." The corners of his mouth were pinched. There had been a beading of perspiration on his forehead as he looked up, skillet in hand.

The mist eddied, revealed a man crouching behind a tree firing steadily. Rives went up behind him. "You seen Ben Bigstaff?" The man drew his sleeve over his black face. "Damned hot in here," he said. "Naw, I ain't seen nothing but this." And he patted his rifle slyly and was crouching again.

Rives ran on. He was talking to himself. They had trained Ben Bigstaff, just as you train a bird dog or a beagle. Sent him out night after night to creep up on men in the dark, shoot them down. Ben had learned all that business but he had been as clean about it, as kindly as a seasoned hunter. He would shoot a picket down in a flash but he would wait five or ten minutes, then crawl back to see if the man was dead. He himself, Rives knew, had always expected to go like that, picked off from behind a tree or shot down in some lonely field. But to be sent in, one of a squirming mass, to be mowed down by grape . . .

It was not grape that had killed Ben. He knew that as soon as he passed the next tree, came to the blackened hole in the ground. The shell had killed two men as it burst and in the same instant had dug one grave for them. There were two heads protruding over the edge of the crater. One would have been bald if shining, black particles had not been grained everywhere into the skin.

Ben lay on his back, one hand upflung. Blood oozed from the corner of his mouth, but except for that his face had a wise, kindly expression. Rives' eyes slid away, went to the man underneath. Matted, auburn hair on a ridged skull. An Alabaman they called Sloppy Jim. A thief and so dirty and lousy besides that nobody would mess with him. One hand was dug into Ben's side. Strange to see the fingers clutching as if the man had died of a gunshot wound. He stooped and with one hand on Ben's shoulder was about to turn the body over when he saw grimed into the pit the tangle of blackened skin, loose flesh, bloody bones.

He sank back on his heels, retched, then came slowly forward again. He raised his eyes, glared at the trees whose foliage was veiled in dull smoke. These men whose flesh was so inextricably mingled must rest in the same grave. The planks had ceased clattering down from the height but there was a high wind keening in his head. *"Judgment Day . . . Till Judgment Day . . ." Judge!"* he screamed, and, leaning forward, grinning, tore with his nails at the shining dirt until it sprayed in a fine black powder over the mangled bodies.

"Steady, there . . . steady . . ." There was a hand on his shoulder. A russet, spurred boot was resting beside his grimy hand.

He got to his feet. The young officer was winking back long

lashes from eyes as light brown, as shallow as a heifer's. "General Hill wants to see you."

Rives walked beside him to where a group of officers sat under a big oak. The man on the gray horse watched them coming, cast another glance at the crater. "Poor fellows," he said perfunctorily, then his eyes went back to the front. The fog had lifted a little and from here you could see a body of men sweeping steadily around the Union left. The General watched them intently. He was shaking his head as men do when they wish to express bedazzlement. "Whose infantry is that?" he asked abruptly.

Rives was limp with fatigue, wet with sweat. "General Forrest's cavalry, sir," he said dully. "I am one of his orderlies."

Into Hill's blue, deep-set eyes came an intent look, the expression of a child who is suddenly promised a treat. He said: "General Forrest! I want to look at him."

One of the young officers was down off his horse and Rives was being pushed up into the saddle. They had to ride to half a dozen places before they found Forrest. General Hill caught sight of him before Rives himself did, and rode up promptly. He raised his broad-brimmed hat, inclined his heavy body slightly in the saddle. His words, delivered in practised tones, cut through the battle roar, reached the other man's ears:

"General Forrest, I wish to congratulate you and those brave men moving across that field like veteran infantry . . ." The words droned on. "Magnificent behavior. . . . In Virginia I made myself unpopular. . . . Never saw a dead man with spurs on . . ."

Forrest turned. He wore no hat. His pistol belt was buckled over a linen duster that reached almost to his heels. His eyes, cold and gray, dwelt on Hill's face for a moment. He raised his hand in brief salute. "Thank you, General." He galloped off to take his position near Morton's battery which just then was being advanced to the open field in front of Cloud's Spring.

14

LONGSTREET and his staff were lunching on the sweet potatoes somebody had dug out of a field and roasted when the courier came with the message from the commanding general. Longstreet snatched the potato which Sorrel handed up on a stick and, still munching, rode off with two or three young officers.

Bragg, surrounded by his staff, was waiting in the shade of a sugar tree. Although the day had grown warm he still wore gloves, but his thicket of beard was awry as if he had been pushing his hand through it, and it seemed to Longstreet that the dark eyes were vaguer, more luminous than usual.

Bragg's staff fell back as Longstreet rode up. The two Generals were left confronting each other. Longstreet saluted, recited formal phrases that had crystallized in his mind as he came along. The progress of the battle though slow was steady and satisfactory. Forty or more field pieces had been taken and a large number of small arms. The Yankee Twentieth and Twenty-First Corps had broken in disorder and were thought to be retreating through the pass of the Ridge by the Dry Valley road . . .

Bragg kept nodding his head up and down. "Yes, General, yes . . . Very gratifying."

Longstreet suddenly felt the heat. He ran his chin around the edge of his sweaty collar, lifted his big chin to stare out over the field. As he had come along his mind had been busy with plans, but now he felt a desire to see the fighting for himself. Bright sunshine and a quiet field here, but out there a dense cloud of smoke. He could barely discern figures reeling through it in familiar, grotesque attitudes. He had suddenly a sense of time passing. The battle had gone on too long. He found himself speaking, with fury:

"Breckenridge's men haven't advanced six hundred yards from where they started and they went in at ten o'clock."

Bragg was startled, then he said, "But they are holding their own, sir."

Longstreet looked so directly into the luminous eyes that they focussed, gave him back his own hard stare. He said: "If you will give me enough troops to hold the ground we've gained I can go down the Dry Valley road and cut Thomas off."

Bragg's eyes darted agonizedly back and forth in his narrow skull, freed themselves from Longstreet, fixed on a distant tree. He appeared to consider, raised a gloved finger judiciously to his lips. He shook his head.

"General, there is no more fight left in Polk's troops, in any of them except your own. You had better stay here and hold your position. . . . My headquarters are at Reed's bridge. You can find me there if anything happens."

He had bowed ceremoniously, was riding off. Longstreet watched him go. As Bragg turned the corner of the fence, his staff jingling on behind him, Longstreet raised his gauntleted hands, smote the pommel of his saddle. He was still shaking with rage and cursing when Colonel Claiborne came up.

"General Longstreet, your orders to Wheeler's cavalry have been sent repeatedly but the cavalry is not riding. . . ."

Longstreet raised a face still suffused with rage but with his little pig's eyes twinkling. "Repeat the order in writing," he said. He threw a hand fraternally over Claiborne's shoulder, yelled jovially at his staff as they swung into the saddle to rattle off in a cloud of dust. His mind raced ahead to the front where his divisions already seemed moving up to do his will. He knew now what he was going to do. Bragg would not abandon his plan of battle; then the left wing would have to get along the best it could. But he would order Johnson to make ready his own and Hindman's brigades. Hood could join on the right. Pull Preston up from the river. Preston, Buckner, Hindman. . . . He would hurl them all in. Knock hell out of Thomas.

15

AT five o'clock General Thomas rode to the left of the Union line, leaving Major General Gordon Granger the ranking officer in the center.

Granger stood on top of the ridge he had just carried. On the slope below, his men were still in line but flat on the ground, panting, most of them, like dogs. Fullerton, the only staff officer he had left—the other four were killed or mortally wounded—sat bolt upright against a tree, his mouth open, his eyes glazed with exhaustion. He did not seem to notice that his right boot sole touched the outstretched hand of a dead Rebel. Granger walked over and looked at the man. About fifty, with prominent brown eyes under shaggy brows, clipped moustache and heavy, sensual mouth. Some kind of lawyer or political leader at home, probably. It occurred to him that the man, except for the lack of beard, looked not unlike himself. He, who was regarded as the least self-conscious of men, had these moments in which he seemed to see himself as he appeared to others. It was perhaps that fragment of a letter he had once seen: "Granger, rough as a bear but with a good heart . . . inclined to insubordination. . . ."

He laughed in his beard. They wouldn't say that any more. No, he could have just about anything he wanted after this engagement.

His mind went back to the morning. The Reserve Corps headquarters had been in a field far to the rear of the lines. He had been on top of a hay-stack, peering through glasses when he heard the roar of Polk's artillery and discerned the great cloud of battle rolling up in the east. He had stood it as long as he could, until it seemed to him that Bragg must be piling his whole army on top of Thomas. He had jumped down then swearing that he would go to Thomas' assistance, orders or no orders. Fullerton had followed him across the field, yelling something about court martial. But they had got the whole command, with the exception of McCook, on the road within twenty minutes. He and his escort had ridden far ahead to escape the dust. Hot as the devil by that time and the column sweeping along like a desert sandstorm. No wonder the Rebs had got wind of their approach. They had been waiting at a bend in the road, to open on the head of the column with three batteries. Fullerton said they were old Forrest's men. He didn't know. The usual rag-tag, bob-tail cavalry they looked, but they swarmed like hornets. He had had to throw his men into line of battle right there. It took two hours to break through and then on the double quick under a heavy fire from a battery and three sections of Napoleon guns.

He had come onto the field, finally, near the house that Thomas had made into a hospital. The Rebels had held it since twelve o'clock. The wounded Union soldiers lying about on the ground cheered as they saw them making off through the woods.

Thomas had sent a young staff officer to find out if the advancing column were friends or foes. He had been fooled once that afternoon, sending the National flag forward to be greeted by a storm of bullets. The boy, as they rode along, jerkily gave news of the battle. The Rebels had been hammering on Thomas since ten o'clock. He had been forced out of his headquarters at the Widow Glenn's, had taken a stand on Snodgrass Hill where a new line was forming. The fighting, the boy said enthusiastically, was as hot as ever he had seen. Bayonets being used—he had never seen a bayonet charge before—and men being killed and wounded with clubbed muskets. The pond where they had got water all morning was no good now, too full of blood.

Thomas was sitting his horse back of some freshly thrown up

entrenchments. His bearded face under the black slouch hat was as impassive as usual but his voice quivered as he shook hands.

"General Granger! Good God, sir, you arrive opportunely!"

The men had hardly got their breath before Thomas pointed to this place on which they now stood and asked if Granger could take it. Granger looked at it, a high ridge running nearly at right angles to Thomas' line. He could see the Confederate divisions forming for assault, make out on the left the battery unlimbering for enfilading fire. He thought that they must have seen the colors of the Reserve Corps approaching for they hesitated though everything seemed in readiness.

He answered confidently that he could take the position, then laughed. "My men are fresh. Besides they are raw troops and don't know any better than to charge up there."

He had sent Aleshire's battery of three-inch rifled guns up to the left. Whitaker's and Mitchell's brigades had been put in the center. They had gone forward on the double-quick, cheering, through weeds waist-high. Halfway up the ridge the men had had to lie down for breath. When they started up again old Steedman was leading the way, a regimental flag in his hand. Five minutes later the Confederates had broken and were flying down the southern slope. The whole business had taken perhaps twenty minutes.

He put up his hand, felt where his hat had been torn half off. Minié ball. Lucky escape. Steedman had been badly wounded, Whitaker perhaps mortally. The worst, though, was that the men were out of ammunition. When he had come up he had given ammunition to Brannan and Wood and that had exhausted his supply. The cartridge boxes of the dead and wounded enemy had long ago been rifled. Thomas as he rode off said he would send ammunition back. But where in the devil would he get it?

He thought of Thomas riding toward the left, finding always the same story. He knitted his brows. It was hard for him to get plans into his head. But he could see Thomas' line as plainly as if drawn in diagram, horseshoe-shaped, but the ends of the horseshoe flattened in until they were in danger of touching each other. And yet Rosecrans had been sending reinforcements all day to this part of the line.

He stood and scanned the woods in front of him, the woods into which the flying Rebels had disappeared. It was surprising how late the leaves stayed green even though it had been a dry August. He found himself picking out with relief the yellow, the scarlet branches that showed here and there. It was the depth, the continued greenness of those woods that made them so ominous. Yes, they would be back, at any minute.

He turned sharply, hearing hoofs in the dead leaves. But it was not Thomas but Brannan riding up. Sweat stood in tiny globules on his fine, aquiline nose. He fixed Granger with angry blue eyes. "General, they are forming for another assault."

Granger glanced at the woods, nodded.

"We haven't another round of ammunition left," Brannan said despairingly.

"Fix bay'nets and go after 'em then!" Granger snarled.

Brannan was off down the slope but two or three officers were bearing down from the other end of the ridge. One looked under Granger's hat, was disconcerted not to find Thomas, emitted nevertheless his angry words: "My men . . . not another round, sir. . . ." Granger shook his head, seemed to push them away with his flattened palm, walked to the edge of the ridge, looked down.

Officers were scurrying about, on foot and on horseback. The men still lay in serried ranks, but there was a turning everywhere, as if in sleep, arms working while legs remained immobile.

In the little silence that he had made about him he looked again at the woods. He could hear far off a confused din but the leaves as yet were unstirred. It seemed a long time before the deep Confederate lines appeared—column of brigades at half distance. He noted approvingly the tactics even as he watched them spread out, swarm up the hillside in an angry flood.

"Forward!" had sounded below. The men were on their feet,

going to meet the charge. A battery to the left kept sending round after round of canister into the advancing column. Each time they were veiled from sight for a little but they kept coming on.

He raised his glasses. Brannan was breaking. The Rebels in massed lines were already swarming around his flank. He called frantically to Fullerton, sent him with a message, but it was too late. On the other side Wood's men were giving way. Granger saw the Rebels strike his last brigade as it was leaving the line. It slammed back like a door and was shattered. Granger dropped the glasses, groaned.

Men were pouring up the slope in masses now, firing as they came. They wore butternut. More men kept coming on behind them.

Fullerton was at his side. "General Thomas says prepare to retire. . . ." His voice rose to a shout. "Get out! While there's time!"

He leaned over, snook Granger's arm, still shouting. Granger rode sullenly off through the woods. His bull-like head was low on his chest. He would not increase his pace for all Fullerton's urging. He thought of the defeat as his own. He did not know that the entire Federal army, except for the few troops on Snodgrass Hill, was flying, routed and disorganized, toward Chattanooga

16

AT ten o'clock that night Rives lay down to sleep under a tree. He slept hard, dreaming of a great pond that stretched from the Chickamauga to the Tennessee River. It was frozen tight but the black trunks of the trees came up through the ice and at the root of each tree was a delicious, bubbling hole into which a man might thrust his burning tongue. At dawn he awoke. He was so parched that at first he thought he was in the grip of fever, then he knew what he wanted: Water. He had been a fool to try to get through the night without it.

He got to his feet, stepped out from the crowd of prone figures. Most of the men were still sleeping but they would all be on their way in a few minutes. Forrest's cavalry would ride toward Mission Ridge at dawn. He himself had permission to stay here on the field until he had found George Rowan's body and had seen to its burial.

He slipped his hand under his blanket roll. Nobody had got at it in the night. The crackers were still there but he would have to wet his throat before he could eat anything. The devil of it was that he would have to walk in search of water. His little mare had broken her leg just before sundown. He had got right off and shot her. Dropping with fatigue then, he didn't want his sleep broken by a screaming horse.

He walked some distance through the woods before he came on the remount, a sleek bay with US branded on his hips. The leaves were torn off the bushes all around him but he was not eating, just standing there dejectedly, head down. He took a look at the saddle, then chucked his own into the bushes and mounted and struck off through the woods. At the head of a hollow the bay smelled water, began racing. Rives saw the creek: a placid ford, spanned by a foot log, bordered on either side by cane. He flung himself off the horse and crouching on all fours drank greedily. The water was cold, not very clean from the débris that collected around the cane stalks. He waded out to a clearer place, stooped and brought cupped handfuls to his mouth. When he had his fill he threw his hat off onto the bank and splashed water repeatedly over his face and whole head.

The horse had moved a little farther downstream and stood in water up to his knees. He had evidently had enough too but he still kept his head low over the water, the nostrils flared out as if at any minute he would suck another drink in. As Rives watched he gave a long sigh, moved slowly to the edge of the stream and still standing in water began to nip the tops off of the tough cane.

Rives went over to the bank and took his crackers out of his blanket roll. He had got them off a dead Yankee late yesterday afternoon. A disappointment—that man on ahead had kept yelling that the bastards had cheese in their haversacks. He wondered if the man had really found cheese in any of those haversacks or whether, wanting some so long, he had just imagined it. There was a dirty reddish-looking border on one or two of the crackers. He flipped it off delicately, taking care not to sacrifice any more of the cracker than was necessary, and leaning back on his elbow, ate slowly and with relish. There were eight crackers in all. He wished there were more. Still he had had enough to keep him going for several hours. He put his hand in his pocket, felt with pleasure the edge of a silver dollar. When the sun got a little higher he would stop at a house, beg something to eat for himself, maybe buy a little corn for the horse. He glanced disapprovingly at the sleek barrel. Stall-fed, like all the Yankees. He would have to put the corn to him if he expected to get over on the ridge by dark. That kind would go down on you quicker than a grass-fed horse if they were suddenly deprived of their rations. He whistled to the horse experimentally.

To his surprise he left the water, came to him. He laughed as he swung up into the handsome saddle. "Old boy, you done jined the cavalry."

The horse trotted nimbly up out of the hollow. On the crest Rives paused long enough to take his bearings, then he saw the first ascending black wings and knew that it must be to the right. At ten o'clock he found the place he was seeking. A clearing on the edge of the woods. It had been yellow with sedge grass once but it was motley color now, with everywhere over it strange swellings. Blue, black, gray, brown. . . . Ten thousand moles had worked frenziedly to throw up these hillocks. Steam went up from them and black wings. It was strange there were so many negroes. . . .

The smell was driving straight at him. His stomach went tight over the crackers he had eaten. He passed his hand over his face, lifted his eyes with an effort, trying to remember what the man in the ambulance had said: "Field full of sedge grass and a little way down from the Yankee breastworks." Yes, this was the place. There were the Yankee breastworks still holding the ridge, and the field would have been full of sedge but for those moles. . . .

He got down, tied his horse to a tree and went forward over the field. The first half-dozen were blue, then butternut. More blue. Butternut and blue in a tangle. He bent over methodically, looked for the same fraction of a second into each face. . . . Too many had their tongues out. . . . His thoughts ran on irritably. Wasting time on the blue and yet you had to look. Mustn't bend too close. That was how he'd missed that one back there under the tree.

He became obsessed with the idea that the body he had not examined was the one he sought. He went back. The man lay face downwards. Jaunty fit to his coat but he had fattened since he left his tailor! The seams were bursting out under each arm. Rives half-bent over, then straightened up quickly. He got a stick, used it for a lever. The black moon of a face came up slowly. Blood and broken leaves masked the eyes but the lower part was smooth, enormously swollen. He made himself look until he saw the yellow beard growing out of the horrible, tight flesh, then turned and made off crazily through the trees.

Over by the fence was a huge mound of fresh turned earth. Living figures moved about it or spilled out over the field. They went in twos. Some carried stretchers.

He walked over. A red-headed giant of a man was just clambering out of the deep trench, naked to the waist and steaming with sweat. He handed his pick to a fellow, growling, "I wouldn't a cared if he hadn't sent me last time. Time before too. Don't matter how hard the ground is, how many there is of 'em. Every time he sends me."

A man on the other side of the trench laughed. "He seen you put Tom Neely on his back the other night. You got too much muscle for your own good, Ed."

The red-headed man shook himself until the sweat flew in bright drops. " 'Tain't fair anyhow. I got a weak stomach, just like anybody else." He pulled a plug of tobacco out of his pocket, bit off a chew, then saw Rives. "Bill," he mumbled, "better git your book."

A boy was coming around the side of the trench, a little red-backed notebook in his hand. Rives went to meet him, "Lieutenant George Rowan, Aide-de-Camp to General Deshler," he said, ". . . Tenth Texas Infantry. . . ."

The boy stared, flipped the pages of his notebook. "I put 'em all down 's best I can," he said hopelessly. "Here, Mister, you want to look?"

Rives took the book, frowned at the greasy figures. Behind him a voice said interestedly, "Tenth Texas. Why don't you look over there under that tree? Just brought in a lot of Tenth Texas."

Rives handed the book back to the boy, went toward the tree. The bodies lay under it as thick as fruit. They were covered, most of them, with dirty canvas or tow sacks. You couldn't look because more kept coming in all the time on stretchers. The man who had spoken had a white handkerchief tied about the lower part of his face. It swayed with his gabbling breaths. He went stooping around, lifting rags of sacks. Rives kept beside him. "No . . . No . . . No. . . ." and then just the indrawn breath that sent you on down the line. George was next to the last, over against the fence. He had to be turned over.

Gabbler was pleased, straightened up. "You can most generally find 'em if you keep at it."

Rives stood with his head bent. He was thinking: Ben Bigstaff and George Rowan had had the same expression on their faces when they died.

Over by the trench somebody was calling: "Hey, Ed, less start putting them in."

Rives raised his head, looked into the glistening bottom of the trench. He said, "My God. . . . You'd think. . . . Not enough graves!"

There was silence; then a spade clinked on a stone. "We can bury him separate if you want," somebody said mildly.

They took George a hundred yards away and buried him near a big sycamore tree. Rives got his knife out, made a cross on the tree in case anybody came looking for the grave. Then he walked back across the field with the soldiers. One had taken the handkerchief from his face and swung his spade as he went. "There's that lady and them niggers come back," he said suddenly. "Got a wagon this time."

Rives looked up, saw the wagon first and then the woman moving toward it. Tall and in black. She came with an odd, hobbling motion but that was because of the canteens, slung one on each side and one across her back.

The bushes parted to the right and a negro stepped out. He had a ragged straw hat, glistening eyeballs. He said, "Mister Rives! What you doin' here?"

Rives said, "Antony!" Then he ran on.

The wagon ahead jolted faster. The girl was coming to meet it. Her hands wove in front of her as she came. She cried out shrilly: "Little Ed! Antony! You didn't need to stay all day."

She saw him and stopped short, the still moving canteens

bobbing back and forth on each side of her. Her eyes fluttered whitely aside for a second, then came back to his face. She cried "Rives," and was in his arms.

The wagon jolted up. A second negro voice cried, "Hi, Mister Rives!" Her lips met his again, then she drew away. She passed a hand over her face. It left her features composed, severe. She said: "Oh . . . it's this way," and ran forward.

He moved beside her. The man lying on the ground had a great bloody bandage wound about his head. The hairs of his moustache were brown against green skin. He stared off through the trees. "Gimme drink!" he said.

She had the canteen up and was bending over. The water bubbled at his lips, spilled down over his chin. "Oh," she cried desperately, "open your mouth."

His lids rose once then fell. "Stay here," he muttered. "Don't want move."

She was on her feet, wringing her hands. "I put the bandage on and I think it's wrong. Maybe no bandage at all. He can't talk."

Rives looked away. "Are those our negroes out there with the wagon?"

"Antony," she whispered, "and little Ed. He always comes with us."

Rives called out in a great voice, "Come here, you boys. Get this man into that wagon."

Little Ed leaned forward, cracked his whip, brought the mules up on the run. The three men lying in the wagon on blood-stained straw stared up sullenly over the side. One was babbling: "He kep' pulling it off. I'd a been all right. But he kep' pulling it off."

"Here," Rives said, "up with him. Quick."

The brown-moustached man rose on the stretcher, came stolidly to rest on top of the pile. A thin boy kept squirming out from under him. Lucy walked so close to the wagon that her skirt was in danger of being caught by the wheels. Every now and then she reached out and prisoned a clutching hand. Rives grasped a fold of her skirt, held it tight, looked away over the field. "Why does Antony keep walking around out there?"

"Cousin Susan said . . . too far gone, not to fool with them. . . . Just water. I send Ant first; then I come with morphia." She looked up, her brows puckered. "Do you think I ought to let him give morphia pellets too?"

He said, "If you've got 'em," and then harshly; "How long have you been on this field?"

Her eyes clouded with the effort to remember. "We got here in the night. . . . Dr. Reynolds . . . was most kind. . . . But he said dangerous . . . so we stayed down the road. . . . *I thought you were dead. . . .*"

He said, not knowing that he was shouting: "It was George Rowan. I buried him over there. Under that sycamore. See, where the fence turns."

She was not looking. Her eyes were fixed on a brown, heaving mass in front of them. She stopped, fell away from the wagon, crossed quivering hands on her breast. "I can't stand it," she cried. "I never could. . . . It is a peculiarity . . . I have tried. . . ."

He had not been aware of the horse's cries until that moment but his pistol was out before she ceased speaking. He walked over, pressed it to the place behind the ear. There was a rumble of gas from the intestines. The horse's head ceased its angry weaving to and fro, sank with a plop into dead leaves.

She was walking on. He went beside her, talking garrulously. "They don't mind. Anything but breaking their legs. It's when they can't stand up. Scares 'em. When they can't stand up."

She put her hand on his arm. "It's over this way."

They crossed a rustic bridge, the wagon rattling on behind. The house, a cabin, with deep galleries front and back, sat on a rise. The ground in front was wooded but to the side and rear a big meadow sloped away. Rives noticed that it was cleft by a dark, cedared ravine.

Her feet took the path up the hill as if they had known it a long time. Wounded men lay thick on either side but they were thicker on the gallery. An army of maimed beggars, in butternut mostly. They lay sprawled on pallets or were set rag-doll-like against the wall. Two leaned over the railing to vomit blood almost in unison.

A fat woman in a dirty Mother Hubbard was lurching forward between the sprawled figures. She fluttered her hands, cried out shrilly: "You cain't bring 'em in here. Not room to step now."

Lucy was looking at him. "Take 'em around to the back," he said.

The wagon jolted on, halted where an enormous network of roots sprang out of baked, white ground. Antony was sliding off his seat, whining: "Cain't git no further'n this, Mister Rives."

He made a threatening gesture, then called out. The negroes were at the side of the wagon. Figures rolled up out of the straw on to the stretchers, came to rest against the trunk of the sugar tree. The man with the bandaged head first, then the thin boy. A hairy face with shut eyes. Rives looked above the heads at the black, ridged tree trunk. A big one. It had been tapped for sugar not so long ago. Shining ants ran about in the little cups left from the tapping.

She was on her knees, looking up at him while her hands tore swiftly at something white. "Your mother's in the house. That first room."

He said, still booming: "I will go in and see her."

He mounted the steps. There was, surprisingly, nobody in the hall, but a half-open door on the right revealed rows of cots arranged hospital wise. There was the smell of blood and purulent matter in the room, a gabbling of high voices.

Two women were in the runway between the cots. One had on a black riding habit; her long widow's veil streamed to the end of her skirt. Steam eddied from the china cup she held in her hand.

Rives stepped up into the room, went down the runway. Bandaged legs. Heads. Closed eyes. One man whose face was a welter of dirt and blood put out a hand, maliciously, it seemed, to stay his progress.

The man threshing about on the bed, moaning, had an enormous arm, swollen darkly red and blistered, where it was not hidden by scraps of filthy bandage. The odor from it was living evil. It crouched above the bed on angry feet, made forays into the room. Rives thought: Nothing like this on the battle field. He stepped back.

His mother was turning around, her nostrils had gone white from being held taut so long. She spoke through clenched teeth. "Rives. . . ." They walked away from the bed. She held his arm, spoke abstractedly yet confidentially: "Poor man. The drug does not seem to have any influence. Your brother, Miles . . . impossible to communicate. . . . Colonel Lawton thought. . . ."

The other woman kept a kind of step with them. "I've torn up all the counterpanes. Do you think those curtains. . . ."

Susan Allard said, "Go in the kitchen. Tell them more hot water."

Out in the hall there was a flurry, a loud, irate voice: "All very well, but you have no authority."

Two women standing in the doorway stepped aside. A figure was revealed. Bald head, red moustache, officer's insignia. He clicked a hand to his brow, frowning: "Madam, this is most irregular!"

There was silence; then from one of the cots came a high, almost negro laugh. Rives met the wounded soldier's gleaming eyes, then looked back at his mother. She was moving to meet the surgeon. You could not see her feet for that long skirt, but she would be on tiptoe; her chin was tilted. She said: "Dreadful . . . not even enough hot water. But we are doing the best we can."

The surgeon's lips jerked under his red moustache. He glared around the room. "Captain Mainwaring . . . reports . . . My God, how many have you got in here?"

She said quietly, "I believe we were the first people on the field. This woman let me bring them here . . . I think her name is Parkins. . . ."

His reddish eyebrows arched up. His mouth opened, then closed. He made irritable gestures of dismissal, was turning to leave the room. But she had him by the arm, was propelling him toward a cot. "This one, Doctor . . . I've been giving him morphia every three hours. I think maybe too much . . ."

He said: "Oh, morphia." He held back, then sank on glistening heels. His sharp nose dived forward, came up, hung, like a dog's on a point. He tapped the distended chest, then rose. He said: "Hear that crackling sound? Emphysema. Got a bullet in his right lung. Doubt if you could operate. . . ."

Antony was in the room, turning his ragged hat around in his hands. "Ole Miss, they's a whole lot of 'em over in the hollow. Some of 'em's 'live."

Rives went through the door. The hall was dark and cool. He passed down it, pursued by a voice, Antony's voice but heard long ago. . . . "Whole lot of 'em, Ole Miss . . . yonder in the hollow. . . ." No, that was black berries. . . .

He came out onto the back gallery, went down the steps. There were more of them under the tree. A small, worried-looking woman went bending about among them with a basin. The man with the bloody bandage had been laid out flat on his back between two arching tree roots. Lucy was crouched on her knees beside him, waving a palm leaf fan.

Rives went up, laid a hand on her shoulder. She got to her feet in a flurry of skirts, handed him the fan. "If you'll just hold that . . . I've got to get my hair back tighter." Her hands went up to the heavy coil of hair at the back of her neck. She was looking straight at him, her mouth a little open. There were little beads of perspiration on her upper lip. His hand slipped from the soft flesh of her shoulder, closed on her wrist. He motioned toward the meadow. "Come on, let's go over there."

She looked at him a second, then she bent and laid the fan on the ground. They went off, stepping carefully among the rows of wounded, toward the dark, cedared ravine.

The summer morning wore on its way. During the next hour more wounded were brought in. The supply of pallets had given out, and the wounded or dying men were laid on the bare ground or propped, as some of them requested, against the trunks of trees. There was about the place a great murmuring. Flies had gathered in swarms and fed on the clots of blood that spattered the ground or on the faces and hands of the wounded. The man whom Lucy had been tending asked to have his position changed and lay with his eyes fixed on the distant woods. He was fearfully turbaned, like an Eastern potentate. He did not seem to mind the flies that swarmed in the great cap-like mass on his forehead, but when they strayed down onto his cheek, he grimaced and sometimes called out. A negro woman moving among the wounded pitied him and breaking a leafy bough from a tree placed it in his hand. The nerveless fingers fell away but she tied the stalk to his wrist. He was able then by moving his wrist slightly to brush the flies away. A man sitting by unable to move because his leg had been broken called out his pleasure at the arrangement: "Now you can keep 'em off, son."

The wounded man grinned back, moving his bough with its drooping leaves faster as if to please his friend. All through the morning it swayed back and forth. The September sky was cloudless now and blue. The man with the broken leg glanced wearily at the sun from time to time and calculated the hour. In the middle of the morning he glanced down and saw the green leaves of the bough fallen athwart his friend's face. He bent near enough to ascertain that the leaves did not stir, then looked up at the sun. He calculated that it must be eleven o'clock.

17

ON the morning after the battle a band of Confederate cavalry came up out of the Chickamauga valley and followed the road which winds along the crest of Mission Ridge. There were five hundred men from Dibrell's brigade and a strong advance guard of Armstrong's men. General Forrest himself rode at the head of the column with General Armstrong.

The cavalcade moved slowly. The two generals kept their horses at a walk while they noted the battle litter that covered the woods on both sides of the road. Arms, saddles, blankets, caissons, wagons and their teams, an ambulance with its broken tongue half driven into the trunk of a tree. Forrest's eyes were bright. "My God, Armstrong, they've left enough stuff to equip a brigade."

Armstrong was looking ahead. "There's something up the road, General."

Forrest withdrew his gaze from the woods. "Rear guard, I reckon. Well, let's give 'em a dare."

Armstrong turned, shouted an order. It was echoed by the men behind and the column swept forward at full speed. The Union troopers stayed long enough to deliver one volley, then fled in the direction of Chattanooga.

The Confederates pursued to a bend in the road, then came to a halt. Here there were even more evidences of yesterday's conflict. Abandoned arms and equipment were thick even in the road and moving on ahead in the dust were still a few stragglers. Some stood and waited to be captured, others made off through the woods and had to be rounded up by the cavalrymen.

Forrest had half a dozen brought over to the side of the road for questioning. Two were Germans who shrugged their shoulders and grunted gutturally. The third, a sharp-faced boy of eighteen or nineteen, suddenly broke off his ready answers, grinning: "Whyn't you look for yourself?"

Forrest and Armstrong looked in the direction of his pointing finger and saw a hundred yards ahead a man swinging from the limb of a tree: a Federal officer, smartly uniformed, with field glasses slung across his breast. He dropped to the ground as they came up, stood grimly while he was relieved of his glasses and pistols. The group of soldiers who led him to the rear suddenly let out a shout of laughter and Anderson smiled.

"What you laughing at?" Armstrong said.

Anderson, still grinning, glanced at the other general. "He said he recognized Old Bedford from his picture and he hoped to God he'd break his neck up that tree."

The sight of the captured equipment had kept Forrest in high good humor all morning. He laughed now, glanced at Anderson's figure and shook his head. "You'd never make it, Charley. I better try."

He was off his horse in a moment. Standing on tiptoe he caught hold of a low hanging limb, swung himself up, then climbed nimbly from one bough to another until he reached the wooden observation platform built into the tree's fork.

Armstrong down below turned up an anxious face: "All right?"

"All right," Forrest said, and raised the Yankee officer's glasses to his eyes.

The scene that lay before him was one of great natural beauty and grandeur. On either side rose majestic mountains. The haze that drifted in front of them made their wooded slopes appear blue even in the morning sunshine, and moving clouds cast a chequered pattern of light and shade over the valley at their feet The valley was wide and green, cleft by the smoothly flowing river which here coils upon itself to form the great bend which the Indians called "The Moccasin."

The Confederate General did not notice how exactly the lazily coiling river reproduces the shape of a giant foot nor did he dwell upon any of the strange effects of light and shade cast by the drifting clouds. His eyes were fixed upon the gap. A long line of tiny figures could be discerned there toiling slowly around the base of Lookout Mountain. The enemy trains were already leaving! And at the river bank there was another group of scurrying figures: workers re-building the pontoon bridge. He readjusted the glasses so that he brought the main street of the town into view. People milled about there on the sidewalks and the streets were choked with moving pieces of artillery, caissons, ambulance wagons, rearing teams. And from the direction of Georgia came a constant procession of straggling figures: What was left of the Federal forces was evidently moving with all speed toward the town.

He turned the glasses to the south, to the valley of the Chickamauga. From this great height the Yankee breastworks were plainly visible. They lay in a semi-circle on a wooded ridge. On the slope in front and spreading far out into the wooded plains about the river was the Confederate encampment, a host of white tent tops, wagons, pack animals, the tinier moving dots that were the figures of men.

The General took the glasses away from his eyes, frowning. In the Yankee camp all was animation and bustle. His own army, it seemed to him, lay torpid at the breastworks as if gorged with conflict.

He bent over and called: "Anderson!"

The aide's upturned face appeared. He was about to climb up but Forrest stayed him with a gesture. "Here's a dispatch for General Polk. I want to be sure it reaches Bragg too."

Anderson looked about for something to write on. Somebody led a horse up behind him just then. He grasped the saddle skirt and holding it taut laid a sheet of paper upon it and wrote at the general's dictation:

"On the Road, September 21, 1863

Gen'l

We are in a mile of Rossville—Have been on the Point of Missionary Ridge

Can see Chattanooga and everything around—the enemy Trains are leaving Going around the Point of Lookout mountain—

The Prisoners captured report the pontoon thrown across for the purpose of retreating

I think they are evacuating as hard as they can go

They are cutting timber down to obstruct our passage

I think we ought to press forward as rapidly as possible

Respftly etc.

N. B. Forrest,
Brig Gen

Gen L Polk

Please forward to Gen Bragg"

Anderson read the dispatch over when he had furnished writing. Forrest listened, looking down through the leaves and frowning: "Anderson, every hour now is worth a thousand men."

At nine o'clock Rives came up out of the valley and headed north along Mission Ridge. He had ridden a mile before the first voice hailed him out of the darkness:

"Who goes there?"

Rives gave the pass word and waited until the picket, trailing his gun, came forward. Joe Robinson. He borrowed a chew of tobacco and leaning up against a tree gave the news of the day. There had been a brush down at Rossville. Dibrell's men had just come back from the gap. The Yankees were fortifying, all right. Captain McGinnis had brought up his guns and shelled them two hours but couldn't budge them. He understood that Old Bedford wanted to take the cavalry and chase the Yankees clean out of the valley but the high-ups were holding him back for some reason.

"Where's headquarters?" Rives asked.

Joe indicated a trail to the left. Rives was riding off when he heard Joe speak meditatively. "Dr. Cowan was by here a while ago."

"Well," Rives said impatiently, "what did he have to say?"

Joe's voice roughened suddenly with laughter. "He said hell was a-popping up the hill."

The scout grunted and rode off. As he made his way through the trees he was thinking of Dr. Cowan and the General. He knew that the surgeon went in fear that Forrest in one of his towering rages might one day injure some innocent person. It was Cowan's custom when he saw the first signs of irritation in his chief to slip quietly about among the men. "Boys, fur's going to fly before the day's over. . . . If I was you I'd step light. . . ."

The trail ended abruptly. He was on the edge of the cavalry camp. It was dark except for the gleam of lanterns at the far end of the clearing. There were no fires going. Still figures lay about under the trees singly or in groups of twos and threes. He heard two men quarrelling as they "pulled blanket" and remembered that he had left his own blanket roll in the ravine. A muffled oath told him that "Beauty"—he named the horse in that moment—was treading dangerously near somebody's head. He dismounted and went toward the lighted headquarters tent. It was empty except for a sleeping figure on a cot, but under the trees a few feet away a cigar end glowed redly and from behind the tent came the sound of measured footfalls. Back and forth, back and forth, ten or a dozen paces each time. The General, probably. When he was thinking out something he often walked that way for hours.

Rives threw up his saddle skirt and was uncinching the girth when he became aware that the red cigar end was moving toward him. Major Anderson's voice came out of the dark:

"Well, Allard, got yourself a new horse?"

Rives nodded, led the horse into the shaft of light from the tent so that the Major could properly admire it. "Saddle too," he said, "rides like a cradle, Major."

"Very pretty . . . very pretty. . . ." Anderson said abstractedly.

Rives finished unsaddling his horse and was turning away when the footfalls behind the tent paused for a second, then came rapidly forward. The General stood beside them.

"Where've you been, Allard?"

Rives told him that he had come from the field by way of the Ridge road.

"Did you pass General Bragg's headquarters?"

Rives mentioned the name of the aide to whom he had reported.

"Any message for me?"

"No, sir," Rives said, surprised.

The General was pulling out his watch. "Nine o'clock. Anderson, what time did you send my message?"

"It's been four hours now, General."

"Four hours!" cried Forrest passionately. "Tell me it takes four hours for a man to ride five miles! No, Anderson, it won't do. He hasn't sent me any message and he isn't going to."

He was walking off. Anderson followed him. Rives could hear the aide murmuring pacifically. The fact that General Bragg had sent no message was in itself an answer; tantamount, in fact, to a denial of General Forrest's request.

Forrest stopped short. "Tantamount, hell!" he said. "I'll go down and have it out with him."

He turned to the scout. "Allard, your horse fresh?"

Rives replied that the Red House where General Bragg was lodging for the night could not be more than six miles away. His horse could easily stand the trip there and back.

Forrest was already in the saddle. There was the creak of leather as Anderson hoisted his big body up. Rives flung the saddle back on his own horse, mounted and followed them out onto the trail. An hour later they passed the sentry and drew up in front of the Red House.

The two officers dismounted, threw the bridles over their horses' necks and stepped up onto the porch. Rives dismounted too. He took the precaution of slipping his bridle reins over the low hanging bough of a tree. His horse seemed tractable enough. Still he might not stand for a new master. He took a few steps back and forth in front of the house, then came to a stop. His legs were so heavy that the effort of moving them made him giddy. Indeed as he lifted his legs he had had for a moment the sensation of moving through water. His whole being, suspended in fatigue as if it had been an element, yearned toward the moment when they would be on the road again. He found himself thinking of a certain dead tree they had passed. Halfway there it must be and after that the place where you left the road and went off on the trace. The picket to pass, another two or three hundred yards and then the tent. He could feel himself sinking onto that ground. Blanket? Hell. He wouldn't need one by that time. Warm or cold, it wouldn't matter. Stretching the body out to its full length would be the greatest luxury of which the mind could conceive.

He squatted down against a tree trunk, not an easy position, but it gave him the advantage of being able to spring to his feet at a moment's notice. This was not one of those times you could snatch a little sleep. Major Anderson would not care but the General would never overlook it.

He arched his back against the tree trunk. The movement tightened the muscles over his stomach. He was faint from hunger. For a second or two he couldn't remember whether he had eaten today, then he saw some crackers with reddish borders and later in the day a hand—it must have been there at that hospital—had held up before him a bowl of steaming soup. At the thought of the soup saliva gushed up in his mouth. He rose and walked quickly around to the back of the house.

There was no movement to be heard, but a dim lamp burning in the kitchen revealed a white-headed old negro man sprawled over a table asleep. Rives tried the door. It was bolted. He knocked on the window pane. The negro sat up, his eyes staring wildly. There was a pane missing in the upper half of the window. Rives stood on tiptoe and thrust his face through it.

"Uncle, this is one of General Forrest's orderlies. Got anything to eat?"

The old man balanced warily beside the table. "General Forrest?" he said. "How come you don't stay around the Gineral then?"

"I do," Rives said calmly. "He's in there now talking to General Bragg."

The old man cupped his hand to his ear. From the room beyond came the rumble of voices. He listened a second, then nodded wearily. "You come on in, soldier," he said. "I'll see if I can't find you somethin' t'eat."

He came out into the hall and unbolted the door, and Rives stepped into the kitchen. The old man went out on a side porch and brought in the remains of a ham and some cold biscuits. He set a plate and knife and fork on the table, added a jar half-full of preserves.

"Thar 'tis, soldier."

Rives sat down, cut himself several slices of ham and made them into sandwiches. He ate rapidly in great mouth-filling bites. When his first hunger was appeased he pushed the plate holding the now denuded ham bone toward the old negro. The old man shook his head. "Ain't no more, soldier?"

"No cold greens, potatoes, tomatoes?" Rives asked.

"Ain't a 'mater on this place. Rebs done even tromp down the vines in the garden. Ain't no hams left in the smokehouse, either. Them Generals et four for their supper."

Rives' eyes brightened at the word "smokehouse." "Whose place is this?" he asked casually.

"It's Miss Libby Shackleford's.... You don't need to be studying about our smokehouse, soldier. Them Generals done already et us out of house and home."

Rives had finished the last of the preserves and cold biscuits. He stood up, tightening his belt. "Well, you tell Miss Libby I sure am obliged for a good meal. And tell her you're a mighty smart old man. If I ever come this way again I'm going to stop and buy you."

The old man sniffed his contempt. "Soldier, you ain't got enough money to buy me."

Rives laughed. "If you're all that valuable you better be careful. The Yanks might get you for nothing."

He went out the back way, pursued by the old man's high cackle and walked around to the front of the house. A lamp had been lit in the room on the left and he could discern figures dimly through the crack between the white curtains. He squatted down against his tree trunk again, pulled out his tobacco and filled his pipe. His back arched itself into the same position it had held a few minutes ago but the muscles felt resilient now, ready to do his bidding. He pondered on the restorative effects of food. A few minutes ago he had been like a man drugged; making it back to camp seemed an almost impossible feat. But now he had command of all his faculties. His mind was clearer than it had been for days.

He relaxed his legs a little, dropped lower against the tree trunk. The events of the last twenty-four hours were taking shape in his mind, clearly but like something experienced long ago. George Rowan. . . . He was dead, and he, Rives, had buried him. There had been a whole field of dead and wounded and later a hospital room filled with the smell of gangrene. A wounded soldier had looked out at him from under a great, bloody bandage. . . . His mind veered away, to the meadow through which he and Lucy had walked on their way to the ravine. As importunate, as passionate as he had been then he remembered looking out over that field as they walked along and noting the sheen on the hay and how everywhere it stood tall and untrampled.

It ended abruptly at the edge of the ravine. The way down was rough and littered with rock. Then they had come in among the first cedars. He had been awkward, remembering the lice, smelling suddenly the stale odors of his own body. "Lucy . . . I'm going over there and wash. . . ."

She had been standing there, her eyes dark with emotion. Suddenly she laughed sharply, threw her head back. *"Dirt!* I've been tending a man with gangrene for two weeks."

He had just stood there stupidly. "Who's looking after him now?"

"Mitty. . . ." She was in his arms.

There was water somewhere below among those rocks. They could hear it all the time they lay there. Her hand kept coming up to brush his face gently. Once her fingers sank into the hollow of his cheek, so hard that inside his mouth he could feel the flesh pressing against the bone. "I can't *bear* to think of you being hungry. . . ." That was after they had been together, when they were just lying there in each other's arms, listening to that trickle far below in the ravine.

She had wanted to talk. Once she raised up, put her hand on his arm. "Rives. . . ." He pressed his lips against her throat. He remembered the fluttering inside as if the words were still trying to get out. . . .

He got to his feet and began walking slowly up and down in front of the porch. He wondered if his mother and Lucy were still at the Parkins' house. They might be on their way back to Good Range by this time. He had passed dozens of ambulances during the day. The field hospitals must be in operation now. There would be no more work for ladies' associations. He grinned, thinking of his mother. You could not set her down as belonging to one of those associations. She was a host in herself. A "captain" the negroes called it.

He had arrived before the two north windows of the house. He stood still. Inside a voice was speaking with passionate intensity:

"We can get all the supplies we want in Chattanooga."

Rives went forward quietly until he could see through the crack in the curtains into the room. General Bragg, in his nightshirt and with his black hair all rumpled, stood at the footboard of a huge bed. He was listening to General Forrest who was standing just inside the door with Major Anderson. Forrest stood with one leg advanced and his whole body bent forward. He was speaking eagerly, persuasively: "General, it seems to me that the river is a help rather than a hindrance. Rosecrans is in Chattanooga. Burnside is across the river. The thing to do is throw our army between them before they can effect a junction."

Bragg shook his head. "That's a rough country, General. And Burnside outnumbers us badly."

Forrest took another step forward. Rives saw his face and was startled. He had not imagined that his General's face could wear such a look. Forrest's eyes were bright. His lips quivered as he enunciated his words. He was like a man pleading for his life. He said: "They outnumber us but they're demoralized. The whole Yankee army is demoralized, I tell you. Thomas' corps is the only one with any fight left in it."

Bragg was half leaning, half sitting against the footboard of the bed. As Forrest began speaking he let his head sink as if in deep thought. "General, what will Rosecrans be doing while we're marching to attack Burnside."

Forrest's face had hardened. His voice was one of strained patience. "What can he do? You've got him bottled up in Chattanooga. We can starve him out or if he won't surrender let him try to get out. There's no way except over Walden's Ridge. He'd find that a hard job."

Bragg still appeared to be considering. He shook his head finally. "General, I do not think the movement you suggest is the correct military procedure. It involves crossing the river into a rough, mountainous country to attack a force superior in numbers."

Forrest started. He fixed his great, luminous eyes on Bragg's face. "General Bragg," he said sternly, "you have an opportunity to destroy the whole Yankee army. Are you going to let them get away? Are you going to take that responsibility?"

Bragg's body stiffened. His dark eyes glittered in the light as he turned his head sharply. His voice was formal and cold: "General Forrest, I shall ask you as I have asked the other general officers to hold your command in readiness for a general advance on Chattanooga in the morning."

"In the morning? Oh, my great God!" Forrest's voice broke on the words. Rives could hear his noisy breathing.

Bragg was climbing back into bed, among his high piled pillows. He sank back then raised himself up. "General, you will excuse me for not congratulating you before on yesterday's success. I have had many reports of the splendid conduct of your men."

There was silence, then Forrest said curtly, "Thank you, General."

A door closed. Rives stepped quickly back into the shadow. A moment later Forrest and his aide emerged from the house. They mounted in silence and followed by the orderly, rode off. After a little Anderson laughed shortly. "Conquering hero! He'll wait till he's sure Rosecrans is out of Chattanooga, then he'll march in and parade the streets."

Forrest spoke in a low, strangled voice: "Anderson, I have written to him. I have sent to him. I have given information about the Federal army and still he will not move. What does he fight battles for?"

They came to the parting of the roads, turned to the right and began the long climb north. The scout kept a little distance behind the two officers. The great valley was below them. In its center the lights of the city twinkled and were reflected in the bosom of the river. Rives fancied that the faint, continuous sound he heard was the chopping of axes—axes that were building fortifications around the remnant of the Yankee army.

Riding behind the two dark figures he raised his clenched hand in impotent fury. When he had first heard the conversation between the two Generals he had been excited to think that he, a private, was receiving information about important manœuvres. That emotion seemed trivial now. The incidents of the morning seemed trivial too, and vain. He thought of George Rowan, dead and buried on the field. He had felt pity for the dead man as he laid him in his grave but now he knew envy. If the Confederate cause failed—and for the first time he felt fear for its outcome—there could be no happiness for him except in the grave.

18

NED was waked by the feeling that somebody was brushing past him. He sat up in his bunk. A guard—the one they called "Old Red"—was disappearing down the corridor. He had evidently just deposited a box on the foot of the bunk. Ned picked it up and examined it. It was empty, except for a neat coil of string. But the box was in good condition, its sides, top and bottom intact. He raised it to his nose and sniffed. It had contained ham. There was no mistaking the aroma. And that faint smudge on the side was surely chocolate, the icing, doubtless, from a cake. He wet his finger, ran it over the stain then licked it but got no taste.

He set the box down and got out of bed. He had gone to sleep at two o'clock in the afternoon. It must be nearly four now. He went to the window and looked out. Over the expanse of ice around the prison walls half a dozen figures moved, prisoners bringing in the night's supply of wood. He had not been on wood duty now for over a week. Thank Blake, the hospital steward for that. Blake and diarrhea. He grinned faintly, and buttoning his jacket up to his neck went down the corridor to Spencer Rowe's cell.

Spencer was sitting under the window on his stool, writing. Ned lay down on his vacant bunk and pulled the blanket up over him. Spencer closed his copy book. "I didn't see you at exercise this afternoon, Lieutenant."

"No," Ned said, "I didn't feel like it."

"That's too bad. A little turn in the air does you good."

"Not in this air," Ned said, "when you're in the fix I'm in. Wind goes through you like a knife."

"Had a bad night?"

"I went to those damned sinks fifteen times," Ned said.

Spencer shook his head. "Hash," he murmured, "Avery's hash. Those that have hash are troubled about it. Those that have none are troubled without it. . . . Would you like for me to read to you?"

"If you won't read poetry," Ned said.

Spencer nodded, flipping the pages of his copy book. "Here is something I wrote only yesterday: Among the hundreds of officers captured at Fort Donelson Captain Winstead is one of the most marked; tall, *distingué,* with classical features, elegant manners, a vast amount of *bonhomie.* Winstead is acceptable to the men, agreeable to the ladies. I became acquainted with Captain Winstead at Camp Chase, in prison Number 3, mess 46, composed of a splendid set of fellows. The mess gave me a grand dinner on my arrival, Captain Winstead presiding. . . . The cards of invitation were playing cards with the names of the guests on the backs. They were distributed through the agency of a tin plate in the hands of George Diggons. . . ."

Ned made an irritable gesture. "Can't you write about anything but prison?"

"Ah, yes, I should have remembered that yours is not an introspective nature. Would foreign travel please you?" He turned the pages. "Ah, here it is: We leave Normandy, with its famous old towers and its beautiful scenery described by a multitude of writers of all kinds and pass on to Paris where much is to be seen. To find Americans you go to the Grand Hotel, the most magnificent and the worst kept in Paris. For elegance and comfort go to the Grand Hotel du Louvre on the Rue Rivoli. We leave the hotel, drive out the Rivoli, cross the Place de la Concorde, look at the site of the guillotine now surmounted by an Egyptian obelisk of Luxor of the time of Sesostris, three thousand years ago. You leave this beautiful square and continue out the Champs Elysées to the Bois de Boulogne. Here you have some of the most magnificent works of art to be found upon the globe, lakes, cascades, a miniature Niagara, artificial banks of roses which fascinate you even to weariness and you turn to gaze upon the brilliant pageant of vehicles, comprising phaetons, carriages, *voitures remises,* filled with the beauty and fashion of Paris. . . ."

Steps were heard approaching down the corridor. A well-set-up man in the uniform of a hospital steward stood in the doorway. "Ah, Rowe," he said pleasantly, then went to the side of the bunk and laid a hand on Ned's forehead. "No fever this morning, Allard?"

"No fever," Ned said wearily, "but I'm weak as a cat."

The steward whipped a small bottle out of his pocket and presented it to Ned with a spoon. "Paregoric," he said, "take it three times a day, but only a spoonful at a time, mind you. . . ." He stepped quickly to the door.

"Blake's a nice fellow," Ned said when his steps had died away.

Spencer looked up absently. "Blake? Ah, yes, our hospital steward is a prince—or shall we say a real snob? Prison brings out his best nature. Or shall we say that prison is after all the one place for your real snob? Now Blake is like many of us. In prison he is natural. Once out of prison he will be artificial. I can see him now as some seedy personage approaches." He raised his voice to a falsetto. " 'Do I know him? Oh, yes, a mere watering-place acquaintance. No, it was not Saratoga or Cape May. Johnson's Island, an obscure watering-place. . . .' "

"Not much water now," Ned said. "It's frozen tight as a drum."

Spencer got up and walked to the window. It was almost dark and a few lamps had already been lighted in the prison. In the streaks of light that they sent out the icy plains that surrounded the prison glittered blue.

He shivered and turned away. "I've often thought that we should not blame the Yankees for their depredations," he said absently. "It's only natural they should be bent on conquest. This country was not meant for human habitation. . . . My boy, did I ever read you my account of my stay on the Riviera? Palms, my boy, palms and blue sky. . . ."

Ned stood up, grimacing. "Read it to me another time. I've got to make a trip now."

Outside in the courtyard the paths to the sinks were full. There were two lines of men in continual movement, one coming and one going. Ned stood in line for half an hour before his turn came. When he came out of the enclosure the line of men returning to the court was in brisk motion. Involuntarily he glanced toward the water tower. From that spot on the parapet yesterday a sentinel had shot a man who lingered on the path. Ned had not been in line at the time but reports of the affair were all over the prison. Colonel Jones, the dead man, was a little lame and was hobbling over a rough place near the water house when the sentinel challenged him. Jones did not hear the sentry's call and continued to move at the same slow pace. The sentinel, a boy of eighteen, had fired immediately. Jones sank to the ground then rolled down the embankment. As he fell he called out in a voice that was heard in all the cells: "Oh, God, oh God, my God, what did you shoot me for? Why didn't you tell me to go on? I never heard you say anything to me."

The bugle was sounding. Men were crowding into the mess hall. Ned followed and stood in line until he had received his dab of salt pork and cup of soup. The pork he swallowed but the soup as usual repelled him so that he set it down untasted, and went back into the yard. A stiff wind was blowing but men were still walking about there, enjoying the brief hour of liberty before time to return to the cells. Ned felt too weak to walk but he wanted a little fresh air. He saw a man he knew, Lieutenant Grover from Alabama, sitting on a bench and went over and joined him.

Grover coughed and moved aside to make room on the bench. "What did they have for supper?" he asked.

"Sow-belly," Ned said, "and bread. Soup, too, but it tasted too much like slop for me."

Grover turned around. His eyes glittered fiercely. "I'm not eating," he said. "I'm not eating any of their slop till they move that."

Ned did not need to follow the direction of the pointing finger. Twenty feet from the wall and not ten feet from the sinks ran the imaginary line called the "dead line" common to all prisons. Ten days ago an officer named Anderson had suddenly broken from the row of men going to the sinks and had made a break for the wall. The sentry had shot him down just after he passed the dead line and they had left his body there as a warning.

For days Ned had trained himself not to look at that spot. He raised his head and stared now. There was only a heap of bones left. The rats had carried most of Anderson off. A good thing. The stench had been pretty bad for several days.

He felt a revulsion against both the dead man and the man at his side. Anderson alive had been a nuisance—the guards were always stringing him up by the thumbs for petty infractions of rules—dead he had still contrived to be a stench in his comrades' nostrils and now this fellow was keeping the stench alive. He would probably be doing the same thing in a few days and there would be another smell to live with.

He thought of Spencer. The first day he had arrived in prison Spencer had proclaimed what he called his philosophy. "Work, my boy, all day and half the night, if the guards will let you. Carve buttons, plait horse hair . . . anything so you're busy. Look at me. Acclaimed by all as the sanest man in this pen . . . ."

Ned got up, nodded coolly to Grover and walked about for a few minutes looking for Spencer. When he did not find him he went to seek him in his cell.

Spencer was sitting on the edge of his bunk. A stoutly built gray-haired man of fifty, Colonel Parham, occupied the stool. The two men broke off a low-voiced conversation as Ned entered. Spencer motioned Ned to a place beside him on the bunk. He leaned over and picked up a sheet from among his papers. "I was just showing Colonel Parham an interesting item in today's news." He read:

"Lost: A little white poodle answering to the name of Fifi, belonging to Mrs. H. Maughersby. This little dog disappeared when Mrs. Maughersby was making her weekly visit to the hospital last Friday. Mrs. M. offers a reward of one dollar for little Fifi. . . ."

Colonel Parham looked a little bewildered, then his big laugh rang out suddenly.

Spencer looked up. "Colonel, you're not the ladies' man I'd thought you." He shook his head. "Too bad about little Fifi. I understand it was Mess Number 7 made away with him. Jenkins tells me he tasted much like veal."

"I wish it had been the old bitch herself," Parham said. "Did you hear what Gahagan told her last time she came to see him? Old Mike was having a bad spell and she hung over him telling him she hoped he saw the error of his ways. Soon as he was able old Mike raised up. 'Madam,' he said, 'I have been a sinner in my day, a drunkard and a wastrel, but I never had chronic diarrhea until I fell into the hands of your government.' "

Parham got to his feet before the other two stopped laughing. He was shaking hands with Spencer, looking at him with peculiar intentness, then after a second's hesitation he extended his hand to Ned. "Good-by—if I don't see you again today," he said.

Ned lay back on the bunk. "I saw Grover down in the yard," he said. "He was still going on about them leaving Anderson's body there."

Spencer had sat down on the stool with his back against the wall. His hands were in his pockets. He stared straight before him. It struck Ned that his cousin looked unusually pale today. Now that his face was in repose the crisscross of fine lines about his mouth was visible. His black eyes were sunk deeper in their sockets than they had been a month ago.

Ned felt remorseful as he looked at him. "Poor old Spence, he feels worse than I do half the time but he don't say anything about it."

A thought struck him. He sat up in the bunk. "What did Parham shake hands for when he left?"

"What?" Spencer asked. "Oh, shake hands. Well, Parham is a ceremonious fellow, you know, Lieutenant."

"That wasn't the reason he shook hands just now," Ned said.

Spencer stood up. His thin face was working. He put his hand up to brush away imaginary flies, a gesture that was habitual with him of late, "Ned," he said, "Parham and I are going to try to get out tonight."

Ned fell back weakly against the side of the bunk. "You can't," he whispered. "You'll be shot and if you aren't shot you'll freeze."

Spencer shook his head. "I tell you Parham is an ingenious fellow. He's got one of the guards fixed. We're to go over in the shadow of the tower. Parham brought me some red pepper just now. We're going to put it inside our gloves. That'll keep our hands warm enough while we're climbing the wall and after that . . ." he shrugged.

"Well, after that?" Ned said.

"Parham's got another man fixed on the outside. It's Red's brother-in-law. You know where that dead tree sticks up out of the ice. He's going to be waiting near there with a sled and a team. . . ."

"Red's brother-in-law!" Ned said hoarsely. "I wouldn't trust him as far as you could throw an elephant."

Spencer shrugged again and was silent. When he looked up the expression on his face had changed. There was a note in his voice Ned had never heard before. "I've had enough prison life," he said. "I've had enough. I've been here longer than you have. . . ."

Ned slid from the bunk and laid his hand on Spencer's shoulder. "Take it easy, Spence," he begged. "Wait till tomorrow. If you still feel like it try it then, but wait. Wait one more day."

Spencer sat quiet for a moment then he gently detached Ned's hand. He rose and going to the window stood with his back turned. "I'm sorry, Lieutenant," he said as he came back toward Ned. "But it's the truth. A time comes when you've had enough. I'm acclaimed, as you know"—he hunched his shoulders with something of his old arrogance—"as the sanest man in prison. But last night I had—a warning."

"What kind of warning?"

"I was standing in the corridor," Spencer said. "Standing there in the middle of the night and I didn't know how I got there. I got back to my cell, all right. It just happened that nobody came along then."

"You were walking in your sleep."

"Maybe. Only I hadn't gone to sleep. I hadn't even lain down. . . . Ned, I'm not going to be shot down like a rat the way Anderson was. If I'm going, I'm going to have a run for my money."

Ned did not answer. Spencer began moving about the cell, straightening his papers. He picked up the copy book containing his "Memoirs" and handed it to Ned with a smile. "If you're exchanged and get home in any kind of shape take that along. They might like to know how I employed my time." He snapped the rubber band that held the book shut. "There's a letter inside. Don't open it till after they sound 'Lights out.' He was holding out his hand, smiling.

Ned got up. "All right," he said. "Good-by, Spence."

When they had shaken hands he went back to his own cell. He sat up in bed for a long while and listened. Once he thought he heard steps in the corridor but he was not sure. The minutes went by. He found himself counting. Up to five thousand then stop and begin over again. The light coming in from the corridor revealed a dark object lying on the foot of his bunk. He picked the copy book up and shook it. A folded paper fell out. Ned unfolded the paper and shook a ten-dollar gold piece out on the blanket.

He held the coin in his hand for a moment then stuck it in his pocket. As he moved he realized that he was drenched with sweat. He pulled the single blanket up and wrapped it tightly around his body. Cold in here, always cold. If a man could only get warmed through once. There were steps in the corridor. Randall was standing in the doorway, peering through the half-dark. "Allard, got half an hour till Lights Out. Want a game of Set Back?"

Ned slid off the bed. His hand stuck in his trousers pocket was still in contact with the coin. He let it fall away from his hand then he clutched it again. "Hell, yes," he said and followed his comrade down the hall.

19

MAJOR ANDERSON had been riding through the west Tennessee country for two days and now at nightfall he came to a fork in the road. There was one dim light burning in the house on the right-hand side. Anderson took a chance that it might be the place he was looking for and rode up to the gate. He had expected to be stopped by a sentry. Instead half a dozen hounds rushed out at him. Anderson had ridden over rough country through drizzling rains all day and he was growing impatient for his bed and supper. When the door opened and a woman's face appeared he did not get off his horse but called curtly:

"I was told that Colonel Basham lodged in one of the houses along this road. Will I find him here?"

The woman stepped quickly backward, letting the door swing to behind her. Anderson swore and was about to ride on when he heard footsteps approaching from around the corner of the house. A face was at his saddle bow, a hard, boyish voice said:

"Will you come around to this side? The colonel is expecting you."

Anderson got off his horse, throwing the reins to another orderly who appeared with equal suddenness out of the dark and followed his guide around the house to a side entrance. A door opened upon a fire-lit room which was littered with blankets, saddles, spurs, canteens, all the impedimenta of the soldier. A big, bearded man in civilian clothes had risen from beside the fire and was coming forward.

"Colonel—Basham?" Anderson asked, smiling.

The big man bowed. "I have been looking for you all day, Major Anderson."

The two men shook hands, then the man whom Anderson had called Basham stepped to a door on the other side of the room. "Mrs. Robinson," he called. The door opened a moment later and a woman entered with a tray that had on it a decanter, a bowl and some glasses. Anderson, who was standing on the hearth unfastening his dripping cloak, discreetly turned his back while the woman was in the room. His host observed the movement. "It's all right," he said. "These people are Secessionists."

Anderson finished unfastening his cloak and laid it on the table. He drew a rocking chair up and spread his legs to the blaze. "A bad night, Colonel, but your quarters here are comfortable."

His host took a steaming saucepan from the fire and going over to the table began mixing some punch. "I've shifted them three times this week," he said bluntly.

He came back to the fire. Anderson took the proffered glass, sighed, sank deeper into his chair. "This is very grateful, Colonel, very grateful." The Colonel had sat down in the chair opposite. Anderson, sipping his hot drink, covertly studied his face. Tyree H. Bell—he called himself "Basham" while he was on this difficult mission—was a handsome fellow, well set up, with a ruddy complexion, bright brown curling beard. Anderson liked the expression of his deep-set eyes—"a fighting eye," he called it to himself. Bell was said to have great influence in this west Tennessee country. Anderson knew that Forrest had promised him a brigadier-generalship if he raised a command sufficient to justify the promotion. It seemed a desperate venture, to try to recruit men in this country honeycombed with Yankees. Still, Bell could do it if anybody could. And after all he was in the same boat with his General.

He recalled the day Forrest came back from his trip to Richmond—some weeks after the quarrel with Bragg. A wet night like tonight. The staff was gathered, waiting to hear the news. Forrest strode in, throwing off his dripping poncho. "Gentlemen, I have been assigned an independent command." There was a shout, but he raised his hand. "We will move at once into west Tennessee, to recruit men." Major Strange was first to realize what that meant. He stared then laughed. "Very handsome of His Excellency, General. He will give you command of an army just as soon as you raise it. That's about the size of it, eh?" Forrest looked grim but he said quietly, "That's the size of it, Strange." He maintained, however, that he was well enough pleased with the result of his conference with the President. He was over near Corinth now recruiting. He expected Bell to come out of this country soon with a sizable force.

Anderson stretched his legs out farther to the fire. "Colonel, the last time we met was at Chickamauga. Much water has flowed under the bridge since then." He looked up with a grin. "Perhaps I should say many heads have gone to the block."

Bell's face hardened. "In my opinion there is just one head that should be lopped off."

Anderson laughed. "The soldiers call General Bragg the man with the iron hand, the iron heart and the wooden head. They are usually just in their final estimate of a commander. It is too bad President Davis doesn't consult them instead of some of the advisers he keeps around him."

"I understand President Davis has been in Chattanooga," Bell said. "Was there any demonstration?"

"Not of enthusiasm," Anderson said wearily, "but that would make no difference to President Davis. He is a peculiar man, Colonel Bell. When once he has given confidence he apparently finds it impossible to withdraw it. He will stand by Bragg to the last ditch."

"He does not bestow his confidence in the right quarters," Bell said. He hesitated a moment then added haltingly, "I have not seen anybody in the know now for several months but, Major Anderson, I still wonder why General Forrest was relieved of command, after his brilliant exploits at Chickamauga."

Anderson nodded. His handsome face suddenly flushed. "I was there," he said. "I will never forget it."

The other man was looking at him expectantly. Anderson stared into the fire as he talked. His voice was bitter. "It was on the twenty-second of September, two days after the battle. They had sent us over on the Hiwassee. We located the Yankees all right and closed in on 'em. Dibrell's men had a very pretty fight. We were chasing 'em off the field when a courier came up. He had a message for the General." He stopped and fished in his pockets. "I've got it here. The General read the damn thing and threw it on the ground. I picked it up." He unfolded a creased piece of paper and read:

"Brigadier-General Forrest, near Athens:
General:
The general commanding desires that you will without delay turn over the troops at your command, previously ordered, to Major General Wheeler. . . ."

Bell was silent for a moment, then he said, "Bragg had to have a scapegoat."

"He had to have several," Anderson replied bitterly. "General Polk—and a braver man never lived—barely escaped court-martial. And what about Hill, Hindman and the others? Feeling ran very high for some weeks. I thought—my God, I thought there'd be a revolution and they'd overturn the government! Colonel, did you know that after Chickamauga a letter was written General Lee asking him to take command of the western forces?"

"I did not know that. Who wrote it?"

"It was signed by Generals Polk, Hill, Brown, Preston and others. I have reason to believe that it was General Polk who actually penned the missive."

"What did General Lee reply?"

Anderson's voice was faintly ironic. "He evaded the issue, saying only that he had been so troubled by rheumatism of late that he feared he could be of little service anywhere. . . . He assured General Polk of his highest esteem. . . ."

Bell nodded. "General Lee is above political intrigue of any kind."

Anderson stirred. "Eh? Oh, indeed yes. One of Nature's noblemen and a great commander." He laughed suddenly. "I always think of what Henry Wise said about the General. General Lee took him aside to try to get him to stop swearing. Young Wise said, 'General, your whole life is a constant reproach to me. But we will have to make a bargain. You do the praying for the entire army but let me do the cussing for one small brigade.' . . ." His voice changed, sharpened with bitterness. "Colonel, we will have to dree our own weird here in the West. No help will come from Virginia. They will not even give us moral support. General Forrest is not a 'West P'inter.' "

Bell laughed, a big man's bluff laughter. "The General told me once that he liked to meet those fellers who fought by note, said he could usually beat 'em before they pitched the tune." He heaved himself up out of his chair. "Well, I've got five hundred men lying out there in the woods now, under she-bangs."

Anderson shook his head to express admiration. "Quite an achievement, Colonel, to keep them together, in this weather, with nothing to do."

"We buck and gag 'em every night," Bell said simply.

Anderson laughed. "Napoleon said fear of the Cossacks kept whole battalions of dead Frenchmen on their feet. I believe that you and the General between you can galvanize even an army of 'homemade Yankees.' "

Bell had stepped over to the table and was mixing another round of punch. Anderson got up and stood on the hearth. The warmth had penetrated his bones, the whiskey was relaxing him after the day's hard riding but it had not brought its customary exhilaration. Standing there in the room cluttered with soldiers' equipment he thought of the conscripted men lying out in the wet woods unprotected except for the flmsy oilcloth coverings with the gags in their mouths and the sticks of wood bound behind their backs. It seemed to him that Bell—and his own chief, Forrest—were trying to do the impossible. You could not fight battles without an army, and a man—two men—could not raise up an army by sheer force of will.

There was a rustling in the corner of the room. A tousled head rose suddenly out of one of the beds. "Who's there?" Anderson called sharply. Bell had finished mixing the drink and was coming forward with the glasses.

"One of my boys," he said. "He's been out three nights running now. I bedded him down here because I wanted him to get some sleep before he started out again."

20

AT nine o'clock Rives got up from a sound sleep in Colonel Bell's extra bed. He ate the supper which Mrs. Robinson provided, then buckled on his pistol belt and cartridge container and went out into the yard where Joe Troup was waiting with ten or fifteen other troopers. Rives put himself at the head of the cavalcade and they took a back trail to the river.

It had quit raining an hour ago and a few stars were out. Later, Joe said, there would be a moon. He had had a snack in the kitchen and a pull at Old Man Robinson's whiskey jug while he was waiting for Rives and his spirits were high. He whistled softly under his breath as they went along. "I feel like we going to git 'em tonight," he said. "Yes, Lawd, I feel like we going to haul 'em in this night."

Rives was still groggy from the sleep in the warm room. "We'll have to haul 'em in faster 'n we been doing if we're going to get away from here by the first of the month," he replied.

Joe looked up quickly. "Who said we going to git out of here then?"

"Major Anderson. Major Charles W. Anderson. Ever hear of him?"

Joe skirted a stump. "Well, now you mention it I believe I have. Bud Tilman and I met the gentleman one night when we was out walking for our healths. He was laying in the middle of the path dead to the world. A teamster come along about then so we just heaved the major up and laid him in the wagon. We heaved him in and then we looked up and who should be standing thar but the General."

"What did he say?"

Joe slapped his leg and chuckled. "He come over to the end board and took a good look. The Major was lying on his back a puffing and letting out a regular steamboat whistle every now and then. Man, but he was full of pine top! Old Bedford he got a sniff of it and he shook his head kind of sorrowful. 'Let the hog lay,' he says and walks off."

The two men laughed, so loud that a trooper riding beside them turned in surprise. Joe thumbed his nose at him, rode closer to Rives and continued the conversation. "You say Major Anderson is here now? I reckon that means we'll be pulling out of here pretty soon. Well, I ain't going to be sorry to leave this country, Allard. I don't like it. I never have." He pointed to a gleam of water ahead. "Ain't that something now to be calling itself a river?"

They emerged from the trail and came to a halt on the banks of the stream. Rives looked at the sluggish water. In the dark it seemed black but he knew that by daylight it was an even tawny yellow. That color seemed to him emblematic of the whole west Tennessee country. Burnt, brown fields, sluggish rivers, the unhealthy green of miasmal swamps. He thought suddenly of a place near Good Range where sparkling water sprang from the face of a black ledge.

"Trouble with this country," he said, "they don't have any rock."

"Trouble with this country they got too many swamps," Joe returned. "I stay here much longer I'm going to turn alligator. . . . Hey, where's Hickman?"

Bud Hickman, the native, who had been acting as guide, came forward. He explained in a low voice that they would have to leave the river and strike a trail through the near-by swamp. They had better ride single file and see that the horses set their feet down in the right places. "This here's called 'Dead Man's Chute,'" he said with a grin. "If some of you fellows was to sink in we'd have a hard time gitting you out."

He slapped his bony mare and she went forward, picking her

way sure-footedly from hummock to hummock. The men followed. Sometimes there would be a splash as two horses made for one hummock at the same time, but for the most part horses, and men, too, understood the procedure and the cavalcade went forward at a surprisingly rapid pace.

After a little the tussocks of grass grew more frequent, united finally to form a deep, resilient carpet. The swamp receded. The cavalcade emerged on a plateau of level land, an island rising out of the heart of the swamp, not more than a hundred feet across, the ground hard baked, with little underbrush but a few big trees standing tall and straight as in a grove. The place was evidently a bird sanctuary for the bare ground under every tree was white with bird lime. Joe looked about him uneasily. "Bet there's plenty bats in here."

At the far end of the grove a single lantern burned and figures could be seen moving about it. Fifty or sixty men were gathered. Rives directed his squad to wait at a little distance and he and Joe rode over to see what was going on. The men stood awkwardly in a circle around a big tree. At its foot a young officer sat writing in a notebook by the light of the lantern: Captain Springer who for some weeks had been in charge of the recruiting stations in this county. As Rives and Joe approached he rose and came forward.

Standing beside a big tree he rattled off the names from the company book roll. As each man's name was called he stepped forward and took his place in the line. Rives, sitting his horse a little way off, found himself studying the faces. Most of the recruits were boys just of conscript age. One, as he swaggered forward to take his place in the line turned to grin at a friend. "I figgered they'd git me anyhow so I jist come on over tonight." The friend nodded. "Well," he said, "I always said I had any fighting to do I'd ruther do it under Old Forrest. . . ."

A man of about forty-five sitting on a stump near-by looked up in disgust. "He ain't here," he said. "They told me if I was to come over to Dead Man's Chute I'd git to see Old Forrest and here I done walked all the way from Boaz and clumb through the swamp to boot and they ain't nothing to look at but a couple of leftenants."

The two boys laughed. "You going to war anyhow?"

"Looks like I ain't got no choice. They tell me they done already mustered me in." He sighed and picked up a heavily laden carpetbag which lay at his feet. "Well, I made a good crop this year. I reckon they's enough corn to last 'em till I git back."

The Captain had come to the end of the roll. He closed the book with a snap, turned the newly organized company over to the lieutenant. He laid his hand on the arm of a ragged, lean youth of eighteen. The two came over to where Rives and Tom were waiting. "Allard," the Captain said, "this is Zack Oakley. He says he knows this country like a book," he grinned. "Er, like the palm of his hand."

Zack grinned too, staring at the troopers. "Reckon I can git you out of this swamp and over to Tallman's store," he said.

Rives and the Captain exchanged glances. "Tallman's store," the Captain repeated. "And Allard, wind the business up as soon as you can. We might have to send you out again before the night's over."

It was nearly eleven o'clock when the band of men rode up to the old sawmill. The building, dilapidated and abandoned for years, stood in a bend of the road. The ground around it was treeless, hard and bare except for some ancient refuse, but on the other side of the road was a stake and rider fence and beyond that thick woods.

Rives measured the distance between the sawmill and this fence with his eye. He turned to the men behind him. "Get in there now and stay as quiet as you can." As they filed past he continued to give low-voiced directions: "The main thing is don't jump 'em too soon. Let 'em get as far as that second bend in the fence. We can crowd in then and pick them up easy. But if you get 'em scattered into the woods we'll have a devil of a time."

There was a subdued clatter of hooves, a subdued grunt or two, and then silence. The men filed slowly around the north wall of the building and came to a halt in its shadow. Rives moved up until his horse's nose just poked around the corner of the mill. He could see the single light in Tallman's store glowing steadily. As yet there was no sound of footsteps down the road. He let the reins fall on his horse's neck, got out a plug of tobacco and bit off a chew. It could not be long now. Zack Oakley had already gone off down the road and was lying hidden behind some bushes. It was arranged that he should whistle —a screech owl's cry—the minute he heard the men and boys leave Tallman's store and start down the road. Joe had been afraid that some of them would take another way but Zack said no fear of that. They were all from the Hazel Fork community and would have to pass the sawmill on their way home, unless, he added with a laugh, "they flew."

The boy had been so eager about the affair, a kind of thing that people didn't usually care to mix in, that both Joe and Rives had grown a little suspicious of him. Joe had been especially impatient. "See here, Mud Turtle, it ain't going to be healthy for you if you're wasting our time. We don't want to be pulling in a lot of frying size chickens just because somebody rocked you home from the store one night."

But Zack had been steadfast. Nobody had ever rocked him home and all the boys at the store were at least seventeen. There were also one or two grown men. One was a particularly notorious deserter. He had joined the army twice, but each time had deserted. "And now he says ain't no conscript guard can git him. Says he knows places to hide cain't *nobody* find."

"He must live in that swamp we was bogged down in tonight," Joe growled.

Rives' eyes left the light, roved along the gray road. This bit of country in here reminded him of a place where he and Ben Bigstaff had lain hidden for half of one spring night. There had been a house with one light showing and just such a road leading up to it and a quarter of a mile away a creek. He remembered that lying there—it was one of his first scouts—he had been obsessed with the idea that the man they sought would come from another direction than the one by which he was expected. Ben had been harsh with the fancy. "Don't ever git the idea folks are going to rush up on you from behind. The idea is to rush up on them. See?" . . . But that had been a long time ago, and in another state.

His thoughts went to the early part of the evening. He had been half asleep in Colonel Bell's extra bed when he heard the rumbling bass voice. He had not at first identified it as Major Anderson's, then he had risen up in bed and there was the Major standing before the fire, glass in hand, his tunic off and a shawl draped over his shoulders. He had seen Rives' head coming out of the covers and stepped back, startled. When he found out who it was he made Rives get out of bed and have a hot punch with him before he started out. The presence of a third person in the room seemed to restore some of his old heartiness. He slapped Rives on the shoulder as he stood by the fire buckling on his pistol belt. "Conscript guard, eh? Well, Allard, you may turn out worse than that before we're through with this business."

He and Colonel Bell had gone on talking while Rives drank his toddy. Anderson kept lumbering over to the table to pour himself glasses of raw whiskey. The firelight shone on his downcast, brooding face.

"Yes, you'll raise an army but what'll it be? Raw recruits and a lot of old fellers with squirrel rifles—and I don't see how you can get even them together in the time that's left. Man, we've got to have the army *raised* by the first of the year."

A whole army to be raised by the first of the year! It did not seem possible. Rives thought of the men lying up there in the woods. More than three-fourths of them were conscripts. The other fourth were men in their forties, cotton speculators, some of them, who had been making money trading with the Yankees and would be at it still if public opinion had not been too strong for them. How could even Forrest weld such rag-tag and bobtail material into an army?

The light up the road winked once, then went out. A moment later Zack's whistle rose loud and shrill. Far up the road but coming nearer every minute was a confused sound of voices. A horse behind Rives shifted its weight and sighed. Rives heard leather creak as the horse's master sat up straighter, tightened his reins. The boys coming down the road were talking, then a voice was suddenly raised in song:

"Oh, Louisiana girls, won't you come out tonight,
Won't you come out tonight,
Won't you come out tonight,
I'll give you half a dollar if you'll come out tonight
And dance *by* the light of the moon. . . ."

Silence except for the tramp of feet and then a voice said: "Moon's done set, Ira."

"I don't care," called the youth who had been singing. "Rather have 'em in the dark, anyhow."

The gray blur of moving forms came in sight, moved slowly forward. Rives waited until they were even with the fence corner, then rode out from behind the mill wall.

"All right, boys," he called. "Just come along quiet now and nobody'll get hurt."

The grayish forms scattered, then came together in a huddle. Somebody called "Robbers!" There was a stampede for the fence. One boy was on the top rail with his leg over. Rives caught him by the scruff of the neck and hauled him down.

The rest of the troopers were out from behind the mill by this time. They formed in a silent ring about the boys. The pale light shone on levelled pistol barrels. A boy in the center of the ring set up a cry: " 'Tain't robbers. It's the conscript guard!"

There was suddenly a shrill squeaking as of rats. One boy doubled up his fists. Two others ducked between the horses' legs, made off down the road. The troopers rode after them. In the confusion those that were left turned at bay. The boy at Rives' saddlebow turned up a white, working face, struck out blindly until Rives' mare reared sharply. "Ain't going to conscript me. . . ." Rives struck his mare with the flat of his hand. She came down with a thud and bucked off down the road.

Rives turned her and came back. The boy was a gray streak in the shadows. Rives caught up with him, grabbed him by the coat collar just as he reached the creek. When the boy hit out he struck him a savage blow across the face. "Take that, you little bastard. You're in the army now."

21

ON the eleventh of February, 1864, an invading army, led by the Federal General William Sooy Smith, left Memphis and proceeded southward through Mississippi, burning and plundering as they went. At Prairie Station, General Smith concentrated his entire command then moved toward West Point. The Union column had gone only five miles when the advance guard was vigorously assailed. General Forrest, who had recently come out of West Tennessee with an army of four thousand men, had sent a brigade under Colonel Jeffrey Forrest with instructions to oppose the enemy sufficiently to develop his strength and purpose.

A short, sharp fight occurred, ending only when Colonel Jeffrey Forrest, about to be overlapped on the flanks by a superior force, retreated south. The Federal forces followed. At West Point they found that the three Forrests—the General, Colonel Jeffrey and Captain Bill—had just left, crossing the Sakatonchee River three miles away.

General Forrest had been directed by his superiors, General Polk and General S. D. Lee, to retire in front of Smith's advance in order to draw him away from his base at Memphis and then to turn on him and destroy him. But the Federals were retiring from Forrest's front now. The General became convinced that they had begun a systematic retreat and that the fight was made simply for the purpose of gaining time. He at once ordered concentration of his scattered troops for the purpose of closing in on Smith. The pursuit was difficult. The roads were soaked with rain and cut up by the passage of the two armies. The Federals, however, were so encumbered with negroes and plunder that their progress was slow. Forrest was able to bring his advance guard into more than one collision with their rear before the day was over and his men went into bivouac.

That night Rives rode nine miles to the Pontotoc bridge with orders for Jeffrey Forrest. He got back to headquarters around midnight. The General was sitting outside the tent on a camp stool dictating dispatches to Major Anderson. A cracker barrel, upturned between their knees, served them as table. There was no need for a lantern. The country for miles around was illuminated by the flames of burning farm buildings and fodder ricks.

After Rives had made his report he went into the tent, pulled off his boots and lay down to sleep on a pallet he had improvised out of saddlebags and coats. As he lay there he could hear the two officers talking. Anderson was evidently anxious to finish the business and get to bed, but the General, who hated writing more than he did—he always said that a pen reminded him of a snake—would not spare either himself or his aide. Rives heard Anderson reading one order aloud in his patient, monotonous bass, and then the General's half-querulous: "No, Charley, that ain't got the right pitch," and after that the sound of crackling paper as the aide tore the message up.

Rives fell asleep. Toward daybreak he was aware that he was being called: "Boy, get up. Daylight."

He sat up and reached for his boots, and pulled them on. As he buckled his holster belt and settled his cap on his head, the only preparations he had to make for the day, he glanced out through the open tent flap. It was dark now but the two figures were still seated beside the cracker barrel.

As Rives stepped out through the tent flap the Major laid down his pen and reached for a decanter that stood beside his chair. He poured himself a glass of whiskey, held it up to the light of the lantern. "Your health, General, and yours, my boy." He tossed the tumbler full of liquor off in two gulps, then balancing expertly on the small stool, stretched himself his full length. "Aaah," he said, "that's something like it." He looked out at the sky, then up at the young orderly. His features, gray and lined with fatigue, broke stiffly into a smile; he had for the moment the air of a man gossiping in the back room of a saloon or in a country store. "The General," he said, his voice leisurely and full, "always puts the time an hour ahead. Now what I want to know is what's he going to do some day when he meets himself going backward. Be hell, eh?" and he grinned boyishly.

Rives permitted himself a laugh and Forrest gave the "Tcchk" with which he greeted humorous sallies from members of his staff. He looked at the sky which showed only faintly gray between the trees. " 'Tain't day yet," he said, "but it's going to be soon." He stood up, spreading his legs wide and flinging out his arms stretched his giant frame until his two companions could distinctly hear the joints in his knee crack, then as if the moment's relaxation were all that he could concede to nature he resumed his erect, military bearing, turned to Rives: "Boy, better see about the horses. Going to be movin' here in a minute."

Rives saluted and went off down the path. He passed the cook tent. The negro toiling over the charcoal stove stepped forward and silently extended a tin plate on which there was a cup of coffee, two hoe cakes and a piece of fried sow-belly. Rives took the plate and ate as he went on to the grove of saplings where most of the horses of the escort were tethered. A lantern was stuck in the crotch of one of the trees. In its light Joe Troup moved slowly about, a sack of corn slung over his shoulders. As Rives approached, he was emptying the sack in front of a huge, iron-gray gelding. "I thought I'd just give this big feller a little extra," he said in his slow voice that always seemed to be making some confidence. "You know whether the General's going to ride him today?"

Rives noted the horse's heavy legs and drooping fetlocks. "I don't know why he ever rides him," he said, "looks slow to me."

Troup kicked some fodder toward the gray's nudging nose. "King Philip's slow," he said, "till he gets steamed up. But when he gits steamed up you want to watch out." His rare laugh rang out suddenly in the gray dawn. "You know what he does? He bites. Yes, sir, this feller'll bite anything blue. I noticed it at Gadsden."

Rives laughed and went on around to where his own horse stood. A little black mare whom he had named Kate. She had finished her rations and was sidling restlessly into the horse next to her. Rives slipped the curb bit into her mouth, threw the saddle on, cinched it and mounted. He let his hand fall on her back in a brief caress as he slid the curb bit into her mouth, then stood for a second wondering whether she would hold up under this, the fourth day's hard riding or whether he had not better try to get another horse. As he stood there, his hands still resting on the mare's back, the horse smell strong in his nostrils, he remembered dawns when he and the other Allard boys would go into the stables to saddle the horses for an early hunt. It seemed a long time ago. He threw the saddle on, cinched the girth, mounted and rode back to headquarters.

Major Anderson, Boone, and the rest of the staff were already in the saddle but the General still paced back and forth on the bare spot of ground where the tent had stood. Suddenly he stopped, throwing his head back sharply as a man might do if he heard a distant call in the woods. His eyes under frowning brows stared straight into Anderson's, who sat his horse a few feet away. Anderson averted his gaze from his chief's face and, whistling softly, sat looking at the ground. He knew and the other men who watched in a silent ring knew that at this moment Forrest was making his plan for the day, no more aware of their presence than of the trees that surrounded him.

Troup was leading up Forrest's horse. He mounted agilely. As he gathered up the reins he turned and spoke to the enormous commander of the escort, Nathan Boone, motioning, thumb outstretched to the right. Boone turned his great hawklike head, spoke to the man next to him; the low-voiced command went down the line, and the sixty mounted men went forward. In those few seconds they had learned the plan for the day's attack. Jeffrey Forrest was moving nine miles away to throw his brigade over the Pontotoc bridge. Barteau, meanwhile, was coming forward. The escort, led by the General, would ride ahead as fast as possible to see how things went at the front.

They jangled out of the thicket of post oaks, took a road to the right. It ran beside a little creek. The water course was bordered on both sides by saplings, poplars and water maples with here and there a huge pecan tree. Beyond this narrow strip of woods was the prairie, flat fields on which last year's corn stalks made from this distance a brown grass. The men had come into this rich country yesterday while it was still light. A yell had gone up at sight of the first stackyard with its huge granary and bursting fodder ricks. Men, and horses too, had eaten full rations when they bivouacked, but they might not fare so well after the battle. That granary and a hundred others had gone up in flames last night.

Joe Troup, riding beside Rives, suddenly rose in his stirrups with a yell, raising his long rifle. At the same moment a mounted man leaped from behind an oak tree down into the road. The horse landed a hundred feet ahead of the advancing column, then fell, half-sidewise, half-backwards. The rider had leaped free and was making off into the woods. Joe Troup sent a shot after him, then leaned over to put a bullet through the horse's head. As he straightened up, his blue eyes sparkled. "Plenty pickets," he said. "I'm going to git me one before we hit that town."

The town was before them, less gray than the prairie, but still shrouded in morning mist. Forsythia was blooming beside cisterns; jonquils ran in yellow waves up to blank front doors, darkened windows. Ahead the hoofbeats of the pickets' flying horses rang hard on the turnpike. A negro sweeping a porch stared after them, turned rolling eyes on the oncoming Confederates. A woman standing in a doorway in her nightgown shrieked and ran back into the house.

More cottages, clapboard with trim walks, an old mansion, deserted in its grove of cedars, negro cabins spilling down toward the railroad. They were out of the town. The Yankee pickets skimmed over the prairie like partridges, were swallowed up in a mass of armed men. The Federals were drawn up in strong lines of battle. Their right rested on the Pontotoc Road, their left in open woods. Joe Troup was leaning forward, peering. "Ain't no telling how many Yankees hid in them woods." Rives looked across the prairie to where, distant at least a mile, another force of armed men could be discerned: Confederates; Bell's Brigade under Barteau.

General Forrest was already galloping toward them. The Tennesseeans had recognized him and were cheering. Men threw their hats in the air, beat one another on the shoulder. The yells rolled out and clashed against the woods like the sound of arms. He was standing in his stirrups to address them. The wind ruffled his short beard, tossed his words to the listening faces:

"Whipped 'em . . . all day yesterday . . . and we'll whip them today . . . reinforcements . . . strong reinforcements coming up. . . ."

Major Strange leaned forward and, without dismounting, tightened the girth of his saddle. His eyes searched the prairie. "If Jeffrey Forrest gets here—and McCulloch." He smiled at Anderson. "And if they don't we'll charge without them. There he goes now."

He put spurs to his horse and rode after the General. The rest of the escort clattered after. Already blue puffs of smoke were spitting across the prairie, then suddenly they ceased. The Union troopers had fired only one volley before retreating behind the first line of cavalry. But Barteau's men came right on. They began firing when they were within a hundred and fifty yards of the enemy, but the Yankee breech loaders were more effective than the long rifles. Twenty saddles were emptied at the first volley. Barteau's men were young and raw, most of them in their first battle. Boys turned to look at one another. One put his arm before his face, ducked and made off across the prairie. The line wavered, broke.

Rives, riding not far from the General saw him stop suddenly beside a picket fence. He seemed unconcerned about the break in his own line. His eyes were fixed on the Yankee front. Suddenly he mounted on top of his saddle and standing there, seemingly unconscious of the target he presented, deliberately studied the field. He was smiling and his gray eyes were alight. "Grierson's made a bad move. We'll ride over him," he called out. Disregarding Major Anderson who just then galloped furiously toward him he gave Rives and another orderly the orders he wanted dispatched. A part of Grierson's line had broken. They must press him before he had a chance to recover. Wilson's and Newsom's regiments would go forward on foot while he, with Barteau's mounted, would sweep around to attack the Federal right.

Rives rode off to deliver his orders. As he skirted the lines he heard wild cheering and looking back saw columns of mounted men advancing from the town and moving on to the field from the south. McCulloch and Jeffrey Forrest had arrived in time. He found the officer he sought, delivered the message and turned back to the place where he had left the General. The battle-field now presented a very different appearance. Forrest's manœuvre had been successful: the Yankees were in full flight.

Several Confederate regiments had become entangled in the execution of the manœuvre. Orders were being given for brigades to halt and reform. In the confusion Rives could not find the General or any member of his staff. He decided to go on and swung into the narrow road. Kate had not gone far before she checked and reared. Rives leaned over, saw a horse's hoof upturned, level with his boot. The way ahead was choked. More dead horses, abandoned caissons, a piece of artillery half drawn off the road and stuck in the mud. He backed Kate and set her at the ditch. She cleared it and worked her way up on the bluff.

Two men were already there, Dr. Cowan and a young officer. Dr. Cowan was using a pair of field glasses. The other stared down at the men milling in the road, occasionally slapping his leg with a sassafras switch.

The Yankees had evidently rallied. Dr. Cowan was reporting quietly. "They're forming on a ridge. Lot of post oaks. Right where the road turns. Those farm buildings will be a help to them. . . . They're tearing down the fences now for breastworks." He broke off as the sound of cheering reached them. "Hey, what's going on below?"

The other leaned over to look down into the road. "Those are Jeff Forrest's men," he said.

He rode over to the edge of the bluff. Rives followed him. The disorganized regiments below were falling back to the side of the road to make way for mounted troopers. They went by in columns of fours, at a slow trot. Their leader rode a little ahead of the first squad, on a black horse, long-legged, slim with coarse, black hair falling to the top of his collar. He turned to give an order and the colonel's insignia on his sleeves gleamed dully through the mud plastered there.

The doctor drew a long breath. "They've got their work cut out for them, if they're going to storm that position. . . ."

"In parallel columns!" the young officer cried. "McCulloch's men are moving up too."

Somewhere ahead a bugle fluted. The trotting columns broke into a gallop, surged forward. Three hundred yards away McCulloch's men moved forward too. Rives saw a trooper in the first column lean forward and thumb his nose at one of the men in the opposite line. Jeff Forrest's men thought they were going to beat McCulloch to the attack.

His eyes went to the ridge. Without glasses he could not make out the figures of men but he could see a dark line running out from some building: the gin-house Dr. Cowan had spoken of and a line of breastworks thrown out from it. Plenty of cover. He watched the blue puffs of smoke roll out to meet the mounting figures.

The doctor had his glasses up again. "They're round that bend in the road. They're over the first line. . . ." He did not speak for several minutes. The lieutenant rapped on his breeches leg with his switch, finally touched the older man's elbow. Cowan gave a start. "Hot firing," he said. "They're going toward the gin-house. . . ." He let his clenched fist fall on his knee. "My God, Chisholm!"

The young lieutenant had seized the glasses from him. "On that black horse?" he whispered. "That's Jeff Forrest."

The two men were down the bluff and off over the field. Rives made for the road. The General was not there. He must be on ahead. But how could he have got the news this soon? Unless he, too, had been in a high place where he could see. That black horse fallen beside the breastworks was visible now.

Where the road turned men in gray were massed thickly. Inside the staring crowd a ring cleared as if for a circus. The General was in the center. He held his brother in his arms. Jeffrey Forrest's head was thrown back. His eyes seemed glued down, his face was the color of greenish wax. The bright blood came from out a wound in the neck. The crowd was parting to let Dr. Cowan through. The surgeon knelt down heavily beside the two figures. His hand went to the bag that gaped at his side, then the hand was withdrawn. He sank back quietly on his heels, let his gaze wander over the ring of faces.

The General looked quickly at the surgeon. Now he was looking down into his brother's face. His arms, slowly moving, brought the body upward till his long black hair, falling over his forehead, mingled with the hair of the dead man. He was getting to his feet, stained with blood, staring as straight before him as a blind man, then his pupils focussed. He took a step forward. "Gaus," he shouted in a loud, passionate voice, "Gaus! Sound the charge!"

He had leaped on his horse and was riding off. Rives had not realized that the firing had ceased until he heard all around him men stirring. They moved about aimlessly, walked up, spoke to officers who stood staring and would not answer.

The bugle sounded, high and clear. Gaus' earnest, high-colored face swept past, rigid as if it had been carved in stone. Mounted figures slipped out from the crowd, hurried forward until there were fifty or sixty coursing over the plain.

Rives, wheeling his horse, came into collision with another rider. Major Strange's eyes were bright with fear. In that silence he was whispering: "Be killed. That's what he wants. Be killed."

Rives' stomach seemed to be shrinking away inside. He put his hand to his belt, tightened it, looked off over the plain. The Yankees had taken advantage of the lull to withdraw. A better place. Trees, not flimsy breastworks. Sixty men couldn't take it. . . . He realized that he was riding. Kate had almost crashed then on that fallen log but the nimble devil landed on her feet, settled into her steady lope. Tears plashed down on his hand. He cursed the officer he had just left. "God damn. . . . Lying . . . dirty . . . *coward!*"

He stood in his stirrups, waved his arms crazily. "He's got the right," he shouted. "Every man. Got the right. To get killed," and then he thought that in a few minutes Forrest would be dead, might even be dead now, and he collapsed on his horse's neck.

"Orderly. Orderly." A big man was galloping up on a bay horse. Major Anderson leaned forward. His lips under the clipped moustache were trembling. "Orderly, get on back there. Get some of 'em up. . . . Rambaut, Duff, anybody. . . . HURRY UP. YOU WANT TO SEE 'EM CUT DOWN LIKE SHEEP?"

Rives wheeled his horse and galloped back down the road. Men were coming up the hill, toilsomely in wavering lines. He caught sight of an officer, dashed at him, shouting: "Rear guard across the road. . . . Nobody up but the escort. Hurry!"

Rambaut's black, French eyes looked out over the field. He put his hand up to his black moustache. He said, "A death trap if I ever saw one. Yes, orderly, tell Major Anderson I'll bring my men right up."

Rives rode on. Across the field were more mounted men. Under an apple tree a wounded officer was being helped onto his horse. One of his hands, swollen with enormous bandages, hung limp at his side. He swore as he gathered up the reins, turned a choleric face on Rives. "What's this, orderly? The General and his escort outridden support? Where's Barteau? Duff's boys? Aaah!"

He was off over the field. A lieutenant had seen him coming and was squealing an order. Men were forming in line. McCulloch rode out in front of them. "Come on, boys," he yelled. The whole brigade was sweeping after him. A riderless horse under the apple tree tossed its head and whinnied as the hoofs churned the plain. Rives put his hand up, wiped black mud from his face, realized that the horse under him was trembling. He laid his hand on her neck. She stopped dead still. He got off, looked back, saw her tail stretch out flat behind her as she went down. He went over to the apple tree, swung up on the bay horse and headed for the road.

They had the start of him. There was no moving thing on the road, only men who sat or lay in stiff attitudes, under trees or fallen against the slope. He pounded across a marshy place, and suddenly figures were coming toward him, men who ran swinging their muskets, gaping. One had his tongue out like a dog. Rives struck at him with his pistol, rode on.

The bullets still sang from the ridge but here at the foot of the slope was confusion. Riders huddled in a mass, horses plunging sidewise, rearing. Men looked up at the ridge, looked at one another. A man at the side of the road intoned softly to himself: "Ain't going up there. . . . Ain't going. . . . Can't nobody make me go up there. . . ." He pulled his horse backward, so sharply that he reared. "Hey you, Dandy," he said in a quiet, natural tone.

Rives followed the direction of the starting eyes saw McCulloch push his way through on his roan horse. He had ridden out a few feet in front of them before he stopped. He held his enormous, bloody right hand up, shook it till drops spattered down onto the shoulder of his jacket. He shouted:

"Men, are you going to stand there and let 'em kill your General?"

He turned his back on them, rode for the slope, the roan's legs doubling like a jack rabbit's. They came after him. The man who had cried was neck and neck with Rives. He leaned forward, pounded his horse's neck. "You, Dandy, git in there. *Catch hell!*"

They reached the gin-house, swung out to avoid it, came upon a cabin. A woman and two children squatted in the corner of the chimney. The woman had a child on each side of her. Her arms pinioned them in her skirts. Her eyes moved like beads on a string, following each bullet as it pinged in the short grass.

A boy careened around the corner on a sorrel horse. He was hatless and his eyes looked out of black rings. He rode halfway into the yard, stopped, sobbing. "Ain't no more ammunition, ain't no more . . ." turned and rode back the way he came.

In the pasture the Yankee cannon chattered out of a grove of post oaks. Their derision was for a line of willows where figures swayed back and forth, contending for possession of a red slash in the ground. Forrest's men had thrown away their useless rifles and fought hand to hand with revolvers But more Yankees kept coming up all the time out of the field. Some of the riders were springing across the gully, were into the midst of McCulloch's men as they came up. A Yankee captain raised amazed eyes, grinned before he slipped out of the saddle. Off to the right a voice was roaring. "Charge 'em, boys. One more time."

The Yankees were scrambling back across the ditch, making for the post oaks. The men with revolvers raised eyes light in powder-blackened faces and cheered. Forrest was riding along the side of the ditch on a big gray horse. He stood in his stirrups, yelling: "Got 'em, boys. On the run!"

Rives was cheering with the others when a hand was laid on his arm. Joe Troup was beside him.

"You hurt much, Bud?"

"Not hurt at all," Rives said indignantly then looked down and saw that his right boot was full of blood.

22

CALLY, sitting at the window, watched Love and Jenny Morris go down the path on their way to the post office. She was startled to notice how much the child had shot up in the last year. Her head came to Love's shoulder. She looked like a young lady, or would, Cally reflected bitterly, if she had had on a decent dress. There had been enough of the blue calico for a bodice but the skirt was skimpy. Without hoops it hung around the child's slim body in dejected folds. "It looks like the dresses we used to make for the little niggers," she thought, "just wide enough to step over the fence." Jenny Morris, however, seemed in good spirits. She was laughing as she looked up at Love, holding on to her arm. Love looked prettier than usual, or was the color in her face just the reflection from the pink parasol she carried? It was in questionable taste for her to be carrying that parasol when she was still in black. She had taken to wearing her black silk dress—the one they had put together for her after George's death—every day now and she had made herself a new collar for it out of scraps of lace from Ma's workbag. Cally watching her through narrowed eyes observed that she paused and looked up and down the street after she had passed through the gate. Yes, there was Arthur Bradley sauntering up from the side street. "Ma," she whispered without turning around, "he's going with them. Well! I wouldn't have let Jenny Morris go if I'd known *he* was going along."

Mrs. Allard did not answer. She often did not answer Cally nowadays. Once Cally had put the question to her directly. "Do you think she's going to marry him?" "Lord, child, I don't know," Mrs. Allard had returned, but later in the same day she had said dryly, "You ought not to go live in a person's house if you're not willing to marry into their family."

Cally, taking up her knitting again, glanced around the room. The cottage, a comfortable four-room brick structure in the corner of the Bradley yard would go certainly to Belle at the old man's death. But it was not hers yet, not by a long shot. The old man was good for many a year yet. Besides, she thought fiercely, we pay him rent. I wouldn't have given my consent to come if we hadn't. She told herself that and then she remembered the night Jenny Morris had seen the face—the black man's face—pressed against the window pane and she knew that nothing would have induced her to spend another night at Brackets. It was just after Cousin Edmund died. Winston was down with pneumonia. They had not heard another sound after that one stealthy stirring of the bushes but they had sat up the rest of the night, Mrs. Allard with an old squirrel rifle across her knees, she herself armed with an axe. No, she thought, I couldn't go through that again. . . .

The gate latch clicked. Mr. Bradley was coming up the walk. Cally watched the spare, agile figure advance and noticed for the thousandth time how the thin, grayish face converged in two sharp lines at the chin. "Old fox," she thought, "old gray fox. That's just what he is. And he goes like one too, jumping from one place to another before you know he's moved. Ma," she called in a low tone, "Ma, here comes Mr. Bradley."

Mrs. Allard was sitting with her husband before the fire which Winston had just kindled. She leaned over and touched his arm. "Fount," she said, "time for your nap."

Mr. Allard had been staring into the flames from under half-closed lids. He sat up straighter, his mouth set in an obstinate line. "I ain't going," he said. "I ain't sleepy."

Cally glanced at her mother. Mrs. Allard shook her head wearily. "Let him stay. Remember last time he made an awful scene when we tried to get him out." She leaned back in her chair. There was a bewildered expression on her face as she listened to the approaching steps. "I didn't know this was the first of the month," she said.

"Well, it is," Cally returned shortly.

She rose and went to the door. Mr. Bradley swept his hat off, bowed slightly before he took her hand in his thin, dry fingers. He was advancing toward Mrs. Allard, bowing again. "A pleasant day, Madam. I hope it finds you well."

"We're all very well here," Mrs. Allard said, "but I thought Fount might be taking a little cold so I had Winston make up a fire."

Mr. Bradley took his seat in the rocking chair she indicated, stretched his hand toward the fire though he was too far away from it to feel any heat. "Nothing like it," he said, "in early autumn. . . . Where is the little girl?"

Cally who had taken her place a little back from the fire did not answer. "She went to the post office with Love," Mrs. Allard said. "Cally likes for her to go out and run around a little between lessons."

Mr. Bradley half turned so that he could face Cally too. "She's very fortunate to have a mother who is such a scholar. Not everybody would be capable of carrying on the child's education."

"I can't teach her anything but the three R's," Cally rejoined, "and not much of them. She'll be lucky if she don't grow up an ignoramus."

"She couldn't do that," Mr. Bradley said. "You've had more education than most, Miss Cally. Didn't you go to that convent up at Bardstown?"

"Cally went to the convent long as the sisters would have her," Mrs. Allard said with a faint laugh. "I used to think when she was a girl she'd turn out a regular bookworm. Why, she used to study her mathematics even in the summer."

"I always did like mathematics," Cally said.

Mr. Bradley turned to Mrs. Allard. "We had fine schools in this country before this war came to interrupt 'em. Now it was different when Fount and I were boys. Old field school and half the time they didn't hold regular sessions. Of course the higher education was of the best, if you were lucky enough to be sent off to the university as Fount was. I had to go to work young to support my widowed mother so I got no more'n the three R's."

Cally got up and made a pretense of getting something from the table. *"Fount!"* she thought. "He never called Pa that before. He never dared."

Mrs. Allard was talking, a low murmur of words, something about an old teacher all three of them had known. Cally looked at her father. The sound of his name had roused him from his doze. He was sitting bolt upright in his chair staring at the caller. "I know who you are," he said suddenly, "Old Joe Bradley . . ."

". . . a very eccentric man, though so learned," Mrs. Allard said. "My father used to say . . ." She broke off as her husband began to rise from his chair. Her hands that had been clasped in her lap tightened on each other till the knuckles stood out white. "Cally!" she cried out sharply, *"Cally!"*

Cally got up and walked out of the room. She shut the door behind her and stood leaning against it a moment. Then she flung it wide and stood on the threshold. "Pa!" she cried in a sharp voice, "Pa, man out here wants to see you about a horse."

Fontaine Allard was standing in the middle of the floor gazing around the room uncertainly. His eye brightened at Cally's voice. He said, "Yes, tell him I'm coming," and walked toward her.

She stood, pressed against the door until he had passed then flung it to behind her. She took his arm and walked with him through the passage to the porch. Old Winston was sitting there in his low chair shelling black-eyed peas. She called to him: "Winston, come here quick and get your master."

He had put his peas down and was hobbling forward. His hand was on Allard's arm. His old black face peered up. "Come on, Marster," he crooned, "come on, less go see 'bout them horses."

They moved down the walk together. She waited until he

turned his head to nod at her reassuringly then she went back into the house.

Mrs. Allard and Mr. Bradley were sitting just as she had left them. Mrs. Allard was staring into the fire. Mr. Bradley rocked a little as he talked. "I'm a person doesn't give up hope easily. Now I believe something could be done for Fount. There's still good doctors in the country, ma'am, and if we could get him to 'em they could probably figure out what was wrong with him. . . ." He coughed delicately, "I don't need to remind you, ma'am, that expense would be no consideration."

Mrs. Allard looked up. "It wouldn't be any use. He's too old. Young people can get over anything like that. But he can't. The damage is done."

Cally, listening to that dry, hard voice almost hated her mother. If Ma, only once, would take somebody else's advice. She had insisted that they pay Mr. Bradley the rent for the cottage the first of every month and had suggested that he call for it in person. But for Ma they wouldn't have to endure this visit every month. He didn't come any other time but he came punctually then. And it wasn't for the money. No, he had found something at last that he liked better than money. He must know what people thought of him, what they said. "Old Joe Bradley, talks mighty pious but watch out for him in a trade. . . ." Yes, he'd had to put up with that all his life. But now he could make up to himself for it. He could come here and see the Allards dependent on his charity, for that was what it came to, see her father the most respected man in the community reduced to imbecility. Oh, he loved it, Old Bradley did. It was keeping him alive, making him younger every day. . . .

There was silence in the room. Mr. Bradley evidently respected Mrs. Allard's opinion too much to argue. He was casting about for some other subject for conversation. "But he'll have to go soon," she thought. "In a minute now she'll give him the money and he'll have to go."

She had taken up her work but she suddenly laid it down in her lap, looked quickly at her mother, then looked away. She knew now what was the matter. There wasn't any money. Her mother hadn't told her but the gold Uncle John had left with them must all be gone. That was why Mrs. Allard had been so queer all morning, why she couldn't believe it was already the first of the month. . . . She picked up her work again, clicking the needles frenziedly. "Never mind. Let's go on and be beggars in name as well as deed. It would suit me better and it would suit *him.*"

He was rising, saying something about the weather. Mrs. Allard rose too. She got his hat from the rack, put it in his hand. He held it pressed against his thin old chest. His eyes, very bright for an old man, were fixed upon Mrs. Allard's. The words, about the cold spell that set in early last winter, came faster. He had shaken Mrs. Allard's hand, pretended not to notice that Cally's was withheld. He was backing away. "If she'd just let him go," Cally thought, but Mrs. Allard was speaking.

"Mr. Bradley . . ."

He stopped with those bright eyes on her face.

"The rent," Mrs. Allard said, "we're going to have to be late with it. . . ."

He raised his hand in deprecation. "My *dear* Madam . . . too old friends. . . ." He was gone in a mumble of words, a series of bows. The door shut behind him. Mrs. Allard drew a long breath, spoke slowly, the words seeming to be drawn from her against her will. "Joe Bradley isn't as hard a man as people think."

Cally watched the spry old back retreat down the walk. "I hate him," she said. "I wish he was dead. Dead and rotten."

23

JIM came into the store by the back way and hung his hat up on the nail by the door. Gosnell, the clerk, was bending over the counter, sorting out a box of nails. He looked up as Jim entered. "Mornin', Mister Jim. Now you here I believe I'll step over and get the mail."

"All right," Jim told him and went around behind the long counter. Gosnell had left the box of nails out. Jim took up where he had left off, sorting out the ten-pennies from the four-pennies. From time to time he raised his head and looked about him. He had been working for nearly a month now, rearranging the stock and getting things in order generally. This morning, for the first time, he was satisfied with the appearance of the store.

Somebody was coming in the back door: Cally, with a basket on her arm. Jim had already seen her that morning when he stopped by the cottage to find out how his father and mother were and he did not greet her now but went on working until she came over to the counter.

He looked up then. "What'll you have?" he asked genially.

Cally was gazing around the way she always did when she came into the store as if there were not anything there she could possibly want. "Have you got any more of those dried apples?" she asked. "Pa seemed to relish them the other day."

Jim said he had. He was going over to the barrel where the apples were kept when Cally suddenly stood aside. "There's somebody coming," she whispered.

A man was coming in the front door, a lean countryman whose boots were caked to the knee with red clay. Cally shrank back. "Don't mind me," she said in a tense tone. "Go on and wait on him.

Jim went over to the man. "Mornin'," he said. "What'll you have?"

The man looked the shelves up and down then his gaze came back to Jim. "Got any coffee?"

"A little," Jim said. He started toward the shelves then turned back. "How you going to pay for it?" he asked.

The man drew out a roll of Confederate bills and laid them on the counter. Jim shook his head. "Sorry, Brother, but we aren't taking them."

The man's Adam's Apple was visible as he swallowed. "I figured maybe you wouldn't," he said. "Well, I got to have a little, anyhow. My wife's mother is down in bed. Heart trouble."

"How many pounds you want?" Jim asked.

"What's it worth?"

"Takes a two-bit shin-plaster to buy a pound," Jim told him.

The man drew the grimy piece of paper out of his pocket, laid it on the table. He shook his head. "I don't know when I'm going to git any more of these."

"Wish I knew where I could get some," Jim said. He wrapped the pound of coffee up in a piece of newspaper and handed it over the counter. The countryman thrust the package into his coat pocket. "You got any sugar?" he asked.

"A little," Jim said. "It's higher'n a cat's back."

The man grinned. "I ain't going to even ask you what it's worth then. That old lady'll have to git along on long shortening."

"Well, it won't hurt her," Jim said. "I been putting molasses in my coffee a long time now—when I got any coffee to put it in."

The man had been eyeing Jim intently. "Ain't you one of old Mr. Fount Allard's boys?" he asked now.

"I'm the oldest," Jim said.

"There was another one, warn't they? Young feller."

"At Johnson's Island," Jim said. "Been there nearly a year now."

The man nodded. "The Yanks got one of my brothers too. Fort Delaware they sent him. Jim Boston his name is. Big, tall feller. You ever hear of him? Long Jim Boston from out near Port Royal?"

"No, I never did," Jim said. "I don't know many folks out that way."

The man settled his ragged hat on his head." And I don't git to Clarksville much," he said. "But I knew you. It was funny how I knew you by the favor. Soon as I came in I says to myself, 'That's one of old Mr. Allard's boys,' and then I says, 'No, he wouldn't be working here in a store.' " He laughed. "I've known Allards all my life but they was all country people. Don't believe I ever saw one in a store before. That's how come I didn't know who you was right at first, even with the favor."

"Well, I don't hardly know myself these days," Jim returned amiably.

The man laughed and went out to his wagon. Cally had retired to the back of the store but she came forward and stood silently in front of the counter while Jim deftly twirled. news• paper into a cornucopia to hold the dried apples. When he had finished she took the paper cone from him. He thought that she was going without saying anything but she paused. "Jim," she said coldly, "I should think you'd be ashamed to take that poor man's money."

Jim tried to be airy. "Why? He wanted coffee and I wanted money. Fair exchange is no robbery."

She hardly listened to what he said. She leaned over and brushed the "shin-plaster" off the counter. She set her heel on the paper and ground it into the floor. "You take the enemy's money," she cried. "You're no better than a spy or a deserter."

Jim's lip trembled and beads of sweat sprang out on his forehead but he kept his voice calm. "Now look here, Cally. I couldn't go to war as you very well know. But I've got to do something. You can't run a store without taking in money and there's no use taking in money that ain't worth the paper it's printed on."

Caily snatched her basket from the counter. "Running a store," she cried. "You, Jim Allard, running a store! No wonder that man didn't know you were Papa's son. Why don't Mr. Bradley put Arthur down here to run this store?"

"Arthur's young," Jim retorted, "and he hasn't got any judgment. If it suits me and suits Mr. Bradley I don't see that it's any concern of yours."

She opened her lips as if to say something else then compressed them and walked hastily toward the door. He was angry now and he came out from behind the counter and followed her. "You think so much of being an Allard, but let me tell you something, Madam. You'll see Allards doing lots of things you never thought to see before you're through with it. You better be glad one of us has got enough sense to keep a roof over your head."

Cally still said nothing, only made a flicking motion with her free hand the while she walked faster. He stood in the doorway watching her until she had disappeared into the house, then he drew his handkerchief out and wiped his forehead. He emitted a long sigh as he turned back into the store. He tried to be patient with Cally but she got harder and harder to manage. It was awkward, with the family all living on Mr. Bradley's property. They paid their way, of course. At least they had so far but Mr. Bradley had been kinder to them than the circumstances demanded. That was why, he, Jim, had been willing to come down and oversee the store. "I'd rather do it," he thought angrily, "than go back to Brackets and fool with a lot of ungrateful niggers."

He stumped about the store, his hands in his pockets, then after a little he walked to the door and standing on the porch looked out over the yard. The brick wall was covered with Virginia creeper. He was surprised to find that it had turned red in many places. Fall, and he had hardly realized that it was summer. But time had a way of standing still lately. In the last months he had almost forgotten that the war was going on. That was why his mother and Cally didn't want to live here. They didn't want to forget the war one minute. And they resented his being able to absorb himself in his work. He glanced down at his shrunken leg. They didn't need to grudge him that. They disliked Mr. Bradley because he too stood aloof from the war. Mrs. Allard—that was before she came here to live—had even aspersed his loyalty—because there was a rumor that he had given a draft on a Cincinnati bank. Joe Bradley a year ago had converted a sizable sum of money into United States bonds. They were deposited in a Cincinnati bank, all right. Old Joe had made no bones about it in conversation with Jim. Confederate currency, he had pointed out, would soon be worth no more than the paper it was printed on: a man's first duty was to his dependents. Jim's brows knit. His mother wouldn't agree to that. A man's first duty, she would say, is to his country. She regarded her husband much as if he had been a soldier struck down in battle; she was proud that Ned was in the service. He knew that she regretted that her older son had not been able to go. Well, he himself had hated it when all the rest of them went off. But that was a long time ago. They had been fighting now for years and what good had it done them? They had better come home and see what they could make of the country, ruined as it was. That was what Mr. Bradley said and he had a hard head.

There was the sound of steps on the gravel. A man was coming slowly around the bend in the path. A tall thin man who had a great shock of beard and bright feverish-looking eyes. He was in dirty, ragged clothes and had a whip curled about his neck, the handle falling down across his chest. A poor starving devil of a teamster, evidently, looking for work. Jim wondered how he got in here. He closed the door behind him, locked it, then stepped down on the walk. The fellow had not spoken so Jim called out: "Good morning. Sorry, but we don't have any work."

The fellow still did not speak but he was coming nearer, glancing around with those unnaturally bright eyes. Crazy, doubtless, from hunger. So many of 'em were these days. "You can come on up to the house," Jim told him. "I expect my wife can find something for you."

The man stopped then in the middle of the path. "Don't you know me?" he said.

Jim looked deep into the sunken eyes. "You're Ned," he said. "Ned, but I'm damned if I'd a known you."

He was beside his brother, embracing him. In his exuberance he clapped him on the shoulder. Ned shrank away from the light blow so hastily that he staggered. He recovered himself and sat down on the edge of the porch. Jim came and stood over him. "How'd you get out?" he asked excitedly.

"I was exchanged a month ago," Ned said. "They sent us to Cairo on the cars. Then they put us on an old tub and sent us down the Mississippi to Memphis. I went to Jackson from there . . ." He stopped, his voice trailing off weakly as if he had told the story already too many times.

"Well, what happened then?" Jim said.

"I found Colonel Martin. I thought I'd ask for a thirty days' leave. He told me not to come back."

"Not to come back," Jim repeated.

"Discharged," Ned said. "They were starting out for north Mississippi. Colonel Martin said no use in my coming, said I was too sick."

"So you headed north then?"

"Why, yes," Ned said. "There wasn't anything else to do. Colonel Martin give me some money but it gave out. I had to sort of work my way across the country. I've been on the road a long time."

Jim had him by the shoulder and was drawing him to his feet. "Come on," he cried excitedly, "come on, let's get up to the house. Won't Cally and Ma be wild?"

24

JIM took his watch out as he rose from the table. "I don't have to go back to the store till two o'clock," he said to Ned. "What say we go out in the yard and sit awhile?" He was aware as he spoke of Cally's eyes upon him—she had been looking at Ned all through the meal and now she was turning that same misty, devotional smile on him. It made him nervous. He looked away from her, to Ned. "The ladies here all take a nap after dinner. We don't want to interfere with that."

Cally was silent. Ned finished folding his napkin, with slow, deliberate movements, then got up and silently followed his brother out of the room. They crossed the yard and stepped up on the little porch of the "office." Jim sat down in one of the chairs ranged along the wall. Ned took his place beside him but after a moment he got up and dragged his chair out into the sun. As he passed Jim caught the odor of his foul breath and involuntarily drew back. Ned had tilted his chair against a pillar and was sitting on the edge of the porch where the hot sunshine beat directly into his face. He had shaved a few hours ago at Jim's instigation. The skin of his face and neck where it had been sheltered so long by his beard looked pocked and blue. "Like a picked chicken," Jim thought, "an old chicken that's been on hand too long." He looked at Ned's hands, crossed on his shrunken knee. They were putty colored except for the knuckles which were puffy and blue. Jim moved irritably in his chair. "You'll bake there, man," he said.

Ned shook his head. "I can't get too hot. I can't even think what it'd be like to be too hot."

Jim gave a "Tchhk" of sympathy. "I reckon that cold got in your bones. What was the coldest it got?"

"It was twenty below a lot of the time."

"Was it that cold the night Spence Rowe escaped?"

"I reckon it was. I didn't notice."

"And he had ten or fifteen miles of that ice to cross?"

Ned had been staring off over the garden. He withdrew his gaze, fixed it on Jim. "Spence didn't get away," he said. "They shot him when he was climbing the wall. I didn't say anything about it before the ladies."

Jim was silent a moment, then he asked belligerently. "How do you know? You say you never saw him again after that evening."

"We heard the shots. One for him and one for Parham."

"Well, how do you know they were for them? Didn't those sentries ever miss?"

"I never knew 'em to," Ned said indifferently. "They shot men for stopping to button their pants on the way from the sinks. I reckon they got Spence, all right."

Jim stole a glance at him. He had a morbid desire to know how much suffering this man whom he could not at the moment think of as his brother had undergone. "I reckon it was pretty bad in those prisons," he said. "Did you ever know any men to eat rats?"

Ned made the dry sound that with him betokened amusement. "When they could get 'em." He shifted his thin leg so that it caught the full rays of the sun. "Johnson's Island wasn't as bad as some places, they told me. One officer came over from Camp Douglas said they used to run to the sewers after every meal to get the raw potato peelings and even then most of 'em had scurvy. Douglas must have been worse than most," he added reflectively. "Those nigger guards there were bad. Used to jump up on the prisoners' backs and ride 'em around the yard."

Jim leaped to his feet and began walking up and down the porch. "Name of God!" he cried. "You'd think human beings couldn't bear it. You'd think they'd dash their brains out against the walls before they'd submit to such indignities." He continued to walk back and forth for several minutes. Ned had not spoken or changed his position. Finally Jim, having paced the length of the porch, came back to his chair. The sick man looked at him. Jim caught the glance and looked away. He had not noticed before that even the flesh of Ned's eye sockets was shrunken, withered and shrunken until there was a deep fold in each lid. It gave the eye a peculiar, hooded look. And the eye itself had changed color. Ned as a boy had had sparkling brown eyes. The brown was shot through with purple now as the eyes of very old persons are. And yet there was something in the glance of the eye that you did not find in an old person. It was as if the man had stopped seeing. Yes, that was what gave the eye that veiled look. He thought of a toad that he and the other boys had found once far back in a cave in the woods. They had pushed it out into the light of day with a stick and it had sat there staring and seeming not to see anything. "What you reckon it lives on?" Spence Rowe had whispered and a shudder had gone down all their backs as they imagined the foul things the creature had fed on.

He conquered his revulsion and sat down. "Have you thought what you're going to do?" he asked.

Ned turned his head slowly. "Why, I haven't had time to think about it much. Where's the nearest place I could join up, you reckon?"

Jim leaned forward, staring. "Join up?" he cried. "Man, didn't you know Atlanta had fallen? And Joe Johnston's been retreating all summer. I tell you it's all over. We're whipped. The sooner we realize it and settle down the better off we'll be."

Ned looked away, off over the lawn where the shadows were beginning to lengthen. "I reckon they're still fighting," he said slowly.

"A few fools like Old Forrest and Cousin Frank are still at it but it's over, I tell you." He looked at Ned shrewdly. "Besides, what regiment'd want a bag of bones like you? You ain't worth feeding, man, and that's a fact."

"I don't reckon I am worth feeding," Ned said after a pause.

Jim tilted his chair back against the wall. He made his tones hearty. "Your soldiering days are over. Best make up your mind to that. Now you want to get into something that'll give you a living. How'd you like to stay here and help me in the store?"

"Store?" Ned said, and then was silent.

Jim let his chair thud to the floor. "Well, what about it?"

"I'm not much in the business line," Ned said. "I reckon I'd better just go on out to Brackets. You been out there lately?"

"Yes," Jim said.

"How'd things look?"

"There were three or four nigger cabins standing and two, three more out buildings. A good many of the negroes are there. I told 'em to go over in the woods and cut down some logs and get 'em up some cabins before winter set in. They've raised a little corn, enough to carry 'em. The women and children made the crop mostly. The men are all gone. I went out there a good deal the early part of the summer, but lately I've just been letting things go. It's no better on my own place. I haven't even got a crop there."

"Where's Uncle John?" Ned asked.

"He's still in Canada," Jim said dryly. "He finds it agrees with his health."

Ned stood up. "Well," he said, "I reckon tomorrow or next day I'll go on out to Brackets."

Jim found himself angry. "What for? I tell you, man, there ain't anything there but a lot of niggers eating their heads off. Ain't even any stock on the place."

They had started walking up the path to the house. Ned was ahead. He turned around so that his dull eyes looked into Jim's. A faint color burned in his sallow cheek. "I reckon the land's still there," he said. "The Yankees couldn't burn that and they ain't strong enough to cart it off."

He was moving up the path. Jim followed. He saw Cally and his mother moving among the flower borders and suddenly called to them. "Well, I reckon you all will be satisfied now. You can go back to Brackets."

His mother stood immobile, with no change of expression. Cally was bending over a bed of geraniums. She straightened up and turned a startled gaze on him. "What do you mean?" she demanded.

He enjoyed her surprise. "Ned says he's going to Brackets. Shape he's in he'll be able to make a big crop."

His mother went quietly over and took Ned's arm. Cally flung herself toward him across the flower boarders. She was sobbing. "Oh, thank God! Thank God!"

The three of them moved ahead of him up the path, the women clinging to Ned on either side. Jim walked slowly behind. He was thinking of Brackets as he had last seen it. The desolate burned-over place where the big house had stood and the three or four windowless negro cabins that were all that was left of the quarter. They would probably move back into the office. They would start packing to go right away, tomorrow, maybe. They had seemed contented enough till Ned came along. But now nothing would do them but to go back to Brackets. His eyes rested on his brother's skeleton form that seemed to be carried along the garden path in the sweep of skirts on either side. The fellow was half dead. It would be a kindness to let him die, go on and die and be buried in the old graveyard at Brackets. But they wouldn't do that. No, they would nurse and coddle him back to some sort of life. He kicked irritably at a weed in his path. Women were the devil. They never knew when they were licked.

25

CALLY was on her knees packing the last trunk when Love came in. She did not look around but called to the girl briskly: "Little more room in here, honey. Got anything you want to put in?"

Love quietly said no, there wasn't anything she wanted to pack. After a little, Cally heard a faint sound that might have been weeping. She turned around. Love was standing by the window looking out over the garden. She had on the same dress she had worn at breakfast. Cally realized that she had not packed any of her belongings.

She got to her feet. "What's the matter?"

Love continued to look out of the window. She was pale and her mouth was firmly set. "Aunt Cally," she said, "I'm not going to Brackets with you all."

Cally stared. "Not going to Brackets! Then where are you going, pray, Miss?"

Love turned. "I'm going to stay here," she said, "with Jim and Belle. They want me. I'm going to stay."

Cally took two or three steps about the room in her effort to control herself. "Want you?" she cried. "Jim don't even know who comes to the table. And Belle . . . well, I reckon Belle wants you, all right."

"I don't see what you've all got against Belle," Love said defiantly. "Belle's been good to me. I like her."

"Belle's been good to me too," Cally said slowly. "I haven't got but one thing against Belle. She's a Bradley."

Love had moved over and was standing with her back against the door. Her breath came hard. Her hands were clenched at her sides. "I don't think so much about blood," she cried stormily. "I don't think our blood is so fine."

"It may not be so fine," Cally said wearily, "but I reckon people are like horses. You breed 'em for what you want to get out of 'em. . . ." She looked at Love. "You going to marry Arthur Bradley?"

Love's lips quivered but she kept her head up. "Yes, I'm going to marry him. I don't care what anybody thinks."

Cally sat down on the sofa, suddenly, as if her legs had given way. "This awful war!" she groaned. "You wouldn't have done this but for this awful war."

Tears were glittering in Love's eyes. "If it hadn't been for the war I'd have married George."

Cally nodded. She was looking past the girl, out of the window. "Yes," she said, "you'd have married George."

There was silence. "I love Arthur," Love said at length quietly. "I love him more than I ever did George."

Cally had not seemed to hear what Love was saying but now she turned her head. Love was appalled by the fierceness of her tear-dimmed gaze. "George is lying out there at Chickamauga," she said, slowly, bitterly. "Don't hardly anybody know where his grave is but I'd rather have him than a thousand Arthur Bradleys."

Love had sat down in a chair near the sofa. She looked at the floor a moment before she spoke. "I know what you mean. Arthur didn't go to war."

"Yes," Cally said quietly. "He didn't go to war. That tells the tale." She bent a sombre gaze on the girl. "There's just two kind of people in the world, those that'll fight for what they think right and those that don't think anything is worth fighting for. Old Man Bradley don't care about anything but making money. And he's got all his money in United States bonds in a Cincinnati bank. The talk is he's traded in contraband cotton and I don't doubt it. . . ." She got to her feet, looking old and tired. "They say we're losing the war. I reckon if we do people like him'll rule this country. You may be glad, Miss, that you married a Bradley. . . ."

Love stood up. "I don't see that you've got a right to talk," she cried angrily. "Your own marriage didn't turn out so well. I don't see that you've got any right to look down on Arthur."

Cally looked at her. Love was frightened when she saw the older woman's face pale. "No," Cally said heavily, "my marriage didn't turn out right. But it wasn't my fault. I did what seemed right at the time." She half turned away then faced the girl. Love saw that her hands were shaking. "I never said anything about it before," she said. "Nobody ever mentioned my marriage to me in the way you've done. But I knew Charley wasn't any good before I married him. I knew it but I was afraid of all the talk and I reckon I was in love with him too. Anyhow I went on with it. That's what gives me the right to talk to you now. . . ."

Love burst into a storm of sobs. She came toward Cally, her arms outstretched. "Oh, Aunt Cally, don't please . . . please!"

Cally put her arms about the girl's shoulder. "All right," she said. "I've said my say. It's over now, far as I'm concerned. She patted the shining, blonde hair, lifted Love's chin to look into her eyes. "How old are you now? Twenty? I reckon it's natural for you to want to be happy. Go ahead. I won't say any more."

Part Four

1

DR. COWAN handed the basin and discarded bandage to the orderly and got up slowly from his kneeling position beside the bed. "That foot'll be all right now if you just give it a chance, General." He wadded a pillow up and stuck it under Forrest's knee so that the leg lay out straight. "Now keep it like that awhile, as long as you can. Gives the circulation a chance."

He washed his hands in the basin of fresh water that the orderly had brought. "You hear what I say, General?"

"Oh, I heard you, all right," Forrest said wearily. "Trouble is keeping your leg stuck out like that. Ever try it?"

The surgeon shook his head. "No, General, but then I've never had a ball traverse the sole of my foot. Very painful wound, I'm sure."

He picked his bag up, motioned to the orderly and went out of the room. Forrest waited till the door had shut behind him then turned to Anderson. "Well, Charley, what does Stephen Lee have to say?"

Anderson was seated behind the little field desk which he had set up as soon as they moved into these quarters a few days ago. He had been silent during the surgeon's visit, studying the sheaf of papers that a courier had just placed before him. As he looked up his eyes were bright. "Big news, General. They're sending out another expedition."

Forrest raised himself up on his pillows. "How many?" he demanded.

"Twelve to fifteen thousand infantry . . . five hundred cavalry. Reliable information. . . ."

Forrest sank back among his pillows. "Who's heading it? They won't send Sooky Smith again, I bet."

Anderson laughed. "Sherman's got a new man. Here's a letter of his Lee got hold of. It's to McPherson. . . ."

"Read it," Forrest said.

Anderson squared back so that the light fell more fully on the copy of the stolen missive. He read in a round voice with relish:

". . . We will not attempt the Mobile trip now, but I wish to organize as large a force as possible at Memphis with General A. J. Smith or Mower in command, to pursue Forrest on foot, devastating the land over which he has passed, or may pass, and to make the people of Tennessee and Mississippi feel that although a bold, daring and successful leader, he will bring ruin and misery on any country where he may pass or tarry. If we do not punish Forrest and the people now, the whole effect of our vast conquest will be lost. . . ."

Anderson chuckled as he finished reading. "General, you certainly have Sherman's good opinion. . . . Well, what's to do?"

Forrest deliberated. "If they leave Memphis the first, they ought to be in this neighborhood in five or six days. . . . Better concentrate Buford and Chalmers in front. And tell Buford to send a hundred picked men to their rear. That'll put the skeer on 'em. They'll think they're being cut off from base right at the start. Better send 'em under Tyler. He'll move fast. . . . I'll be on the road myself tomorrow."

Anderson glanced at him. He seemed about to say something but checked himself. He rose. "All right, General. I'll get the message to Buford and Chalmers right away. Tyler too."

"Better send that boy, Allard," Forrest said. "He rides faster'n most of 'em."

"He ain't here," Anderson said. "Don't you remember he got hit in the knee, at Okolona."

Forrest moved restlessly on his pillows. "Well, send Troup then. Any of 'em you're a mind to. . . . What you standing around for, Charley? Didn't you hear the doctor say I must get some sleep?"

"All right," Anderson said hastily. He paused to draw the blinds then tiptoed from the room.

Forrest raised himself a little and bracing his shoulders against the headboard for a moment managed to slide his whole body far down under the covers. He gave a sigh of relief. That was better. Trouble with having so many of them around all the time a man could hardly grunt when he felt like it. He closed his eyes. If he was to get on the road tomorrow he ought to take advantage of this chance for sleep. But sleep would not come. His thoughts were already on the coming engagement. . . . This would be the third expedition they had sent out against him, first "Sooky" Smith, then Sturgis and now these two new men, Andrew Smith and the young brigadier, Mower. Sherman was promising Mower a major generalship if he was successful. "Go out and follow Forrest to the death . . . if it takes ten thousand lives and breaks the Treasury." He opened his eyes and stared at the wall opposite. They said that the authorities at Richmond didn't appreciate him. Well, he would take his praise, when he got any, from the Yankees. Sherman, for all his book learning, went right to the point. He wondered what Sherman would think if he knew that he owed his most brilliant success to one of those stolen telegrams! He sat up in bed, oblivious of the pain in his foot and leg. The blood surged hotly through his body. Brice's Cross Roads! A fight to hand down to your children and your children's children. Yes, he would take his stand on that battle. He liked to look back on it. Every detail was as fresh and clear in his mind now as on the day itself. . . . But he might not have fought it the way he did but for Sherman's telegram.

The ninth of June. They had arrived at Booneville in the midst of a torrential rain and rain had kept up all that night. He had sent Anderson to Lee the day before with a message, saying he was ready to make an expedition against Memphis. Anderson came back that night with the news that he must retrace his steps. An expedition—eight thousand strong under Sturgis—had left Memphis on the first and was moving through north Mississippi. Lee's telegrapher had intercepted a message from Sherman ordering the advance. Anderson had a copy of the message.

There were half a dozen young officers in the room. Forrest had had them all cleared out so he could think. Young Morton had been making a map for him. It was still there on the table. He had walked over to study it—he could never plan any movement till he got the whole lay of the land in his mind. As he passed around to the other side of the table he looked down and saw the stolen telegram where Anderson had left it. Two phrases had leaped out at him: "Go out and follow Forrest to the death . . . if it takes ten thousand lives and breaks the Treasury."

He saw that and realized something that he had never realized before. The Yankee expedition was not moving out to plunder the country or to reinforce Sherman's rear. It was coming against him, Bedford Forrest. He had been deathly tired that night but the realization had cleared his brain like lightning. He felt as if he were already in the midst of a battle. The plan of it had come to him in that moment, complete almost in every detail.

He studied the map. Sturgis, according to reliable information, was encamped that night on the Ripley road. His own forces would be moving the next morning along the Guntown road. He put his finger on the spot on the map where the two roads intersected, at the farm of a man named Brice. He knew then that the battle would be fought there.

He walked up and down the floor for an hour marshalling his forces in his mind. The artillery and Rucker's brigade, seven hundred strong, were here with him at Booneville. Johnson's and Lyon's brigade were at Baldwyn, six miles away. Bell, with 2700 men, was farthest away, at Rienzi. He had figured it all out, walking up and down in that room. A close shave to get them there on time but he would have to chance it. He sent the couriers out around eleven o'clock with the orders. At twelve o'clock he went to bed and to sleep.

The men were on the road the next morning as soon as it was

light enough to see. A hot day even then with those gumbo roads sucking at the horses' hooves every step of the way; they were foaming before they'd gone five miles. At eight o'clock he pulled up beside the head of Rucker's column. He told Rucker then that he felt pretty sure that the fight would be at the cross roads. "They'll make slow progress along that narrow, muddy road. The cavalry'll be there three hours in advance of 'em. I aim to whip the cavalry before the infantry gets there."

Rucker looked up at the sun, a nasty bronze color already. "It's going to be hot as hell."

"That's what I'm figuring on," Forrest told him. "As soon as the fight opens they'll send back to have the infantry hurried up. Coming on the run for five or six miles over roads like these they'll be so blowed we can ride right over 'em."

Rucker nodded—he had a bull-dog look on him all that day. "And you think the fight'll be at the cross roads."

"Yes," Forrest said, "I never took a dare from 'em yet and I ain't going to do it today. I'm going ahead now with Lyon and the escort and open the fight."

But Lyon had already opened the fight. His advance had collided with Waring's a mile beyond Brice's house on the Baldwyn road. When Forrest rode up messages were already coming back to the rear: the Yankee General had dismounted a whole brigade and thrown it on both sides of the Baldwyn road. A good place, too, just on the edge of a field and well protected by blackjack thickets.

That for him had been the most ticklish moment of the fight. Rucker was still two miles to the rear and Johnson yet behind Rucker. The Yankees had two thousand men dismounted and already on the field. They might have sense enough to charge in force now. If they did they could run over his small command before Rucker and the others came up.

He knew he had to do something and do it quick. He couldn't think of anything better than the old trick he worked on Streight. As soon as he got on the field he dismounted Lyon's troops and threw them in line on the edge of the woods. He had men tear down alternate panels of that old worm fence too as if he expected to come through in force any minute. Then he ordered Lyon to make a show of force, throwing a double line of skirmishers out into the open field. It worked, all right. The Yankees opened with small arms and artillery but cautiously. Lyon's men held them there with the feint for an hour.

While Lyon was holding them he ordered Barteau to take the Second Tennessee and go across the country through the woods until he struck the road over which Sturgis must pass on his way to the cross roads. Barteau had two hundred and fifty men of Bell's brigade with him. They could play hell if they got into the Yankee rear.

It was eleven o'clock by that time and getting hotter every minute. He remembered looking up at the sun and thinking it looked like it might melt and run down out of the sky. But he was glad of the brassy heat. He was counting on it to help whip the Yankees. Rucker came up about that time and a few minutes later Johnson. A lot of his horses had given out on the way. Bell hadn't got there but Forrest knew he must carry out his plan just the same. He rode out in front of the dismounted cavalrymen and told them that the next attack would be a real one, no feint this time.

The bugle sounded. The three skeleton brigades went forward. Johnson on the right, Lyon in the center, Rucker on the left. From the little hill where Forrest was watching it looked like they were running a race to see which would get to the Yankees first. Rucker made the first impression. He struck that line fully a hundred yards ahead of Lyon and Johnson. The enemy concentrated their fire on him. Forrest rode to the front. The men were staggering, some of them dropping flat on the ground, some hiding in gullies. Rucker and Lieutenant Taylor dashed in and ordered them back in line. The fire was still pretty deadly and they hung back. Then somebody yelled, "Pull out a tree, boys." They jerked a bushy topped blackjack out by the roots and the Seventh Tennessee poured through the gap. Some of 'em clawed the brush off the top of that fence to get at the Federals. It was too close by that time for firing. They were using pistols and clubbed muskets.

The Yankee center gave way slow but it gave way. Some of their troopers must have mounted again. You could see horsemen making off over the field and then there was a lot of confusion and the sun flashed on arms so bright it hurt your eyes. The Yankee infantry was on the field.

He waited till he was sure before he rode back behind the lines. He was wondering then if maybe he hadn't run his calculations too close. He'd done what he'd planned, beaten the cavalry before the infantry came on the field; but it wouldn't do him any good if his artillery didn't get up in time. And then he saw them coming, at a gallop, the horses' bellies bloody from the spurs. Eighteen miles but they made it just in the nick of time. He rode up to Morton, shouting his orders. They placed the guns to the right of the Baldwyn road, in Lyon's rear. He stayed long enough to see John open up on 'em with double-shotted canister, then he rode over to where Bell was.

Bell moved forward about two o'clock and the battle started up hotter than ever. You could tell that the infantry was on the field now, all right. The small shrubs and bushes were being cut off to the earth as close as if a cradler was at work. Bell's men held their ground but their ranks were being thinned out too fast. Then they broke in one place. The Yankees took advantage of it and advanced all along the line.

Forrest got off his horse, dismounted all the escort and sent them in. He had fifty of Gartrell's Georgians with him on headquarters duty. He slung them into the breaking line too. It stiffened and held. Just then Colonel Wisdom came up, with two hundred and eighty of Newsom's regiment. He threw Wisdom's men in on the left. That checked the Yankees all right.

It was four o'clock by this time. The battle would have to be won before dark set in but he couldn't do anything till he was sure Barteau had got into the Federal rear. He rode back to a position on the extreme right from where he could overlook the field pretty well. He sat there and waited till he saw a sudden movement in the Yankee cavalry around Brice's house. He wasn't sure even then, so he waited till he heard musketry off near the creek. Barteau had come up. He rode back fast to Bell and told him that in a few minutes he would order him to charge on the left.

Then he rode out in front of the men. Usually when he made them a speech he thought out what he would say beforehand. This time he just told them what in that moment he knew to be God's truth. "If you do as I say I will always lead you to victory. I have ordered Bell to charge on the left. When you hear his guns and the bugle sounds every man must charge and give 'em hell."

They were pretty hot by that time—some of 'em drinking water out of the sponge buckets, a thing he'd never seen before —and they didn't waste breath cheering. But they had the right look on their faces. He rode back to where Morton was with his guns. Morton saw him on the brow of the hill and left his post. He said, "General, you'd better get down that hill. They'll hit you there."

"All right, John" he told him. "I believe I will rest a little." He dismounted and sat down at the root of a tree. Morton came over and stood in front of him. He told him he was going to order a charge all along the line and he pointed out the place where he intended to double 'em up. He told Morton that when the charge sounded he wanted him to hitch up his guns and charge without support. "Give 'em hell, John," he said, "right yonder where I'm going to double them up."

John said, "Yes, sir," like he always did. All hell couldn't rattle that boy. Rice had come up and was standing near them. Forrest heard what Rice said as he turned away. "Captain Morton, you reckon the General meant for us to charge without support?"

"You heard the order, Captain Rice," Morton said. "Be ready."

Forrest was mounted again by that time and riding toward Buford's position. He gave him final instructions and told him what part artillery was to play in the charge. Buford thought it was dangerous to throw the guns forward without support. Forrest knew it was dangerous but he knew too it was the thing to do. "Buford," he said, "all the Yankees in front can't get to Morton's guns the way we're going to charge."

Lyon was coming to meet him. A reckless fellow. He laughed out loud when he got his orders: "Charge and give 'em hell and when they fall back keep charging and giving 'em hell. I'll soon be there with you and bring up Morton's bull pups."

He left Lyon still laughing and rode back down the line. He had never in his life felt surer of anything than he was of the happenings of the next few minutes. It was pretty to watch it work out. The minute the bugle sounded the Confederate line leaped to its work. Morton's four guns charged down the road and unlimbered just as the Yankees came out of the woods. They threw charge after charge into 'em until the Yankees fell back. The artillerymen began pushing the guns forward by hand and giving it to 'em hotter all the time. He himself had got back a little, far enough to see Johnson sweep forward and throw the Yankee wagon train into confusion. The wagons parked in the field west of the Ripley road began moving to the rear then. Meanwhile Rucker, Lyon and Bell were herding the Yankees back toward Brice's house. The Confederate lines, massing, got stronger as the Federal line weakened. By the time the artillery got into them they were running to the rear and toward the creek. There was a dismounted regiment of cavalry there, reinforced by a negro regiment. They tried to stem the tide but it didn't do any good. Morton captured six of their guns. He promptly turned three of them right back on the Yankees. This increased the panic. A wagon was overturned on the bridge. The Yankees crawled over it or swam the creek or drowned. Forrest's escort had passed over a little way down the stream. They came up, charged into the mob and captured a lot of them as they came over.

The sun went down but they kept up the pursuit. He came upon a squadron of his men at a creek. They were looking at the bodies of some negro soldiers lying on the bank. Dead as door-nails but two or three of 'em hadn't a scratch anywhere; died of fright, Strange said.

They captured the rest of Sturgis' wagon train, several ambulances and fourteen more guns. Sturgis tried to make a stand at Ripley but they flanked him out of there pretty quick. Forrest sent the horseholders ahead then to keep up the pursuit and allowed the rest of the command to sleep from one o'clock till three. They struck Sturgis again at Stubbs' farm and drove him into the Hatchie bottoms. He was worse scared by that time than the niggers. A Yankee deserter said that Bouton was trying all the time to hold the rear with his colored troops. This man said he heard Bouton ask for a white regiment to help him lift the wagons on to better ground. Sturgis said: "For God's sake, if Mr. Forrest will let me alone, I'll let him alone. You have done all that you could and more than was expected of you and now all you can do is save yourselves. . . ."

He grinned. Opening his eyes he saw Anderson standing at the foot of the bed. Anderson looked perturbed. "General, I've been talking to Dr. Cowan. He says you can't ride horseback tomorrow with that foot."

Forrest sat up. "Who said I was going to ride horseback?" he demanded. "I'll travel in a buggy. Prop my foot on the dashboard. What you standing around here for? Why don't you go out and git me one? We've got to move away from here and move fast."

2

THEY were still dancing in the parlor when Rives and Lucy came out on to the porch. He had brought his blanket roll out with him and laid it with his pistols on the bench that ran alongside the wall. "This shindig will be breaking up in a few minutes now," he said. "We'll have to be on the road by eleven o'clock." She made no comment and they had stood there together for a little while gazing out into the dark. Then he remembered that he wanted to have a last-minute talk with Uncle Mack. He had wanted her to walk with him down to the quarters. But she refused, pleading her thin slippers as an excuse.

She stuck her foot out before her and turning it in the light from the window noticed that the thin kid had broken in two more places since she put them on. Her last pair of shoes. She might never have another. "But then," she thought, "I will probably never dance again."

She sat down on the bench. She was very tired. The preparations for the party tonight had been going on since yesterday. When Mrs. Allard had announced that she was going to give one last dance for the soldiers before they went away, nobody could see how she would manage it. There had not been a dust of flour in the house for months and of course sugar these days was unheard of. But the cakes had been made—of meal bolted till it was as fine as flour—and flavored not with cane syrup or sorghum but with the juice of watermelons. Susan had had a hundred melons brought up from the patch and the women of the place had been busy all yesterday afternoon squeezing the slices through sacks and then boiling the juice down in the great outdoor kettle. The result had been a bright golden syrup which Susan pronounced to be as good as any made from cane. It had flavored the cake nicely but at the last minute there had been another serious complication: no oil for lamps or tallow for molding candles. Mitty had been on the point of tears. "You can't have a dance without lights, Ma!"

"And why not, pray?" Susan had demanded sharply. But she had been pleased when Lucy had discovered her substitute for candles: balls of the sweet gum tree floating in shallow bowls filled with melted lard.

Lucy looked into the parlor where the improvised lamps sat one on each end of the high mantel. They flickered with every breath of wind and the light they gave off had an odd, wavy translucence.

Her eyes sought her mother-in-law's face. Susan Allard's great chair had been drawn up between the two west windows. She sat far back in it, her small feet well off the floor, her hands folded one over the other in her lap. There was a fixed, bright smile on her face, and her eyes followed the dancers with an almost childish absorption. Lucy drew her breath in sharply. "She's happy," she told herself. "Everything has gone just as she wanted it."

She shifted on the hard bench, tried to concentrate on the dancers. There were half a dozen of them before the window now. The Rawlins' boys and the Petersons and those girls from Oak Grove. The soldiers danced with abandon. Their booted feet shook the floor and even the rafters of the old house as they whirled their red-cheeked, bright-eyed partners about in the maze of the dance. Every now and then three or four would get together and clap till the fiddlers started their favorite tune up again:

> "When Johnny comes marching home again . . .
> Ta Ra! Ta Ra!"

She and Rives had been in there with them until a few

minutes ago. But he could not dance because of his injured knee. He had sat with the old people in the chairs ranged along the wall while she danced first with one, then another of the young men. Each time she passed he had been sitting with folded arms staring straight before him. When she had at last come over to sit beside him he had stood up abruptly. "Let's go out on the porch." She had known then that he had only been waiting for the time when the party would be over.

Rives' face came before her, dark and set as it had been each time she glimpsed it in the whirl of the dance. When she had first known him, long ago—oh God, how long ago!—at Brackets, it had been a square-cut, boyish face, almost heavy. Now it seemed actually longer but that was because there was no spare flesh on it. The bony structure showed everywhere as if during these last four years the flesh had been slowly whittled away. It was the sucked-in hollows of the cheeks that she minded most and the deep lines graven from the nostrils to the corners of the mouth.

Once, turning over in bed on a moonlight night, she had caught a glimpse of his face on the pillow and had bent swiftly over. The bitter line was there, even in sleep. Later that same night a hard voice had spoken suddenly out of the dark: "We've got to get out of here, Joe. If he won't come stick him and leave him."

When she had succeeded in waking him he said that he must have been dreaming he was "on the road." All the rest of that night she had lain there wakeful. The brutal words seemed to reverberate in the room. Lying there she had been troubled by persistent fancies. Spies—and Rives was to all intents a spy—were not like other soldiers. They had strange things to do. She felt a sudden revulsion from the man at her side. Raising herself on one elbow she had studied his face. The light coming in at the window illuminated his features: the high, aquiline nose, the eyes set in their deep hollows, the stern mouth. In the moonlight they were like marble. The kind of face that might be carved on a tomb. She drew a quick breath, sank down beside him, after a little reached over and laid her fingers on his nerveless hand. It comforted her to find it warm.

She was thinking now of the day he came home. In February. They had taken Little Ed and the spring wagon and had met him at Dalton. Two man had carried him off the cars on a stretcher. He had seen Lucy and his mother before they saw him and had raised himself on the stretcher to show that he was all right, that it was only his knee that was hurt. He had not been shaved for days and powder was still grimed on his cheeks. His eyes had been as bright as if he had fever.

They laid him on the mattress that had been placed in the bed of the wagon and piled quilts about him—he was shivering though it was a warm day. She had sat low on the wagon floor beside him, holding his hand, while Little Ed plied his whip and shouted to the oxen. They had come home by Wayman's because the road was easier. She remembered pointing out some pussy willows in a swamp to Rives. He had raised himself a little on his elbow to look at them. There was hardly any green along the road and yet it seemed to her that she had had more conviction of spring then than in all the months of its flowering. She raised her eyes to the trees that crowded up to the house. They were fully leaved, had been for two months. She hardly knew when that had happened. It had been a year without seasons, the longest year of her life.

She forced her mind back along the months. That first night when they had got him onto the great bed in the downstairs room. He had been tender then. . . . Or had she merely imagined it? No, he had turned to her often in the night and by day he had wanted her to bring her sewing and sit beside his bed.

The change, whatever it was, had come over him later when he was up and around. That day Bob Acree was there and Rives had taken two or three steps across the room to show that he could walk almost as well as ever.

Bob had laughed. "If that bullet had gone a little nearer the joint you'd a been all right."

"All right?" Rives repeated.

Bob laughed again. "Well, this way you'll have to be going back in a week or two, won't you?"

There was a dead silence. She had not realized what was happening till she saw Bob take two hurried steps backwards. He was still laughing, but awkwardly. "Say, I didn't mean anything."

Rives was breathing hard. He let his clenched fist sink to his side. "Well, you'd better go home," he said.

Bob got up and walked out. Rives turned his back and stood at the window looking out. She went softly up to him. He did not seem to know that she was there. After a little she let her shoulder press against him. He raised his arm; it fell about her shoulders, but it lay there nervelessly. She had felt him exert his will to tighten it. It was then she had run out of the room. He had not come after her.

The door on the porch opened. A young man and a girl came out. They did not see Lucy at first and moved toward each other, then the girl caught sight of the form on the shadowy bench. She came forward, into the light, humming a tune, putting up a hand to rearrange her hair.

"It's cool out here," she said.

Lucy did not answer and after a moment they moved off together down the walk. When they had gone Lucy went down the steps and stood looking down the other path. There was no one in sight yet, but she thought she heard the sound of footfalls and yes, that was the clink of the gate chain. She walked slowly back, took her seat on the bench.

He came up on the porch slowly with his halting step. He went over to where his knapsack and pistols lay, took one of the pistols up, held it in his hand a minute, then laid it down and came and sat beside her. Under the voluminous ruffles of the old, much washed chambray her body was rigid. The hand that lay on the bench between them trembled. She told herself that she would not speak first, then heard herself speaking, "Well, how is Uncle Mack?"

He was sitting with his clasped hands swinging between his spread knees. He did not look up. "All right. He complains of rheumatism, of course."

She rose and walking over to the opposite end of the small veranda, broke a spray off the clematis vine. She held it in her hand, turning it this way and that to catch the light. "He wanted your mother to sell him the other day," she said.

He was looking up now. There was surprise on his face. "Uncle *Mack?*"

She nodded carelessly. He was still staring at her. She waited a moment then said: "It was funny. He found out somehow that Mr. Billings wanted to buy him, so he came up and urged Cousin Sue to sell him to her. He said the negroes were all bound to get free, anyhow. And he'd rather Mr. Billings would lose the money than Miss Sue."

He laughed shortly. She looked at him with malicious eyes, then as the surprised look died out and his face assumed its heavy despondent look, her own expression changed. She forgot that she had wanted from him surprise, laughter, tears, anything that would break that mask-like calm. She went over and sat down beside him, so close that their bodies touched and slid her hand under his. "Rives," she whispered.

He said, "Yes, darling," but his hand did not tighten on hers. She resisted the impulse to take her hand away, leaned back against the bench. "Are you sure you have everything?" she asked in a low voice.

He was still staring out into the dark. "New jacket," he said, "comb, all that soap, the medicine, and the extra blanket. Hope I can hold on to it. . . . Lucy, I'll try to write oftener this time."

There was a flurry in the hall. Voices. A door in the back of the house opened. Somebody called "Ten o'clock," and another voice drawled, "That isn't possible." They had remembered the time. They were gathering their things together. It would take them five minutes, three, two . . . no, they would be out here at any minute!

"Yes," she said, "I know how hard it is . . . but if you could . . . we worry. . . ."

They were on their feet, moving side by side to the place where his belongings lay in a dark pile. He had taken up the pistol belt and was strapping it on. His eyes were bent down. There was a frown on his face. "The trouble is that I'm always thinking I'll get time to write a real letter. . . ." He paused, fumbling with the buckle, "but even a note is better than nothing, I suppose."

The pistols settled into their leather jackets, one on either side of his waist. His face was still bent down. She put her hands behind her to hide their trembling. She said: "Yes." You are going away. I may never see you again, but I will desire you all my life. "Yes," she whispered, "even a note."

Steps in the hall. They were all coming out on to the porch. The youngest Rollins girl kept saying, "Joe . . ." Back in the house a soldier laughed. "But I tell you I got two. . . . You might as well have one. Cousin Sue, you come here, you tell him. . . ." Rives was standing beside Mitty. She had her arms around his neck. You could hear her crying. He put her arms down gently, went to his mother where she stood in the doorway, kissed her. He was coming back.

Lucy moved to one side where the light would not shine on her face. He was in front of her, was bending over. His lips were warm on hers and hard. Her face was wet with tears. She held it up for his second kiss.

Good-by, Rives. Good-by. Good-by. . . .

3

RIVES awoke with a start. For a moment he lay rigid, staring at the dark wall opposite, then he shifted his gaze to the tent flap. It had been black when he lay down on his pallet, but now it was pearly gray. Dawn could not be far off. He closed his eyes and was about to go back to sleep when he heard outside the tent the sound of slow footsteps. He sat up quickly. A dark figure was visible for a moment, silhouetted against the gray light, then it passed on and the slow, regular footsteps resumed.

Rives lay back against his wadded-up blanket roll. He told himself that it would be time to get up in a minute; he had better make the most of the few minutes left. But the footsteps continued to make their round of the tent. He listened to them and all desire for sleep left him. He felt as if he had been awake for hours. After a little he got up, lit a lantern, pulled on his boots, armed himself and left the tent. He walked about for a few minutes then sat down on a stump, placing the lantern on the ground beside him.

It seemed darker now than it had been when he woke. But that was because of the lantern. It sent yellow streaks of light across the snow, covered the tent wall with the shadow of trees. His own booted feet loomed there, enormous. He shifted his feet idly and as he did so felt in one of the soles the nail that all day yesterday had pricked him. He took the boot off and examined his foot. The nail standing almost upright in the boot sole had worn through the layers of toughened skin and the leather was stained with blood.

He got out his knife and with the heavy handle began hammering on the nail. He had worked for several minutes before he was aware that he was not alone. The General had come from around the side of the tent and was standing motionless beside a tree. He had on his black slouch hat and over his uniform he wore one of the ponchos that had been captured from the Yankees a week ago. He stood there for a few minutes staring into the lantern flame, then without speaking turned and resumed his solitary pacing.

Rives replaced his boot and laced it up. After a little he reached into his pocket, brought out a piece of hardtack and munched it slowly. As he ate, his eyes wandered over the scene. Off to the south was the town of Murfreesboro. His brother, Miles, was there, sick, lodged at the house of Dr. Nelson. He shifted his gaze to the north. He could not make out the fort—a thick grove of trees intervened between it and the camp—but he was conscious of its presence there on the horizon. He had been one of the men who had ridden with the General when he made a reconnaissance yesterday and decided that it was too strong to take by direct assault. But there would probably be a battle or skirmish of some kind before the day was over—the General would find some way to lure them out. He could not visualize the approaching battle. He was more interested in the weather. The light was getting brighter now. There was a stiff little wind, but it came from the north. He puffed his breath out. It hung before him in a little cloud, then slowly vanished. He kicked at the snowy ground under his feet. No sign of thaw. The earth was frozen as tight as a drum. He thought of Joe Troup. Joe was keeping a sort of calendar on the sassafras stick that, dandy that he was, he used for a toothbrush. Fifteen notches on it, Joe said. That meant that it had rained or hailed or frozen every day they had been in Tennessee.

His mind went back to that day when the dispatch had come, in early November at Corinth. They were trying to get out of Mississippi over roads that were hub deep in mud. The head of the column had just reached the town when the dispatch came from General Beauregard. He himself had brought it to General

Forrest. He had searched for him up and down the line, had finally found him at a blacksmith shop a little off the road. Horseshoes and even nails had given out by that time. The General was watching the manufacture of some shoes from tires that had been stripped from farm wagons along the way.

Major Strange was with him. Forrest read the telegram, then handed it to Strange. The aide read it and handed it back. His eyes rested a moment on the General's face, then went back to the road. There was a temporary halt in the line; a horse had just fallen. They had hauled him to his feet and his fifteen companions—it took sixteen horses now to pull a single cannon—were being cut out of the traces. Strange watched the wretched animals being led to the side of the road, waited while the yoked oxen moved slowly forward to take their places. There was a hard smile on his face when he turned to Forrest:

"Better late than never, General. I congratulate you. You are now in command of all the cavalry of Hood's army."

Forrest was gazing over the heads of the floundering men and beasts at some distant woods. He said: "It's a gamble for Hood to go into Tennessee but it's no bigger gamble than for Sherman to march through Georgia."

"General Sherman," Strange began, "is marching through a rich country, and laying it waste, I understand, in unprecedented fashion . . . but what forage is there here?"

Forrest did not wait for him to finish. He turned and roared at Rives: "Boy, hurry up. Find Captain Boone. Tell him to take two squads and scour the country. Go fifty miles each side if he has to. Take brood mares this time and two-year-olds, whether they're broke or not. Tell him I want him to meet me at Bolivar with enough horses to mount five hundred men."

That was on the twelfth of November. They had pushed on as fast as they could to Florence where the General assumed command of the new forces. The bad weather had begun after that. The fords of all the rivers were swollen far out of their banks and the roads were ice and mud. So many of the infantrymen were barefooted or else had nothing but pieces of sacking to tie on their feet. The General had ordered hundreds of them into the wagons. Hell on the teamsters, of course.

It was after a week of this that they had their first sight of any body of the enemy. They had come upon them while it was yet light, a considerable body of dismounted cavalry who were just saddling and setting about cooking supper. The General ordered Chalmers to advance and sent Kelly with the old Forrest regiment around to the rear. Then he put himself at the head of the escort and rode in on them. It was almost dark and the escort all wore the rubber overcoats and leggings captured along the way—the Yankees had not known what was happening until they were fired upon by pistols at short range. That Manning boy and Captain Wuthers had been killed and several wounded but they had captured about sixty horses and as many prisoners. The Yankee pickets, hearing the shots, had come running in like geese and were captured too.

They had pushed on next day at top speed. Most of the fighting and it seemed, looking back, that there had been skirmishing every foot of the way—had been done on foot, a hard country that for cavalry. Rocky and covered everywhere with cedars. It had been a relief when coming down out of the mountains they saw before them the blue plains and the little towns, Columbia, Spring Hill, Franklin . . . Franklin! He leaned forward with his hands swinging between his spread knees. "If I live through the war," he thought, "live to be an old man I will tell people 'I was in the battle of Franklin.'" There had been skirmishing all that day before the Yankees yielded their position and headed west. The cavalry had fallen back at dark, to feed their horses and bivouac out of range of the enemy pickets. He had been on his way back to headquarters after taking a message to General Jackson when he saw two men he knew parching corn by a good fire and got off to warm himself a little. While he was standing there a tall man wandered up and asked what division this was.

"Cleburne's," Bud McGuire called without looking up from his cooking. But Ed Johnson watched the man making off through the trees. "That's a Yankee," he said suddenly. They were up and after him. When Rives came up they had caught him and were sitting on a log dividing the contents of his haversack. They had given Rives a cracker and a piece of cheese the size of a half-dollar. It had melted deliciously in his mouth as he rode down to the pike.

He halted there in the bushes long enough to see what was happening. The Yankees were up, all right. Wagons going by and guns and finally a strong column of infantry had come marching. He took a short-cut he knew of and was back at the cavalry headquarters within twenty minutes.

But the General was not there. Rives had then ridden to the headquarters of the commanding general. Forrest and General Stewart were just leaving. General Hood had come out on the steps with them. He was drunk or not waked up properly, for he kept repeating the same thing:

"But I tell you, Cleburne and Cheatham were to have remained in position."

Forrest did not seem to be listening to Hood. He said: "Buford and Chalmers haven't got a cartridge left. Jackson has only what he captured late this afternoon."

"How many rounds?" Hood asked eagerly.

"Oh, twenty—thirty maybe."

"Send Jackson then," Hood said. "Let him throw his whole division across the pike."

Forrest had said curtly that he would send the order to General Jackson and had ridden off to make application himself for more ammunition. The cavalry—all except Jackson's division—had then gone into bivouac around eleven o'clock. All that night they heard the roar of guns and the ping ping of musketry but they knew even before the couriers began coming in in the morning that it was useless. That heavy column of Federal infantry pressing on to Franklin had been too much for Jackson's men. They had been able to harass them and force them to abandon a lot of wagons—but they had not been able to keep them from getting to Franklin.

The General had been in the saddle for four or five days then, but he had walked around the tent that night much as he was doing now. When Major Strange came into the camp the next day he went to meet him, his face lined and old-looking. "No use," he said bitterly, "the fox has gone to earth. Hood let them slip past in the night."

The fox had gone to earth, all right. When they moved into Franklin the next day they were confronted by as stout breastworks as he had ever seen—a complete bridge-head encircling the town.

General Hood came on the field at one o'clock. Forrest took Rives and Major Anderson with him when he galloped up to report the result of his reconnaissance. He told Hood that the Federal position was formidable. It was his opinion that the works could not be taken by direct assault. He said that and then he added, "Without great loss of life."

While they were talking Rives had been watching the commanding general's face. They were saying around the camp that he was drunk last night and that was why he let the Yankees slip past him so easily. Well, he wasn't drunk today. But he looked surly, as if he might have a head. Surly and dogged. He listened impatiently to what General Forrest said, then shook his head.

"General, I do not think the Federals will stand direct pressure from the front. This show of force they are making is only a feint to stop pursuit."

Forrest looked at him hard and a muscle at the side of his mouth quivered. He said, "General Hood, if you will give me one strong division of infantry with my cavalry, I will agree to flank the Federals out from their works within two hours' time."

But Hood would not agree. He had divided the cavalry, sending a force out on each flank. Rives had been lent to General Jackson that day. Some hot skirmishing there by the river, but it didn't get them anywhere.

The cavalry withdrew south of the river at dark. The battle

was over by that time, men streaming down the pike and over the fields. He had shared a blanket that night with an infantryman lost from his command. Not much sleep for either of them, for the fellow was feverish from a bad wound in the shoulder. When he wasn't tossing he told about the battle.

He had never seen stouter breastworks, he said. Still things looked all right when they first went up. There were quite a few Yankee regiments left outside the works. They must not have been expecting an attack so soon or maybe they were green. Anyhow they broke like paper. That cheered the boys up and they went in yelling. All the fighting he saw was inside the works. With muskets mostly. Guns standing in the embrasures idle. The bastards didn't dare use them for fear of killing their own men. It was hard to get room even to fire. But Brown's and Cleburne's men were all over the place, were even manning the guns. Then all of a sudden a lot of Yankee reserves came up. The officer leading them was on foot. The fighting worked over toward the gin-house then. It was hottest, he reckoned, between there and the pike. Yes, he had seen General Cleburne. Coming up over the works on horseback. He stopped a bullet and rolled fifty feet. General Adams was killed about the same time. He didn't see Adams but he saw his horse. A bay. It was dead on top of the works with its front legs toward the inner side. Adams' body must have been somewhere outside. They were piled up three deep by that time. When he himself was wounded a little later it was somewhere near the gin-house, for he remembered looking up and seing a big pipe over his head. He was lying on his back for a while and they kept stepping on him, then he managed to crawl off and get behind a tree. There was a wounded Yankee sergeant lying near who was talking all the time. He said his colonel couldn't write and he had to make out all the reports. He couldn't figure how the Confederates kept coming on. Said he counted thirteen distinct attacks before he was hit and if he lived till morning he was going to see that the Old Man got it into his report, by God. . . . Rives wanted to know how many killed? God Almighty alone could tell when they were piled up on top of each other like that. . . . Funny thing. Most of those that weren't killed got away. Old hands, that is. The conscripts, of course, were afraid of being fired on by their own men so they had to stand and take it. He expected the Yanks scooped in plenty of them by the time it was dark. . . .

Rives stood up. A man was coming toward the tent. An orderly from the artillery camp. The General, when it was possible, always messed with the artillery.

Rives watched the soldier come forward over the snow. He swung each foot out with an awkward ducklike motion. That was because of his boots, made out of a piece of rawhide and laced with a leather thong. Rives remembered when the men got those boots. On the march up from Duck River. The Yankees, fleeing, had had to abandon their cattle. But some of them had already been driven too far. The minute they halted they fell to the ground as if they had been shot. The infantrymen were on them like tigers. A whole steer would be skinned three minutes after the knife had been drawn across its throat and then you would see the men standing, one foot in the center of the smoking skin while they drew the heart-shaped outline for the boot with their knives.

The orderly passed the tent, stopped. "Captain Morton's compliments. He says tell the General he's got coffee for breakfast, with sugar."

Rives went over to the General, came back with the message that he would breakfast with the artillerymen. The orderly was gazing off over the plain. You could make out the fort now, pale in the morning light. The man gazed, spat on the ground. "They tell me there's ten thousand of them bastards shut up in there."

"Must be," Rives said.

"Well," the orderly said, "I heard 'em talking over at camp. Looks like there'll be something doing today."

Rives nodded as he turned back into the tent. "Looks like there might," he said.

4

THE artillery fight had already begun when Rives rode down toward the creek with a message for General Buford. He could hear the guns thudding all the time he was hunting Buford along the dry creek bed. He found him warming his hands at a fire in the shelter of a brake.

"All right," he said impatiently, "all right. Tell the General I'm ready to move, soon as he gives the word. Tell him I better move pretty soon or the horses'll freeze in their tracks."

Rives galloped back, past the ranks of waiting horses whose breaths went up in a great cloud on the chill air. The General, he was thinking, would not give the word for some time. He wanted the Yankees to get some distance out from the fort before he sent Buford's and Jackson's men in to cut off their retreat. The Yankees were coming on strong when he left. But it was only artillery duelling; no infantry engaged as yet. You could tell by the sound.

He came up over the hill where smoke was beginning to settle. Over on a little knoll the headquarters flag fluttered stiffly in the wind. He made for it. The General was there, surrounded by half a dozen of his staff. A hundred yards away there was furious activity—men toiling with picks and shovels to throw up great mounds of earth while others ran about bringing in rails and logs, flinging them down, darting back for more. The little knot of officers seemed completely disengaged from all this activity. They sat, many of them with glasses to their eyes, studying the farther scene.

A wood and in front of it dull shapes of metal that stood, doggedly belching black smoke. When he had been on this hill a while ago those guns had been surrounded by marching figures, but the figures seemed to be pouring away now into the wood.

He was puzzled and glanced at the officers to see what they made of it. Major Anderson and Major Strange were among those who sat there waiting. Strange, though he had been up for hours, seemed not to have got warmed up yet. His shoulders were hunched and his bitter face was blue with the cold. Anderson had a gaudy woollen scarf wound about his neck. His cheeks were bright as apples. He had a pair of glasses to his eyes. He put them down now on the pommel of his saddle.

"They're coming out on the other side of the woods," he said.

The General had let his own glasses fall and he stood in his stirrups gazing intently as if his naked eye could give the only authentic report. "You're right," he said. "They're forming. Double line. Right across the road. Hell, Anderson! This changes the looks of things."

He put his hands in his pockets. Instead of looking at the woods he gazed intently at the ground. He raised his head. His eye fell on Rives. "Here, boy," he called, "go down and tell Major Bassett to stop that entrenchment. Tell him to form his men there on the other side of those breastworks. We'll be moving here in a minute."

Rives raced off, and met Major Bassett coming around the end of the long trench. He stared disgustedly when Rives gave him the order. "Lord, what have we been digging for all morning?"

Rives wheeled his horse quickly, in order to avoid smiling in the officer's face. He knew now what these manœuvres meant. The Yankees had come up close enough to get a look at the entrenchments and had decided they were too strong for direct assault so they were forming on the other side of the wood. He grinned. The fools! To think they could outflank Old Bedford!

He hurried back. The General was still there, with Major Anderson and Major Strange. The rest of the staff were making off over the slope, carrying messages to the division commanders. All about him were excited shouts, the sound of trampling feet.

From the south came the thud of wheels and singing through it the hiss of leather on hide: the artillery was coming up to take the new position. Four guns bounced by, horses straining under the whip, men clinging to the caissons. The youthful captain of artillery, John Morton, grinned from the carriage of one of his "Bull Pups," raised a hand in salute to the General before he vanished around the side of the hill.

The General let the hand he had raised fall to his side. "Double-shotted canister," he said. "John'll get up close as he can." He turned to Rives, spoke as if they two had been alone in a quiet room. "Boy, you see General Bate?"

Rives pointed out the infantry commander on a tall horse, riding up and down in front of the line that was just forming. Forrest rode toward him. They talked for a moment, then Forrest rode out in front of the infantry lines. Rives pressed up until he was within earshot. Forrest was hatless. He stood in his stirrups to fling his voice out on the cold air:

"Fifteen minutes . . . that's all I ask of you men. . . . Hold 'em fifteen minutes. . . . That'll give me time to get in the rear with the cavalry . . . capture every last man."

There was a long, answering shout from the men. The Yankee cannon opened before it died away. The Confederate guns just coming into position howled back. Regimental officers shouted. Musket fire blazed along the line.

Forrest was riding back to where Strange and Rives sat under a tree. Strange had his glasses to his eyes. He shouted through the din: "Cavalry's coming on fast. . . . Looks like Wilson's men to me, General."

Forrest sat silent, watching. The smoke from the cannon drifted down and hung in a great cloud over the field. Sparks from the musket-fire played along it. The Yankee flags moved steadily forward, rosy through smoke. You could make out figures on horseback, the noses of cannon. . . .

The smoke in front lifted suddenly. The front ranks of the

Confederate infantry were revealed. But they lacked the coherence they had had. They moved in a maze, clinging together in blocks or bunches or dissolving to form a nucleus somewhere else.

Strange put his glasses down. He yelled: "Great God! They're breaking!"

Forrest turned. He had a gray face, eyes that were incredulous yet stricken. He said, "Strange, go find Ross and Jackson. Tell them to come up and fetch all they've got. Tell them everything depends on the cavalry."

He was riding for the infantry lines, his staff crowding on behind him. General Bate was there, too, crying out wildly to his men. Forrest pushed past him and was in among them, shouting and slashing with his sword. A wave of fleeing men hid him from sight for a second, then he was seen again, towering, on his gray horse. Tears streamed down his face. He implored them, his voice breaking:

"Rally, men, rally! For God's sake, rally!"

But they would not listen. They broke around him and fled, orphan chickens scudding before a hawk over the plain. Some ran straight for the rear. Others went dodging as if to throw off pursuit. One bunch, compact even in panic, was making for a thicket not far from where Rives was.

Rives whirled his horse and made for the copse, took his stand against it. They came on. The man in the forefront had an open mouth, starting eyes. One of his hands was held up stiffly. Something pink fluttered over his shoulder.

A voice behind Rives was muttering: "Dirty coward," and then in snarled surprise: *"Color bearer!"*

Rives drew his pistol. The man was coming faster now. Rives aimed at a button on the wet jacket. The man coughed and began to fall. Rives swooped by, snatched the flag from him as he hit the ground.

He rode back toward the front. Morton's guns were still firing but they stood alone except for the bending, dogged figures of the gunners. The infantry was pouring away in panic over the slope. Some men brandished weapons, others struck at the air with their hands, looked back over their shoulders, howled. Rives' anger drenched his throat, beat in his temples. But he had the flag. His fingers closed over the wood that was still warm from the dead coward's hand. He set the pole hard against the pommel of his saddle, rode at them yelling and firing.

They swarmed past him. And now they had faces. One came up at his saddle bow: white eyes ringed with black. The man grinned insanely and caught at Rives' arm. Metal flashed in his hand. He ran past.

Rives felt a jagged branch strike his hip. He looked about for the tree but it was not there. A sharp pain vibrated through his whole body, then it was sweetly gone. He tried to ride faster but it was difficult now to hold the flag staff. It kept slipping from the slick leather. He closed his eyes. When he opened them he was still in the saddle but he might have been walking along a road, or trying, still holding the flag, to climb a wall. In the saddle still, but he had legs that would not be lifted. . . .

The blood from the severed artery gushed out and stained all his trouser leg. He could not see. And then he was falling. A fleeing soldier sprang aside to avoid the body as it sprawled out of the saddle and struck the ground.

Then men fell away on all sides to make way for a frenzied rider. Forrest checked his great horse, so sharply that hooves became paws, grazed dodging shoulders. He was out of the saddle, his hand was on the flag, where it lay near the outstretched fingers. His eyes went to the dead face. He said to the man behind him, "It's that boy, Allard!" He was back in the saddle.

The horse galloped forward. The rider sat rigid, staring straight ahead. The hooves, striking hard on the icy ground, seemed to ring out the names of all the fallen. . . . Pat Cleburne, dead at the foot of the breastworks. . . . Strahl, himself dead and so wedged in by the dying that his stiffened arm still curved upward in the gesture of command. . . . That boy's face, dark against the trampled snow. . . . No, it was a brown prairie and a ring of staring men . . . Jeffrey! Jeffrey! . . . He raised amazed eyes to the milky sky. Death. It had been with him, beside him all the time and he had not known. . . . But they had all known. Hood, Bragg, Buckner, Floyd, His Excellency. . . . Those men who weighed and considered, looked to this side, to that. They had whispered their constrained "No's" not to him but to that dog, Death. They had seen Death there at his heels, at Chickamauga, at the Cross Roads, at Franklin, even at Donelson. . . .

He turned and looked behind him. The field was gray under the icy sky, dirty with trampled snow. He was aware of glittering eyes upon him, could discern in the eddying mass, faces contorted with fear and shame.

He put spurs to King Philip. The great war-horse bounded forward. Forrest stood in his stirrups. The rose-colored flag danced above him then dipped. It veiled his face for a moment from the men's sight but they heard his voice sounding back over the windy plain and saw him gallop toward the fort.

5

AT four o'clock Mitty went out to the kitchen to give old Rivanna some directions about supper. Lucy was alone in the chamber. She had been spinning steadily since two o'clock and now she thought she would go out and walk about a little before night fell. But the long-continued work had tired her. She felt a disinclination to face the cold air. She went over to the hearth. The fire had dwindled to a bed of embers. There were logs in the wood box on the porch. She could call Uncle Mack to bring one in for her or she could struggle with it herself. But either effort seemed too great. She turned from the hearth and went to the window.

There had been a severe freeze a few days ago. The black branches of the tree beside the window were cased in ice. Lucy's eyes went to the field beyond the fence. It was bare of green, gullied at the northern end. "Humph, I'd hate to live in a country where my grave was already dug for me." Her grandfather's mother had said that long ago, descending before this house.

"Piney woods country," she thought, *"If I could once again see Kentucky!"*

A figure on horseback was approaching. Molly had ridden for the mail that afternoon in spite of the bitter weather. Lucy was about to go out to meet her when she heard the front door open. Susan, her shawl over her head, went swiftly down the walk. She was beside the girl, had taken the mail bag from her. There was only one letter. She held it clutched against her breast as she struggled back against the wind. Lucy opened the door and stepped out into the cold hall.

"Is it for me?"

"For me," Susan said, and walked past Lucy into the room.

Lucy stood on the hearth, watching the small, gnarled fingers fumble with the envelope. Susan had the single sheet out and was holding it up. She read, then the letter sank to her lap.

Lucy bent over her. "Who is it from?" she asked angrily. "Tell me. Who is it from?"

"It's from a Major Anderson."

"Is Rives dead?" Lucy asked.

Susan raised her head, winked to clear her vision. "I don't know," she whispered. "He says . . . deep sympathy . . ."

Lucy put out a hand, took the letter from her. It seemed a long time before her eyes found the words: "killed in action on December 7, at Murfreesboro." There was more. She read on and then realized that she did not know what she was reading. She laid the letter carefully on the mantel, then as carefully returned it to Susan's lap and stood, her back to the hearth, staring at a picture on the wall.

"In action," she said, "December 7. Murfreesboro."

She walked over to the window. Behind her Susan read from the letter:

" 'General Forrest . . . wishes . . . communicate . . . deep sympathy. Your son held a position of peculiar trust . . .' " The voice faltered, then became full and proud. *"Lucy . . ."*

"Yes," Lucy said.

"He has never been absent from his post of duty and has shown true and uniform gallantry on many fields. . . ." The voice sank, then became proud again. "He was killed instantly while carrying the colors forward against the enemy."

"Instantly," Lucy said.

She had been staring at the dark woods that rimmed the horizon. They took strange shapes, a boy in a peaked cap fleeing a giant along a forest road, a man on horseback contending with a dragon. She turned around. The letter had slid from Susan's lap to the floor. She was bent forward, sobbing.

"She has never seen him die before," Lucy thought.

She told herself that she must go to the weeping old woman, but she had no words and she lingered at the window, held by a wonder as to how this death he had died was different from the other, imagined deaths. The sun dropped behind the pines. She watched the light go from the sky and knew that when she saw the green fields of Kentucky again they would be as alien as the gullied, pine-clad slopes outside the window.

THE END

CAROLINE GORDON (1895–1981), was a native of Todd County, Kentucky, the locale of much of her fiction. She began her literary career in the 1920's after her marriage to the poet Allen Tate. Her first short story appeared in 1929. *Penhally*, her first published novel, appeared in 1931. It was followed by eight other novels, including *Aleck Maury, Sportsman* (1934), *The Garden of Adonis* (1937), *Green Centuries* (1941), *The Women on the Porch* (1944), *The Strange Children* (1951), *The Malefactors* (1956) and *The Glory of Hera* (1972). *None Shall Look Back* was published in 1937. She published two collections of short stories, *The Forest of the South* (1945) and *Old Red and Other Stories* (1963). She was also the author of *How to Read a Novel* (1957) and, with Tate, of *The House of Fiction: an Anthology of the Short Story* (1950).

EILEEN GREGORY holds the Ph.D. from the University of South Carolina and currently chairs the Department of English at the University of Dallas, where she was a colleague of Caroline Gordon. She has published numerous articles and is the editor of the *H. D. Newsletter*.